Eloise lowered her eyes as Lord Drake climbed inside the carriage and sat down opposite her. "Do you realize what sort of establishment you have come to, Miss Goodwin?" he asked.

She swallowed uncomfortably. "Yes."

"Are you seeking a different position than that of companion to a spoiled young lady?"

"Not the kind of position you're referring to, I'm certain."

"Well, you did come to a bordello."

The dancing fire in the depths of his deep blue eyes sent heat flushing through her body. With a faint smile of acknowledgment he pulled her closer and kissed her.

His lips brushed across hers until she responded, her mouth softening, opening at his urging.

He slipped his hand up beneath her cloak and stroked his knuckles in the barest caress just below her breasts.

"Perhaps one day," he breathed against her parted lips, "we will meet at a more appropriate place and time so that I could properly—or improperly—tempt you."

"You've tempted me enough," she whispered.

Also by Jillian Hunter
(*published by Ivy Books*)

THE SEDUCTION OF AN ENGLISH SCOUNDREL
THE LOVE AFFAIR OF AN ENGLISH LORD
THE WEDDING NIGHT OF AN ENGLISH ROGUE

The Wicked Games of a Gentleman

A Novel

Jillian Hunter

BALLANTINE BOOKS • NEW YORK

The Wicked Games of a Gentleman is a work of fiction. Names, characters, places, and incidents are the products of the author's imagination or are used fictitiously. Any resemblance to actual events, locales, or persons, living or dead, is entirely coincidental.

An Ivy Books Mass Market Original

Copyright © 2006 by Maria Hoag
Excerpt from *The Sinful Nights of a Nobleman* by Jillian Hunter copyright © 2006 by Maria Hoag

All rights reserved.

Published in the United States by Ivy Books, an imprint of The Random House Publishing Group, a division of Random House, Inc., New York.

IVY BOOKS and colophon are trademarks of Random House, Inc.

This book contains an excerpt from the forthcoming edition of *The Sinful Nights of a Nobleman* by Jillian Hunter, published by Ballantine Books. This excerpt has been set for this edition only and may not reflect the final content of the forthcoming edition.

ISBN 0-345-48760-5

Cover illustration: Iskra Design, Inc.

Printed in the United States of America

www.ballantinebooks.com

OPM   9   8   7   6   5   4   3   2

For Jacqueline, with all my love

Chapter One

❦ ❦

Lord Drake Boscastle had less than two hours to suffer through the party before his assignation with one of the most sensual women in all of Europe. If the evening went as well as he expected, he would make the celebrated English courtesan, Maribella St. Ives, his next mistress. He certainly hoped she would prove to be worth the rigmarole required for their rendezvous, or he would feel like a hell of a fool. He had spent a month corresponding with her and had presented her with a small fortune in gifts to prove his sincerity. Maribella's private agents had conducted an investigation to research his character. The last Drake had heard, even his cook had been questioned on what his master ate for dinner.

His indigo blue eyes darkened with irony at the thought. Any thorough check into his past would have yielded a treasure trove of scandals and indiscretions. It seemed, however, that Miss St. Ives was not put off by his reputation. Apparently he had met whatever qualifications she desired in a protector. He had been summoned to meet her tonight in a private suite at Audrey Watson's salon on Bruton Street. Salon, of course, being a euphemism for the exclusive bordello that its half-world hostess, Audrey, maintained.

His valet had efficiently packed a few personal necessities and a fresh change of clothes, not bothering to ask whether his master would be home before morning. Drake was rather hopeful he wouldn't return for a week. His life had been curiously devoid of pleasure lately, sex included. His capacity for enjoyment seemed to be diminishing by the day. He couldn't put his finger on the precise reason for his sense of dissatisfaction, but he was half-decided that if this affair with Maribella did not improve his outlook, he would return to soldiering.

"Counting the minutes?" his younger brother Lord Devon Boscastle asked from behind him.

Drake glanced around, grinning in reply. A small flock of debutantes stood gazing in breathless anticipation at Devon, whose openly playful charm made him appear far less of a threat than his more intense older brother. "I'm down to seconds at this point," he said dryly.

Devon lowered his voice. "Do let me know if Miss St. Ives has any sisters in the market for a protector. That is, if you can talk coherently at the end of the evening."

Drake shook his head and cast a sardonic glance across the room. "I'm going to be talking all night. Haven't you heard that she's famous for her wit?"

"And that's why you're interested in her? For conversation?"

He punched his brother on the shoulder. "Go dance with the debutantes, Devon. They're dying for you to ask."

"I can't dance with all of them at once. Why don't you help me out?"

He shook his head in amusement. "I'll leave the innocents to you. Anyway, I think I ought to conserve my strength."

One of their mutual male friends sauntered past them. "I suppose we won't see you at the auction tomorrow, Boscastle," he said to Drake in an envious voice. "Damn lucky devil."

Drake's answering laugh was suddenly drowned out by the blood rousing strains of a country dance. He cast a halfhearted glance about for a partner. He'd prefer the sister or wife of a friend rather than a timid debutante who would gaze at him in hopeful trepidation or chatter her empty head off after the set.

His restless gaze lit on a young, nicely built brunette in a plain lilac dress who was staring across the dance floor. She looked lost and . . . maybe a little frantic. She had an interesting sense of panic about her and an even more interesting silhouette. Good enough for what he had in mind. He only wanted to squander a few pleasant minutes with the woman, not marry her.

He strolled up behind her, clearing his throat at the cursory glance she granted him before turning away. Ignore him, would she? That was a challenge his devilish impulses could not turn down. "Lost a sheep?" he asked quietly, his chin brushing her ear.

Her soft white shoulders stiffened. He knew perfectly well she was aware of him, even if she refused to turn to meet his regard. "Yes, in a manner of speaking," she answered distractedly.

At that point another man might have taken the hint and melted away. Instead, he studied her profile, the imperfect patrician nose, her stubborn chin, a lushly shaped mouth. His gaze drifted in lazy appraisal down her shoulders to the ivory curves of her full breasts above her neckline. "Shall we look together?" he inquired, masking his thoughts behind a polite smile.

She angled her head slightly to regard him. Her oval face bore an expression of practiced disdain that slipped as her eyes slowly met his. She blinked. He stared at her, enjoying his own rush of pleasant surprise. She was really quite lovely. He saw her bite the edge of her full bottom lip a little nervously before she retreated in a half step. She wouldn't ignore him now. She recognized a threat to female virtue when she saw it.

"Come on," he said, gently taking her arm. "We'll hunt for your sheep on the dance floor. It just so happens that I'm good at hunting."

She stared down guardedly at his hand before returning her shrewd gaze to his face. The shadow of a smile lifted those lushly curved lips. "Wolves usually are."

He laughed, pleased but surprised at her response, and drew her forward. She gave a strong twist of resistance, although there was no room for her to escape. Guests had already filled the void where they'd been standing. The ballroom was thronged elbow-to-elbow with elegantly dressed lords and ladies. Loud ones, too. Drake was reminded of a barnyard filled with clucking hens and braying asses, which didn't exactly speak well of his opinion of Society as a whole.

He could barely hear what his reluctant partner was attempting to say above all the chatter and music of the orchestra. "Tell me about him later," he said in answer to her distressed look.

He didn't particularly want to talk, or dance for that

matter. He simply wanted to pass time with this pretty stranger before a night of bliss-inducing sex with a courtesan he'd met only once; and even during that meeting he and Maribella had not exchanged more than a few provocative words. This whole affair hinged on rumor and innuendo, which was what probably made it so intriguing.

"It's not a him," his partner said rather forcefully as he drew her resisting figure into the steps of the dance. An unexpected surge of arousal stirred his senses at the pliant warmth of her body. There was a pleasant sturdiness about her that appealed to him. She was an accomplished enough dancer to follow the pattern without seeming to pay attention. She seemed to be more concerned with looking for whomever it was she'd lost than with his efforts to disarm her.

His hooded gaze studied her as she faced the stage. She wore her hair back from her face, a heavy cluster of chestnut brown waves that enhanced her creamy skin. No jewelry except for a pair of pearl earrings. Her lilac muslin dress hadn't been designed to impress anyone, either. In fact, she looked like a governess, or a lady's companion. Which would explain why she was looking for lost sheep. He'd probably get her dismissed for dancing with him.

A middle-aged gentleman bumped into her as the set reconfigured. Drake gave the man a look and reached out his arm without thinking to steady her. Her full breasts pressed through his white linen shirtfront, another flagrant shock to his senses. He allowed his hand to fall to the rise of her well-rounded backside. Oh, yes. She felt very nice, very promising. He preferred a substantial woman in his bed.

"I beg your pardon," she said, reaching back to pluck his hand away. "Someone's fingers are straying where they don't belong." Her pretty oval face reflected a frowning disapproval that made him smile. She had hazel eyes, he realized. Dark brown and green dappled light at the same time. Intelligent and not entirely innocent.

"You don't need to beg me for anything." All of a sudden his thoughts went a little wild. "Why don't you enjoy yourself for a moment?"

She looked as if she'd swallowed a boiled onion whole. "Enjoy myself?"

He caught her wrist. "Aren't you allowed any pleasure at all?"

"I've lost my client," she said in vexation before the dance parted them again. "And I'm not here to enjoy myself."

"Do you want to go outside and look for her?" he asked quietly, the epitome of chivalrous concern. It was as hot as an inferno in the ballroom, and he wouldn't mind leading her astray in the dark for a minute or two.

"Outside," she muttered, her arched eyebrows drawing into a deep scowl. "I'll throttle the wits out of her if that's where she's gone."

He started to laugh. He really wasn't making much of an impression on her. He trusted he'd have better luck later in the evening. "Do you always have this much trouble keeping your missing lamb in line?"

"An army of Hussars couldn't keep that girl in line," she said in exasperation. "Not that she wouldn't enjoy challenging them, mind you."

"Is that what you do?" He followed her to the French doors that led to the garden, welcoming the excuse to leave the stuffy room. "Keep unruly persons in line?"

"That describes my present position." She stopped abruptly, reaching behind her for the door.

A proper gentleman would have stepped back to allow a respectable distance between them. Drake did not bother with the pretense. "Perhaps you could keep me in line?" he said, provoked by some inner demon to tease her. "Quite a few people have called me unruly."

"I'm sure they have. However—"

He slipped his hand around her waist to open the door for her. For a moment he thought she would finally react.

"—you're about two decades older than my most unruly clients," she finished instead in a dismissive voice. "I'm afraid you're on your own. Self-discipline, and all that."

He laughed in feigned offense. "Two decades? Suddenly I feel like Methuselah."

The doors swung open. The damp night air counteracted the heat that rose between them. "Actually," she murmured, glancing out into the shrubbery with a faint smile, "I think Mephistopheles is more what I had in mind."

"Mephistopheles?" he asked, guiding her outside.

"Yes." She stepped out onto the terrace where several couples lingered in conversation. "The devil."

"I know who you mean," Drake replied. He led her casually toward an unoccupied corner of misty moonlight. "I don't think it's fair to label me thus on such short acquaintance, though." If she got to know him better, she would undoubtedly have ample justification to call him any number of names.

"First impressions are quite reliable in my experience." She peered over his shoulder as a cluster of guests drifted past them.

"I don't seem to be making much of an impression at all," he said with a good-humored grin.

He touched her flushed cheek with his gloved knuckles. He demanded—and suddenly received—her full attention. "Couldn't your duty be delayed for a few moments?"

She looked up into his face, her hazel eyes hinting that she might not be as immune to him as she wanted him to believe. "Do you have any idea how much trouble a woman might find in a few moments?" She shook her head, a note of reluctant amusement in her voice. "That was not an invitation. I was referring to my client."

He bent his head to the curve of her chin. "May I at least kiss you before you go?" he asked, determined to satisfy his curiosity if nothing else. That soft mouth of hers could not taste as delicious as it looked.

He did not wait for her permission. Capturing her strong chin in his fingers, he slanted his mouth over hers and took possession of her tempting lips. She drew in a breath and stood immobilized, silent, and oh-so-enticing. He felt a quick flair of answering fire in his blood. She gave a faint sigh, the merest exhalation of breath, as he shifted his weight, molding her to the hard contours of his body. How long had it been since he had felt even the slightest tug of temptation?

"That," she whispered in an uneven voice, angling her head to the side, "will be quite enough, thank you."

"You're more than welcome." He lifted his hand to her soft rounded shoulder. "But it wasn't quite enough."

"Yes, it was."

"No, it wasn't."

"It—"

"—wasn't," he said in a coaxing undertone. "Look, I'll prove it to you."

She turned her face slowly back to his. This time when he kissed her, she parted her lips, allowing his tongue to penetrate her mouth. She buckled unexpectedly. He caught her without a second's hesitation, aware that he was in peril of forgetting where they were.

"I told you," he said thickly.

She shivered lightly, looking dazed and desirable. "Told me what?"

He closed his eyes and summoned his control, crushing her to him for one final second of self-torture. When he let her go, her eyes shimmered with a bewildered passion, and her breasts rose enticingly with the quickened measure of her breath.

"If you don't mind," she whispered, putting her hand to her heart, "I'm going to leave you now. Thank you ever so much for the dance, but it so happens that I'm occupied for the rest of the evening."

"So am I." He smiled down ruefully into her moonlit face. The moist fullness of her mouth invited another kiss. "Although unplanned pleasures are the most gratifying, in my experience," he said, aching to pull her back into his arms.

Her answering laugh surprised him. "I'm sure you've experienced plenty of them."

He grinned as she gathered her skirt in hand to edge around him. He was glad that they would part as friends. "I won't deny it."

"I doubt you deny yourself anything," she retorted.

He grasped the delicate lace of her sleeve, gently tugging her back toward him. "Then why deny myself now?" he asked, gratified at the shiver she gave as their bodies touched.

She stared back at him as if she saw straight through his invitation to the hollow core of his heart. "Sometimes denial is good for the soul."

"Wait—at least tell me who you are. My name is Drake."

She hesitated. He lowered his hand and lounged back against the stone wall, realizing that he was going to lose her. It seemed that he should at least know her name. He liked that she had a mind of her own as well a sensuality that begged a man to bed her, and that she was neither painfully insecure nor full of herself, like the other ladies who were brave enough to flirt with him. It made him wonder whether she'd ever taken a lover. Devil that he was, he wouldn't have minded being her first.

"I don't have time for the sort of games that wicked gentlemen like to play," she said, her smile dismissive. "I work too hard to give in to temptation."

At least he thought that was what she said. He watched her as she slipped back into the ballroom, vanishing into the crush of guests. For a moment he considered going after her. But he didn't want to get her in trouble. If he hadn't had such grand plans for the night, he might have pursued her. God knew he was tired of whores and vapid young girls who giggled or blushed at every word he uttered.

God knew he was tired of life, actually.

Chapter Two

❧ ❧

Eloise Goodwin paused inside the ballroom, taking a second to recover her wits. She felt warm and pleasantly discomforted from the inside out. The dancers moving in the shifting gold shadows of candlelight only made her head whirl in another dizzying wave. Well, that charming diversion had not helped the situation at all. Her client could have sneaked off anywhere, with anyone, during the few illicit moments that her overtaxed chaperone had been waylaid by that rogue.

Breathtakingly handsome beast, she thought grudgingly. Her heart fluttered against her ribs. She'd known the minute she looked into his beguiling dark blue eyes and strongly sculpted face that his smile invited capricious pleasures. Hadn't he cared he'd been dancing with a mere companion? An impoverished gentlewoman who was at her wits' end and had no time for seduction? Or maybe that was why he had singled her out in the first place. She was a plump pigeon ripe for the plucking in a sea of graceful swans.

She released a rueful sigh. At least he was accomplished at the art. Eloise could not remember a single instance during her career when she had been anywhere near as tempted to submit. Of course none of the country gentlemen who'd pinched her bottom or followed her into the pantry to steal a kiss had possessed a fraction of this man's finesse. *His* kiss had absolutely devastated her.

She glanced back unwillingly at the doors leading to the garden, wondering if he had returned to the ballroom. She'd glimpsed a moody disposition behind his handsome mien. It beckoned, as darkness often did, but it also put her on guard. One must have no sympathy for the devil.

Nor would one have sympathy for a woman galloping around the dance floor when she had been employed to act as a chaperone and companion. Heaven forbid that a future client should observe such unseemly behavior. Fortunately for Eloise, it seemed unlikely that anyone would remember her in this crush.

A woman in her position wanted to be anonymous. She had spent years purposefully hiding in the shadows and had no desire to draw any undue attention to herself. She did, however, have a raging desire to strangle Miss Thalia Thornton with her bare hands for sneaking out of the ballroom. Eloise had merely bent down to retrieve a fan that a stout baroness had dropped upon the floor. When she looked up again, Thalia had disappeared from sight.

She bit her lip. Now that she thought about it, her young client had seemed rather overanxious to attend this ball tonight, which meant there was a man involved. In Eloise's experience, there usually was when trouble visited, and troubles seemed to define Thalia Thornton's life. In fact, Eloise would never have chosen to work for her client. She had more or less inherited the position.

Two years previously she had been quite contented

serving as a companion to Thalia's great-aunt, Udella Thornton. When Udella peacefully passed away at a Christmas party last year, Eloise had been prepared to pack her bags and seek employment elsewhere.

But Udella's nephew, Lord Horace Thornton, had interceded and begged Eloise to serve as a chaperone to his unmarried sister, Thalia. He had promised that the position would last only until he married off Thalia. Eloise should have heeded the initial instinct that warned her to refuse.

Thalia, with no parents to guide her into womanhood and a brother who had already gambled his inheritance into the ground, was—well, there were no kind words to describe her—a petulant brat.

"Did you find her?" a concerned female voice asked from behind her.

Eloise drew her gaze from the garden doors with a pang of guilty pleasure. It was time to forget her rogue and his stolen kisses. Reality stood before her in the dowdy form of Miss Mary Weston, a fellow companion in her thirties employed by the stout baroness who, by dropping her fan, had set into motion the evening's chain of events. "No," Eloise said, fresh panic flooding her. "She wasn't in the cloak room?"

Mary shook her head, whispering, "No one has seen her. Do you think you ought to try the conservatory? Or one of the rooms upstairs?"

"I wouldn't know where to begin," Eloise said, turning white at the mere suggestion of barging into private bedrooms. And what would she say if she caught Thalia in the act?

"She wouldn't be that foolish, would she?" Mary asked in a worried undertone.

"Of course she would," Eloise said with grim certainty.

"But she's engaged to be married—"

"To a man she claims she cannot love." And it was this poor besotted baronet who had offered a generous bonus to Eloise to keep an eye on his "spirited fiancée" until he returned from Amsterdam. The rather unattractive man was undoubtedly aware that he didn't cut a dashing figure in comparison to the young bucks of the ton who were attracted to Thalia. Eloise wouldn't have been at all surprised if Thalia weren't deliberately trying to sabotage her own engagement.

"What about her brother?" Mary glanced around them. "Lord Thornton escorted both of you here, didn't he?"

"I doubt his lordship even remembers he has a sister, let alone cares that she has vanished."

Eloise broke off in agitation. A young man and woman had just made a discreet return from the garden into the ballroom, their faces aglow with intimate secrets as they separated. She knew immediately that the lady reentering the room was not Thalia. Nor was the tall gentleman at her side the blue-eyed rake who had distracted Eloise from her duties. For some irrational reason this soothed her agitated mood. It was nice to think he was a little discriminating in whom he chose to lure astray.

Mary gave her a nudge. "You'll have to catch her before anyone else does."

The thought galvanized Eloise back into action, reminding her that a companion had no business spinning fantasies about scoundrels. "Believe me, I intend to."

* * *

Drake sauntered through the upstairs gaming room in search of his younger brother. Perhaps the boy had enjoyed better luck with one of his smitten flock of sparrows than he'd had with his lovely if elusive lady of dutiful self-denial. He commended her control, amused that she had excited him at a time when precious little did.

He smiled at the pleasurable memory of their too-brief meeting. The warm temptation of her body against his lingered in his blood like smoke. Given more time he would have found a way to penetrate her defenses. Well, she was better off having escaped him. As talk went in the ton, by the time a young lady was seen in Drake's company, her reputation was already ruined.

"Evening, Boscastle," a man murmured from the depths of a wing chair. "Is this the last any of us will see of you alive?"

"If I'm lucky," Drake replied, not stopping to indulge idle curiosity. Maribella St. Ives rarely took on a lover without fanfare, and her temperamental behavior was often reported in the newspapers. He preferred keeping his affairs on the private side himself.

He took stock of his surroundings. An intense game of ecarte was in progress at a window table. He recognized two of the players in the candlelight. One was an upstart cousin of his, Sir Gabriel Boscastle, a dark, hard-seasoned soldier who had been wounded in Spain; the man opposite him was Lord Horace Thornton, the ne'er-do-well younger brother of one of Drake's late friends.

Gabriel looked as detached and unreadable as only a Boscastle could; Horace was chalk-faced and drinking heavily, losing, too, to judge by the desperation in his eyes. Competitive by nature, Gabriel would probably take him for every last halfpenny. Drake turned away, embarrassed for Thornton. He didn't feel like witnessing the downfall of a man he didn't particularly respect.

He didn't feel much like anything, which seemed to be at the heart of his dilemma. In the past several months he'd begun to realize that his malcontent was growing more acute. He wasn't sure why, although he traced it back vaguely to the anniversary of his younger brother Brandon's brutal death. Drake and his last mistress had parted company that same month. He thought that his moodiness had probably contributed to the death of their affair. She'd accused him of being an uncaring bastard. He didn't deny it.

He was drawn suddenly from his thoughts by the deep pulsing silence that swept through the room. Before he'd turned around to investigate, the clash of angry male voices resounded from the gaming table at the window.

His cousin had risen from his chair to grab Horace by his silk cravat. Gabriel's thin-lipped expression revealed only an unforgiving fury. Horace shook visibly as if he were fighting back tears. Drake assessed the situation in a world-weary glance. There had to be more to life than this.

"He was cheating," Gabriel said at Drake's questioning scowl. "Look at the edges of his cards. I demand satisfaction."

Horace eased himself free, knocking a glass of port across the table. "You will serve as my second, Drake? I know that my brother defended you once on the field."

For an instant Drake was too astonished by Horace's presumption to react. Not to mention his sheer stupidity for getting into this situation in the first place. What sort of idiot thought he could cheat a Boscastle and not get caught? And why in God's name would Drake wish to become involved in a duel of dishonor against his own cousin? True, he did not particularly like Gabriel, and he had every reason to assume that the feeling was mutual.

A year or so ago he would have thrashed Horace on the spot for embroiling him in a public display. After all, Gabriel was a blood relation, albeit a ruthless one who seemed to take pleasure in rubbing Drake the wrong way. Cheating was unacceptable by any standard. Yet there was something so pathetic about Horace, and his brother *had* been a good friend, a man to count on until he'd lost his life in the cavalry.

Gabriel looked up darkly at Drake. "It's good to see you again, cousin. I'm sorry I missed Heath's wedding. By the way, I will not be offended if you accept this fool's request."

Drake could not help laughing. "Why not?"

"Join me for breakfast if we both survive?" Gabriel asked, motioning for a footman to bring him his coat. "I'm not in London often."

Drake hesitated; he wasn't entirely sure of his plans for the following day. He assumed it would be a continuation of spine-tingling sex and stimulating conversation with Maribella. Besides, he wasn't sure he wanted to spend time with Gabriel. He suspected they were too much alike to trust each other. "We'll see."

Gabriel's mouth curved into a hard smile. He'd inherited the same Boscastle blue eyes as Drake, but with a darker cast. "Enjoy yourself tonight."

Drake nodded wryly. He wondered if there was a single male in his set of friends who had not heard that

Drake Boscastle had been selected for the enviable position of Maribella's new protector. He could only hope that she deserved her reputation, and that he could live up to his.

Gabriel turned aside as Horace made his way to the door. The younger man looked so pathetic in his self-induced shame that Drake almost pitied him. "Go home and get some sleep, for God's sake. You'll need it for the morning."

Horace swallowed. "With any luck I'll be dead before dawn."

Gabriel laughed. Drake shook his head in disgust. "Your older brother would probably kill you as a point of pride. It's only out of respect for him that I am even talking to you."

"I know," Horace said in a voice laden with self-remorse. "I don't suppose I could ask one more favor of you?"

"Don't do it," Gabriel warned Drake in scornful amusement.

"I'm not lending you any money," Drake said flatly. "Your debts were a disgrace before tonight."

"Not that." Horace lowered his voice. "I only want you to see my sister home. You remember Thalia, don't you?"

Drake groaned. "Are you referring to the hideous little brat who was hitting everyone in the shins with her hairbrush the last time I saw her?"

Horace managed a weak smile. "She's still a hideous little brat. However, she's getting married soon, and hasn't taken a hairbrush to anyone in several years."

"I have plans for the evening, Thornton," Drake said

stonily. He was well aware that Gabriel was enjoying this whole thing.

"All I ask is that you see her home," Horace said tiredly. "I don't have the heart to face her. You can drop her off on your way." He edged around Drake's unmoving figure, adding as an afterthought, "You might want to be careful around her dragoness, though. The woman breathes fire. I'm scared to death of her myself."

Drake caught the smirk that played across his cousin's face. "I have no idea what you're talking about. Where is Thalia, anyway?"

Horace seemed to shrink in size as he reached the door. Every pair of eyes in the room regarded him with contempt. His disgrace tonight marked the end of him in Society. "She's at the party," he mumbled. "Dancing, as far as I know."

Gabriel broke into a grin as Horace disappeared from sight. "I think you and I will be facing each other alone tomorrow, Drake."

"Good," Drake said with grim humor. "It will give me a chance to avenge myself on you for annoying me all through the years."

Chapter Three

ॐ ॐ

Drake gave a loud cough from behind his hand, then stood back in the shadows of the conservatory to allow Thalia and the man kissing her to disengage. After a few moments, however, it became clear the amorous couple did not care that they had an audience. Watching them made Drake feel distinctly uncomfortable. He reminded himself he had his own pleasures to seek.

He tapped the oblivious Lothario on the shoulder. "All right. That's enough."

"Not now," the man muttered, waving him away.

Drake wrenched him around by the arm. He wasn't at all surprised to discover that the scapegrace was Percy Chapman, a boastful, young debaucher of debutantes whose boyish charm hid a callous disregard for others.

Percy glared up at him with a belligerence that quickly evolved into respect when he realized who had interrupted him. "Hell, Boscastle. It's you. Can't you see I'm a bit busy at the moment?"

"You're finished," Drake said, smiling coldly.

"Come on. It's not as if she's one of your sisters." He straightened, pulling Thalia's hand from his arm, and smiled faintly. "I'd think that you of all men would understand."

"I understand that you are done," Drake said without a trace of empathy. "Now leave. Alone. She will not return to the ballroom in your company for everyone to see."

"Fine." Percy shrugged, his mouth sulky. "Whatever you ask."

Drake turned impatiently to Thalia, who was standing with a petulant expression in front of the potted fern. Her paisley shawl lay on the tile floor. He picked it up. "Put it on."

"Why should I?"

He raised his brow. "Shall I count to three?"

"Do you know how?"

He laughed. "You're really asking for trouble."

She pulled off a fern frond and flicked it at his nose. "But I didn't ask for your interference, did I?"

Eloise pressed her hand to the painful stitch in her side. The conservatory was the last place at the party for her to look. She hurried past the fair-haired figure who strolled toward her, twirling his filigree watch fob. Percy Chapman, she thought in contempt, pretending not to recognize him. Well, at least he wasn't with Thalia. She'd caught the pair of them sneaking off at another party.

She entered the conservatory, her gaze going straight to the shadow of a man standing with Thalia between a cluster of ferns. His chiseled profile and broad-shouldered silhouette sent a shock of awareness through her anger. Oh! The blackguard. *Her* blackguard. The beautiful blue-eyed scoundrel who had shamelessly kissed her on the terrace. He certainly hadn't wasted any time looking for another chance at seduction. Look at him—trying to put Thalia's shawl over her arms. He'd probably taken it off in the first place.

"You!" she exclaimed, marching her way between the two figures and the curly fern fronds. She snatched the shawl out of his hands. "Isn't this a surprise? I should have known."

He turned and gave her an indolent smile. "And *I* should have known this is the twit you were looking for earlier." Dark humor kindled in his eyes as he gazed at Eloise. "My God, *you're* the fire-breathing dragoness."

"I beg your pardon." Thalia narrowed her eyes in indignation. "Who are you calling a twit?"

"You," Drake said without looking at her.

"I think you deserve a good slap for that." She threw Eloise a beseeching look. "Eloise, you have my permission to slap him."

"Oh, slap him yourself," Eloise said, still trying to catch her breath. The stitch in her side did not bother her half as much as the disappointment of finding her dark seductor in the middle of another seduction, and with Thalia, of all people. Was her client the plans he had mentioned for the evening?

He crossed his arms over his chest and glanced challengingly at Thalia. "I think you ought to be spanked while we're on the subject of corporal punishment. Miss Dragoness, spank your client."

"It seems to me you're the one who is asking for some discipline," Eloise said under her breath.

"I did not lay a blessed hand on her, thank you for asking." He shot Thalia a black scowl. "You might want to step in at this point to confess the truth."

Thalia stubbornly refused to utter a single word.

Eloise studied him in undisguised suspicion. He stared

back at her, dark, a little defiant, and all too attractive. Well, who was she supposed to believe?

"The truth," she said in a crisp voice, "is that I have found the pair of you alone together and Miss Thornton visibly disheveled. Am I mistaken?"

Drake was insulted, actually, at the mere suggestion of seducing a bird-wit like Thalia. He knew that the pretty dragoness was only doing her job, and an unpleasant one it must be. No doubt she was overworked and underpaid. Her plight aroused what little sympathy he was capable of summoning these days. In fact, the woman was quite talented at arousing him in general.

"Ask Miss Thornton," he said, bracing his hip against the wall. "And while you're at it, you might ask the coxcomb who was making a full-course meal of her face."

Her lush mouth puckered in on itself in reproach. "That wouldn't be Percy Chapman, would it?" she demanded of her client, who by this time was tapping the toe of her slipper in simmering resentment. "I am *so* disappointed. What did we discuss before we left the house?"

Thalia stared at her in defiance. "You asked me not to dance with Percy. And I didn't." She cast a sly look at Drake. "Was I dancing?"

"Hard to tell," he said in a bored voice, picking a fern frond off his cuff. "From where I stood you were moving together as one."

The dragoness paled and closed her eyes. Drake hoped to heaven she wouldn't faint on him. He was going to be late for his assignation; it would be hellishly inconvenient to fetch a footman to attend to her. He decided it wouldn't hurt to give her a gentle shake to be sure, though. The moment he touched her, however, he wished he'd ignored the impulse. Her shoulders yielded softly under his hands, a pleasant disturbance to his senses. He knew when he'd kissed her in the garden that he wanted to hold her again. This wasn't quite what he'd had in mind.

"Dragoness," he said in mild alarm, "are you all right?"

"Would you be under the circumstances?" she whispered, then opened her eyes to search his face. "They were fully clothed, weren't they?"

"They were when I found them," he said calmly. "I've no idea what they were doing before."

"That isn't reassuring." She glanced down suddenly at his gloved hands. "Why are you holding on to me so tightly?"

"I thought you were going to faint."

"What made you think that?" she demanded.

He felt like a bit of a ninnyhammer for bothering. "Because you turned white and closed your eyes, and that's what women do when they start to swoon."

She lowered her voice. "You might feel like swooning if you'd been entrusted to keep Miss Thornton out of trouble until her wedding three weeks hence."

"By her brother?" he asked amusedly, drawing her away from Thalia to talk in private.

"Her fiancé." She hesitated. "Not that I should be revealing this, but he's a little afraid that she will change her mind at the last moment and ruin herself with a rake." She paused meaningfully. "There seems to be a score of them in London this season."

Drake glanced past her to the young woman in yellow silk who was a wanton-in-training if ever he'd met one, and he had met quite a few. In fact, a professional wanton was waiting for him at this moment. He released his grip on the companion's appealing shoulders. He couldn't imagine anyone wanting to marry a twit like Thalia, but what did he know? He had an attraction to her dragoness.

"I wish you luck in your challenging endeavor. Good thing it's only three weeks until the wedding."

The cold glitter of cynicism in her eyes caught him off guard. "Do you have any idea how much trouble a man and woman can find when following their undisciplined instincts? Do you have any notion at all of the sins that can be committed in twenty-one days? Not that I'm keeping count."

Drake decided not to reply; he could have written an encyclopedia on the subject of following one's lowest instincts. For now, however, he was safer playing the gentleman.

He extended his arm toward the steps. "Ladies, I have been asked by Lord Thornton to escort you home."

Thalia regarded him with an evil smile. "I know where you're going tonight," she said softly. "Everyone at the party was talking about *your* assignation."

He glanced at the other woman from the corner of his eyes. His dragoness had a pretty name. Eloise. Her gaze lifted to his face in silent appraisal. He realized then that a woman as comely as she was and in her position had probably been offered more than one opportunity to sin herself. Hadn't he given her the chance a little while ago? He wondered what it would have taken to persuade her.

"Your brother was caught cheating at cards tonight, Thalia," he said in an appropriately disapproving voice.

"He is to fight a duel in the morning and he has asked me to serve as his second."

Thalia glanced so helplessly at her companion that Drake almost felt like a dog for telling her about her brother's disgrace.

"He's done it again, Eloise."

"We have stayed at the party long enough," Eloise replied evenly, taking the girl by the arm. "Don't forget you're having breakfast with your future mother-in-law tomorrow." She paused before murmuring, "Assuming your brother manages to survive this duel with his life if not his dignity."

Chapter Four

❧ ❧

Eloise slipped off her cloak at the window of Thalia's bedroom as the black carriage below swept into the shadows of the London street. She had been so intent on getting the girl safely home that she had not properly thanked the gentleman for his courtesy. He would be late for his assignation, she thought. Despite their dalliance in the garden, he had given the impression during the short ride to Lord Thornton's leased Hill Street town house that he could not wait to discharge his duty.

Unfortunately Eloise knew exactly how he felt. Only three long weeks, at most, of this torture, she consoled herself. Three more harrowing weeks of guarding Miss Thornton from temptation before delivering her in a marriageable state to her unsuspecting fiancé. Eloise fervently hoped that his "golden-haired angel" would go untarnished to the lovestruck middle-aged merchant Sir Thomas Heaton, who obviously had no idea what a she-demon he had offered for.

The baronet had taken one look at Thalia across a crowded assembly room and tendered a proposal to her brother on the spot. Thalia had mocked his ardent interest to her friends until she discovered that her admirer had amassed a minor fortune in the spice trade. Eloise thought that the poor man deserved better, but Thalia's beauty had blinded him to her flaws. It was none of her business, in any case.

After all, the opinion of a companion was neither sought nor appreciated. And she had her own uncertain future to consider. She had already applied for her next position, that of instructress in the private academy that Emma Boscastle, the Viscountess Lyons, had opened here in London after closing her small but acclaimed school in Scotland. Her preliminary interview with Lady Lyons a few weeks ago had gone well. Eloise had been invited back to tea and assured that she was under serious consideration.

Foolishly, perhaps, she had pinned all her hopes on working for the viscountess, whose high standards in regard to the social graces were widely admired by those who cherished refinement. Eloise aspired to develop such standards of behavior herself, even if her client challenged that dedication on an hourly basis.

She had managed to thwart Miss Thornton's penchant for poor judgment at every turn. At least so far. But the effort had exhausted her emotional reserves. She lived in a constant state of terror that Thalia would find a way to disgrace them both before the wedding.

She glanced over her shoulder. Regrettably Eloise understood too well the pitfalls that a girl might encounter on the road to wedlock, having fallen into a nasty pit once herself. And having pulled herself out through sheer resolve. She was absolutely determined to walk Thalia to the altar in handcuffs if necessary. The effort required for this made her feel that she deserved the money the baronet had promised her, a severance pay if you will, although Sir Thomas had hinted that he might desire her services when he and Thalia produced an heir.

What an unappealing prospect. Eloise would rather scrub floors in Lady Lyons's elite academy than chase wild children around a country house while fending off the advances of amorous neighbors who thought that a governess was fair prey.

A soft thunk behind her broke into her troubled thoughts. She glanced around in faint irritation. Thalia was dragging a small trunk across the room to her armoire. Eloise watched her for a moment.

"What on earth are you doing?"

Thalia paused but did not turn around. If Eloise had not been so deeply mired in her thoughts, she would have sensed something amiss. But her defenses had been lowered. The hour was late, and Lord Thornton had still not returned from his disgrace. There would be a duel in the morning, and breakfast with the baronet's mother at her hotel. Eloise required a full night's rest to face the challenges of the next day.

"What are you doing?" she repeated a little sharply. She wondered what the baronet would think if she tied his bride-to-be to her bedpost until her wedding day.

"I'm looking for something suitable to wear for breakfast tomorrow."

Eloise turned as Thalia tossed a silver tissue dress onto the bed. "Surely you aren't wearing that—that handkerchief. One can practically see your limbs through the skirt."

"Then one shouldn't look." Thalia swung around, her pretty face petulant. "You may retire now, Eloise. I'm perfectly capable of selecting my own clothing."

Eloise retreated to the door. The case clock on the

nightstand showed the time as past midnight. Only twenty more days. She was so elated at the thought that she did not pause to consider Thalia's activities even a little suspicious.

Of course she could blame her distracted frame of mind on the man who'd brought them home. Would she ever see him again? Perhaps when she settled into bed she would have the privacy to think of the handsome stranger who had left a permanent brand on her lips with his kisses.

She was still thinking about him almost a full hour later, after she'd washed her face, scrubbed her teeth with tooth powder, and said her prayers.

An ominous clatter from the garden disturbed her pleasant yearnings. She flew out of bed to wrench open her window.

She stared down blindly at the ladder on the grass, her heart plunging in dread. Dear God, the girl had eloped, right under her nose. While Eloise had been mooning over a rake's kisses, her client had run away.

And with the ungrateful peagoose went her hard-earned reward from the unsuspecting baronet. Not to mention her reputation as a responsible companion.

She thundered back through her room and down the hall to Lord Thornton's chamber, bursting in without a thought to propriety. Not that he deserved propriety, or that it mattered much at the moment. He wasn't there to notice.

His bureau drawers had been pulled onto the floor and emptied. His wardrobe door hung open. She could only assume he'd decided to sneak into the house to remove his essentials, taking the coward's way out of his disgrace by running away. She picked up one of his dueling pistols from the floor.

"I'll kill him," she said at the top of her voice. "I'll kill everyone and be hanged in a madwoman's cage."

White-lipped, she clattered down the stairs to the small servants' hall where Freddie, the only footman Lord Thornton could afford, stood quaffing his nightly pint.

"Crumbs, Miss Goodwin," he exclaimed as he recognized her. "Where's the fire? And, my God, is that a gun in your hand?"

"She's gone." She looked at him in panic before dropping the gun on the table. "They've both gone. Lord Thornton's run off to avoid a duel, and his sister has finally made good on her threat to elope. At least I think she has."

"God's truth." He banged down his mug on the table beside the pistol. "There goes your money."

Bluebell, the ever-cheerful kitchen maid, popped her tousled head around the door. "Pipe down, you two. You'll wake up the entire bleedin' house."

"The entire bleedin' house is gone," Eloise said in a distraught voice.

The maid glanced at the footman in alarm. Miss Goodwin never swore. "What's the matter?" she asked, squeezing around the door with a worried frown. "Where have they gone then, miss?"

"God only knows." Eloise sank down disconsolately onto a hard oaken chair. "I've got to think. That stupid girl could not have gone far."

"Stupid girl?" Bluebell repeated, intrigued at this description of their inconsiderate mistress. It went without saying that they all shared this opinion, but the composed companion had never spoken so openly before. "Who did she run off with, miss?"

"A rake named Percy Chapman. I don't know where he lives, or what to do." She pounded her fist on the wall. "How could she do this to me?"

"Lord Thornton has to come back to make it all right," Bluebell said in a hopeful voice. "He can't just walk away from all he owns."

"All he's lost, you mean," Eloise said, her head starting to ache. "He gambled away everything but his cravat tonight, and got caught cheating at it into the bargain. He's gone through all the money he borrowed from the baronet."

"He cheated and still lost?" Freddie asked with a disgusted look.

Eloise narrowed her eyes. "Incredible, isn't it? He—"

The three of them glanced up simultaneously at the quiet but persistent rapping at the front door. The town house was modest, its staff small and struggling on poor wages. None of them had another decent position lined up. The servants had been counting on Eloise finding employment at Lady Lyons's academy and making connections with wealthy homes in which they could work.

If Miss Thornton had run off and gotten herself ruined, then they might well be prowling the streets together for employment. The scandal would taint the lot of them. It was bad enough being supported by a man caught cheating at cards.

"Who's here at this hour?" Bluebell asked, not budging an inch to find out.

Freddie looked at Eloise for guidance. "It might be the creditors. His lordship has been holding 'em at bay for weeks. What should we do?"

Eloise rose from her chair, her back rigid with dread.

"Perhaps something has happened to Lord Thornton or his sister. We cannot be cowardly."

"Why not?" Freddie wondered aloud. "It's not as if we've done anything wrong. Wot's the point in riskin' our necks, I want to know."

She brushed past him, refusing to surrender to fear. She could shake Thalia like a pullet for her scandalous turn. How would she ever explain an elopement to the baronet, or the behavior of Thalia's brother, for that matter? More important, how would she and the servants survive? Eloise had no friends in London to help her. Her relatives had disowned her nearly six years ago over her own secret scandal.

Her secret scandal.

That was what she'd come to call the fall from grace that had brought her to her current position. Only rarely did she think of her broken engagement, and her subsequent lapse into temporary insanity. A blithe young girl of nineteen, who lacked confidence and experience, she had been shattered when she'd discovered that her suitor was betraying her with another young woman he was affianced to in a nearby village. Her parents had expected her to swallow her betrothed's deception with a pained smile and to gracefully fade away into spinsterhood. She'd been expected, as an unassuming magistrate's daughter, to merely suffer in silence when she'd found out that handsome Ralph Hawkins had been playing her for a fool. The other woman, who had discovered the betrayal and notified Eloise, was a raging virago named Mildred Hammersmith. She had the temper of a tigress and made Eloise look tame in comparison.

Together, the pair of them had unleashed their shared wrath on their betrayer like avenging angels before leaving the shocked village on separate paths. Ralph had been lucky to escape with his miserable life after she and Mildred had finished with him. At Mildred's urging, the two women had confronted him in church before a speechless congregation. Actually Eloise had never been so embarrassed in her life, but Mildred had not been content to stop at a public shaming. She and her male cousins had stripped Ralph down to his skin and tied him to a dog-cart at the crossroads for the world to see. As if that were not enough, Mildred had then dragged Eloise to Ralph's cottage and set fire to his bed.

The following day the two scandalous women left the village on separate stagecoaches and never saw nor had contact with each other again.

"For heaven's sake, Eloise," Mildred said as they parted, "do not sniffle over Ralph. The man isn't worth a toad's tear." Mildred had produced a wrinkled handkerchief from her reticule. "It isn't as if you're completely ruined, are you?"

"No." Eloise blew her nose and gazed past Mildred at the smoke-blackened chimney of Ralph's cottage. She'd kept thinking that if she had married him, they would have slept in his burned bed every night. "Are you ruined, Mildred?" she asked, not really wanting to know the answer.

"Don't worry about me." Mildred tossed back her cascading coal black hair. Even then she'd seemed mature and beautiful, and Eloise had been a little in awe of her. It wasn't really surprising Ralph had been attracted to her. "I had no desire to stay in this boring little backwater, anyway. I may only be a tavern keeper's daughter, but I will not tolerate betrayal, Ellie, and you must promise me that you won't, either. Find a man who loves you enough to be loyal."

For the first few months following her departure from Titchbury Eloise wrote infrequent letters home to her family. They never invited her back, or even replied, and as the days passed she had less and less desire to return.

Finally she came to the decision that she'd rather work for the rest of her life than face the gossip she would engender by going back. Not that anyone seemed to miss her. It was as if she had ceased to exist to her family.

She had made a living as a governess and worked hard to establish good references. She rarely thought about Ralph, although she did wonder a little fondly what had become of Mildred Hammersmith.

Her secret scandal was all in the past, anyway. However, if she did not rise above her present crisis, she would be no better off than she had been six years ago.

She hurried through the narrow corridor to the front door, the creaky-kneed butler, Heston, hobbling a few steps ahead of her. "I'll answer it, miss," he said in a gruff voice. "It might be bad news."

Bad news. Countless unpleasant possibilities crowded her mind. Lord Thornton had committed suicide. Thalia had crashed in Percy's carriage. Creditors had come to claim the few valuables in the house, most of which had already been sold off to pay debts.

She paused at the hallstand, holding her breath in suspense as Heston cautiously opened the door. The shadow of a man stood against the moonlight, a lean, arresting figure. Her heart gave a rather frightened leap in response. She could not make out his features, but there was something familiar, compelling, and intensely masculine about his stance.

She exhaled in relief, rushing forward to prod the motionless butler into action. "Well, don't just stand there gawking, Heston. Where are your manners? Do let the gentleman in."

"But he's a stranger, and it's past midnight—"

Eloise had to restrain herself from wrenching the door off its hinges. It was him, she thought in giddy relief. The self-assured, handsome scoundrel-friend of Lord Thornton's who had kissed her and brought her home. She recognized the crisp, black hair, the impressive physique in an elegantly tailored greatcoat, which reminded her that it must be chilly outside at this time of night because he had been wearing only an evening jacket earlier—she took control of her scattered thoughts and frowned at the startled butler.

"Don't be a dolt," she said under her breath. "He would not be here at this hour unless he had urgent business. Bring him inside this instant."

Chapter Five

❦ ❦

Drake allowed a smiling young maidservant to remove his evening jacket while he greeted a group of acquaintances in the receiving vestibule of Audrey Watson's exclusive salon. He was a frequent visitor to the house; indeed, only a favored few of London's Society were granted the privilege. Audrey adhered to more stringent restrictions of admission than even Almack's, but then the pleasures she offered came at a steeper price.

For years Audrey had harbored a genuine fondness for the Boscastle family, as well as for those elite men and women in all walks of society who possessed either great wealth, wit, or beauty. Drake Boscastle claimed all three attributes, as did most of his relations. It was no secret to Audrey that he had been discontented lately, and that he was considering rejoining the military. It was rumored that he would travel to India. She and his ardent admirers had discussed in depth how concerned they were over losing one of their favorite visitors.

Drake took the glass of burgundy a footman brought him. Fine wine, excellent food, stimulating conversation, sexual pleasure—all could be experienced in this private establishment. He wasn't in the mood for much of anything all of a sudden, aware only of a need to either appease or numb the gnawing ache inside him. In the past, he'd known how to relieve it. Tonight, well, he was suddenly unsure of what would satisfy him. The woman he had anticipated with such pleasure?

Audrey approached him, her auburn hair drawn back elegantly onto her nape. She studied him in unconcealed pleasure as she took the goblet from his strong hands. "Drake," she said in a combination of delight and despair, "I wasn't sure if you had changed your mind. You're terribly late."

"A problem arose." His dark blue eyes scanned the room. "Are her feelings wounded?"

"She's offended. A woman of her worth isn't accustomed to waiting. This does not bode well."

His firm mouth curved into a wicked smile. "I shall have to make it up to her, shan't I?"

"Lucky Maribella," she murmured. She laid her fingertips against his arm. "Have you given this much thought? She's difficult to please."

His eyes glittered devilishly. "So am I."

"She's so expensive."

"Then it's a good thing I can afford her." He straightened his shoulders. "Where is she?"

"In the small room next to the Venetian chamber you'd requested. She didn't care for the view."

He wasn't at all surprised. "A lady who asks for what she wants. I shall have to be on my best."

Audrey examined him with a sardonic smile. "You shall have to merely breathe and be yourself. Some women I know would pay *you* for the privilege."

He leaned down to brush his mouth against her cheek in an affectionate kiss. He counted her among his truest friends. "An exaggeration, surely. I cannot even stand myself of late. I hope I can coax her into a pleasant temper."

She gave him a reluctant nudge into the torchlit tapestry-lined hall. "She won't even see you if you make her wait any longer. Go, darling. There's a small fortune at stake on the outcome. Everyone is betting on how this affair will unfold."

Drake gave a deep laugh. "I'm curious to see how it plays out myself."

And yet he felt little more than a restless curiosity as he walked down the hall and stood before the closed door behind which his fate, or at least a sexual detour, awaited. He wasn't sure why his anticipation had dulled in the past few hours. Well, he was always in the mood for sex.

He opened the door.

Maribella was reclining with her back to him on a crimson-silk-draped Duchess bed, her unbound bronze red hair and bare white shoulders the first details to attract his notice. She was surprisingly on the slender side, more fragile than he'd imagined she would be, but there was no denying the smoldering sexuality in her smoke-gray eyes as she turned to study him. Her full red lips lifted into a practiced smile. "I thought you might have changed your mind."

She had a low, sultry voice, and most men would have responded to it on the spot. Drake could not deny her physical allure, but he was aware of a fleeting sense of disappointment. She was beautiful, yes, with dramatic coloring and finely carved features. She was also as cool as ice and rather detached despite the rumors of her volatile nature. His last mistress would have been throwing pillows or knives at him for being late.

He was cool, too. A few people considered him cold. "I apologize for being late. I didn't mean to slight you."

She sat up slowly, her ivory tissue gown clinging to the curves of her body. "As long as there wasn't a woman involved."

There had been two of them, actually, but Drake had no intention of telling her that. Not when he'd gone to so much trouble to arrange this meeting. He'd be the laughingstock of his friends if it turned out that he'd ruined his tryst to help a lady's companion. Miss Eloise Goodwin, he mused, her image suddenly vivid in his mind.

He grinned inwardly as he remembered the chagrin on her face when she thought she'd caught him with her client. And her look of embarrassment when she realized her mistake. The pretty dragoness would glare him dead if she could see him now. She probably had only the vaguest idea that establishments like this existed. Then again, he could have underestimated her. She'd been sharp enough dealing with him. Perhaps she did know.

And she had smelled like soap. Not some costly French-milled fragrance, but a pure old-fashioned Castile soap that scrubbed away the sins of the world. She hadn't seemed like a sinner.

He was one, though. He doubted all the soap in the world could wash his soul clean. He'd whored and killed in a hellish war. He had drunk himself into a daze more times than he could recall. He had drunk in sorrow when he'd lost both his parents and the younger brother the entire family adored. He had drunk in celebration as his siblings had abandoned their hedonistic ways for wedlock.

The sensual touch of a woman's fingers on his shirt-front interrupted his reverie. He drew a deep breath, closing his hand over her wrist. "Looking for something?"

She smiled up at him, but there was a detachment in her eyes that most men would never notice. "I thought I'd make you more comfortable."

"We could start by talking about you."

He saw the flicker of hesitation in her eyes. "I've taken three long-term lovers in the course of my career. Anything else you may have heard about my affairs is probably untrue. What else do you want to know?"

She sank down against the gold-tasseled bolsters. The tops of her breasts swelled over her bodice, and he saw that her nipples had been rouged. In the past, the mere sight of a woman such as she would have stirred his senses into black lust. Tonight, for no reason he could name, her efforts to arouse seemed mundane. If she was to be his mistress, she would have to learn that his preference leaned more to the understated.

He suppressed a sudden urge to smile. He'd read that she'd given lavish parties in her villa at Naples and allowed her pigs and chickens to roam at will in the ballroom. He didn't think it was an appropriate comment to initiate an affair, though, so he merely said, "I read that you've recently returned from the Continent. Is that true?"

He noted the faint tightening of her mouth. He decided there was more to her than he'd been led to believe. "I read that you are a dangerous man, Drake Boscastle. Is that true?"

He smiled. "That's up to you."

* * *

Eloise concealed her disappointment behind a wary look as the caller stepped into the entryway. He bore a superficial resemblance to the other gentleman and was handsome in his own right, with his cropped black hair and dark brooding face. But she had never seen him before in her life. She took an instinctive step back from the door.

Heavens above, she had just admitted a complete stranger into the house at an ungodly hour. Which meant that Heston the ancient oracle was right. This man could only be the bearer of bad news. She braced herself for the blow. He hadn't come to the door to rob them; she wondered fleetingly if he was a friend of the family whom she had never met before.

"I am Miss Goodwin, employed in this household," she said with a guarded formality. "Is something wrong? Has Miss Thornton been found?"

The stranger's black eyebrows shot up. He'd taken her meaning with uncanny perception. "Is she missing?"

She could have bitten off her tongue. "I mean, has her fan been found? She mislaid it tonight at the party."

"I see," he said after a pause.

What he saw was that she was lying through her teeth, Eloise thought, although he appeared to be gracious enough to let the deception go. "Have you come to see Lord Thornton?"

He glanced appraisingly around the hallway. Eloise and Freddie exchanged uneasy looks. He didn't behave like a bailiff, but, in these uncertain times, who could tell? "I don't know if Thornton has mentioned my name. I am Sir Gabriel," he added at her blank look. "Your employer is supposed to fight a duel with me in the morning."

Eloise raised her chin in disdain. So this was the other gambler, the duelist—

"He isn't here," she said, swallowing her distaste. "I'm not sure when he'll return."

"Ah." His gaze assessed her with polite curiosity. "What a pity. I wished to give him a chance to make a public apology for cheating. Perhaps I should wait?"

She sagged back against the wall, noting irrelevantly that the wallpaper had begun to peel off and ought to be replaced. Not that she or even her employer would be present to see it done. "He's gone," she repeated, shaking her head. "I don't know when he's coming back, or where he's gone."

"Desperation brings out the worst in a man," he said awkwardly.

It brought out the worst in a woman, too, Eloise had discovered. No prospective employer would be impressed by her background when it was revealed that she'd worked for a debtor, a cheat, no less, and had lost his sister, her charge, into the bargain. How many competent companions lost their clients? No one would take into account that Thalia was hell-bent on ruining her reputation. Eloise would be blamed; at the very least it would not look impressive on a résumé. Nor could she use as a reference an employer who had vanished.

She stared past Sir Gabriel into the misty gaslit street. Only twenty days. "I'm sunk if she doesn't come home soon," she thought aloud. "Her fiancé will be furious, and his mother—dear me, what will I tell her in the morning?"

Sir Gabriel looked at her in puzzlement. "Are you referring to Miss Thornton again?"

She scowled at him. It wasn't polite, but there was no point in keeping up the pretense indefinitely. "Yes," she practically snapped at him. "She's run off and so has her brother. She was to be married in a few weeks, but she met a man at the ball tonight—"

"Percy Chapman?"

Eloise nodded in resignation. Self-pity would never do. If she went to gaol, she could feel sorry for herself all day long. "Yes. I believe that's who she's with."

Gabriel seemed to be holding back a smile. He was quite an attractive man, she thought, although she had come to the conclusion he was something of a rogue himself. He knew Percy for one thing. He gambled and fought duels for another, and she suspected by the way he looked at her that he was no stranger to seduction, either.

"I don't know what to do," she said, shaking her head. "Perhaps the gentleman who brought Miss Thornton and me home has an idea of where to find his lordship. But I don't know where to find him, either. His name was Drake—"

Sir Gabriel gazed down at her in disbelief. "Drake? You're talking about my cousin. Of course. Horace threw himself at Drake's mercy. I was there."

"Does your cousin have a surname?"

His laughter held a dark ring that sent a little frisson of foreboding down her back. "I'll say. He's a Boscastle. We both are, but he happens to be several steps higher than me on the family ladder. Lord Drake Boscastle," he mused, his eyes gleaming with irony. "Horace's late brother was close to the brood."

A shock of detached horror gripped Eloise. Well, wasn't that the jewel in her crown of rotten luck? Lord Drake Boscastle, one of the viscountess's notorious brothers. She had kissed, insulted, and practically assaulted the brother of the one person in London she was desperate to impress.

What if Lord Drake mentioned tonight's events to Lady Lyons at a family supper? Did scoundrels discuss their attempted seductions with their sisters? Why of all people had he singled her out? And why had she allowed it?

"I've heard of your family," she murmured numbly.

"Hasn't everyone?" he asked in a dry voice.

She nodded, her mind reeling. Was Drake the Boscastle brother so frequently embroiled in scandal? Or were they all wicked in their ways? Drake Boscastle. Drake, Drake, Drake. Which brother was he, anyway? The elder brother, whose name escaped her, had gotten married last year after some sort of wedding scandal. She thought that there were three other brothers. Or was it four? One had died, hadn't he? She searched through the archives of her mind for all the trivial social knowledge she had accumulated.

All of the Boscastle males were alleged scoundrels, popular in the haut ton and the half-world. One of them had gotten swept into notoriety only months ago.

There had been a cartoon in the gossip sheets of a certain Boscastle brother. A nude cartoon that had depicted parts of his male anatomy in scandalous detail. Eloise had caught Thalia and her friends giggling in delight over the wicked caricature, and she'd ordered them to toss the papers in the fire. Now she wished she had taken a better look herself. Not that she would be able to draw any similarities between the man in the cartoon and the one she had kissed.

"Drake might know where Lord Thornton is, I suppose," Sir Gabriel said in a thoughtful voice.

"But do you have any idea where we might find your cousin?" she asked, biting her bottom lip.

Gabriel's gaze flickered to her mouth. If Eloise had not been so intent on begging his help, she would have listened to the small inner voice that warned her not to trust him.

"He is attending a private party in a house on Bruton Street," he said slowly. "I meant to return there myself. It's possible that I could persuade him to address your concerns. In the interest of time, you could . . . well, I suppose you could accompany me there."

"That's bleedin' kind of you, sir," Freddie said with an anxious glance in Eloise's direction. "Isn't it, Miss Goodwin?"

"Please guard your language, Freddie." She realized she had gone to pieces earlier this evening. It was improper, even dangerous, to venture out this late at night, and with a virtual stranger. But if she did not bring Thalia, or at least her brother, home, then her reputation would not matter. Her greatest concern was that the girl would come to great harm, and her ruination would fall on Eloise's conscience.

She put on the cloak and gloves that Heston had brought her. The housekeeper, Mrs. Barnes, and two other servants, awakened by the sound of voices, gathered in the shadows of the hall, regarding her in concern. Eloise nodded at them like a soldier about to go off into battle.

"Do be careful, miss," Mrs. Barnes said in an anxious voice, then, "Oh, that wicked young girl, to put us through all this worry."

Eloise managed a nod and turned to the door. She was so distressed she'd forgotten to pin back her hair, and it tumbled rather untidily over her shoulders in a manner she could only describe as wanton. No matter. She was not a woman to be noticed, and she had a mission to accomplish—rescuing a confused young girl from a rake's seduction. She felt her lips tighten into a grim line. No one in this household would guess that she had personal experience dealing with a rake. Or that her heart had been broken by a deceptive man and she had become stronger for the experience.

Chapter Six

❧ ❧

As a rule, Colonel Sir Gabriel Boscastle did not examine his conscience. When he sinned, it was usually with a consenting woman, and when he gambled, he played against an equal match. He might not be one of the passionate and popular London Boscastles, but the devilish family blood ran hotly through his veins, and he'd done his share to contribute to the line's reputation for the pursuit of wicked pleasures.

For some reason he and Drake had repeatedly found themselves in competition at various times in their lives, frequently over a desirable woman. Only last evening did it occur to Gabriel that it wasn't as much their differences as their similarities that had pitted one cousin against the other. Theirs was a convivial rivalry. Although, to Gabriel's amused disgust, Drake always managed to beat him to the finish line.

It was difficult to compete with a master, as devoted as Gabriel was to hedonistic delights. Ironic that the two of them would meet on a dueling field later that morning, for the pretense of satisfying honor. God knew neither he nor Drake wished to shoot the other. He wouldn't mind shooting Horace, though, and he suspected Drake probably felt the same way.

Or perhaps Drake had completely forgotten about the duel, lost, no doubt, as he was in the sexual splendor of his latest mistress. Gabriel had caught a glimpse of Maribella St. Ives once in her carriage and had been instantly smitten. He could not get through her cadre of bodyguards to introduce himself, however.

"I cannot tell you how much I appreciate your assistance," Miss Goodwin murmured as she settled down on the edge of the carriage seat opposite him. "And your discretion," she added in an anxious voice.

"I won't tell a soul," Gabriel assured her. He wouldn't, either, and the more he looked at her in the moonlight, the more he realized how very pretty she was, especially with that mass of wavy brown hair falling waywardly over her shoulders. He sensed there might be a voluptuous figure underneath that plain attire. His cousin must have noticed. Gabriel had not missed the faint blush on her cheeks when she had spoken about Drake. Hell, he wouldn't mind having a companion like her himself. Or a mistress like Maribella St. Ives, a woman who had made the study of sensual arts her calling.

"Bruton Street," Miss Goodwin said, peering out the window. "I suppose I should be grateful we're traveling to a decent neighborhood."

Gabriel glanced out the window. Decent neighborhood it might be. But their destination? He had managed to gain admittance to Audrey Watson's salon earlier tonight, but no one was allowed in the upstairs sanctum of private rooms without a special invitation. The establishment catered to a wide range of pleasures, earthly delights that Miss Goodwin probably never dreamed could be sampled. The callow young footman on the box outside, however, whom she had brought along for protection, would no doubt think he'd died and gone to heaven if he glimpsed some of Audrey's entertainments.

The coachman slowed at the end of the street behind another parked carriage. Gabriel heard Miss Goodwin give a sigh of relief. "Is this the house?" she asked as she appraised the elegant brick façade.

He sat forward. "Yes."

"Well, it looks very nice. Quite respectable."

He masked a smile. "It does, doesn't it?"

"I cannot tell you how relieved I am," she added, folding her hands in her lap. "A few unpleasant possibilities had entered my mind."

He gazed at her. His cousin was going to kill him for this. "Really?"

"London does have its decadent side," she said, turning her head slowly to look at him; for an uncomfortable moment he sensed that she knew he'd walked on the decadent side a few times himself.

"All right then." He shrugged off the guilt that had threatened to detract from the pleasure of the dirty trick he intended to play on Drake. "I shall fetch my cousin and dispatch him to you posthaste."

The seams of Eloise's full mouth pressed down into a worried line. "I do hope he won't mind being disturbed."

Gabriel suppressed an evil grin. Mind? Drake would be out of his mind with blazing anger. Still, this was too good a chance for Gabriel to get a close look at Maribella, if not a personal introduction. Revenge and sex. Could anything be sweeter? "Right. I'm off to Mrs. Watson's."

"Mrs. Watson?" Eloise said with a frown. "Where have I heard that name before?"

He leaned toward the door. His footman and Freddie

already stood on the pavement, both gazing up in awe at the house. "Probably in the papers," he answered vaguely.

"The papers?" she asked in reflective voice. "Is she a Society hostess?"

Gabriel stepped down onto the pavement and straightened his coat. Far be it for him to inform her that her hero Lord Drake was most likely at this moment deep in the throes of passion inside one of London's most exclusive bordellos. It was hardly a secret.

Still, he'd leave it up to his cousin to inform her. And take advantage of the situation in whatever way he could. After all, Gabriel was a Boscastle, too, and it was time he scored a point in his favor.

Drake rose from the bed to pour himself and Maribella a glass of wine from the lacquered cabinet that sat beneath the heavily draped window. Maribella, playing a harp, was posed on a stool in the corner. Her long, flame red hair flowed down her back like that of a Celtic enchantress. She had rubbed his shoulders with a light but erotic expertise, claiming he needed to relax. There was no denying her ability to put a man at ease or to arouse his senses, but something vital was missing.

Was it him? Or her? Was she merely too practiced or was he jaded beyond redemption? He had never particularly desired to be redeemed. Sinning was something he excelled at, if no longer enjoyed, and he felt quite ambivalent about the recent loss of his three siblings to a fate he had always considered worse than death: falling in love. Losing what little control one had over one's life.

Maribella twanged a false note on the harp, swore

aloud, and rose from the stool. To quell the urge to laugh he pushed open the drapes to study the street below. She glided up behind him, slipping her nimble fingers inside his waistband. "Why were you late, anyway?" she asked huskily. "I don't like it when a lover makes me wait."

"Nothing personal, darling," he murmured, not moving a muscle. "I was doing a friend a good turn."

But strangely it was not Horace Thornton or his impertinent sister he thought of as he answered. It was the beleaguered companion, and the sweet crush of her body against his. Those direct hazel eyes of hers intruded on his memory. He remembered the unexpected sting of arousal he'd felt when he kissed her. Her image was so clearly imprinted on his mind that it was almost as if she were with him at this moment—

He blinked. He shook his head. There was a carriage parked below the window, and he could see a woman's face peering out from the folds of the leather curtain. It wasn't possible, of course. It was an illusion. Either that, or someone had slipped a fantasy-inducing mushroom in the wine. But—he narrowed his eyes.

He could swear the woman sitting in the carriage was Miss Eloise Goodwin. Which couldn't be possible because a proper young gentlewoman would not be caught within screaming distance of such an establishment unless— Lord God, what a laughable possibility—did she conduct a secret life as a courtesan? Was she supplementing her meager income as one of Audrey's girls? He realized that sort of thing happened, but it was too much of a coincidence that he'd met her earlier in the demure position of companion only to discover that she led a double life as a provocative counterpart.

Maribella's fingertips traced a path across his rib cage to his forearm. "Why do I have the feeling that I don't have your full attention?" she whispered.

He shook his head again. "Because I'm"—the murmur of voices in the hallway, punctuated by a quiet but insistent knock, interrupted him—"I'm listening to that," he said, gently lifting her hand from his arm. "I gave instructions that I was not to be disturbed unless it was an emergency." Or a war.

The only people who would dare disturb him here were his brothers. The members of his family acknowledged few rules or boundaries, and he was going to have someone's head unless the interruption proved to be a true crisis. He glanced back curiously at the carriage parked outside, but his mystery woman had retreated behind the curtains. Or come inside.

He gave Maribella an apologetic smile as he strode to the door. She had returned to the canopied bed, half reclining behind the curtains. She looked dramatic, alluring, and more than a little annoyed. She played the part of pampered courtesan to the hilt.

He cracked open the door, his face as friendly as frost. "Whatever this is, it had better be justified. It—What in the name of God?"

His cousin Gabriel stood before him, a brash grin on his hard, sun-bronzed face. Behind him hovered Audrey Watson, the proprietress of the house, and two of Maribella's unsmiling bodyguards, who were flexing their arms as if to physically remove Gabriel at the snap of their employer's fingers.

"What the devil are you doing here, Gabriel?" he demanded.

Audrey shouldered her way between the two bodyguards. "What could I do? He insisted it was an emergency, and he is family."

"Barely," Drake said, glaring at his cousin who, he realized, was doing his best to steal a peek inside the room. He wedged his body against the door to thwart the view. "This had better be important, Gabriel."

"Did I come at a bad time?" Gabriel asked guilelessly. "Perhaps you should let me into the room so that I can speak my piece in private. No point in everyone knowing our business."

Drake's face darkened dangerously. "Do you want me to thrash you? It wouldn't be the first time, as I recall."

"I'm bigger now," Gabriel said pleasantly. "I really think you should allow me—"

Audrey interrupted him. "No quarreling in my home, and that goes for the Prince Regent as well as the Boscastles. The next thing I know you shall be fighting a duel, and my dignity will be offended."

"We are fighting a duel," Drake said in a disgruntled voice. "I think I might go ahead and kill him after this."

Audrey glanced over his shoulder, whispering, "Not over Maribella already?"

"No," Drake said. "Over a man."

"A—"

Gabriel threw up his hands as if to surrender. "And that's why I'm here," he said under his breath so that only Drake could hear. "I went to Thornton's house to see if he would apologize in public so that I wouldn't have to shoot him this morning, and it turns out he's disappeared, and so has his sister."

"What the blazes do you want me to do?" Drake asked in disbelief.

"I don't particularly care, but that companion of

Thalia's has gotten herself in hysterics over it and begged me very prettily to find you."

"Well, I'm not coming," Drake said, aware that Maribella had risen from the bed to glare at him. And that Gabriel was practically breaking his neck to stare at her. "Tell her I'll visit her tomorrow."

Drake glanced back at the window. It couldn't be, but he knew now that it was. That appealing, pretty face. The woman who had been ready to thrash him because she thought he'd been seducing her client, and whom he'd stolen a kiss from at the ball. She ought to see him now.

"You brought that young woman, a lady's companion, to a brothel?" he asked Gabriel in a clipped undertone.

Gabriel gave him a cursory glance. "I brought her to you."

"You're a bastard, Gabriel," he said.

"I'm a Boscastle." Gabriel retreated a few steps as Drake began to advance on him. "Wait. What was a gentleman to do? I felt sorry for her. She's easy on the eyes, you know, and I've never been able to resist a damsel in distress."

Drake shoved him out into the hallway. "Being such a compassionate soul."

"Well, since you'd helped her earlier, and she thought you might be inclined to help again, I assumed you'd want me to perpetuate the myth of your saintliness."

"I'll perpetuate you, cousin or not."

Drake scowled and stopped in hesitation. Audrey and the two guards were standing at the end of the hall as if to prevent the two men from continuing their argument in front of their other guests. Maribella had folded her slender white arms across her chest and was staring at him with glacial indignation. *"Ma chère,"* he said, shrugging helplessly, "it's not my fault. I'll be right back to explain everything."

"Don't bother," she said between her teeth. Then she slammed the door so hard that even Gabriel jumped back in alarm, and the echo reverberated through the walls.

Chapter Seven

❧ ❧

It had taken Eloise several minutes to realize exactly what sort of establishment the respectable-looking façade concealed. She'd watched with a prickle of suspicion as Gabriel hurried up the steps of the house, to be admitted only after a lengthy interrogation by two liveried servants at the door. She had caught a glimpse of an elegant candlelit wall with mirrored recesses; with slow-dawning alarm she recalled that when the names "Mrs. Watoon" and "Bruton Street" were mentioned together in the newspapers, it was not in reference to a poetry reading or musicale.

Well, it often was, but always with the underlying implication of another sort of more carnal entertainment. Sex, pure and simple. Expensive. Exclusive. Excessive.

She snorted softly, startling Freddie out of his dreamy trance as she stepped out of the carriage beside him. "It's a—a—"

"—bordello," he said in a wistful undertone. "Among the finest of its ilk in London."

"Which is of small moral reassurance."

"I'd give my eye teeth to work 'ere."

"Oh, honestly, Freddie."

"Yes, honestly." He smoothed down his thicket of

red-blond hair, which Eloise had always thought gave him the startling appearance of a human mop. "Sir Gabriel's been inside a bit long. Do you think I should check to see if 'e forgot you?"

She grabbed him by his coattails. "Don't you dare go inside that house," she said in the authoritarian governess's voice that she reserved for times of emergency. "We have come here for only one reason, and that is for help finding Lord Thornton and his sister, after which I shall most likely shake them both into a stupor."

Freddie eyed her with concern. "I've never heard you so upset, miss. This evening's got you all undone."

Her voice rose. "It doesn't help that I begged to be brought to a House of Venus. Or—" She broke off, releasing Freddie's coattails and diving back into the carriage.

She'd recognized him the moment he appeared at the front door, his lithe figure advancing in powerful strides. His lean face was obscured in shadow; Eloise found herself so lost in appreciation of his magnetic presence that it did not immediately occur to her that he was missing his evening jacket. And his beautifully starched cravat.

He descended on the carriage with the graceful wrath of a fallen angel; the closer he drew, the more obvious appeared the irritation on his hard, chiseled features. In a startled glance Eloise noticed that his well-tailored white waistcoat was unbuttoned, as was most of the shirt beneath.

"He's half-undressed," she said in a disappointed voice through the door, unable to tear her gaze from the sight. "What on earth could he have been doing?"

Freddie cleared his throat. "Perhaps he was boxing, miss. The sport is very popular with the swells."

"Boxing, Freddie. In a brothel at this time of night. Do I appear to be a proper idiot?"

Eloise did not hear his reply, nor was she sure he even made one. All her attention centered suddenly on the hard-visaged man who flung open the carriage door to address her. For a moment every sensible thought flew out of her head. He looked intense and understandably perplexed. Yet as he met her eyes, he appeared to curb his temper. The forbidding hardness eased from his expression, only to be replaced by what she recognized from personal experience as thinly veiled exasperation.

"I have to apologize," she said in embarrassment. "I would not be here if the situation were not desperate." Or if Sir Gabriel had warned her exactly where he was taking her, demon that he was.

She watched him draw a controlled breath. "Miss Goodwin."

She indulged herself in a moment of illicit pleasure at the sound of her name being spoken in such a suave, albeit exasperated, voice. Actually Goodwin was not her surname at all, but Eloise had wanted to start life afresh in London. Goodwin was a family name, the name of an elderly aunt on her paternal side, to be precise. Surely one could forgive the slight distortion of the truth for the sake of burying past transgressions.

She shook her head. "I would never have disturbed you had I known—"

Had she known what? Faced with his faintly disheveled state, perhaps it was better that she did not know exactly what she had disturbed. Unfortunately she had more than an inkling. She was certainly not as unworldly as most people assumed her to be. Naïveté in a companion proved to be more a liability than an asset.

A woman in her profession was expected to anticipate moral pitfalls without ever having fallen into them.

She had learned a bitter lesson from her own experience, although for the life of her she did not completely understand what that lesson had been. That a woman had to be on constant guard against deception? That all men who professed undying love were suspect?

"What is the matter?" Lord Drake demanded of her, his dark gaze drifting over her before she could reply.

She lowered her eyes as he climbed inside the carriage and sat down opposite her. Who would have believed that she would be asking the help of a man who had just left a brothel without even bothering to finish dressing properly? She stared at his strong bare throat.

How uninhibited of this gentleman to appear in public unbuttoned. Of course he'd been in a house where inhibitions were discarded, along with clothes, at the door. She was fortunate he had not exposed more.

He leaned toward her without warning, his knees touching hers. Eloise felt her pulses jump as he asked again in a low if understandably impatient voice, "What is the matter?"

She glanced up from her inappropriate absorption of his throat. The proximity of his face, his disconcerting blue eyes, flustered her thoughts. "You aren't properly buttoned," she said as if he were unaware of the fact.

His heavy eyebrows rose fractionally. "Did you come all the way here at this time of night to tell me that?"

She sat back against the squabs. "Of course not. "How could I possibly know the state of your apparel in advance?"

"Do you realize what sort of establishment you have

come to, Miss Goodwin?" he asked, and to his credit, there was no mockery in the question.

She swallowed uncomfortably. "Yes."

His brooding eyes traveled over her with renewed interest. His deep voice dropped to a seductive pitch that sent a tingle down her spine. "And you still came here?"

He leaned forward before she could reply and positioned himself on the seat beside her. "Are you seeking a different position than that of companion to a spoiled young lady?"

"Not that kind of position you're referring to, I'm certain."

"How do you know until you apply?"

"I'm not applying for a position!"

"Well, you did come to a bordello."

The dancing fire in the depths of his deep blue eyes sent heat flushing through her body. And somehow he knew. With a faint smile of acknowledgment he pulled her closer and kissed her.

She strained against his arm, then subsided, shivering lightly. He drew her into the warm, solid wall of his chest. She felt her hand lift slowly to his shoulder as she closed her eyes. His lips brushed across hers until she responded, her mouth softening, opening at his urging.

He murmured his approval, and the intent of his kiss deepened into an unmistakable invitation to darker pleasures. Shifting lights and shadows flickered behind her closed eyelids. He slipped his hand up beneath her cloak and stroked his knuckles in the barest caress just below her breasts.

"Perhaps one day," he breathed against her parted lips, "we will meet at a more appropriate place and time so that I could properly—or improperly—tempt you."

"You've tempted me enough," she whispered.

His voice vibrated with wicked humor as he swung back onto the opposite seat. "Why the bloody blazes are you here, if you'll pardon me for asking? And just what is it that you want of me?"

She wanted suddenly to strangle him. She wanted to bang open the carriage door and tell every thoughtless lord and lady in London to go to the devil. But sanity, a sense of desperation, prevailed. "Lord Thornton has left home," she said, her voice breaking at the end.

"I'm not surprised."

"And so has his sister." The words came out in a rush. She was afraid she'd lost her chance to enlist his help. "I fear that she's run off with the rake she met at the party. Her life will be quite ruined, you see, unless I find her. Her fiancé will never forgive her if he finds out. She doesn't know what she's doing."

He studied her in utter silence. Perhaps he was appalled at her lack of judgment. Perhaps she had shocked him speechless, although the glitter in his eyes indicated a more sophisticated response. "I am sorry," she added, to fill in the awkward quiet that had fallen. "You were helpful earlier, and I did not know who else to ask. I don't wish to see either of them hurt for all their rash behavior. I would never have come to you for help if—" If you hadn't danced with me tonight, she thought. "Well, if you weren't friends with Lord Thornton."

She turned her face to the carriage window, her cheeks burning. Imagine sitting outside a School of Venus. If anyone recognized her, she would never be able to explain it.

"Miss Goodwin." He offered her a roguish smile as she glanced back at him in hesitation.

She felt a tight, aching sensation in the pit of her stomach. His smile wielded an unfair advantage. How often had she warned Thalia against succumbing to the lure of a handsome man?

"I thought you might know where to find him," she added, as if he cared that she lived on a mere pittance, that she could not afford to buy even one pretty dress for herself. Or that Thalia was probably being seduced out of her pretty dress at this very moment while her frazzled companion sat here pleading with a rakish gentleman who was probably anxious to go back inside the brothel and take off his harlot's dress. If he hadn't already.

"I should never have come."

A smile lingered at the corners of his firm, masculine mouth. "No, you should not. But now that you're here, I suppose I'm obligated to help you."

She could barely conceal her relief. "Oh, thank you . . . Lord Drake. I didn't know before how to properly address you." She hadn't known he was a Boscastle, either.

Which reminded her that he was as unlike his respectable sister as was a lion and a lamb. It hardly went without saying that Lady Lyons would be shocked to learn that Eloise had summoned her brother from a seraglio to help her find her missing client.

His amused voice roused her from her troubled reflections. "Is there anything else about me you wish to know? It might spare you some embarrassment in the future."

She met his ironic gaze. She could not envision a more embarrassing situation. "I think I know all that is necessary for now," she said with a quiet sigh. "A bordello speaks quite eloquently for itself."

* * *

For the life of him, Drake could not understand why he was not more upset that she had ruined his evening. He had the infamous Miss St. Ives waiting for him, a woman who could bring a man to his knees with a look, and he'd paid extravagantly for their arrangement. He could hardly blame Maribella for slamming the door in his face. He'd be insulted if she deserted him in the middle of a seduction for . . . for what? *What* exactly had he gotten himself into?

He studied Eloise across the carriage. Her hair had fallen across her shoulders in a tumble of thick waves that made him think of sex. Hell, it wasn't surprising, considering they were parked outside a house of pleasure. He felt like punching Gabriel for bringing her here.

His gaze darkened in speculation. He didn't know quite what to make of her. She was outwardly sensible, and within, well, there might be more to her than anyone knew. He wouldn't mind spending time alone with her to satisfy his curiosity. He rubbed his jaw. God, he must be beyond jaded if he found a lady's companion tempting when he had a professional courtesan waiting for him. Or not. He'd have to make amends to Maribella if she was ever going to speak to him again.

He leaned toward the door. He had just noticed his cousin Gabriel exiting Audrey's house, which meant that the sneaky bastard had not gotten the meeting with Maribella that he had wanted. Served the swine right, too. "Excuse me, Miss Goodwin," he said. "I have a private matter that has been left dangling, you might say."

She vented a deep sigh. Drake had the surprising sense that she'd grasped the innuendo a little too quickly.

Gabriel stopped at the carriage door just as Drake

stepped outside to confront him. "Don't bother, Drake," he said, shaking his head. "Your ladybird has just left by the back passageway with her bodyguards."

Drake swore under his breath.

Gabriel grinned. "Oh, she told me to give you a message: No one abandons her for another woman. No one."

Eloise stuck her head out the carriage door, studying Drake in chagrin. "You have another woman? Two in the same night?"

Gabriel cleared his throat. "You're the other woman, Miss Goodwin."

She opened her mouth, but nothing emerged. At least not for several seconds until she said, in a rather choked voice, "Your personal life is not my business, Lord Drake. And I do hate to seem so persistent, but I am rather desperate to bring Miss Thornton home."

"I agreed, didn't I?" He stared at her with his most forbidding smile. "Although, not to sound rude myself, but I must be short a sheet to go along with this."

He had to give her credit. Her voice sounded remarkably steady when she replied, "Goodness is its own reward."

"Not in my experience, although I can't honestly say I've had a great deal of practice. And I shouldn't, but I have to ask—have you ever considered that Thalia may not want to be found?" Just as he didn't want to be rewarded. He only wanted the darkness that hung over him to go away.

He smothered the spark of guilt that flared inside him as Eloise looked down at her lap, presumably appalled at his outburst of cynicism. He could have told her that living a decent life didn't matter in the least. His mother had been the sweetest woman in the world, and she'd suffered a slow death from a lingering disease. His brother Brandon had been brave and young, and he had been ambushed and brutally murdered.

Miss Goodwin had apparently deceived herself into thinking that he was some sort of gentleman, despite their heated interlude in the garden. Well, better she face the truth now rather than later, because he found her a little too attractive for her own good. "All right," he said. "I agreed to help. I'll try to find your missing employers, but in the meantime I insist that you return to the house and await word."

Slowly she lifted her head. He felt a disconcerting sensation steal over him as her gaze met his. Good God, he must have gotten his brains shaken loose in the war. He was an idiot to help her without expecting something in return. What could a woman in her position give him, anyway? His inner demons stirred. He knew what she could offer.

"Thank you," she said simply, her relief obvious.

His cousin pushed himself away from the carriage. "Where are you going? Do you want company?"

Drake frowned in displeasure. He knew why Gabriel had brought Eloise Goodwin here, that she'd been used as an excuse for his cousin to meet Maribella. He might just shoot the bastard in the knee later on to show him that he did not appreciate the low-handed trick.

He drew his gaze away from Eloise's face. "Percy is known to frequent the home of a mutual friend who lives nearby," he said. "Perhaps I'll find him there with the absconded twit. And, no, I do not want company. Especially not yours."

"You might want to put on your evening jacket," Miss Goodwin murmured from the depths of the carriage.

Drake glanced at the young straw-haired footman who was standing on the pavement, absorbing every word that had been spoken. "Would you please take her home? This is no place for a gentlewoman to be."

He was several paces away from the carriage when he heard her voice calling out again in soft disparagement, "It is no place for a gentleman, either."

Drake did not bother to defend himself, but instead quickened his pace. He was not proud of it, but the fact was that he'd probably spent as many nights at Audrey's house as in his own. He owed no one an explanations for his behavior. If any of his closest friends had dared question his habits, he would not have responded. Still, he was rather tempted to react when a wicked voice inside him urged, "Ask her where you do belong then. Ask her if she'd make a place for you against those pillowy white breasts, or better yet, in her bed. Ask her."

He raised his dark, angular face to the sky and realized that it had begun to rain. He decided he would not return to the house to put on his evening jacket. The cold would not bother him. He wasn't sure he would even feel it. Or if he would feel anything again.

"Repent, sinner," a man in a ragged gray cloak shouted at him from the street corner. "Repent, or find yourself in Hell."

Drake graced him with a mordant smile. "Bit late for that, my friend."

Chapter Eight

⚜ ⚜

Eloise slept in brief snatches throughout what was left of the night, awakening every half hour or so to check whether either Thalia or her brother had returned home.

Just before dawn she finally arose, washed briskly with Castile soap and cold water, then dressed in the dark. She had no idea how she would explain Thalia's disappearance to Sir Thomas's mother. She brewed a strong cup of sage tea and brought it into Thalia's room, which seemed empty and abandoned. Despite her annoyance, she had come to care about the girl and was worried about her.

When, and if, Thalia returned from her impetuous escapade, she would never be the same. Her innocence would have been compromised, if not lost. Eloise and Lord Thornton had failed to protect her. It did not matter that Thalia had sought her own destruction. Eloise had accepted a responsibility, and she had proven herself inadequate.

She set her tea on the dressing table and wandered to the tall walnut armoire in which Thalia had stuffed her collections of old letters and scandal sheets willy-nilly. Within minutes she had accumulated in her arms a stack of well-worn gossip rags. She carried them downstairs to the parlor. She did not have to read far to find mention of the Boscastle family.

Lord Drake figured prominently in a number of past scandals. A prudent-minded woman would have tossed such filth in the fire.

Eloise was still reading, cramped, stiff, and thoroughly engrossed an hour later, when she heard an insistent knock on the door. She sat up, the blood flowing back into her limbs.

Was the duel over?

Had Thalia returned, or, worse, been discovered in some alleyway?

She rose, several of the scandal sheets still gripped in her hand. When she reached the door, she was hesitant to unlock it.

Who came to call so early in the day that even the scullery maid was not awake?

She eased open the door and knew instantly that the slouched figure in a shabby dun-brown coat was not Lord Drake, nor even his cousin. The caller's face was turned toward the gray-shadowed street, but she could tell by his furtive posture that he carried unwelcome news.

The duel in the park. Surely it had not been fought. She braced herself, her throat dry, as the man turned his head to smile at her.

A chill of recognition slid down her back. She went to slam the door, but Ralph had anticipated her reaction, wedging the worn toe of his boot against the jamb. She shoved the door harder, but he did not budge.

"Hello, Ellie," he said in a sly voice, gazing past her shocked, white face into the hall. "By damn, it's good to see you again. Have you missed me?"

She stepped back into the hallstand. "Get out of here this instant, or I shall have his lordship throw you out. I shall summon a constable—"

"Hush, you silly thing. We both know his lordship isn't home." He squeezed his wiry body between the crack, and then closed the door behind him. "And you've certainly had a busy night. My, my, Ellie. A fancy ball, then a gentleman caller and a brothel. To think you were always the shy one."

Footsteps echoed in the unlit corridor behind them. Eloise glanced around in distraction and saw Freddie come to a halt, the sleepy look on his pale, freckled face slowly replaced by suspicion. "What is it, Miss Goodwin? Whatever is wrong?"

She took a breath, resisting the urge to tell him. Freddie was a sweet young man, a proper gent at heart even if he was a footman and the son of a drunkard. He had risen above his gutter upbringing, and she would not involve him in her problems. "It's all right," she said, hoping he couldn't hear the unsteadiness in her voice. "Go about your duties."

The man standing in front of her laughed, a grating rasp of sound that raised the fine hairs on her nape. "Leave us alone, lad. Eloise and I are old friends. She'll be fine with me."

Eloise drew up her shoulders, not allowing Freddie to see how upset she was. Perhaps if she pretended to be strong, Ralph would go away. "Tend to your business, Freddie. Everything is all right."

As Drake had predicted, Horace did not bother to appear at Hyde Park for the early-morning duel. Drake barely made it there himself, having spent the better part of the night prowling about town. For all his trouble he could only conclude that Percy and Thalia had probably not left London, having been seen together at a late party, and that Horace had not visited any of his favorite gaming hells. The consensus of opinion among his acquaintances was that he'd escaped for a lengthy country sojourn. For Drake's money it meant the damn coward had deserted his dependents without a qualm.

He would have to break the news to Miss Goodwin after breakfast and a stiff drink to get his blood going. The letter of apology he'd sent Maribella late last night had already been returned. He might actually kill his cousin on the dueling field and consider it a favor to mankind.

Gabriel grinned at him from his waiting place under a tree. The sun was rising over the park, and a small crowd of onlookers had already assembled on the dewy lawn in anticipation of bloodshed. The audience included stragglers returning home from a night of excesses, a ragman, a husband and wife in a post chaise with a sleepy child. Two surgeons stood in attendance with their instrument cases.

Drake and Gabriel assumed their positions, walked their paces, and awaited the signal to fire.

Gabriel spoke without moving. "Did you see Maribella again last night?"

Drake scowled. "No, you devious bastard. Did you?"

"Only in my dreams," Gabriel said, and laughed.

"Do you know," Drake said with a heartless smile, "that I may not delope at all? I might just shoot you through the head and save myself future aggravation."

"That's all right, cousin. As long as you don't shoot me in a part that gets regular use. Especially the part that I would need should I ever find myself alone with Miss St. Ives."

At the signal they both turned with languid grace and fired straight into the air. The spectators, voicing their disappointment that neither of the duelists had dropped dead on the grass, dispersed in various directions to begin the day.

"Damn," Drake said, as a servant hurried forward to bring him his gloves and pewter gray morning coat, "I missed. You still have your head."

Gabriel flashed him a grin. "And you still have your female admirers." He motioned to the small carriage and four that had drawn up behind a thin stand of trees. "At least one of them has come to make sure you survived."

Drake unhurriedly rebuttoned his coat. "I never like to disappoint a lady. What a shame I shall have to miss our breakfast together. Another time?"

"I shall take Maribella off your hands if you decide you do not want her," Gabriel called as his cousin began to walk toward the parked vehicle. "Or the companion, for that matter. Perhaps that's her again in the carriage. Or did you scare her away for good last night?"

Drake knew, of course, that it was not Eloise who had come to the park. She had probably not even recovered from the events of the previous evening. He smiled at the memory. Too bad he hadn't had the chance to collect repayment for his efforts. Who would have thought he'd find her so damned fetching, anyway? She didn't have the vaguest notion how to flirt or play the games he was accustomed to playing.

It only went to show what an unpredictable devil desire could be. And that he did not know nearly as much about passion as he believed.

Two bewigged footmen in tight scarlet breeches opened the carriage door for him. He stepped inside, his gaze lifting to the lone female occupant. Ah, the beautiful Miss St. Ives. He caught a glimpse of her bodyguards at the end of the path, pretending to look away. He had to wonder whether she'd created most of her own mystique.

She was dressed in shimmery aquamarine silk, and the scent of attar of roses wafted in the air when she shifted languidly on the seat. "You won the duel?" she asked coolly, her gaze moving over him, presumably in search of wounds.

He sat down opposite her. "It was a travesty." He paused. "I thought you never wanted to see me again."

"I'm not sure that I do."

A taunting smile curved her lips. She was an alluring woman, he could not deny that. Even in the daylight she resembled a distant moon goddess with her perfectly symmetrical features and icy grace. But there was something lacking. Although whether it was within him or her, he still could not decide.

His mouth lifted in a cynical smile. "Then to what do I owe the honor of this unheralded visit?"

"I'm not sure that I don't want to see you again, either. I might be convinced to forgive you."

He laughed. "You're very generous, Maribella."

"I'm not, actually. I'm greedy and selfish."

"No one is perfect, darling."

Her smile faded, and he felt her examining him with an intensity that did not speak as much of sexuality as it did of shrewd assessment. There was more to Miss St.

Ives's character than that of an unusually beautiful woman who had become an exclusive courtesan.

He leaned his head back and closed his eyes. He wondered all of a sudden when a woman's character had begun to matter to him, and why, when he should be thinking about exploiting Maribella's sexual expertise, his mind was wandering off again to that other female.

It was insanity to pursue a woman who would be more inclined to tuck him into bed than to share one with him. Maybe he was going insane.

He opened his eyes in amusement at the touch of a light hand on his knee. "What," Maribella asked, her mouth pouting, "are you going to do to make it up to me?"

He glanced down at her hand. For a moment he thought he'd detected a curious hint of country dialect in her voice. Hadn't the papers claimed she'd been raised in the Italian Alps? He supposed he should know. With all the mystery that enshrouded her, he would be wise not to take her as his mistress without investigating a little more of her background, although Audrey had never misled him before.

Certainly Maribella was not a spy, and Drake no longer harbored secrets of much value to the political world. He had enjoyed a little subterfuge when his country was at stake. He did not particularly want to trust a woman who misrepresented herself to him, however. A mistress served as a confidante, as well as a lover. He would not sleep with a woman he could not trust. Well, at least not on a regular basis.

"What sort of retribution do you desire, Maribella? Monetary?"

She drew her hand back into her lap; he still found

himself remarkably unmoved. Of course he was tired, and—

"My wardrobe needs to be replenished," she said, her gaze challenging his.

He laughed. The familiar ground of a frivolous if demanding female was one he understood and could even appreciate. "Well, why not?"

She looked faintly mollified. "Today?"

He wavered. The truth was, he couldn't say exactly why he'd delayed playing his hand. Did hesitation enhance the outcome, heighten the sense of anticipation that preceded a sexual affair? Perhaps, but this felt off. He suspected she had as dark a side to her soul as he had. He wasn't sure whether that would make for a satisfying affair.

"Not today," he murmured. "I have foolishly agreed to help a friend."

"Is this friend of yours a woman?" she asked directly.

He laughed again. He thought he'd glimpsed a hint of her infamous temper in her eyes. "What a suspicious mind you have. The truth is that I'm trying to find the man who caused the farce of the duel I just fought." And if she sensed that there was more to his story than his simple explanation, she was wise enough not to ask.

Chapter Nine

※ ※

Eloise forced herself to look steadily into the face of the man she had almost married. She sensed that to show him fear would give him an advantage. Still, she had to restrain herself from taking him by the lapels of his threadbare dun-brown coat and shaking him like the rodent he was. How had he found her? She had changed her identity and believed herself at last lost if not happy in the mass of lower-class humanity that populated London. For the first time in years she'd begun to hope that she was free of her past life.

"My God, Ellie," he said, stretching his scrawny arms over the back of Lord Thornton's sofa, "it is good to see you after all these years."

She frowned at the muddy footprints he'd tracked on the carpet. "I cannot say I return the sentiment."

He snorted. "Still using all them fancy words, are you? Well, I see it's paid off. You've done well for a country girl, you have."

Eloise noted the watery dawn light that penetrated the drawing-room draperies. There was a duel being fought at this very moment between two of the most stimulating young men she had ever met in her life. Lord Drake Boscastle and his cousin. There was no comparison between them and the vulgar intruder sprawled so rudely before her.

"Ellie, Ellie, Ellie," he said with an unpleasant smile as he looked her up and down. "It is good to see you again. You've trimmed down nice, I see."

She stared past him to the window. A wooden cart rumbled through the street as vendors hurried to market. It was a day in London like any other, and yet Eloise knew that with Ralph's reappearance, her life would never feel as safe again. Last night she had been swept into a glittering world she had always known existed but had only glimpsed from afar, as if she'd been watching a play. She had danced recklessly with a man she would never forget. No, she wasn't quite the timid, vulnerable girl she had been six years ago.

"What do you want, Ralph?" she asked in an even voice.

She noted the uncertainty in his look as her gaze held his. Who would have guessed that her background as a governess and companion would have given her this much confidence? Did he hope to humiliate her? She had endured years of humiliation and drawn strength from her trials.

"What do you want?" she asked again.

"Just a bit of cash here and there. I wouldn't want to spoil things for you, but times are hard, with another young one on the way."

"How many does that make now, Ralph?"

"Five," he said vaguely, forcing another smile. "It could have been you and me raising brats together. Do you ever think of that?" He got up awkwardly when she did not react. He had to realize they were not alone in the house. "Have you heard anything from Mildred?"

"No, Ralph. I have not."

She frowned, realizing she was still holding the scandal sheets that she'd found in Thalia's room. "And I wish I hadn't heard from you, either."

He studied the painting above the mantel. "I've been watching you in private for a week now. That was a fancy gent you went off with last night. But oh, my, Ellie. A brothel. If your father knew. Not that I'd tell anyone back home. It'll be our little secret, eh?"

Absurd as it was, she found herself clutching like a shield the scandal sheet that depicted Lord Drake Boscastle's brother. How foolish to think of a rakehell's dalliance as a sort of talisman against a man like Ralph Hawkins. Yet she did. There had been magic in that man's kisses last night. Magic and power. "Leave now," she said, her voice brittle.

He tapped his battered felt hat against his knee. "Fine then. I'll come at another time."

Her mouth firmed. "No, you won't."

He smiled, showing his pointed ferret's teeth. How could she have ever thought him dashing and attractive? "Sure I will, pet. And you'll pay me, Ellie, or else."

She stared at the teapot on the table and took pleasure in the thought of bashing him on the head with it. "Or else what?"

"Well, I'll spill the soup, that's what. I'll tell your fancy employers what a wicked thing you and Mildred did to me. No one wants to have a madwoman in their employ, Ellie. No one wants a loony working in their home."

Surprisingly she fell asleep again not long after he left. The excitement of the previous evening, then the anxiety of finding Ralph Hawkins showing up on the doorstep after all these years, like something nasty a stray dog had deposited, had done her in. Quite simply she had worried herself into an exhausted state, to the point where she no longer cared about anything.

Thalia could have run off with a chimney sweep. Lord Thornton could have thrown his useless self into the Thames along with the other flotsam and jetsam of life. She could well end up selling pies on the corner, or throwing them at former employers. She was fortunately too fatigued to follow her dire imaginings to their unhappy conclusion. There was nothing to be gained by going into hysterics. So she went to sleep.

She slept deeply, dreamlessly, slumped over the table in the morning parlor where everyone in the house could see her. She slept the sleep of a condemned man who realizes all hope is lost. There was a profound relief in no longer fighting life. There was—

—the most handsome man in all of England on his knees before her, shaking her by the shoulders and ordering in an urgent voice, "Miss Goodwin, for heaven's sake, are you all right? Speak to me, woman. Can you hear my voice?"

"Ummm . . . what . . . what—"

"You haven't taken an overdose of laudanum, have you?"

"Have I what?" she mumbled, frowning down at him like a mole.

His face came into focus. Eloise sat up with a start, suddenly wide awake and unable to breathe properly. The papers in her lap spilled to the floor. She tried to stand, only to feel his firm hands slip under her arms to support her, and a good thing it was because she felt quite wobbly at the sight of him. Lord Drake Boscastle, on his knees before her. Heavens, had she been snoring? Drooling?

"I—oh, my," she said, nearly knocking her head against his. "What time is it? Did you fight the duel? Are you all right?"

He was more than all right. He was absolutely gorgeous, clean-shaven and elegant in a pewter morning coat and black pantaloons. Even after a long night he presented the very picture of inborn elegance, except perhaps for the faint smudges of fatigue beneath his eyes, which only enhanced his air of wicked appeal. His square jaw was drawn into terse lines.

He frowned as she straightened in the chair. Her mind was beginning to clear. She silently reviewed the upsetting events leading up to this moment. Lord Thornton and Thalia's disappearance. Ralph at the door like a vermin who scented impending death.

"I'm so sorry," she said. "I had no idea you were here. Would you care for some tea? Some—oh, heavens, did I ask you—is the duel over?"

"Yes, and not a drop of blood spilled," he answered, visibly relaxing. How long had he been trying to awaken her, anyway?

"Was Lord Thornton there?" she asked in hesitation.

He shook his head. "I'm afraid not."

"You fought your cousin alone?"

"I would hardly call it fighting. I've probably come closer to killing him during a sack race than I did today."

"A what?" She couldn't have heard him clearly. She was still worried about whether he'd caught her snoring.

He grinned. "A sack race. Once or twice a year the entire Boscastle family meets in the country for a fortnight of torture. Gabriel always tries to best me. So far he never has."

Eloise smiled a little wistfully, even if she suspected there was more to this rivalry than he had shared. Her own family had rarely taken time out for pleasant activities. Her father had had too many responsibilities as a busy magistrate to play with his children, and her mother had worked long hours as a needlewoman to supplement their income. Even now Eloise felt slightly guilty when she had a spot of free time. But there was warmth again in his voice when he spoke of his family. It made him more attractive than a mere rakehell who stole kisses at a ball. He couldn't be a complete devil if he cared so much for his family, could he?

She stood in uncertain silence, wondering for a wild moment what she was supposed to say next. He solved the problem for her, although in an unexpectedly embarrassing way.

"Well, well," he murmured, in a deep, sardonic voice, "what do we have here?"

She blinked. She had no idea what he meant until he bent to retrieve one of the papers scattered on the floor. The scandal sheet. The cartoon of the scandalously proportioned Lord Heath Boscastle as Apollo. She had completely forgotten she'd fallen asleep holding a nude likeness of his brother in her lap.

She could only hope he would not recognize it.

He did. One dark eyebrow lifted in surprise. He pursed his lips and studied the drawing without saying a word. Eloise wasn't sure which was worse, that he'd caught her with a caricature of a naked man, or that the naked man was his brother.

"My goodness!" she exclaimed. "If I've told Miss Thornton once, I've told her a hundred times she should not read this filth. And leave it lying about."

"I believe it was on your lap," he pointed out, a smile playing on his chiseled lips. "My, my, Miss Goodwin. What *were* you dreaming about when I awakened you?"

She cleared her throat. Heaven forbid he thought her one of those women who pretended to be proper, but who enjoyed looking at pornographic drawings in secret.

"I was curious," she said, snatching the paper from his hand.

His gaze caught and held hers, dark with amazement. "About my brother?"

"I was looking through Miss Thornton's things," she retorted. "I was hoping to find a note from Percy hinting where they might have gone." Well, that wasn't the absolute truth; in fact, it didn't even come close. But she couldn't very well admit she'd wanted to find a few tidbits of gossip about him.

He paused. "I personally don't find a thing wrong with a woman who likes to look at erotic pictures."

"I wasn't looking at the picture!"

"There's no need to be embarrassed. Except that it is my brother. You've never met him, have you?" he asked curiously.

"No, of course not." She cringed when he turned the paper over and that drawing stared her in the face again. "But I've seen—"

"—quite a lot of him," he finished, his blue eyes twinkling with humor. "The whole of England has."

Eloise bit the tip of her tongue. "I meant that I've seen his name mentioned in the papers infrequently. He doesn't seem to have been involved in many scandals." As you have, she could have added.

He grinned. "This was scandalous enough."

"I don't doubt it. What an embarrassment for a gentleman."

"Embarrassment does not even begin to describe the trouble that drawing caused." He shook his head in reflection. "It was never meant to be published, as I understand. To this day no one knows exactly how it reached the press. I don't think his wife will ever live down her artistic indiscretion."

"His wife?" she asked in surprise. "His own wife drew that?"

Drake studied her for several moments before he answered. How could he possibly explain the unconventional and incalculable underpinnings of his ancestry? He didn't understand it himself, but he was a cog in the whole damned machine, and had resigned himself to it. "I'm afraid so. The Boscastle men tend to be attracted to exceptional females. The women in our family tend to do very wicked things."

"And . . . this is accepted?" she asked in a quiet voice.

Drake had to remind himself to pay attention to their conversation. Damn if she didn't look even prettier than she had last night. Her skin was still flushed from having been asleep, which naturally made him think of waking up beside her. Even in her ordinary green muslin dress that buttoned so primly down the back she managed to make him think about undressing her. "Yes," he said, finally bringing his unruly thoughts back into line. "We're an accepting lot in general. You have to be accepting in a family where sins are committed almost every day." He cleared his throat. No point in letting her know what a devilish brood they were. "What about your family?" he asked in a blatant attempt to divert her interest.

"Not quite that accepting," she answered, glancing away. "I'm almost afraid to ask—did you find out where Miss Thornton might have gone?"

He wasn't about to admit that Thalia was the furthest thing from his mind; he was wondering suddenly where Eloise had come from and where she'd lived before working in this house. Had she been an orphan? Perhaps she did not have any family left to discuss.

"I don't know where Thalia is," he said honestly. "I'd guess she was still in London. You can hardly blame yourself for her behavior."

She glanced up. The warmth inside him flared into a fierce heat. "I won't be able to cover for her disappearance indefinitely. Her fiancé's mother will suspect that something is amiss. They're supposed to have tea in a few hours."

"For all we know Thalia will return and no one will be any wiser."

She shook her head. "Society isn't always as forgiving of a woman's mistakes as your family seems to be."

He pulled off his gloves and dropped them onto her chair. "Spoken as one who has experience?" he asked casually.

She hesitated. "None of this nature."

Some part of his mind noted the evasion. "You mentioned that she is to be married soon. Were you planning to work for her indefinitely?

"I'm not sure what I'll do after her wedding."

He nodded, considering her reply. He wasn't even sure why he asked. "There are probably easier ways to make a living."

"I suppose that depends on what one considers a hardship." She paused. "Have you been friends with Lord Thornton for long?"

"I don't know that I've ever considered Horace a friend. His brother was."

"Then why are you helping him?"

He lifted his hand to her face and brushed his thumb across the curve of her cheek. "Why do you think?" he asked musingly.

She swallowed at the naked fire in his eyes and blurted out the first thing that popped into her mind. "I asked you first."

For an unbearable moment she was afraid he would laugh at her. And then he lowered his head and answered her with a kiss that swept her into warm, swirling darkness. She stood motionless and closed her eyes, rendering no resistance at all. It was quite shaming, really. She didn't even put up a token protest. The instant she parted her lips, he drove his tongue deep inside her mouth with a pulsing sensuality that took possession of her entire body.

"My God, Eloise." His mouth burned like a conquering flame across her face, then down her throat to where her breasts swelled above her bodice. "I kept telling myself I'd imagined how much I wanted you last night."

Shivers of raw desire chased down her spine. She'd heard such seductive confessions in the course of her career before, but it was her own reaction that named this a novel experience. The danger of this man lay not in that he took what he wanted, but that he made her want it, too.

"This is . . ." She lifted her hand weakly to his wrist. Was she holding on to him or pushing him away? Was it possible to do both at the same time? Was it possible to pretend she didn't know what she was doing?

"What?" His bare hand slipped down her shoulder, raising shivers on the untouched territory of her skin. "What is it? Tell me."

"I don't know."

"I don't, either," he whispered back, "but I like it very much."

She felt his hands skim her ribs before rising to shape her breasts with a knowing touch. His fingertips circled the aching peaks through her dress. She would have died before allowing another man to do this. But because it was him, she arched her back and closed her eyes, silently asking for more.

He rubbed his jaw across her breasts. "Are you this soft everywhere?" he asked in a husky voice. "I want to know."

She swayed into him with a moan, aroused by the decadent allure of his voice. How effortlessly he made her desire him. She'd known last night not to give him her sympathy. Hadn't she sensed that he would demand something more valuable? He certainly hadn't kept his intentions a secret. The surprise was in her response, and the liberties she was allowing.

His mouth closed around her nipple and suckled it through the thin muslin of her gown. A wave of wanton pleasure flooded her senses with melting heat. Heaven only knew what she would have permitted next had a carriage not lumbered over the cobbled street outside. The disturbance brought them both back to sanity. He withdrew from her with an unsmiling stare that sent an involuntary shudder down her back.

"I'm going to help you," he said slowly. "I think now we both know why."

Eloise could not bring herself to break the intensity of his stare. Yes, perhaps what he felt for her was mere lust. But did lust mask itself behind the gentle, knowing touch of a strong man who offered support when all other hope was lost? Of course it did, a very annoying voice promptly answered in her mind. Temptation would not entice if it did not arrive in an appealing package.

"What do you want in return?" she asked.

"I didn't say I'd expect anything, did I?" He looked directly into her eyes. It was disarmingly like looking into a mirror. The reflection did not deceive, but it was a little too well guarded.

"I'm not that naïve," she said.

He smiled. "I didn't think for a moment that you were."

Chapter Ten

※ ※

She was justified, actually, in assuming that there would be a cost for his help. There usually was, Drake mused cynically as he left the unassuming house and began the walk home. The frightening part of this situation was that Eloise assumed she would be the debtor. He wasn't so sure himself. He wasn't sure of anything in his life these days, although he knew that his involvement with her had little to do with Horace Thornton. Perhaps he was simply bored. A man couldn't keep drinking, whoring, and dueling forever. Or could he? There were worse ways to die. Christ knew he'd seen his fill of senseless deaths on both sides of the battlefield. As far as he could tell, the world wasn't any better because of all the sacrifices it demanded.

Still, he was already starting to regret his offer to find Thalia Thornton. What did he care if the chit ruined her life? She'd hit him with a silver hairbrush and flicked a fern frond in his face, for God's sake.

"Hell's bells," a deep voice drawled behind him. "Do they really let people like you prowl the streets nowadays?"

He glanced around at the offending voice. He was hoping that he'd been insulted by a stranger because he thought he might feel better if he could get in a good fight. But it was only his younger brother who had jumped out of a carriage full of friends to join him on the pavement. He shook his head in chagrin as Devon sidestepped a pea-seller, roasting hot green peas. The pea man started to curse, but stopped at the apologetic grin Devon flashed him.

That was Devon all over. He could charm a smile out of a stone. The same boyish ways that got him into so much trouble worked even better in reverse. Who else but Dev could have pulled a stint as a highwayman only to have young aristocrats all over England imitating his impetuous crime? And young ladies hoping he would rob them of kisses late at night? It hadn't mattered to the haut ton that Devon had been forced to go into hiding until the scandal of his behavior had blown over. It probably hadn't mattered much to Devon, either.

Devon waved a newspaper at him. "Look at this."

Drake grunted, and pushed the sheet from his face, recognizing the work of a popular satirist. "If that's another naked cartoon of Heath, I'm not interested. I've had my fill of Apollo's attributes this morning, thank you all the same."

Devon's white teeth gleamed in a grin. "Well, this isn't about Heath. It's about you."

He snatched the sheet from Devon's hand. "It bloody well better not be. At least not naked."

"Er, no, there aren't any illustrations, actually. Not that I've seen. I'd wait for tomorrow's edition before I go all hysterical."

"Have you ever seen me go all hysterical?"

Devon thought for a moment. "Not that I can remember."

"Then why did you warn me not to?"

"Well, I suppose because I didn't want your first time to be in the street."

"My first time? Am I a virgin, Devon?"

"I wouldn't think so. Certainly not according to the paper."

Drake scowled and scanned the nonsense, which was the usual salacious gossip with a grain or two of fact buried between layers of inaccurate description. He couldn't believe anyone paid to read this sort of thing, but there it was, in print. An exaggerated accounting of his night of passion with a celebrated courtesan, followed by a brief mention of the duel that would be fought at dawn, over which two Boscastle cousins would contest the aforementioned courtesan's favor.

"Bloody hell," he said, shaking his head. "Wait until Grayson reads this. Ever since our dear brother got married, he's become so moral I hardly know him. I think I'll get him a pulpit for his birthday."

"It's true though, isn't it?" Devon asked, bumping against him. "You did make an arrangement with Maribella, and you fought a duel this morning? I meant to come, by the way, but I had personal matters to attend. I'm glad you weren't killed."

"Gabriel and I didn't fight over Maribella, for God's sake. Don't you remember what went on at the party last night? Thornton got caught by our cousin cheating at cards. And then he disappeared. You were there, Dev, unless you were you more potted than you looked."

"I wasn't potted at all. And I'm not a total nitwit. I simply assumed that after what happened at Audrey's, it might have become a little more personal between you and Gabriel."

Drake tossed the paper into the street. "How do you know what happened at Audrey's?"

Devon breathed out a deep sigh. "Well, you know how the girls like to gossip."

"*You* like to gossip," Drake said. "It's very unmanly." Except that no one had ever questioned Devon Boscastle's manhood so it was a moot point. "I don't suppose you've seen Thornton in your nocturnal travels about town?"

"No. Can't say that I have."

Drake glanced at him with exasperated affection. Devon was about an inch taller than Drake, lean and angular, although he'd been all bones, knees, and elbows growing up. Yet by some blessing of nature he had evolved into a strong, well-favored young man. It was his easy temper and wicked grin that deceived those who did not know him. His boyish appeal concealed a complex nature as well as a depth of emotion that few people ever recognized. And women absolutely adored his playful ways.

"Where are we going, anyway?" Devon asked, eyeing the plump backside of a walnut girl who almost dropped her basket when she looked around and saw him.

"I'm waiting for my carriage so that I can search for Miss Thornton and her seducer Percy Chapman. I've been looking for her half the night."

"Do you mean Thalia?" Devon asked, finally glancing away from his comely nut-seller and back to his brother.

Drake folded his arms across his chest. Talking to Devon, trying to get his full attention was one of the most frustrating experiences in the world. "Do you know where she is?"

"She visited a hotel on St. Albans Street last night." Devon looked back at the walnut girl with a heart-broken expression. "I think she was with Percy, now that you mention it."

"Now that I mention it." Drake threw up his hands in exasperation. "Why didn't you tell me in the first place?"

Devon grinned again. There was no point in getting angry at him. He never meant offense; he did not know how to dissemble. "I thought you wanted to talk to me about Maribella. I had no idea you were interested in Thalia Thornton."

"My God, Devon. Why would you think I was interested in the twit?"

"Well," Devon said slowly, "you told me you'd been looking for her half the night, and you walked out on Maribella in front of witnesses at Audrey's house. What is a man to think?"

The disturbing part of this was, the way Devon phrased the events of the evening, his deduction made a shallow kind of sense. How was Drake to explain his actions? He was almost afraid to analyze them in case he disliked what he discovered. Sometimes it was better for a man to remain in ignorance. "I'm not looking for Thalia for myself," he said carefully. "I'm trying to help a friend find her."

Devon didn't say anything for several moments. Unfortunately Drake knew better than to trust his silence. Devon, for all his lighthearted appearances, had to suspect that Drake would never sacrifice an entire evening merely to help a friend. He must have guessed there had to be more at stake.

"Oh, my God." Devon staggered back a step, grinning like an idiot. "There's a woman involved. Another woman. You're doing this for a woman. What a surprise."

"Don't be damned absurd," Drake said between his teeth.

Devon regarded him with a look that hovered somewhere between fascination and pity. "I have to meet her. Who is she? What is she like? She has to be something to see if she's already usurped Maribella."

"There isn't a woman, dammit. Wouldn't I tell you if there was?"

"I don't know," Devon said. "Would you?"

"What do you think?"

They stood shoulder to shoulder, staring out at the street together, neither man saying another word. And both of them knowing that for the first time in their lives Drake had lied, not only to his brother, but to himself.

Chapter Eleven

❦ ❦

It had been an unpleasant shock for Eloise to find Ralph on her doorstep early that morning, and with the exception of being surprised by Lord Drake Boscastle, who unsettled her in an entirely different way, her day had not improved at all. Three creditors in a row came demanding payment for Lord Thornton's unpaid debts. A tailor's assistant threatened to hold hostage all of the coats Horace had ordered for the season. Eloise asked him if he'd like a pair of pantaloons to keep the captive coats company. She and the other servants had become experts at the art of inventing excuses for their master's reckless irresponsibility.

Inventing an excuse to explain Thalia's disappearance to the girl's future mother-in-law, a rather sweet silver-haired lady, was far more difficult. Eloise liked Lady Heaton, and it pained her to have to explain that Thalia would not be able to have tea with her and Sir Thomas's three elderly aunts in Piccadilly.

"Is everything all right?" Lady Heaton asked, her brown eyes full of concern.

Eloise suppressed a sigh. She couldn't tell this gentle-woman the truth, and the truth was that Eloise didn't know where Thalia was, or if she was all right. "She was called off on an emergency, I'm afraid. A heart condition."

"A family member?"

"Er, a dear friend." More like a rotten bastard, actually. Eloise might not approve of swearing aloud, but she did tend to curse a colorful streak to herself in times of crisis.

"That's so kind of her," Lady Heaton murmured. "I hope it isn't fatal."

Eloise made a noncommittal noise in her throat. It might be fatal, at least to Thalia, if she were ever able to get her hands on the girl. And this escapade would certainly be fatal to Thalia's reputation if the scandal became known.

And so she waited on pins and needles for the remainder of the day. She waited for her prodigal employer to come home. She waited for the bailiff to allow creditors to take away the furniture. She waited for her odious former fiancé to return to ask if she'd decided to pay him for his silence.

And throughout all these unpleasant worries she waited for the dark and dangerously elegant Lord Drake Boscastle to return and whisk her away from her troubled existence to his fairy-tale world of sin and seduction.

"Eloise," he would say, "I knew my heart belonged to you from the moment we danced together at the ball."

And they would laugh together, reminiscing fondly over how she had insulted and mistaken him for a rakehell. He would confess that until that night he had never visited a brothel, and wasn't it amazing, but her faithful young footman had been right. Drake had not been consorting with a *fille de joie* in his unbuttoned shirt at Mrs. Watson's. He had been boxing with a friend. Truly!

She snorted out loud at her wistful silliness and busied herself sorting through the post and organizing letters into tidy piles, listening all the while for a knock at the door until it was time to go to bed.

No one came during the night. Nor were there any visitors the next day, although she waited again anxiously until it was almost dusk.

Then when she finally realized she was to be neither rescued nor evicted, at least not immediately, she took a long, hot soak in her hip bath while deciding what to have for supper. No one was home. The staff had gone off with her blessing to watch a play. She could indulge in wine and crumbly cheese for all anyone knew. She sank beneath the water to rinse out her hair. Soaking always helped her think, even though she knew there was no thinking herself out of this situation.

She wondered how her life had come to this. Was it her fault she had almost married a cad? Or that the man she currently worked for appeared to be little better? Or that she'd lingered in the bath so long that her toes and fingers had wrinkled up like currants?

She rose from the lukewarm water in reluctance, reaching around for the chair she had placed behind the bath. The air had grown cool. She wanted to put on her night rail and pull the bedcovers over her head, hoping that when she woke up in the morning her situation would have miraculously improved for the better.

"Where is that chair?" she muttered, and twisted her thick brown hair into a rope before squeezing the moisture from it. "Heavens, it's not enough that I've lost my client, possibly my position, and now a chair. I'm losing my everloving mind as well. Eloise, Eloise, I do despair of you."

She flung back her hair and marched across the irregular wooden floor to the single window. It had still been light when she'd undressed. Now the sky showed the loveliest lavender-gray dusk that muted the sins of the city it canopied.

"I love London," she whispered in an uncharacteristic moment of abandon. "There's no where like it on earth. Please, God, don't make me have to leave. I know it's wrong to love a wicked place so much."

She smiled self-consciously and shook her head. She was not in the habit of saying her prayers in the nude, but her chemise, corset, and clean muslin drawers were not on the chair where she had placed them. She looked around again in puzzlement. As a matter of fact, the *chair* was not where she'd left it, and even at her worst, Eloise was a very precise person, consistent in her personal habits.

She felt a little shiver slide down her back as she revolved slowly on her bare feet to regard the shadowy form sitting in the corner. "Oh, my," she said, her throat dry. She was seeing things, she told herself. She must be. The alternative was too awful.

She closed her eyes, refusing to give in to panic. But when she opened them again, Drake Boscastle was still there. And she was still bare. As bare as a bone, in fact. And she decided it would not be inappropriate to give in to panic.

The scandal of it. Waltzing about without a stitch in front of a man. She wondered if she had embarrassed him into that unnerving silence by parading back and forth in her natal suit. Embarrassing, however, did not begin to describe the elemental look on his face.

Illicit. Intent. Unabashed.

Furthermore, this was her room, and *he* had intruded on her privacy, not the other way around. Lord Drake Boscastle or a dustman, there were certain standards of decency that he obviously had chosen to ignore.

She huffed out a breath. "I'm speechless," she said in a choked voice. "Absolutely struck dumb. This is unacceptable, my lord. Unconscionable, scandalous, mortifying. I do not think I can express what it feels like to discover that one is being watched by a Peeping Tom. As if I were Lady—Lady—"

"Godiva?" he supplied helpfully, his gaze traveling over her in unwavering absorption.

"Yes. Yes. Well, no." She frowned. "There was a horse involved in that instance, and an element of choice, and—"

"Taxes?" he asked, his eyes gleaming.

"Taxes. Yes, there were taxes, and I . . . I'm speechless. Quite at a loss for words."

"I should be rather afraid to meet you in a loquacious mood. Although"—his deep voice sent a wave of boiling heat down the back of her legs—"I find words a little inadequate to convey what I'm feeling myself at the moment."

She inched toward the washstand. "I'm quite at a loss—"

"—for a towel?" he asked, not managing to hide a grin. "And your undergarments?" He rose indolently from the chair and came toward her with her clothes, taking his time about it, too.

She narrowed her eyes. She could not reach the wardrobe or even the bed for a sheet without exposing her backside to him. She couldn't dart behind her dressing screen, either, because it stood directly to his left, and she would have to pass him to reach it. Of course she could hardly stand here in the altogether, with her hands shielding her pertinent parts.

"Throw me the towel!" she shouted.

"I beg your pardon," he said, coming to a sudden stop. "What did you say?"

"The *towel*!"

"There's no need to shout." He made a pretense of lifting the towel to show her exactly where it was. "It's right here. And there's certainly no need for me to throw it. My heavens, that would be entirely rude."

"And sneaking into my room while I was bathing is not?"

"I did knock," he said with maddening complacency, "but no one answered. I was afraid that during the course of the day you might have been evicted. Thornton is in grave debt. Can you blame me for being concerned?"

She had to admire his defense. The other servants *had* taken the night off to see a play. It *was* possible that he'd knocked and become suspicious when no one came to the door. It could even be considered heroic of him to have entered the house and . . . watched her from a chair in the corner while she bathed? Oh, how could she excuse his behavior?

She stepped behind the washstand. He watched, the towel still draped over his arm. "Would you please leave?" she said crouching behind the ceramic pitcher and basin.

He looked surprised. He was also looking his fill. "I

thought you wanted me to bring you your clothes and towel?"

"What I'd like to do is get dressed," she said through her teeth.

"But you're soaking wet," he pointed out. "You need a towel."

"I need privacy to dress!"

"I only wanted to help you, Eloise."

"I can do it—"

Her mouth dropped open as he strode forward and snapped the towel like a whip around her waist. She could only be grateful that twilight had cast a veil of shadows over the room.

"—myself," she whispered, swallowing a gasp. "I can do it myself."

"Of course you can," he said with a condescending smile. "But isn't it so much nicer to have a helping hand?"

"That really depends on what the hand is helping itself to," she said stonily.

"My valet helps me to dress all the time."

"Does he now?" Her voice rose again.

He nodded. "I'm amazingly helpless when it comes to tying a neck cloth."

"Perhaps I could tie it for you," she said. "Into a tight little knot around your neck—"

"Look at you," he chided. He drew her damp body against him. "You're shivering. This will never do. Turn around before you catch your death."

"If I die, it is *not* going to be from cold." She was naked in his arms, trapped against his steel-hard thighs by her own towel. She felt a flash of warmth, a warning, an aura between her temples, before the blood rushed from her brain in a dizzying surge.

"You aren't going to faint again?" he asked in alarm.

"I didn't faint before," she whispered as she fought against another wave of light-headedness.

He tightened his grip on the towel. His face looked down at her in genuine concern. "Perhaps I should carry you to the bed."

Her eyes flew to his. "*No*. It's really not necessary."

"Your toes are turning blue from the cold." His big hands kneaded the rise of her bottom, a part of her body, she thought faintly, that had little to do with her toes. "I might as well make myself of use while I'm here, Eloise."

"Why are you here, anyway?" she murmured.

"Let's get you warm before we discuss that."

He pulled the towel loose and brushed it up her back and shoulders, then across her breasts, slowly circling the rosy aureoles until she stood shivering, immobilized by his touch. "Why, you've practically caught pneumonia," he said in a stern tone. "We're going to have to do something to get you warm."

She made a sound that was somewhere between a whimper and a groan of dissent. She wasn't sure herself what it meant. She only knew that the naked woman she could see in the mirror couldn't possibly be her. The towel slid to the floor. He gripped the firm globes of her bottom as she twisted awkwardly to reach for it. "Did you say something?"

"I don't know," she whispered. "Did I?" She couldn't move.

His strong fingers danced up and down her spine. "I knew your skin would feel this soft," he murmured huskily. "Are you still cold? Wet? Lie with me on the bed."

She wanted to say yes. She wanted to feel his sinful hands all over her body. The hollow between her thighs grew achingly moist. She shivered against him but not from cold. She shivered as his hard arousal branded her belly, then again as he pulled her tighter until she was practically straddling his thigh.

"I only want to touch you," he said, his deep voice weakening the few defenses she could muster. "I want to touch you inside where you're even softer. And wetter." He exhaled and looked down at her, lifting his thigh against her soft mound. "Only for a moment."

She stared up at his face. The unrepentant desire in his eyes dazed her senses, made her so damp below she thought he could feel it. She opened her mouth to object only to gasp in helpless surprise as he lifted her into his arms and carried her to the bed.

"Exactly what do you think you're doing?" she whispered.

He laid her down beneath him. "Making you warmer than you've ever been before."

She moaned, raising her arm to her face.

"What did you say?"

She swallowed. "I didn't say anything."

"You didn't say no."

"I didn't say yes!"

He grinned. "Is it yes or no?" His blue eyes glittered knowingly. "Or is it maybe?"

"I'm not going to talk about this," she whispered.

"Fine. Words are superfluous in a situation where the senses have taken control, anyway."

She lowered her arm a little. "That isn't what I said."

"I know." He smiled consolingly. "We've already established that words aren't needed to express what we feel."

He smiled inwardly at the look of indignant bewilderment she gave him. She would never have believed him if he had admitted that he wasn't nearly as self-possessed as he pretended to be. Or that he hadn't come here to seduce her. Well, at least not consciously. He couldn't deny that the possibility hadn't entered his mind.

He might even die of his desire for her, he decided. Her body was a soft, sensual enticement. He pulled off his cloak and dropped it on the floor. His gaze drifted over her plump breasts to her belly and lingered at her mons. He wanted to nuzzle her sweet fluff with his mouth, to breathe in her most intimate scent and wear it on his skin for the rest of the night.

"What will you allow?" he whispered, inhaling in anticipation.

She closed her eyes. He bent his head to her breasts. He flicked his tongue across one tender little tip. She gave an uncontrollable shudder and half lifted her hips off the bed. He was a man who followed his instincts and indulged them often. He enjoyed the game of seduction, but this was different from the usual challenge of conquest.

She's a danger to me, he thought, his heart beating fiercely at the realization.

"Tell me when to stop," he murmured. He licked a trail from the hollow of her throat to her navel. "Now?" he asked.

She shook her head. He sighed in pleasure.

Slowly he eased his finger between her thighs to separate the dewy petals of her sex. She gasped and tightened involuntarily. His finger sunk deeper. "Should I stop?" he whispered, sending her a merciless smile.

"No," she breathed, her hips shifting restlessly.

"You're quite sure?" He laid his face against the silky cushion of her thigh. Her pearlescent fluid scented his fingers. He closed his eyes and breathed deeply of her fragrance. "I'm not certain I heard you, Eloise." He pressed another finger inside her and skillfully stretched her sheath. She was tight and temptingly soaked.

She groaned.

He rubbed his thumb over her hooded nub, his fingers probing even deeper. "What was that?"

"Don't . . ." she whispered. "Oh, God, what have you done to me?"

His jaw tight, he deepened the pressure of his thumb against her swollen bud and deftly quickened the movements of his fingers inside her. She convulsed with a sob of grateful surprise, riding his hand as her belly quivered with uncontrollable spasms.

He opened his eyes and watched her; her full breasts were thrust forward, the silky rose nipples taut, her thighs spread open. His hand was absolutely drenched. In his lower body, blood pooled and left him aching relentlessly for relief.

He inhaled to steady his erratic heartbeat. So close. Too close. It wasn't what he'd come here for. He'd had no idea he would find her in such a desirable state. He had merely meant to tell her that he knew where Thalia was. No, that wasn't entirely true. He'd wanted to see her again. But now that he was here, now that she had let him pleasure her, he could barely remember his own name. This was more than any desire he'd ever known. Something unfamiliar and threatening. It beat down upon him like a dark-winged beast that beckoned from a shadow realm against his shield of indifference.

He gazed at Eloise and knew that he should leave this house and never return. Her soft voice interrupted his thoughts.

"Please," she whispered, pulling the sheet out from under his arm. "Please turn your back so that I can get up from the bed and dress."

He sat up with his face to the wall, not bothering to mask the sinful pleasure in his eyes. In the pier glass he glimpsed her graceful back and white bottom as she bolted across the room to the dressing screen. He grinned. God, he loved a woman with a well-rounded arse. Something to hold on to when sex turned hard and wild. She was curvy all over, with the sweetest nest of dark curls under her rounded belly.

"You forgot your personals," he said over his shoulder.

"As if they'd do me any good now," she muttered.

"Would you like me to help you put them on?"

Eloise did not bother to respond, reappearing a minute later in a rose woolen walking gown with a double row of pearl buttons. "Not bad," he murmured, "although I have to say, I preferred you before."

Eloise squared her shoulders. She had never put on a dress without wearing at least a chemise underneath, but this was an exception. What was the point in pretending that a layer of undergarments mattered after he'd laid her bare and shameless? Her mind was so unsettled it was surprising she could even talk.

"Why are you here, anyway?" she asked. She fumbled with the second row of buttons at her back.

"I've found Thalia."

"Is she all right?"

He rose from the bed and walked up behind her, re-buttoning her gown with a frown. Eloise tensed slightly but allowed him to finish. The man was obviously talented when it came to using his hands. "She and Percy spent the last two nights together with friends of his in Chelsea," he said quietly.

"Two nights. Together. Do you think they—"

"Played tiddlywinks?" He stared down at her as she swung around to face him. The blueness of his eyes stole her breath. "Of course they did."

She released a disheartened sigh. "Then I have failed in my duty. As much as her fiancé adores her, I do not think he'll understand this. I don't understand it."

"Perhaps all isn't lost," he said. "When a man is in love with a woman, he—"

Eloise looked up at him with a combination of hope and skepticism. "He what?"

Drake shook his head. "Hell, I don't know. I suppose I should say something profound and inspiring, but I'm probably not the best person to talk of love."

"No?" she asked.

He shook his head again. "I'm not the least bit understanding myself, and I certainly wouldn't be if I were Thalia's fiancé." He paused. "To be truthful I can't even imagine anyone wanting to marry her in the first place."

Eloise refrained from commenting, having entertained similar thoughts herself more than once. "He really loves her."

Drake shrugged. "Then we can only hope he won't hear about her misadventure until after they're married."

"And then what?" she asked hesitantly.

He grinned. "It's not our concern."

It was too tempting to be swept into his devil-may-care attitude. She made a conscious effort to appear disapproving. "Is she downstairs, or did she go straight to her room?"

After a long silence, he said, "She isn't here at all."

She blinked.

"I wasn't prepared to force her to come home in the event she resisted," he said. "In fact, she never even saw me. This is a situation that her brother should handle."

Her lips tightened. "Except that he isn't here to handle anything. Well, there's no choice. I shall have to bring her home myself. There's no one else to accept the responsibility."

He straightened in alarm. "No, you won't. This was not a genteel house party she and Percy attended."

"I didn't for a minute think it was," she said. "But someone has to bring her home. I'll take Freddie along for protection."

He snorted. "And who the devil is going to protect Freddie? He must weigh all of ten stone. You can't show up on the doorstep of a place like that. The young bucks would take one look at you and—"

Drake stopped. They would probably try to do what he wanted to do himself, but he wasn't about to let that happen. He could hardly allow her to place herself in a vulnerable position.

She looked up at him levelly. "Was this an orgy?"

He hesitated. "Orgy might be a bit strong a word to describe an impromptu party in a bachelor's town house, but it wasn't a refined family reunion, either." Certainly Eloise would have been disgusted at the degree of sexual liberties taken. Once such entertainments had offered mild amusement. Now they offended him. He knew exactly why Percy had taken Thalia to that party. He'd participated in more than his share of similar revels in the past. And it went without saying that the women he'd known had never lamented their loss of innocence.

"You aren't going there," he said firmly. "I'll bring her back myself."

"I thought you just said that it wasn't your responsibility."

He felt that dark-winged beast lurking behind him again. Perhaps if he refused to acknowledge it, it would disappear before he could identify what it was. "That doesn't mean I won't help you."

She looked at him for a long time before she smiled. "I don't know what to make of you."

He bent to pick up his cloak from the floor. "Let's hope for your sake as well as mine this is only a momentary deviation from my customary nature. Ask anyone who knows me well. Ask my family. I'm quite irredeemable."

He thought he detected a fleeting smirk on her face as he straightened. "If you say so," she said.

"Everyone says so."

"Do they?" she asked softly.

She didn't believe him. God, the stories he could tell her. "Ever since the day I was born."

Chapter Twelve

❧ ❧

Drake was halfway to the front door when he heard hesitant footsteps behind him. He turned to the scrawny, mop-headed figure who stood in the hall to the basement stairs.

"Oh, it's only you, Freddie," he said. He put on the gloves he'd left at the hallstand. "I thought you'd gone off to a play."

The young footman stepped into the entry hall, glancing up the stairs before he spoke. "I came home after the first act. I didn't feel right leavin' Miss Goodwin by herself. Not with all that's gone on."

Drake smiled. It was hard not to admire such loyalty, although the lad hardly looked capable of defending even the doorstep. "That's undoubtedly a wise idea."

"Thank you, my lord." Freddie did not return his smile, his thin face grave. "Are you going to help her?"

"It appears as though I am," Drake replied, a little amused at this interrogation.

"Are you going to protect her from that man?"

That man? He paused. The boy must be talking about Thalia. Well, he shouldn't be surprised that the servants knew about Thalia's indiscretion with Percy. It would be nearly impossible to keep that kind of secret in a small house. Especially a house in which the master had deserted his dependents.

"I hope so, Freddie. Miss Thornton has her companion very worried."

"Miss Thornton . . . yes, but I meant—"

Drake stared at him. "You meant what?"

Freddie shook his head. His gaze dropped to his feet. "I meant, well, my lord," he muttered, "I know it ain't my place to interfere, but I meant no harm."

Drake raised his brow as the boy almost tripped over himself to open the front door. Dusk had deepened into early evening. The lamplights of a passing carriage bobbed like fairy lights in the mist. There had been a man standing on the corner when Drake had arrived at the house. He was now gone. A creditor, perhaps. He had intended to remind Eloise to be on the alert. Witnessing her rise from her bath like a voluptuous sea nymph, however, had virtually incapacitated his mental faculties.

As, oddly enough, his intended mistress Maribella St. Ives had not. Why? God, hadn't he promised to take her shopping this afternoon? Or had it been yesterday?

"The crows are closing in for the kill, Freddie," he said as he put on his tall, black silk hat. "I speak in monetary terms, of course. Predators always sense imminent death. Thornton's creditors will predictably fight for their share. Not that there appears to be much in this house to be shared."

"Picked to the bones." Freddie's young voice sounded unsteady.

"Don't answer the door again tonight," Drake advised him.

"I won't, my lord."

He stepped outside, sensing that the boy wanted to

say more but had held back. Drake glanced up at the third-floor window and smiled at the indistinct shadow that moved behind the curtains. Who would have guessed that such a sensible woman could stir his blood without even trying? Or that he was about to launch out on a preposterous mission to save a young girl who presumably did not want salvation? He who had charged into battle with the cavalry with no thought to loss of life or limb. The choices presented in his fighting days had been far less complicated. Victory or defeat. Survive. No surrender. There had been little time to brood or sink into this melancholy. His smile faded.

Damn if he didn't prefer staring death in the face than wrestling with his own dark nature.

Predawn darkness blanketed the river. Drake paced before the plain redbrick Georgian house that rose beyond the dark shore of the Thames. A few lights flickered through the half-opened shutters, and an occasional faint-hearted cheer drifted from a bedchamber. A figure cloaked in a monk's garb flitted behind a window.

Devon stamped his booted feet on the shore. "I hope there's a damned good reason why we're here."

"We're heroes, that's why. Two valiant lords who intend to save a damsel in distress. Even if the damsel has brought her woes upon herself."

Devon shot him a jaundiced look. "I said a good reason, not a bloody bedtime story. I assume this damsel is someone near and dear to your heart?"

"Hardly." He grimaced. "It's Thalia Thornton."

"Oh, my God," Devon said. "I'm freezing my ballocks off for that chit?"

"There's a little more to it than that. I'm keeping a promise I made."

A damp breeze blew up from the river. If Devon detected a vital omission in his brother's explanation, he was wise enough not to question it. "Do you want a mask?"

Drake stared down in amusement at one of two black velvet dominoes his brother had slung over his arm. "Mementos from your highwayman days? Or do you carry them around as the well-prepared lover would a French letter?"

Devon grinned. "Mock me all you like, but a man never knows when a mask might come in handy. Some ladies enjoy the notion of being seduced in the dark by a stranger."

Drake took the hooded cloak in his hands, examining it with a grin. When had his young sib grown up to be an expert in seduction? "I had no idea you were so well versed in sexual matters, Dev," he said wryly.

"How could I go wrong with you and Gray as my shining examples?"

"Follow me, and you could go very wrong," Drake said, throwing on the cloak with a laugh. The dark folds swirled around his legs as he strode toward the house. A wooden sign crudely nailed to the front door read:

LADIES BOARDING SCHOOL
FRENCH LESSONS GRATIS
INQUIRE WITHIN

"French lessons?" Devon said, whistling softly. "I like the sound of that. Perhaps the night won't be a total waste, after all."

Drake shook his head. How could he not love Dev? "I'll take the upstairs. You go below."

No one appeared when he opened the door. No one stopped him on the stairs, or as he made a brief search of every bedroom for Thalia. She was half-asleep when he found her in the last chamber he checked, curled uncomfortably on a chaise in her rumpled party gown while Percy snored away fitfully in the corner.

She stared up at his masked face in slow-dawning alarm, pressing her shoulders back into the chair. "Go away, or I shall scream the house down."

He nudged Percy with the toe of his black leather boot. The man made an incoherent sound in his throat, his eyes rolling upward. Drake backed away. Had he looked like that in his wilder days? He was afraid he knew the answer.

"Put your shoes on, Thalia," he said in a quiet but firm voice. "We're going home. And if you meant to scream, you should have done it a day or so earlier."

She sat up, her hand at her throat, her eyes bright with hopeful recognition. "Lord Drake?" she whispered. "That isn't you, is it?"

"Yes." He found one of her shoes on the floor while she wrested the other from under the cushions. He studied Percy's pale, bloated face in disdain. "My God, what a pity. It still lives."

She straightened her gown, her voice contemptuous. "Barely."

"Do you want me to throw him over the windowsill? I'd say it would be a favor to mankind."

She swallowed and stared up at his masked face. "I don't want you to get into trouble over me. I—I want to go home, please."

He took in her disheveled dress, her tangled ashen hair, the fresh tracks of tears on her cheeks. She shivered as their eyes met; he frowned and picked up her thin shawl from the floor to place around her shoulders. "You're the one who's in trouble by the look of it."

"Lecture me," she whispered a little brokenly. "I deserve it."

He sighed. "That's not for me to judge. Come on. I've got to find my brother before *he* gets into trouble."

Which Devon seemed unable to avoid by nature. Drake located his younger brother in the library, a young redheaded Cyprian draped quite comfortably in his lap. Drake cleared his throat. "Studying the classics again, Devon?" he asked from the doorway.

Devon sat up with a guilty grin, gently setting his new admirer on her feet. "We were discussing our missing friend. Alice here believes she's upstairs with Percy."

"She's standing right behind me," Drake said dryly.

Devon readjusted his domino. "I was only trying to be helpful."

"I could see that," Drake said with a bleak smile as he turned away.

Devon surged to his feet and blew his red-haired lady friend a farewell kiss. "It was lovely meeting you. I hope we have a chance to deepen our acquaintance in the near future."

Eloise was awake and dressed at dawn. She could hardly have been expected to sleep well, not after what had happened between her and Lord Drake. She couldn't stop thinking about him. The subtle warmth that still pervaded her body mocked her attempts to even try, and it didn't help matters that she had spent years persuading other young women to avoid similar situations. At twenty-five years of age, she should have known better.

She had just made herself a cup of tangy spearmint tea and taken it into the parlor when Freddie burst into the room to inform her that her lost sheep had been brought home.

She rose from her chair. She wasn't sure that she would be able to control her anger at Thalia even if it was not her place to criticize. How blithely the girl had been willing to sacrifice a man who adored her for a foolish interlude. And yet Eloise wasn't entirely unsympathetic. The moment she saw Drake Boscastle standing in the doorway, she was reminded of how easily a man could lead a woman down a dangerous path.

Her heart pulsed with currents of pleasant awareness that she could feel throughout her entire body. She stole a glimpse at his hawkish profile and cloaked figure, thinking of the beloved fairy-tale heroes of childhood, those shining knights who rescued ladies fair. Yet when he turned to regard her, she knew there was more darkness in her knight's countenance than light.

Was she afraid of the dark? Or was she attracted to it? Perhaps it didn't matter. She knew perfectly well that it would be easier to empty the Thames with a teaspoon than to redeem a man of his reputation.

Thalia rushed past her to the stairs, whispering, "I know what I did is unforgivable and that you'll never understand. But please don't hate me."

Eloise stood in silence as the girl broke away to retreat to her room. Only then did she take notice of the younger man who stood behind Drake. "Perhaps I could offer you some refreshments?" she asked. She felt inadequate for even offering. She could never repay Drake for what he'd done to help her.

The man who stood behind him stifled a yawn. "It's too early for coffee. Or too late. A brandy might be nice. I'm Devon Boscastle, by the way, Drake's brother. And—"

"*Eloise,*" Thalia said in a peevish voice from the top staircase. "I thought you would come upstairs with me. I need to talk to you."

She shook her head in apology. "Freddie, please bring the gentlemen whatever they would like." She turned, adding over her shoulder to Devon, "I'm pleased to make your acquaintance, my lord, although I do wish it had been under better circumstances."

Devon gave her a smile that added strength to the claim of the Boscastle family charm. He was a little taller than Drake, with similar chiseled masculine features and a magnetic warmth. "I do believe," he said, ignoring the scowl Drake sent his way, "that I would be pleased to meet *you* under any circumstance."

Chapter Thirteen

※ ※

Only a few hours later, life for Eloise had resumed at least a semblance of normality. Lord Thornton may not have returned home, but a message finally arrived from him stating in vague terms that he was settling his accounts and would send for his household as soon as he established a new residence. The letter was not delivered by a postman, but by a sweeping boy who ran off before anyone could ask if he'd been sent directly by his lordship.

Eloise was relieved that Lord Thornton had not done away with himself over his debts. However, she was not at all comforted by his promise to settle his accounts. She suspected this plan of his involved gambling, and if they joined him anywhere, it would be in the poorhouse. Still, she could not worry about him. Her immediate concern was to see that his sister took her wedding vows. She and Eloise had made an unspoken pact that Thalia's escapade would never be mentioned again. It was a good thing that Sir Thomas planned to live in the country, and would hopefully never find out what his bride had done before their wedding.

Later in the afternoon Eloise took her tea out into the garden and fed the sparrows bits of crust from her breakfast toast. She was savoring her peace before Thalia woke up and directed the rest of the day. There were a hundred details to attend to before the wedding. In light of Lord Thornton's abandonment, Lady Heaton had been kind enough to offer her son's help in closing up the house when he returned from Amsterdam.

But for now, just for a moment, Eloise sat in the watery English sunlight and closed her eyes. If all went well, she would be working for Lady Lyons by the end of the month. She wondered whether Lord Drake would put in a good word on her behalf and how she would manage if she were ever in the same room with him and his sister. She would have to maintain her decorum, of course. Pretending all the while that he'd never seen her bare bum or kissed her into oblivion . . . or shown her a delight that still sent flushing waves of heat through her body. Such encounters were probably commonplace to him, but not to her. Perhaps it would be better all the way around if they pretended they didn't know each other.

"There you are, Eloise," a gruff male voice announced from the garden gate.

She opened her eyes in regret. A heavyset man in a military jacket had just appeared on the gravel pathway. The sparrows on the sundial flew off in fright. She rather wished she could join them. The intruder was Lord Thornton's next-door neighbor and frequent uninvited visitor, Major John Dugdale, a retired infantry officer.

At least it wasn't Ralph, or that tailor's assistant again demanding payment on past accounts. Major Dugdale was at worst a blustering busybody, not a blackmailer or betrayer of women.

Still, he wasn't Drake Boscastle, either, a faint but disappointed voice whispered in her mind. He was a middle-aged nuisance who never had a kind word for anyone.

She lifted her face in greeting. She resented having to leave her secret fantasies about Drake Boscastle unfinished. "How are you today, Major?"

He frowned. "I am concerned about *you*, Eloise. I know that Lord Thornton has disappeared and left you and his sister unprotected."

She said nothing. It would be improper to malign her employer, selfish and stupid sod that he had proven himself to be. "We are managing, sir."

"Are you?" She jumped slightly as he banged his cane against the bench. "I've noticed a man coming to and from your house at odd hours."

She averted her gaze. Did he mean Ralph? She swallowed the sour taste in her throat. Had he been prowling about since the morning she'd ordered him to leave?

"He was a Boscastle," he added in the tone of voice a priest might use when exorcising a demon.

Eloise was taken aback. "Have the Boscastles done something to offend you?"

"Did the sun rise this morning?"

"I beg your pardon."

"Eloise, my dear," he said in a patronizing voice. "In view of your defenseless position, I feel obligated to warn you what sort of family the Boscastles are."

"What sort of family are they?" she asked, hoping she did not sound overly curious.

"A family prone to excesses of passion. A family given to scandal. To duels and sinful affairs practically every other month of the year."

She gazed past him to the garden wall, willing herself not to smile. "One cannot believe rumors."

"One cannot believe *this*," he said, and produced from his waistcoat the very caricature of Heath Boscastle that had taken London by storm.

"Is *this*—this naked Apollo not the young man who has been visiting you at all hours?"

She looked up at him accusingly. "Shame on you, Major. Have you been spying on me again?"

"Only in your best interests, my dear. Is this or is this not the same man?"

"I have never seen Lord Boscastle without his clothes," she retorted. Although he'd seen her completely nude.

"I should hope not," he said in horror.

She took the sheet and turned it toward the sunlight, murmuring, "There is a certain resemblance, I have to admit."

"A resemblance?"

"Between the brothers, although I doubt that Drake has such an enormous . . ."

"An enormous . . . ?"

She trailed off, afraid she was going to burst into irreverent laughter. Well, gracious, how *was* she supposed to think clearly when she was staring at a sketch of a man's tallywag? She didn't know what to say.

"Eloise!" Major Dugdale rapped his cane again. "What were you going to say? An enormous—"

"—tallywag." Her eyes widened in embarrassment. "Scallywag, I mean. His lordship is not such an enormous *scallywag* as to allow this sort of smut to circulate in public."

In private was anyone's guess. But, apparently, naughty behavior ran in the Boscastle family. She still could not believe that Drake's sister-in-law had drawn this caricature. Eloise could not imagine *her* mother drawing a picture of her father's unmentionable parts, and if she had, certainly no one would have paid to see them in the papers.

The major looked doubtful. "I sense an unhappy change in you, Eloise. This is not at all the reaction I expected from a lady of your remarkable propriety."

"I have no idea what you mean." But she was afraid she did, and that he was right.

"Boscastle hasn't tempted you, has he?"

"To do what?"

"I cannot say," he said.

"Then you cannot expect me to defend myself." She rose to her feet and handed the sheet back to him. "I do appreciate your concern, but I think—" She gave a gasp of surprise as he settled his hands on her shoulders. His cane dropped to the ground. The sheet flapped against her face. "What on earth has come over you, Major?"

"As a friend and neighbor, I feel compelled to protect you from—"

The tread of footsteps came from the gravel path behind them. Major Dugdale swiftly removed his hands from her shoulders and swung around rather guiltily. Eloise leaned to one side to see who had saved her from an embarrassing situation.

"Protect her from what?" Drake asked with a cool smile as he came through the garden gate.

His gaze narrowed in displeasure as Eloise and her silver-haired companion pulled away from each other. It hadn't exactly looked like a romantic moment, but the older fellow's hands had been on her shoulders. Eloise stood with a disconcerted expression on her face. Drake wasn't sure what had been going on between the two of them, but he knew he didn't like it.

He shot the older man a disgusted look for good measure. Protect her, his arse. The rascal had probably been waiting for ages to take advantage. Thornton's desertion had left his household vulnerable to every sort of predator. Why else was *he* here? he wondered cynically.

He walked to the end of the path. He deliberately ignored her disgruntled companion and focused his attention on Eloise. She darted a nervous look at the sheet of paper in the old fox's hand. God bless her. She was as open as a dictionary and just as easy to read. No deception on that pretty face. Whatever had been going on had not been her doing.

He recognized the paper instantly. And grinned. "Amazing what some people read for entertainment these days, isn't it?" he asked in amusement.

The man holding the caricature frowned. "This is a wicked, wicked world. I am Major John Dugdale, and you are—"

"—not the person depicted on that paper." Drake caught the faint smile that flitted across Eloise's face. "Although I have been told that I closely resemble him. That's my brother."

"Ah. I see," the major mumbled, his brows drawing into a frown.

"And now that we are properly acquainted," Drake said, determined to make his point clear, "I am going to ask you to leave me alone with Miss Goodwin. You don't mind, do you?"

Before the major could even open his mouth to protest, Drake slapped his hand on his shoulder and steered him toward the gate. "It really was a pleasure to meet you," he said, then added in an undertone so that Eloise could not overhear, "but it's more of a pleasure to see you go. Stay away from her, won't you?"

The man's face turned as red as a boiled crab. "Stay—"

"Don't worry. I'll find a proper protector for her. Lord Thornton would have wanted it that way, don't you think?"

"I hardly know what to think," the man sputtered.

Drake closed the gate and pivoted to find Eloise standing exactly where he'd left her, a look of amused chagrin on her face. She looked fetching in her pale violet frock, her lush mouth resisting a smile. He smiled back to counteract the surge of desire he felt. It almost knocked him to his knees. No wonder that old blunderbuss had been touching her. The sight of her brought all his own male instincts into play. Subdue. Seduce. Protect.

It was quite clear to him that his desire bordered on obsession, a realization that should have sent him running into the street. But Drake's reckless streak had a habit of rearing its head in the most unlikely situations. His past obsessions had been fortunately few and far between. He'd rarely regretted their pursuit, having discovered the greater the risk, the greater the pleasure.

She moistened her lips. "Is something the matter?"

"Yes," he said starkly. "Or no. I suppose it depends on you."

"What depends on me?"

And that was the moment he realized that his obsession was not like anything he'd ever known. That it might be more than he bargained for. The challenge oddly made it more enticing. It was a novel feeling, being attracted to a woman who wasn't as bloody jaded and tired of life as he was. And yet she could hold her own with him.

He motioned to the stone bench. "Why don't we sit down together?"

He took both her hands and drew her down next to him. Her skin looked like buttercream in the light, paler still beneath the violet ribbon-laced bodice where her cleavage disappeared into the deep valley of her breasts. His hooded gaze traveled over her in pleasure. What a waste for this warm, desirable woman to be waiting on other people.

She cleared her throat. Her hazel eyes glinted with humor. "Did you have something to tell me?"

"Yes."

She waited. "Well?"

The problem was that he hadn't planned what he intended to say. He hadn't even known he would see her today until suddenly he'd found himself standing outside the gate a few minutes ago, wondering what the devil he was doing when he was supposed to be at a garden party with Devon.

But then he started to think about how she'd looked as she rose unaware from her bath, glistening with moisture. He'd had only a sample of her, and he wanted even more. He wanted to lick her silky pink nipples and part her soft thighs to bury his face between them. He wanted to savor the sense of lightness that stole over him when they were together.

And that was how he had found himself here beside her. But it wasn't the sort of confession a man could offer and hope to make a good impression.

He noticed her gaze drift to the paper that lay beneath

the sundial. He glanced in the same direction to see what had caught her interest.

The caricature of his brother Heath stared up at him in all its vulgar infamy. It struck him as rather unfair that a distorted picture of his brother's rod would intrude on what should have been a meaningful moment.

"Have you given any more thought to your future?" he asked, looking back at her.

"Yes. I hope to take a position at Lady Lyons's Academy here in London."

He felt an evil urge to laugh. "Emma? You aspire to serve the Dainty Dictator? My own stone-hearted sister?"

"She was quite gracious when I met her."

"Perhaps when you're not the recipient of her one-hour lectures. The woman goes on like a senator of Rome." He paused. This was another first. A seduction thwarted by a picture of Heath's privates, and an offer of employment from Emma. His family was ruining his chance for romance simply by existing.

"Do you really want to work for others all your life, Eloise?"

She smiled wryly. "Of course I do. I enjoy having people order me about and humiliate me. Wouldn't everyone?"

He did laugh then. "You don't have to work, you know. That old rascal happened to be right. A woman in your position needs a protector, someone who could ease you into retirement."

"Ease me into *what*?"

"Retirement."

There was complete silence except for the sparrows rustling in the trees and the muted clatter of traffic in the street. He wondered if she understood what his proposition meant, or if he even understood it. She had turned him inside out from the night he'd met her at the dance. His friends would think he was out of his mind for walking away from Maribella. But his friends had never met Eloise. And he wasn't particularly eager to introduce them. This was one woman he wanted to keep for himself, and he didn't relish the thought of exposing her to his world.

She gave a heavy sigh. It didn't sound like the sigh of a woman who was about to say yes. "Are you suggesting what I *think* you're suggesting?"

"I think so." He smiled at her. "I'd like you to become my mistress."

She pursed her lips, looking a little flustered and very desirable. "That's what I thought you meant."

Another silence lengthened. She looked less surprised at his offer than he might have expected. But then her lack of sexual experience didn't mean that she was unworldly in other ways. He doubted he was the first man who had offered to take her into keeping. Was she tempted? She hadn't exactly leapt up from the bench in enthusiasm.

Still, he could see the delicate throb of her pulse at the base of her throat, and he thought he had caused it. He knew she was attracted to him and that he had to convince her. But the usual ways he would use to persuade a woman didn't seem quite appropriate.

"Eloise?" He leaned his head close to hers. She lowered her eyes, but he noticed that she was biting the edge of her lip. "What are you thinking?" he asked with a teasing smile. "Give me a hint. Is this the first time a man has made you such a proposition?"

Her eyes lifted to his, bright and unveiled. She didn't answer. There was no need. He saw the truth.

"I didn't think it was," he said with a wry laugh. "Having resisted previous offers, you must view mine as the devil's bargain."

She laughed a little, too. "Would that stop you if I did?"

"Not at all."

"I thought as much."

He felt the subtle heat that radiated from her body and resisted the urge to pull her into his arms. She was sweet and strong at the same time, an enticing contradiction. "In that case, you won't be surprised to hear I'm going to take it as a personal challenge to persuade you."

Her lips parted. "Do I stand a chance?"

"No," he murmured, his strong fingers sliding up her elbows to grip her upper arms.

Her head fell back. His mouth slanted over hers. He pulled her closer. To hell with resisting his urges. He needed to hold her if nothing else, and he knew damned well his kisses were persuasive.

"Do you think I make this offer lightly?" he asked as she shivered against him in a way that inflamed his blood.

"Does it matter what I think?" she whispered.

"Just tell me you accept." He scattered a trail of quick kisses down her throat to the soft mounds of her breasts. No matter what she told him, or tried to tell herself, her response to him betrayed her. He knew what his reputation was. He knew that any woman who valued her virtue would sooner sell her soul to the devil than to him.

Value me above virtue.
Want me as much as I want you.
Trust me even if I am unworthy of your trust.

"Please, Eloise," he whispered. He traced one hand across her throat and then in lazy circles to her breasts, his thumbs caressing the elongated tips through her gown. "Don't refuse until you've thought about it."

She heard his voice like a pleasant echo from far away. Her eyelids had lowered in the heavy languor that had stolen over her. She didn't want to open them because then this dreamy moment would end. She would have to make it end. He couldn't be serious. And she couldn't be seriously considering his offer.

Had she ever been asked before? Yes, twice, in fact. Had she ever been tempted? Not until now. Now temptation made itself known in tiny pulses of pleasure that arose from the secret depths of her body.

No doubt he was accustomed to ladies who granted him carte blanche and considered it a privilege. In shaken silence she opened her eyes and stared at him. The contours of his face seemed starkly shadowed in the daylight. The desire in his eyes was underlaid with an even darker emotion.

She felt like a mermaid who had been washed to an unfamiliar shore and found herself out of her element, unable to breathe, to move, to return to the warm safety of her world.

His gaze gleamed with pleasure. "I'm going to love every minute of persuading you."

She began to put her thoughts back in order. "It might be better," she said a trifle unevenly, "if you practiced your persuasion in a more private—"

"Don't move," he said. His voice sounded so different from the previous moment that a chill went down her back. He was staring past her at what appeared to be the ivy trellis. "We're being watched."

"By whom?" she asked, shivering again.

His face had hardened into a forbidding mask. It seemed hard to believe he was the same man who'd been seducing her a moment ago. "I'm about to find out."

Chapter Fourteen

❦ ❦

He surged up from the bench, breaking into a run before she even knew what he was chasing. She couldn't imagine what or who could be hiding in this rather neglected garden. The worst threat Eloise ever encountered besides thistles, mice, and unpaid tradesmen was—

Ralph, she thought in horror. Could Ralph have returned to demand more money? She sprang up from the bench. She had to stop him from meeting Drake. It would be too humiliating to explain how she had been betrayed and sought revenge on Ralph Hawkins.

A black-clad figure had just leapt up from a crouch behind the trellis and was attempting a frantic escape for the gate. Drake would have caught him easily had it not been for the wheelbarrow that the intruder pushed onto the path at the last moment.

And perhaps, had it not been for Eloise, who impulsively cried out, "Wait! Just let him go. He might—"

His gaze wild, Drake wheeled around to stare at her. So did the intruder.

She caught only the barest glimpse of his face. A blur. It wasn't Ralph. That was her first thought, a relief. This was a man she'd never seen before, tall and long-limbed, with an unexpectedly friendly face and broad shoulders that could have pulled a brace of oxen. Her mouth hung open. She realized Drake was waiting for her to finish.

"He might—he might hurt you."

He flung her a furious look.

The intruder grinned, then promptly disappeared around the garden gate with surprising agility for one of his size.

"Jesus," Drake muttered, and swung around to give chase.

She hurried after him, pausing only briefly to look back as the kitchen door behind her flew open. Lord Thornton's small household staff appeared on the path. Thalia, still in her dressing robe, led the pack.

Freddie reached Eloise first, waving a broom over his head like a sword. "Creditors, Miss Goodwin? We're not being evicted, are we?"

She grabbed the broom from his hands. The lease on the town house was due to expire, but she wasn't sure exactly when. "I don't know who it was, Freddie," she said. Or what Drake planned to do if he caught him. "Lord Drake is chasing after him."

She went through the garden gate to the street.

Freddie came up behind her on the pavement. "I don't see hide nor hair of them, miss."

It was true. The only sign of any disturbance in the street was an overturned wagon and an irate vendor collecting his scattered onions from the gutter. At the corner a costermonger ran after an escaping head of cabbage.

"Should I go after them to 'elp?" Freddie asked, already rolling up his sleeves, which, Eloise noted with despair, were stained with soot.

"Yes. Yes." She passed him the broom. "You might as

well take this. If it doesn't serve as a weapon, it might come in handy cleaning up after Lord Drake."

"Good thing he was with you, miss," Freddie said. "You need a man like 'im to protect you."

"Protect me from what?" she murmured.

She turned at a commotion behind her and saw the butler consoling Mrs. Barnes, who had taken one of her turns and was sitting on the sidewalk, her stockings sagging around her thick ankles, which were swollen from having to work so hard with scant help. For a moment Eloise wondered how different her life might be if she became Drake Boscastle's mistress. She would be able to take the staff with her. They would not be turned out on the street, and Mrs. Barnes could rest her feet.

She could ask Drake for a decent carriage. She would never worry about creditors pulling the chair out beneath her because her employer hadn't paid his bills. Instead of hiding behind the curtains when a collector called, she would hold court at one of the private parties that the mistress of a nobleman would be expected to throw.

Tempting.

Then again she would lose her chance to gain a measure of security on her own terms. True, she would have to work hard at the academy, training spoiled young ladies how to navigate the perils of polite society.

But she would be the mistress of her own fate, so to speak. She would keep her hard-earned dignity, proving to herself if not her estranged family that she was not the ignominious young woman they had cast out into the unwelcoming world. She wished she did not care what they thought. She wished that the pain of their rejection would go away.

"El-oh-*eeeeze*!" Thalia cried from the garden gate, her white face petulant and puffy. "What *are* you doing in the street? I *need* you this very moment. Have you forgotten me?"

She sighed, shaking her head, and cast a final look around her for a sign of the man who had made her a most indecent offer.

So very tempting, indeed.

Drake spent almost an hour in pursuit before he realized that his prey had disappeared somewhere in the labyrinth of mews and alleyways that provided countless means of escape for the London underworld. He'd knocked over three produce carts and a lace-seller's stall in the process. At one point a pair of constables, recognizing him, had joined the chase. But they'd become too winded to keep apace, and Drake had lost them several streets back outside a public house where they had stopped to break up a brawl.

He would have been satisfied believing that the man he'd chased was merely an unscrupulous creditor who'd come to the house to reclaim his losses. But it seemed unlikely that a creditor would lurk in the ivy to observe a private moment.

And there had been something familiar about the man's unusual build that nagged at his memory. He knew him, and yet he didn't. They had never met. Drake's mind wouldn't rest until he remembered.

He slowed his pace and stood on the sidewalk for a moment, so intent on pursuit he hadn't realized that he'd circled Berkeley Square to reach Bruton Street. Audrey Watson's house stood directly to his left.

"What the devil," he muttered.

How had he ended up here of all places?

At any rate, he'd lost his quarry. He'd know that face if he saw it again, though, and he wouldn't be caught off guard next time. Still, it rankled that he'd have to return to Eloise and explain he'd failed when he was trying to impress her as a potential protector.

Which brought up the problem of Maribella St. Ives and how he was going to explain to *her* that he was not interested in pursuing an affair. And that he trusted she would understand how these matters worked and forgive him.

He grimaced. Not bloody likely. She would fly into the boughs in a wicked temper, and he couldn't blame her. He didn't think she was the sort of woman, however, who would sit about gathering moss. But, well, *he* wasn't interested, and he'd never been the sort of man to pretend. His brutal honesty hadn't always made him popular with his friends. Or even his family, for that matter.

Oh, God. His family. It never ended. Here came one of them now.

He glanced away from the house to see his brother Devon strolling backward from the opposite direction, so engrossed in flirting with a pretty girl in a passing curricle that he didn't notice Drake until he walked right into him.

"Oh, sorry—" He straightened, his beguiling grin in place. "Drake, fancy bumping into you outside a brothel. Are you coming or going?"

Drake stared past him. "I'm looking for a man."

"In Audrey's?" Devon considered this. "For what purpose, or is this one of those secrets about you I don't want to know?"

"It's a man I caught spying on me and Miss Goodwin in her garden a little while ago," Drake said curtly. He wasn't about to give his younger brother a complete explanation on the street.

"Spying on the pair of you?" Devon made a face. "Bloody impertinent. I won't ask what you were doing."

"Good. I wouldn't tell you, in any case." He gave Devon a nudge toward the front door of the respectable-looking house. All the windows were tightly shuttered as if to conceal the sins committed within. He wondered suddenly if the man he sought had somehow gained entry. It was unlikely, but worth a try.

Devon stood beside him as Drake lifted the heavy brass knocker. "What are we going to do if we find him?"

"Invite him to tea." Drake shook his head in exasperation. "What do you think, Devon?"

"I think you're a damn moody swine."

"I never claimed to be a bloody ray of sunshine."

The door opened. Audrey's imposing butler, who had served briefly under the Prince Regent in Brighton before she stole him away, stood gazing at them in pompous silence before he recognized who they were. It didn't show, but Drake knew the man carried a pair of flintlock pistols underneath his long-tailed black coat.

"Good afternoon, my lords," he said through his nose, sketching a stiff-arsed bow. "Please come in. The mistress is not home. May I personally attend to your needs?"

"I'm looking for a man," Drake said without preamble.

The butler's eyebrows flew toward the ceiling. "A man, my lord?"

"That's what I said."

"Perhaps you might visit Mrs. Rutherford's establishment by the Strand. I understand she caters to a variety of appetites."

"I don't want this man for pleasure," Drake said in annoyance. "I want to kill him. He has given me offense of a confidential nature."

"And you believe he may be in our house?" The butler's nostrils quivered in indignation. "Describe the miscreant to me, my lord."

"I only caught a glimpse of him," Drake said. "Tall. Well built. He had a cheeky monkey's face."

"A monkey's face," the butler said with a frown. "I can think of several men who fit that description."

"But has anyone like that arrived here in the past hour?" Devon asked.

"I shall ask Mrs. Watson's personal attendants. Please make yourselves at ease while I inquire."

"He may have entered by the back passage," Devon called after him.

"And he may have gone out that way, too, while we stand here chatting like schoolgirls," Drake said, striding impatiently through the lower hallway. "Come on, Miss Muffet. Upstairs."

He and Devon separated to make a quick search of the private upstairs salon. Only two visitors were present, one a popular Drury Lane actress in an emerald silk gown, who sat sipping champagne, the other a respected member of parliament who nodded cordially upon recognizing the Boscastle brothers.

"On to the rooms," Drake said. He was aware that enough time had elapsed for his quarry to sail halfway to Cornwall. Why had Eloise tried to stop him, anyway? That moment of distraction had cost him the chase.

Devon put his hands on his hips. "Look, we don't *know* that he came in here."

Drake didn't spare him a look. "He might be hiding in one of the rooms."

Devon straightened his athletic frame in alarm as Drake cut toward the private hallway. "You can't very well go knocking on doors while people are doing the dirty."

"You have a point," Drake muttered. "We won't knock."

"He might have gone to the house down the street."

"He might have. Except that I have a hunch about him, Devon."

Devon followed him down the corridor. "I don't think you or Heath have ever had a false hunch."

"I'll start at the right."

Devon shook his head in resignation. "Just remember to duck when objects start flying."

Drake flashed him a grin. Damn, but he didn't know what he'd do without the young bastard. "With any luck the only missiles they'll have time to throw are pillows."

"Nobody makes a fool of Maribella St. Ives." A volley of tasseled pillows flew across the room like a meteor shower. "Do you mean to tell me that I'm being jilted for a mere companion?"

Albert dug his hands into his pockets and gazed down gloomily from the hotel window into the street. He was sure he'd lost Boscastle, but, God, what a chase. He'd never run so far and so fast in his life. He shuddered inwardly. "He looked bloody fit to kill me."

"I'll kill him," she said, her gray eyes smoldering. "What sort of game does he think he's playing?"

"Hold still, madam," the young maid on the floor cried in frustration. "You've sloshed rose water all over your lovely carpet. If you want to be beautified, you can't be dancing your feet like a racehorse."

She lifted one delicately arched foot into the air and swore. "What is this companion's name?"

"Damned if I know," Albert replied, hunching his shoulders. "The house is leased to a Lord Horace Thornton. He and his sister live there, but I gather he's gone off to evade his debtors."

"Never heard of either of 'em." She frowned down at the exasperated maid on the floor. "Are you sure Lord Drake didn't call while I was asleep?"

"Yes, I'm sure, Miss St. Ives," the maid replied for at least the tenth time that day. "He sent an apology claiming that he'd been delayed again."

"Delayed. He's been delaying, all right. How horrifically insulting. Dallying with a—a virtual domestic while I sit here all alone."

Albert frowned at her. "There's an earl and two other titled gentlemen waiting downstairs for you to appear."

"The Earl of Chesleigh?" Her face cleared. "Did he come bearing more gifts?"

"You'd have to ask him yourself. I'm only supposed to be a bodyguard." He frowned at her over his shoulder. "Boscastle's going to kill me if he ever sees me again."

"I told you not to let him see you," she said, picking up a copy of a Parisian magazine.

"I was well enough hidden. I swear he has the instincts of a wolf."

"So I understand," she said a little sourly. A reluctant smile curved her red lips. "A lady's companion. I wonder if that's the same woman he had waiting in the carriage the night we met, the devil. I knew the moment I met him that we would not suit."

"He's worse than a devil," Albert said, ducking the magazine she heaved in his direction. "I knocked over two elderly women escaping him and damn near castrated myself scaling a wrought-iron gate."

She looked distinctly unconcerned. "Do you remember where this woman lives?"

He grunted. "Of course I remember. I'm not going back there, though."

"No." She dipped her toes back daintily into the bowl of scented water. "But I might."

Two hours later, as Eloise was sitting down to tea and a healthy serving of almond trifle with Heston and Mrs. Barnes, a note arrived from Lord Drake warning her that he hadn't caught the culprit in the garden, but that everyone in the house should be on guard in case he appeared again. Eloise was relieved he had not been injured in his wild pursuit. Who had been watching them? Not Ralph Hawkins. Was it too much to hope that he had disappeared?

"Goodness," Mrs. Barnes exclaimed, putting down her spoon, "we have a champion in Lord Drake. A *protector*."

Then she looked frankly at Eloise, who resumed digging into her trifle as if she had no idea what the woman meant, although it was obvious that Mrs. Barnes understood exactly why Lord Drake had been paying Eloise so much attention. What wasn't obvious was how Eloise would handle the situation. Her heart wanted to accept his offer. Her mind warned her that to abandon her principles could only bring unhappiness. She had always hoped that one day she would marry, but could she let him go?

She was still pondering her options three hours later when a footman arrived at the house and, in front of Mrs. Barnes, Thalia, and Freddie, presented her with a letter on expensive vellum along with a bouquet of long-stemmed hothouse lilies. Eloise was delighted enough with the flowers, but was rendered speechless when she realized that entwined in their white silk ribbon was a necklace of baroque pearls.

The letter read simply:

> *I knocked over enough flower carts today to fill a meadow.*
> *I'll give you time to think.*
> *Let me know the moment you decide.*
> *But decide soon.*
>
> *Drake*

"What's it say?" Freddie asked, staring over her shoulder.

She pressed the letter to her heart. "Er, nothing. Not much. His lordship knocked over several flower carts while pursuing that intruder today."

Mrs. Barnes cleared her throat. "He didn't knock over a jeweler's shop, did he?"

"Pearls from Drake Boscastle," Thalia said softly,

coming up behind her. "How perfectly wicked. Do you realize how many women I know would be envious? He must be infatuated. Oh, Eloise, what are you going to do?"

Eloise shook her head. "What *should* I do?"

"Put them on." Not caught up in herself for once, Thalia lifted the necklace to Eloise's throat. "It doesn't hurt to see what they look like, does it?"

Eloise almost smiled. Since Thalia's return, she seemed to have changed in subtle ways. Eloise could only hope the girl had learned from her experience. But what of herself? For all she had struggled, she was not sure what lessons to draw from her own life.

"What luster they have!" Thalia exclaimed. "How well they look against your skin."

"How impractical," she murmured. "Putting on pearls to go to bed. As if anyone could admire them."

But several minutes later, after everyone had retired for the night, she sneaked back into the hallway and tried on the necklace. She studied herself in the cracked mirror that hung on the wall. She did look quite nice in pearls. Not common. Almost fashionable if she pinned up her hair and changed her serviceable brown muslin for silk. A fashionable impure. That was what she would be called. She wondered whether she would come to not care.

"A mistress or a schoolmistress?" she mused aloud. "Practical or pampered? What will Eloise decide?"

"She's a fool if she lets a gentleman like Lord Drake get away," Mrs. Barnes said from the door to the parlor.

Eloise spun around, blushing in embarrassment. She suspected that Mrs. Barnes had taken to tippling Lord

Thornton's brandy before bed, and drinking lowered her inhibitions. Well, Eloise had been known to take a few sips herself here and there after a trying day.

"Of course I can't accept the pearls," she said. She struggled to undo the clasp, which seemed to have developed a mind of its own. She could not unfasten it. "Don't stand there dispensing bad advice, Mrs. Barnes. Kindly help me remove this symbol of sin and seduction from my neck."

"Sin and seduction," Mrs. Barnes said, breathing out brandy fumes like a drunken dragon as she came to Eloise. "I call it security and protection."

Eloise lifted her chin. "Are you encouraging me to accept an indecent offer?"

Mrs. Barnes, normally a sorceress with her fingers, frowned when the clasp resisted her deft handling. "Indeed, I am. Better a rich man's mistress than a poor man's wife. Or a schoolmistress, as you said when you were talking to yourself."

Eloise had never heard the woman speak to her so frankly. She was glad that Thalia could not hear this conversation. "Consider the shame," she said lightly.

Mrs. Barnes snorted. The necklace remained in place. "Yes. Consider the shame should all of us end up begging in the gutter because you chose, selfishly, I might add, to become a schoolmistress when we might have been living in a palace."

"Lord Drake does *not* live in a palace."

"Close enough. Better than debtor's gaol, at any rate. You've never stayed in an almshouse, my dear. I have, and it wasn't pleasant."

"Poverty never is." Eloise put her hands to the back of her neck. "You did something to the clasp, didn't you?"

"I did not."

"It's stuck."

"It's fate. Face it, Eloise Goodwin, fate is offering you a once-in-a-lifetime chance at wealth and ease."

Not to mention love, lust, and heartbreak, Eloise thought wistfully, lowering her hands from her neck in resignation. "I shall have to go to a jeweler's shop first thing in the morning to have this removed," she muttered.

"You're making a mistake," Mrs. Barnes said, one thick white eyebrow lifted in ominous warning. "A person should heed the signs of fate."

"A person should mind her own business!" Eloise retorted.

"It's a sign, mark my words," Mrs. Barnes insisted in a forceful voice.

Freddie emerged from the steps of the lower floor, rubbing his eyes. "A sign of what? The end of the world? Lord, you two are making enough racket to signify the Apocalypse. What's the matter now?"

"I cannot remove this necklace," Eloise said. "The clasp is stuck."

"I'll fetch a bottle of brandy," Mrs. Barnes said, veering toward the parlor.

Freddie plopped down on the bottom of the stairs. "Does brandy loosen clasps?" he asked with a disinterested yawn.

"No," Eloise said crossly. "It loosens tongues."

But by the time the three of them had polished off the rest of the bottle and a plate of biscuits, having given up on the necklace, Eloise had graciously accepted Mrs. Barnes's apology, if not her advice. In fact, they were all in a convivial mood as they wished one another pleasant dreams and Eloise went into the parlor to read before bed.

And no one heard the furtive knock on the front door or noticed the man who stood listening to their laughter for a long time before he melted back into the night.

Chapter Fifteen

❧ ❧

Drake had decided to spend the evening alone. He would have liked to visit Eloise, but it was rather late, and he'd promised her he would wait for her decision. He thought he might walk to work off his restless energy. He was a large man and looked forbidding enough that even late at night he was usually left alone. In fact, he'd been assaulted only once, when he had been mistaken for his brother Heath. Even then Drake had gotten the better of his assailant.

The incident reminded him of Heath's infamous naked caricature, and how it had stared him in the face when he'd kissed Eloise in the garden. For a moment, the memory of her flooded him with irrational need, and he wasn't sure all of a sudden how long he could wait for her decision. He realized he had to get a firm grip on himself before he frightened her off. They barely knew each other, but he knew what he wanted. And how to get it. He didn't consider the possibility that she would turn him down, but she might drive him mad in the interim.

Where? Where had he seen that man in the garden before? At the club? A waiter there? A footman of a friend?

He knew, and didn't know. Had he been watching Drake, or Eloise?

He slowed his pace. He was only a few minutes away from his brother Grayson's Park Lane mansion. Once one of London's most scandalous scoundrels, Gray had recently settled down with his warm-hearted wife, Jane, and their infant son. Grayson had a calm head when it came to life and women. He'd seduced his share of them, but to this day even his past mistresses would defend him to the death.

Grayson was anything but calm when Drake arrived. In fact, the entire house was in an uproar. Servants were running up and down the stairs, brandishing cold wet compresses and bottles of expensive sherry, puppets, and poultices.

Weed, the senior footman, grabbed Drake by the shoulders as they met on the landing. *Nothing* upset Weed, and he had to be at his wits' end to put his hands on a member of the family.

"Thank heavens, you're here," he said half-hysterically. "The marquess is in such a state."

"Is he ill?" Drake asked, glancing up at his brother's suite of connecting rooms.

"No, Lord Drake. It's his son. The young lord has a fever, and we are most distressed."

"Have you summoned a doctor?"

Weed threw up his hands. "We've summoned every physician in London."

A few moments later Drake located his older brother in the nursery where enough beeswax candles to illuminate the entire West End blazed in every corner. Grayson, a tall, majestic-looking man with disheveled golden hair and bare feet, was pacing the floor in his black silk dressing robe. His infant son lay swaddled in his cradle, red-faced, pudgy, and fretful.

Grayson spun on his heels, looking for all the world like an agitated sultan. "Oh, it's only you," he said in disappointment as Drake closed the door. "I thought you were the godblasted physician. I shall have his periwig for making me wait. Did you see the herbalist on your way here? The apothecary?"

Drake stared at his brother in helpless surprise. He could not remember seeing Grayson this frantic, this distraught. He didn't know what to say. Neither of them had any practical experience with children. "Where is Jane?" he asked. He thought that Grayson's wife would take better charge of the situation than his brother. Grayson was falling apart.

Grayson bent over the cradle, staring at his son in utter bewilderment. "She's with her parents. I've sent word for her to come. What should I do in the meantime? My God, what if he dies before she gets here? Don't stand there staring. Tell me what to do."

Drake was afraid to go to the cradle. "I have no idea what to do. The only experience I've had with sickness was on the battlefield. Usually fever followed a bayonet wound."

"That's helpful, isn't it?" Grayson snapped. "Do you think I'd allow my son to play with a bayonet? What the hell do you want, anyway? You don't care about anyone. Drinking, whoring, war. That's your life, isn't it? Do you want to die alone?"

Drake's face remained impassive. He knew Grayson was upset, but there was enough truth in the assault to feel its sting. "Where is the nursemaid?"

"I dismissed the damned woman!"

Drake was beginning to feel a little frantic himself. He took an instinctive step toward the restless form in the cradle. He supposed that any help was better than none. "Why did you dismiss her?"

"She let my son contract a fever, that's why! I'll see her hanged by her damned toenails. Or her tongue. The damned woman talks too damned much anyway. If she'd been paying attention to my son instead of talking . . ."

"Perhaps I should see if I can hurry that physician along," Drake said. His brother's fear was contagious. "Don't forget that Devon had frequent fevers as a child. And he survived to torment us all."

Grayson looked as if he were a drowning man who had just been thrown a lifeline. "I forgot. Devon and his infernal fevers. Mama thought he was dying every time he took sick."

Drake worked up the courage to walk over to the cradle. The plump, red-faced family heir looked like an uncomfortable little perisher but he didn't remind Drake of any of the dying soldiers he'd attended. "You've got him swaddled up like a caterpillar in a cocoon!" he exclaimed.

Grayson looked up defensively. "He was crying when I came in. I was afraid he'd hurt himself."

"In the cradle?" Drake asked blankly. "How?"

"Well, he might have fallen out."

"He can't sit up yet, can he?"

Grayson laid his large hand against the child's cheek. The baby arched his back in agitation. Drake wasn't sure, but he might have broken wind. He hoped it wasn't Grayson. "Devon climbed out of his cradle almost every night."

"Before he could crawl?" That didn't sound quite right to Drake.

"I don't know," Grayson said, throwing his large body into a chair. He had exhausted himself.

Drake leaned over the cradle and loosened the three swaddling blankets that imprisoned Rowan. The baby kicked furiously, expelled a fart, and stopped fussing, his blue eyes wide and curious. Drake touched his cheek. "He doesn't feel hot to me. I think he had a fart."

"A fart?" Grayson said, rising in relief. "Are you certain?"

"Well, that's what it sounded like. Anyway, I'd feel hot, too, if you smothered me in all these blankets."

Grayson scooped the infant in his arms and snuggled him to his shoulder as the door behind him flew open and his wife, Jane, the Marchioness of Sedgecroft, burst into the nursery. She looked elegant if visibly upset in her lemon yellow watered silk evening gown, a diamond choker on her slender white throat.

Her parents, Lord and Lady Belshire, crowded in behind her. Hot on their heels followed the Scottish physician, an herbalist, the apothecary, and the indignant Irish nursemaid. Everyone seemed to be talking at once.

Drake had never felt so out of place or useless in his entire life. A child had caused all this chaos and concern. A human being who had not even existed a year ago. An unplanned product of love and passion and God knew what else thrown into the pot. The intensity of emotion in the room staggered him.

Jane wrested the infant from her husband's arms. "What have you done to my son?"

"I saved his life, Jane," Grayson said, as arrogant as ever now that the crisis had apparently passed.

She scattered kisses over the baby's bald head, his fat cheeks, his neck. "What was wrong with him?"

Grayson blew out a sigh. "He had the stomach grippe and a raging fever."

Jane narrowed her eyes, suddenly noticing Drake standing in the corner. "My brother summoned *you* here because Rowan was ill? What did he expect you to do?"

"I'm not convinced, actually, that Rowan was really—" Drake broke off as Jane's mother, Athena, jostled him aside to fuss over her recovered grandson. Jane's father, Howard, had spotted the bottle of sherry on the windowsill and was looking around for a glass.

Jane gasped. "You didn't give him sherry, did you, Grayson?"

"That was for me, Jane," Grayson said defensively. "I needed it to help our son fight his illness."

"Why did you send Mrs. O'Brien from the house?" she demanded.

"Because her infernal lullabies disturbed the boy."

"They calm him down, Grayson." Jane shook her elegantly coiffed head in maternal disapproval, passing the child to her mother's care.

Jane's sisters, Miranda and Caroline, burst into the room, tears of emotion in their eyes. Clearly they had been told the situation was dire. Drake expected his own sisters, Chloe and Emma, to arrive at any moment.

"There's a crowd gathering in the streets," Caroline said from the window. "They're looking very sober. One would think the life of a crown prince were in peril."

"Wave to them, Grayson," Jane said, her voice softening as she glanced at her husband. "Let them know all is well."

Grayson strode to the window and waved one of his

son's nappies. The small crowd cheered. Then, as if suddenly recovering his wits, he pivoted and gave his attention to Drake, a reserved witness to this family crisis.

"My God," he said, and walked to where Drake stood. "You did not come all the way here for nothing. Did you wish to talk to me? Is something wrong?"

"No, Grayson. It can wait." Drake felt quite exhausted himself from all the drama.

Grayson lowered his voice and placed his arm around Drake's shoulders to walk him to the door. "You do not weaken in a crisis, and such strength was exactly what I needed to see me through. Thank you. Now let me return the favor. What is it you needed of me?"

"Nothing." Drake shook his head and backed into the hallway. "It's all right, really. I understand."

"Do you?" Grayson followed him, looking completely helpless. "I gave way to panic. I never panic, but when I thought I might lose him—Do you understand? It was Brandon's birthday last week. I believe that remembering him, and what it feels like to lose someone you love, undid me."

Drake felt a sense of unwelcome heaviness steal over him. Brandon's death had left a scar on the heart of the family. For better or worse, and it was often the latter, the Boscastles were a fiercely close band who loved and lived hard, and mourned with a passion that few of their friends understood.

"I had not forgotten," he said quietly, and wondered, not for the first time, if his own unresolved anger over Brandon's murder had not contributed at least in part to his recent emotional unrest.

"I could lose my son," Grayson said, his voice raw with imagined grief. "I would rather die a thousand deaths by torture than lose him or Jane. Love is horrible, Drake. Horrible. Don't let it happen to you. Why did I let it happen? *How* did I let it happen?"

Grayson stood in the doorway, his powerful figure framed in the blazing candlelight of the room behind him.

"I don't know how it happened." Drake retreated deeper into the darkness of the hallway. This was anything but the calm advice he had sought. "But you haven't lost them."

"I know." Grayson closed his eyes. He drew an enormous breath and his great body shuddered as he exhaled. "I was wrong. Don't listen to me. Love is a wonderful thing. I hope that one day you—"

He opened his eyes. Drake had disappeared. He turned to find his wife standing beside him, their baby active and content in her arms. Her long honey-colored hair had come unbound in a bewitching tumble down her back.

"What was your brother doing here, Grayson?" she asked quietly. "Was something else wrong besides your falling apart the moment I left you?"

He slanted her a sharp look in return. "I never fall apart, and, to be honest, I'm not sure what Drake wanted."

"Then perhaps you should have found out instead of the commotion you caused in the nursery," she said lightly.

"He did seem troubled," Grayson admitted.

Jane gave him a reluctant smile. "Perhaps it's time to find out why."

"Yes, perhaps." He was gazing down in fierce tenderness at his son. "Damn little devil scared me to death."

"I do love you, Grayson," she said ruefully. "But I will never leave you to watch our son again."

Drake hurried down the stairs of Grayson's mansion, nearly colliding with the lanky, familiar figure coming the other way. "Am I too late?" Devon asked, his cloak spangled with mist. "I got here as fast as I could."

Drake shook his head. He wanted to escape from this house, to escape his own emotions if the truth be told. He needed a bottle of brandy, and a bracing walk in the night air. "It's all over. Everything is fine."

"What happened?" Devon asked, handing his gloves to a maidservant who had just come up behind him.

"Nothing. Grayson thought the baby had the stomach grippe. He had gas. It was the usual family pageant." He made to move down the stairs.

"Are you saying all this fuss was over a fart?"

"Yes."

"Well, in that case, do you want to go to the club?"

"No." Drake heard the impatience in his voice. "Not tonight."

"You're in a mood, aren't you?" Devon asked, staring at him.

"What if I am?"

"Nothing." Devon shrugged, never one to provoke an argument. "I was merely pointing out that you seem to be in a bad humor. Is there anything wrong? Does it involve Eloise Goodwin?"

"Stop it," Drake said with an irritated scowl.

Devon shook his head. "Stop what?"

"Stop being so damned annoying."

"I didn't mean to be annoying. I asked about a woman. How was that annoying?"

Drake glanced away. "It annoyed me, that's all."

Devon looked mystified. "I ask you questions all the time, and they have never seemed to annoy you. Well, not this much, at least. You've always acted as if you didn't care. Unless—" A knowing gleam kindled in his eyes. "Unless—"

"Unless what, you idiot?" Drake asked, leaning back against the railing.

Devon lifted his shoulders. "Unless, well, nothing."

Drake's face darkened. "Unless what, dammit?"

"Well." Devon stared down at his boots, mumbling, "Unless you *do* care."

Drake pinned him with a long, lethal stare. "Unless I care about what?"

"About whom," Devon said under his breath.

"Are you suggesting—" Drake pushed himself off the railing, glaring at his brother, who by refusing to meet his gaze rendered the glare infuriatingly ineffective. "I hope to God that you're not suggesting what I think you're suggesting."

Devon lifted his gaze. "I'm not suggesting anything, really. Far be it from me to suggest that you might be a little touchy on the subject."

Drake's eyes smoldered like coals. "And the subject is?"

"I believe," Devon said, quite bravely meeting his older brother's regard, "that the subject is that rather fetching woman you introduced me to earlier today."

"It isn't true," Drake said quickly.

"What? That she is the subject, or that you're touchy about her?"

Drake put his hand over his eyes. "I'm going to count

to five, and if you're still standing here when I'm finished, I'm throwing you headfirst over the railing."

He counted to five. When he opened his eyes, Devon was gone. And if Drake had not been in a dark mood before, he found himself caught under a veritable eclipse now.

He went downstairs into Grayson's study and found a bottle of French brandy on the sideboard. He had visited this room often as a boy, hoping to receive a word of approval from his father. It had never come. Not a crumb. Not a smile, nor pat on the shoulder.

He'd always known that he was his father's least favorite child; they had fought constantly, and Drake had been forever in trouble for fighting or disobeying. He still remembered his mother whispering to him after a particularly shaming scolding from his father, "He punishes you because you are so alike. He struggled all his life with his private demons. I think he means to exorcise them from you."

"It didn't work," he said, opening his eyes. "The demons survived."

His father, Royden Boscastle, had been passionate and moody, protective and tyrannical at once. To this day Drake felt that he had never known the man, or understood him any better than he understood himself. But they had been alike. Everyone in the family said so. It wasn't an encouraging thought.

He left the house.

He supposed he ought to visit Maribella St. Ives this evening. He'd planned to tell her face-to-face that he did not wish to pursue a relationship. Not long ago he would have pursued her, if only to dispel his depressive state with the distraction of sex. The prospect of seeing her made him feel even worse.

Still, if he visited Maribella, then perhaps Eloise would be safe from damnation. Grayson's words echoed in the back of his mind.

You don't care about anyone. Drinking, whoring, war. That's your life, isn't it? Do you want to die alone?

He walked without stopping to the Hill Street house. Rain glistened on the cobbles. A lone carriage rumbled past. He hadn't meant to come here, and perhaps if he hadn't seen the light in the parlor, he would not have stopped.

He knocked at the front door of the unassuming house. He hadn't decided what he would do if someone other than Eloise answered. He didn't even know how he would explain visiting her this late at night when he had promised he would await her decision. Oh, what the hell. He'd just make up an excuse.

"Who is it?" a soft voice asked cautiously from inside the house. Her voice. Thank God. Her. It was her.

"It's me. It's Drake."

She opened the door and stared up into his face. Again he sensed that she could see beyond the superficial. She did not even look surprised that he had come.

She stood in darkness, the pearls he had sent her glistening with promise at her throat, a book in her hand. "Is something wrong?" she asked hesitantly.

"May I come in?

She glanced around as if considering her answer. There was no one in the hall behind her. "Yes."

He followed her into the parlor. He shrugged out of

his coat and stared at her, not bothering to disguise his restless thoughts with polite conversation. He saw her eyes lift again to his in question. She might as well know what he was from the start. If he was to be her lover, she would have to accept his darkness, his restless moods, the whole damned mess of him.

Chapter Sixteen

✣ ✣

Eloise took his coat from his hands. He caught her by the waist before she could turn around. The dark angles of his face were shadowed with an intensity that made her heart falter. He pulled her against him. She went, his coat slipping from her fingers to the floor. His arm tightened around her as if he sensed that she welcomed his embrace, that she had thought of nothing but him since their last meeting.

His lips slanted over hers in a demanding kiss. She strained against him and felt his body harden in response. His tongue slipped inside her mouth and sent a heated shiver dancing over her from head to bottom. "What is it?" she whispered. "Why are you here so late at night?"

"For you. No other reason."

"Where have you been?"

"To my brother Grayson's house." A reluctant smile eased the tension on his face. "He thought his infant son was dying."

"Dying?" she said in alarm. "Is he all right now?"

"There was nothing wrong with him but gas in the first place." He shook his head in amusement. "I should not laugh at my brother except that both of us were behaving like a pair of helpless idiots until his wife came home."

"You thought the baby would die of gas?" she asked gently.

"Frightened to death until he farted," he admitted. "What do I know of babies? Will you let me stay awhile?" he asked. "Although be warned, I may be bad company tonight."

She'd known the instant she'd opened the door that something had upset him—he had been worried about his nephew. And he'd come to her. That meant more to her than pearls or promises.

"Do you want something to drink?"

"No, I've already—" He lifted his fingers to her throat, his eyes warming in victory. "You're wearing the pearls I sent you. Does that mean you've decided to be my lover?"

Her lover and protector. She drew a breath at the weakening desire that swept over her, then shook her head in chagrin. "What it means is that the clasp wouldn't come undone."

His mouth quirked into a smile. "Really, Eloise, you don't expect me to believe that."

"It's true," she said, a blush rising to her cheeks.

His eyes glowed with laughter. "Then it's fate, isn't it?"

"No, it's—" She tilted her head back to look at him. "Did you have the clasp designed to lock like this?"

He moved one hand idly down her back. "Darling, that would make me too devious, don't you think?"

"Devious or determined," she said with a rueful smile, aware that he was making a leisurely exploration of her backside beneath her dress.

"I might be both." He smiled back at her rather wickedly. "Of course I am compelled to point out that you put the pearls on in the first place."

Eloise did not reply. She really couldn't think of a way to deny it.

"And trying on pearls might be construed as an acceptance of my offer." He cleared his throat. "Or not. Do you mind if we sit down?"

His hand drifted across her bottom. She felt a wicked trail of warmth burn in the wake of his touch. His quiet exhalation of breath brushed a tendril of hair at her temple. "If you like," she said, thinking that her legs probably wouldn't hold out much longer, anyway. At least if she sat down he wouldn't be able to tell how badly she was trembling.

Of course, once they reached the sofa, she realized that she hadn't solved the problem at all. He leaned into her, his long, lean-muscled body overshadowing hers, and her knees still trembled.

"What were you reading?" he asked casually, his thumb rubbing across her knuckles.

"Reading? Just a book of country cures."

His fingers raised little flames across her wrist. Before she knew it, he had walked a path up her arm until he stopped to flirt with the undercurve of her breast. "It's a shame you weren't with me earlier in the evening when I visited Grayson. I'll bet as a governess you've had a lot of experience dealing with sick babies."

"Mostly with ill-behaved young boys," she said unthinkingly, distracted as his hand caressed the shape of her breast through her dress. How could he talk so calmly when he was arousing this wild desire inside her?

"And men?" he asked curiously, lifting his face to hers. "Have you had much experience with men?"

She was drawn into the dark eroticism of his eyes. "No," she said faintly.

He murmured, "Good," and kissed her again, sliding one arm around her shoulder to position her to his advantage.

Her eyes drifted shut. He was brushing his fingers rhythmically back and forth across her nipples until she moaned in melting arousal against his arm. Shudders of raw sensation traveled from her shoulders into the base of her spine.

"Eloise." He pressed a kiss against each corner of her mouth. "I wasn't going to see you again until you sent for me. Please, may I keep touching you?"

"I don't—I don't know."

She wasn't ready to open her eyes to look at him again. Just for a moment longer she wanted to concentrate on the sexual heat that shivered through her. The secret place between her legs had begun to pulse unbearably; a sense of loss left her sighing when he drew his hand from her swelling breasts. But then slowly she felt the cool invasion of that same hand under her skirt, and loss turned into longing. She felt her body opening, aching, inviting more of his touch.

"Drake," she whispered in a breathless voice.

"Tell me when to stop, sweetheart." He groaned softly. "But, please, don't say so yet." God, not yet, he thought, his hand drawn to her heated cleft. He could practically taste the musk-scented moisture of her arousal.

She thought that this was probably the sensible time to tell him to stop. But when his long fingers suddenly parted the damp folds of flesh between her thighs, sinking deeply into her aching crevice, she found she could not speak. Hot shocks of pleasure streaked into the secret reaches of her body. Instead of resisting, she arched with her thighs opening to invite him.

"This is a warm welcome," he whispered in a raw voice. He worked another finger into her wet passage and stretched her wide.

She sank against his hand, drenching him with her desire, unable to mount a defense. Her body would have betrayed whatever protest she could have made, anyway. Every private fantasy she had suppressed clamored for satisfaction. He made her so aware of her sensuality that there was no room for shame.

She shifted restlessly and moved her hips. He seemed to understand what she wanted and pressed another finger deep inside her. She ached for more but couldn't ask. But then he plucked the sensitive hood of her sex between the thumb and forefinger of his other hand. She fell back gasping against his arm. Her swollen cleft wept with need.

"Please, Drake," she begged, pressing her face into his shoulder. "Please . . ."

"You will be mine," he whispered, unlacing the back of her gown and her chemise with one hand so that her breasts spilled out, soft and ivory pale. He leaned down and sucked a taut pink nipple into his mouth. Wild with desire, on fire for him, she gave a soft cry and arched against his other hand.

His fingers quickened, sinking even deeper, stretching her virgin sheath until pain and pleasure blurred. The muscles in her belly tightened with maddening tension. The need for relief built unbearably until she reached for him in desperation.

"Your answer is yes, isn't it?" he asked, his voice raw. "You can't refuse me, Eloise. I know you wouldn't let me touch you otherwise."

He silenced her muffled sob with his mouth. How could she stop him when she was stricken with the same insatiable hunger that she saw in his eyes? She laced her arm tightly around his neck and drew his dark face to her breasts. She needed for him to ease this helpless longing. He pulled her bodice down to her waist as if she were a wanton. Even then she couldn't tell him to stop. She was beyond thought, offering herself to him, inviting his possession. The damp warmth of his mouth on her breasts only intensified the pulsating ache between her legs. She was half out of her mind when she felt him pull back . . . felt him push up her dress to expose her woman's place to his scrutiny.

"Drake," she gasped as he forced her knees even further apart. His tongue scalded her, drove between her plump folds in merciless enjoyment. She shuddered, throwing one arm across her face. She could not bring herself to look at him, to watch him suck and nibble at her hidden pearl. She twisted her hips, shocked and aroused at the same time. He slipped one hand beneath her bottom and held her immobile as he ate at her.

"You taste so sweet, Eloise," he murmured, his voice thick with desire. "Just let yourself enjoy it."

Her mind drifted into darkness. There was no fight in her. Her hips arched involuntarily, and his tongue drove into her core, the stabbing pleasure more than she could bear. Her breath caught on a broken cry, and then, oh, God. She shattered in complete abandon.

Drake could have died with pleasure himself when he felt her body stiffen and convulse in climax against his face. Her musky fragrance intoxicated him and he struggled to suppress his own desire, his control challenged as never before. As badly as he wanted to ease his erection inside all that honeyed warmth, this was as far as he would go until he was certain of uninterrupted privacy. It was enough she understood what pleasure he could give her even if his nerves were frayed raw with frustration.

He laid his face against her inner thigh and inhaled her womanly perfume. Faint aftershocks of pleasure still quivered through her lower body. He sighed. He'd loved watching her lose control, loved knowing that he could wring such sensuality from her.

She struggled to sit up. Her hand rested on his shoulder. He lifted his head and stared at her, unable to hide a smile. She looked spent and more than a little dazed. "Are you all right?" she asked hesitantly.

He regarded her with wry resignation. "I might be in a few hours."

She shook her head, a smile lurking on her lips. "I don't know what to say."

He leaned forward and lightly kissed her, his mouth still bearing her fragrance. "I think I understand." With another sigh he drew her dress down around her knees.

She put her hands to her loosened chemise and gaping bodice. "I don't know what would have happened if we'd been caught."

"I would claim that you made me shameless."

She laughed. "As if anyone would believe that."

He shook his head, laughing, too. "Your answer is yes?"

She bit her bottom lip. "You promised me time to think."

He nodded slowly. A black despair had brought him to her door tonight. Now that too-familiar darkness had lifted, even if his body ached like the very devil with unfulfilled desire. Her answer would be yes. He would patiently pursue her until she relented, and when they were together his patience would be rewarded.

"I ought to leave," he said softly, glancing away from her. "I don't suppose you've heard anything more from Thornton?"

She frowned. "No. Not after his one message."

He bent to kiss her once more before he rose. "All the more reason why you need a protector, Eloise."

Throughout the remainder of the night she wrestled with her thoughts. After the past week, she could not deny the advantage of having an aggressive protector like Drake Boscastle. Perhaps she would have to compromise her principles. They had not served her particularly well thus far.

By becoming Drake's mistress, she would not merely cross the line of respectability, she would leap over it and never be able to return. She would go from being an impoverished gentlewoman to a nobleman's paramour whose sole purpose would be to fulfill a rake's desires.

Quite obviously it would be the most demanding position she had ever held. And the most enjoyable. Her body flushed with feverish longing at the thought of lying with him. She'd be deceiving herself if she denied that deep in her heart she wished to accept his offer.

She had simply never thought of herself as a woman who could play the role of seductress.

By the next morning all she had really decided was that she had to come to a decision soon.

Perhaps later in the day.

The entire household had started off on the wrong foot. Everyone overslept, and no one was in a good mood over breakfast tea because there was no money to pay the coal man. The downstairs rooms were freezing, and Heston claimed that someone had broken into the house and stolen a carving knife. He knew because he'd just had it sharpened the other day. Then Mrs. Barnes came thundering into the parlor from the kitchen like a war horse because creditors had snatched a copper pot right out of her hands.

"Bloody 'ell," Freddie said, running into the room with his jacket pulled on over his nightshirt. "Now we don't even 'ave the proverbial pot to piss—"

Eloise held up her hand. "Enough. Hide whatever valuables are left. Especially the rest of the silver carving knives."

"They're all gone now," Mrs. Barnes said with a wail of misery. "I have nothing to chop vegetables for soup."

Eloise turned pale. "I thought Heston said only one was missing."

"That's right." Mrs. Barnes folded her beefy arms over her stomach. "I threw them at the bill collectors for taking my pot."

Anarchy, Eloise thought. The household had gone to hell in a handbasket. "Freddie, put some clothes on, please. The constable will probably come to ask why the housekeeper, like a country fair performer, is throwing knives at people. Not that it really matters, I suppose. We won't be living here much longer."

"Where will we be living, miss?" Heston inquired, his

back creaking as he spilled the last of the broken coal onto the hearth and halfway onto the carpet.

She hesitated, awash in sympathy for the whole sorrowful lot of them. No one in his right mind would hire a butler who looked liable to drop dead at a dinner party. Or a housekeeper who had a secret calling as a performer in Astley's Royal Circus and kept a brandy bottle in the pocket of her apron.

None of them had pensions, or relatives willing to provide shelter until they got back on their feet.

"Not to worry," Mrs. Barnes said with a hopeful look at Eloise. "Your fancy gentleman will find you a nice house in Piccadilly, I reckon."

"My fancy gentleman, indeed."

Lord, they were all looking at her like a herd of starving deer during a famine, Eloise thought in annoyance.

"If she decides to take him on, that is," Freddie said under his voice.

"You could all come and work for me." Thalia appeared in the doorway, her cheeks as white and puffy as balls of pastry dough. Clearly she had overheard the conversation.

Eloise turned around. It gave her chills, the thought of living at Thalia's beck and call for the rest of her days. "That's most kind of you, but I'm sure Sir Thomas already has a staff of his own."

"I have an uncle who owns a bar in Blackfriars, come to think of it," Mrs. Barnes said.

Heston straightened his back. "I might open a tavern myself one of these days."

"Better make sure it's next to a graveyard," Freddie muttered. "People'll perish of thirst waitin' for you to serve 'em."

Thalia tapped her slippered toe on the floor. "Has everyone forgotten that *I'm* the one supposed to be served? I've been waiting an eternity for my breakfast tray. And you, Eloise, you have to do something about your hair for Lord Mitford's anniversary ball."

"What ball?" Eloise asked in consternation.

Thalia subjected her to a long-suffering stare. "The one I told you about last month. Lady Heaton and her brother are escorting us. Aren't you the one who insisted I should go?"

"And so you should," Eloise retorted. "But I don't have a decent dress to wear." Besides, the last thing she wanted to do was sit against the wall listening to spinsters discuss their bunions and boils.

"Borrow one of mine," Thalia said. "The crimson ball gown covered in silk poppies absolutely swims on me. You should be able to fit into it if we let out all the seams."

"Lady Heaton will be there to chaperone you," Eloise said, frowning. "This will be a good opportunity for you to grow close to her before the wedding. I should only be in the way."

Thalia planted her hands on her hips. "But you're paid to be my companion."

"We haven't been paid in a month," Freddie said, ignoring the warning look Eloise gave him.

"You haven't?" Thalia's eyes grew red and watery. Her nose quivered. "I didn't realize. I'm certain that Lady Heaton could be persuaded to pay your wages."

Eloise felt her annoyance melt away. What a gratifying surprise to see the spoiled girl showing signs of becoming a thoughtful young woman. "That's very kind of you. I wouldn't ask for myself, of course, but for the others—"

"Good. Then it's settled," Thalia said, rubbing the tip of her nose. "You can ask Lady Heaton yourself at the ball. I don't want to spend my whole evening talking to her, anyway. She bores me stupid."

Eloise looked at Freddie as Thalia flounced back upstairs to await her breakfast. "I'm not quite sure how that happened."

"My God, miss." He shook his head. "You're too soft, that's how. Still, an evening out won't do you any harm. No pleasure sitting about on that old sofa every night."

Her eyes strayed to the aforementioned old sofa. An illicit image flashed through her mind before she could stop it. Drake's shadowed face between her legs. Her body straining against him, his dark blue eyes drugged with desire. Oh, there was pleasure for her on that sofa, all right.

A door banged open upstairs. Thalia's shrill whine trembled through the house. "El-oh-*eeeze*! I thought you were going to help me go through my gowns. Will you *please* come upstairs this instant? I need you."

"Cor," Freddie muttered, "sometimes I'd like to take the flat of my hand to 'er scrawny backside and—"

"Really, Freddie," Eloise said. "One does not speak of one's employer that way—"

"Are you coming or not?" Thalia shouted.

"—even if one thinks it," she muttered, stomping with clenched jaw up the steep stairs to Thalia's bedroom.

She wondered whether this really was what the future held for her. Was she destined to fulfill a calling to refine the uncouth young Thalias of the world? Would she devote her life to dignity and duty? Or would she submit to the lure of the wicked and become Drake Boscastle's lover? Would pearls and a pampered life take precedence over her principles? She paused at the top of the stairs.

"Help me, Eloise," Thalia shouted from the bedroom door, and a pair of shoes went flying into the air. "Everything I own is so horribly outmoded. And you, well, all I can say is that if you're going to be a fashionable impure, you shall have to consider your appearance."

Several exhausting hours later Thalia had decided on what to wear to Lord Mitford's ball. A silver-white gown and tissue overskirt whose clinging lines embued her with the elegant silhouette of a Grecian sylph. Her moon-blond hair took another two hours to arrange until each scented ringlet hung just so on her slender shoulders, rather, Eloise thought happily, like a cluster of spring lilies in half-bloom.

None of Thalia's inexpensive but attractive gowns fit Eloise properly. In contrast to Thalia's sleek, long-waisted figure, Eloise possessed a body that was mostly bosom and bottom. After squeezing in and out of a selection of dresses, she was breathlessly reduced to choosing the stiff red brocade ball gown emblazed with huge poppies. She felt as if she were wrapped in the parlor carpet.

"It belonged to my great-grandmother," Thalia said nostalgically. "Try not to spill anything on it. She was wearing that gown when she drew her last breath, and it has special meaning to me."

"If I sit down tonight," Eloise said, "I think I may be mistaken for an armchair."

Thalia threw her arms around her in an impulsive hug. "I am going to miss you, Eloise. In fact, I will beg Thomas unceasingly to send for you once we're settled, unless you become Lord Drake's mistress. Have you decided?"

She disentangled herself from Thalia's arms in alarm. "You don't think he'll be there, do you?" She moved stiffly to the mirror in the ball gown of Thalia's deceased great-grandmama. "If he sees me in this dress, he'll probably retract his offer."

Thalia raised her brow. "If he sees you in that dress and still desires you, you will have to know that he deserves your love, and there really won't be any decision to make."

Chapter Seventeen

❧ ❧

The ball had gone fairly well. Thalia had been on her best behavior, attentive to her future mother-in-law. Eloise had privately fended off four inappropriate advances, scolded a footman for snidely asking her if she was Queen Elizabeth's ghost, and sneaked her third glass of champagne between sets. The champagne soothed her jangled nerves and lifted her into a floatingly pleasant if detached frame of mind.

How many days left until her client was married? She'd lost count. Blame it on a Boscastle. Ever since meeting Drake she had lost track of time. Was he here tonight? she wondered. She wanted to see him, but not like this. She'd scare the daylights out of him looking like . . . like the Virgin Queen's ghost.

She scanned the ballroom for a sign of his dark, broad-shouldered form. She was standing against the wall with Lady Heaton's relatives, attempting to fade into the background unnoticed. Perhaps people would think she was a Flemish wall tapestry.

Suddenly there was a buzz of excitement amidst the older matrons seated around her. Lady Heaton surged to her feet and gasped, her blue-veined hand over her heart. "He's here. Oh, my heavens, he's here. The darling boy did not alert me of his return."

Eloise turned in mild curiosity to examine the slightly plump young man plodding awkwardly across the floor toward them. By no stretch of the imagination did this lumbering barrel-chested figure cause a similar consternation in her heart. Yet he did seem vaguely familiar—

"It's Thomas," one of Lady Heaton's maiden sisters said, clapping her hands in glee. "Oh, where is Thalia? She'll be beside herself at this happy surprise."

Lady Heaton glanced in agitation at Eloise. "Would you please find her, Miss Goodwin? I vow she was on the dance floor with my brother only a few moments ago."

Eloise could have sworn the same thing herself. In fact, Thalia had not made a single misstep the entire evening. She'd danced with only one or two of the most decent, if boring, young gentlemen. And now, in the middle of a country reel with her betrothed's uncle, she appeared to have vanished into the ethers.

There was no reason to panic. She had probably ventured off for a lemonade, to chat with a friend, to preen. There was no reason to believe that history had repeated itself.

"Where could she have gone?" Lady Heaton wondered aloud, watching as her beloved son stopped to greet a group of old acquaintances who had recognized him.

There was no reason to panic.

"I think she may have gone out onto the terrace for lemonade with Lady Woodbridge," Eloise said, squeezing her cumbersome skirts between the row of chairs. "I'll find her."

"I didn't see Lady Woodbridge," Lady Heaton's sister said in an aggrieved voice. "You would have thought she'd bother to ask after my health."

Eloise broke into a run the instant she left the ballroom, no easy feat in the heavy brocade that dragged her down like a coat of armor. No wonder Thalia's great-grandmother had taken her last breath in this dress. It was a contraption of torture.

She hastened down a side hallway on instinct and walked straight into the snide-faced footman who'd insulted her earlier. "Well, well, if it isn't Queen Lizzie's ghost a-haunting again," he said derisively.

Eloise grabbed him by the lapels of his livery coat. "Help me find Miss Thalia Thornton or I'm going to tell on you."

"For what?"

"For finishing off the champagne left in the glasses you've been collecting."

He pulled his coat free. "How do you know?"

"Because you're a footman, that's how, and I saw you sneaking enough drinks to fill a fountain."

"She was going off into the garden a minute or so ago," he said reluctantly.

"Alone?"

"I don't give out that sort of information," he said, then narrowed his eyes. "Not unless you're willing to pay for it—"

"Never mind," she muttered, sweeping around him.

"Happy haunting to you," he called after her with a rude snicker.

Eloise stopped in her tracks to glare haughtily over her shoulder. "If I were Queen Elizabeth, I'd have your bloody head on a platter, you insolent popinjay."

* * *

Drake lounged back against the massive column, staring distractedly down the shadowy corridor. There was some sort of commotion around the corner, but he was too intent on his private conversation to pay much attention. He'd only come to the ball tonight because his sister Emma had asked him to escort her and none of his brothers were available for the duty.

He would have preferred to spend another evening with Eloise and press his advantage. After last night, he knew he was close to persuading her, but he would rather that she think the decision to submit was hers. It was, he thought, only a matter of time.

"There is little to report from Elba," the gray-haired man who stood before him said. "Napoleon receives his visitors. The only oddity of note is that he has requested buttons."

He started, aware that his thoughts had been wandering. And that the information imparted to him by the other man, Sir Jeremy Hutchinson, a member of the War Office, at least deserved his attention.

"Buttons? Did you just say—" He broke off abruptly, his gaze riveted on the familiar figure that had just rounded an oversized Grecian urn and was barreling toward them. "Hold on," he murmured, "we're not alone."

Sir Jeremy guffawed in amusement. "My God, I'd no idea this was a masquerade ball. What a hideous dress."

Drake started to laugh. In fact, he was laughing so hard by the time Eloise reached them that Sir Jeremy took a step away from him in alarm. "I take it you know this woman?" he asked in curiosity.

Drake wiped the edge of his eye. "I confess that I do."

Sir Jeremy coughed. "I'll be at the club tomorrow for an hour or so. Drop by if you want to hear some other opinions. It appears that your mind is occupied at the moment."

Drake nodded absently, his shoulder braced against the column. He wondered when Eloise would notice him, and what on earth she was stalking in that unattractive costume. She looked determined and displeased, her gaze cutting across the room first to the empty alcove, then to the unoccupied tapestried bench, and . . . ah, at last. To him.

She came to a halt, her soft hazel eyes widening in astonishment. "You!"

"*You,*" he murmured, anchoring his finger in her old-fashioned boned bodice and drawing her behind the column.

He gave her no chance to resist. Before she could say another word he silenced her with an openmouthed kiss that sent blood surging to his groin in heated anticipation. "I suppose it's too much to hope that you were looking for me?" he murmured, shifting his body to overshadow hers.

"Actually—"

His hand wandered in a possessive caress down her back as his mouth captured hers again. With no effort at all he had trapped her between the hard porphyry column and his body. She couldn't move if she wanted to, and to his approval, she didn't even try.

"I didn't expect to see you again this soon, Eloise." His mouth teased the curve of her jaw as he shifted to cover her completely from view. She feigned to escape, then apparently changed her mind and smiled up at him, her body softening against his.

"Someone," she whispered, pressing her palms to his chest, "ought to teach you to behave yourself. It isn't polite to waylay young women."

He smothered a laugh. "Somebody ought to buy you some nice clothes. That dress—"

She pulled her hands to her sides. "Do I really look that hideous?"

"You don't." He bent his head to her neck, blowing gently across the creamy skin of her throat. "The dress does, though. Let's get rid of it."

"Here?" she asked in alarm.

He glanced up, his eyes dark with temptation. "Do we dare?"

"No."

She shivered and leaned her shoulders back against the column. He stared at her with a pleased smile. "I notice you haven't taken off the pearls. Is the clasp still stuck?"

She smiled evasively. "I don't know. I didn't try it again."

His eyes burned with the elemental instinct of a predator who scented victory was at hand. "And I thought this would be another boring party. Be ready for me in the morning."

"I can't," she whispered awkwardly. "I have another appointment."

He drew back, his brow lifting. "Then break it."

"I can't. I made it before I even met you."

"With whom?" he asked softly.

She looked distinctly uncomfortable. "Who is it, Eloise?" he asked in a low voice.

She cleared her throat. "You know. Your sister. We discussed this."

"Of course, Emma. Again." This was rich. His brothers would roar in laughter to learn he was in competition with his sister for a woman's devotion.

"Yes." She sounded utterly serious. "I have an interview for a position at her academy."

He broke into a grin. "Do you want me to give you a personal reference? I can vouch for how very delicious you—"

"Don't you dare," she said, her breasts quivering in her horrible dress.

"Eloise," he said, more relieved than he could possibly show, "didn't I tell you that you don't ever have to work again? No more old ladies prodding you with their canes. No spoiled young misses to rescue from rakes—"

"Oh, dear God." She groaned and glanced over his shoulder.

He smiled at her in puzzlement. "I am almost afraid to ask you what's wrong."

"Thalia. Rakes. I'm supposed to be looking for her at this very moment. Her betrothed arrived home today from Amsterdam and came here tonight without telling anyone, and she disappeared from the dance floor."

"How many days until the wedding?" he asked wryly.

"I lost count."

"Why the hell doesn't he go looking for her?" he demanded.

"We're talking about Thalia, Drake. And she's disappeared. Do you understand why I don't want him to find her until I do?"

"You can't keep her out of trouble forever."

"Only until the wedding. After that she is her husband's problem."

She gave him a distracted kiss on the cheek. He exhaled slowly, drawing his hands away from her. It was killing him to let her go. He felt her move around him while he stood, a virtual captive of the hardest erection he'd ever experienced in his memory.

"Drake?" She hesitated, her hand touching his arm.

He hoped for a moment that she had changed her mind.

He turned and pulled her back against him, certain she could feel his rod pulsing through her ridiculous dress to her belly. "I need you," he warned her in such a fierce whisper that her eyes widened. "And if you don't leave right now, I'm going to carry you out of this house in front of everyone."

She swallowed, backing away from him. "I was only going to ask for one small favor."

He sighed. "Which is?"

"Please don't tell your sister how you feel about me."

He watched her hurry off, his heart beating a tattoo in his chest. He was dying to be her lover, and all she could think about was making a bad impression on Emma? Well, this was the punishment that his father had promised him all his childhood and which he probably deserved.

The horrifying truth was that he knew he had *never* felt like this. His physical desire for her had grown emotional roots that reached somewhere into the region of—his heart?

The realization sent a chill up his spine into his scalp. He straightened, shaking off the thought.

It couldn't be. He wasn't going to let it happen. He desired her, that was all.

He stood in the shadows of the column as she disappeared down the corridor, her skirts dragging in her wake. She was as different from his past lovers as chalk was from cheese. He didn't think it was even possible for him to fall in love. In fact, the more he contemplated it, the more he reassured himself that he had nothing to worry about.

He desired her, that was all.

Chapter Eighteen

꧁ ꧂

Several minutes later, Eloise discovered Thalia skulking outside in the garden behind a statue of Pan. Her white gown made her easy to spot. "What in the world are you doing out here?" she asked in vexation. "And don't you dare tell me you're meeting another man, tonight of all nights, or I shall shake you. Yes, I will."

Thalia dragged her around the fishpond. "I'm not meeting anybody," she whispered frantically. "I'm hiding. Stand in front of me so I'm not seen."

"Hiding from whom?" Eloise demanded in alarm. "Not from Sir Thomas? You do know he's here? If you've changed your mind about marrying him—"

"I know he's here," Thalia said, tears choking her voice. "But so is Percy, and he and his friends are completely potted and saying vile things about me to anyone who'll listen."

Eloise felt an unbridled surge of panic. The agony on Thalia's face was genuine. This was an ugly consequence of her escapade with Percy that neither she nor Thalia had foreseen. Percy could ruin Thalia with his vicious tongue. Eloise would be ruined, too. She and Thalia could well end up as beggar women in St. Giles unless she could stop Percy.

"Drake." This seemed like the kind of situation he would know how to handle. "He was here a minute ago. I have to find him."

Thalia started to cry. "How can you think of yourself at a time like this? You are the most selfish person sometimes, I swear."

Eloise shook her then. She couldn't help herself. Thalia looked so taken aback that she fell into an immediate and gratifying silence. "I meant that we should find Lord Drake to deal with Percy. He wanted to take care of him once before, as I recall. I should have encouraged him to do so."

"Where is he?" Thalia asked in a mollified voice.

"He's leaving. Or he has already left. I'm not certain. I shall have to hurry to stop him."

"No," Thalia cried. "Don't leave me here alone with Percy and his friends. I'll go after Boscastle."

Eloise nodded in reluctant agreement. Thalia was hardly in any state to return to the party. "All right. But go through the gardens, so that no one sees you, and hurry. I'll have to find a way to distract Percy. Where is the fiend, anyway?"

Thalia gazed past Eloise with a gasp. "He's just come out onto the terrace, and I think he saw me."

"Then find Lord Drake as quickly as you can."

Thalia put her hand to her mouth. "Don't let Percy ruin me. Not only will Thomas break off our engagement, but I'll end up a spinster like you, Eloise."

"No, you won't," Eloise said, giving her a shove onto the garden path. "No one is going to find out anything, if I have to—to do something dreadful."

Thalia stared at her in trepidation. "What do you mean?"

Eloise didn't answer. She had already turned around to confront the enemy, a lady's companion turned knight errant. She hadn't a clue what she was going to do to keep her promise to Thalia. It seemed doubtful she could reason with a drunken wastrel. However, she had to do something to prevent him from running into Sir Thomas.

Suddenly Percy was standing on the path before her. She retreated into the stone rim of the fishpond. He regarded her with lurid insolence. "Well, well, look at this," he drawled. "Where is your little lambkin? The last time I looked she was in my bed."

Eloise leaned away from him. He was inching steadily toward her, and she had nowhere to go. "I'm warning you," she said softly. "If you breathe one word of what happened, you will regret it."

He smirked at her. "Would you like to pay me off? Do you have something to buy my silence?"

"Don't be revolting."

His gaze raked her in crude appraisal. "That's the ugliest dress I've ever seen. Let's find out if what's under it is any better."

He reached down to raise her gown, and Eloise felt the last thread of her temper snap. "You are pure filth," she said as he stuck his hand under her skirt, "and there's nothing for filth like a good washing."

He was unsteady enough on his feet that it took little effort on her part to unbalance him. She knew she would regret it later, but this was one of those moments when the chance for revenge was simply too sweet to resist. With a slight push of her hand on his shoulder, he toppled headfirst into the fishpond.

She watched him sink in detached horror.

What had she done? Probably destroyed any chance of ever finding another position in London. At least as a companion. Perhaps she could work as a barmaid who served double-duty as a batman.

His head emerged from the water, his yellow hair plastered like yarn across his forehead. Eloise cringed at the curses that he spewed at her. Even worse he'd managed to hook his hand around her knee. "I'm going to wash out that dirty mouth of yours," she said in a determined voice.

"You bloody mad bi—"

She lifted her other leg, positioning her foot on his shoulder, and forced him back into the pond. He struggled and broke his head through the surface again, screaming, "Help! A madwoman is trying to kill me," and grabbing her leg again.

"It's not polite to yell in a lady's face," she said. "Let go of my leg, little man."

He spat a stream of water over her shoulder. "Let's see you make me."

He'd gotten up on his knees, and his grip on her grew stronger. She felt her balance giving and braced her feet firmly around the base of the pond. She leaned into him, a woman who had grown a spine by governing beastly boys. "Have you learned your lesson?"

He ripped off the lace hem of her drawers and tossed it defiantly in the air as his answer. Eloise gasped, dimly aware of footsteps on the flagstone path, of voices from the terrace above them. Her skirt was soaked. Her hair had come undone. And suddenly a strong pair of arms lifted her into the air and set her squarely onto the path.

Drake stared down at the torn lace on the ground, then looked up into her face. "Did he do that?"

She bit her lip. "Yes."

Percy's white, dripping face registered dread as he recognized who had come to her rescue. "God, she's a wild one, Boscastle," he said quickly. "You should have seen her attack me. Give me a hand up, won't you? But watch your back—"

Drake planted one leg on the stone and stretched toward Percy. Percy flashed Eloise a look of pure malice, and then his head went down. Several times.

Shaking with anger, she bent to wring out her skirt. When she straightened there were two other men at the pond. The first she recognized as Drake's handsome younger brother Lord Devon. The other man, a little older, was also remarkably attractive and well-built, with cropped dark hair and a compelling demeanor, although he did not physically resemble the two Boscastle brothers.

He gave her a sympathetic smile. She managed a wan nod in return.

"What is Percy doing in the pond, Drake?" Devon asked casually.

And just as casually Drake replied, "Bobbing for apples. Do you want to join in?"

Devon glanced at the man beside him. "It looks as if we're bobbing for apples, Dominic. Care to play?"

The man named Dominic stepped forward, rolling up his sleeves to reveal muscular forearms. "Perhaps you shouldn't watch," he advised Eloise gently. "Bobbing for apples can turn a little rough."

Drake wrenched Percy out of the water by his collar. "You don't look at all well, Chapman. I suggest a long rest in Wales to restore your health."

"Wales?" Percy sputtered. "But it's so bloody wild and I don't have any relatives—"

"All right," Drake said, his voice soft and lethal. "Scotland then."

"I prefer Italy myself," Dominic said, his voice deceptively pleasant.

Drake's broad shoulders blocked Eloise's view of the dunking. He studied her with a long worried look. "Go and wait in my carriage."

"I shouldn't." Lady Heaton might wonder where she'd gone, although chances were that Eloise would scarcely be missed in the excitement of Sir Thomas's surprise return.

Still, she couldn't reappear in the ballroom in this unkempt state. And it was clear that Drake didn't want her to watch what he was doing. Nor did she, actually. What *was* he going to do to Percy?

She retreated into the hedgerow. A few guests had spilled out onto the terrace. She considered hiding behind the statue of Pan until they returned to the ballroom. She could only hope that no one noticed her, and that Thalia would have the sense to ask her betrothed to take her home.

She turned and found herself unexpectedly standing face-to-face with a beautiful young woman in an elegant ecru-white satin evening dress. Her vivid blue eyes and glossy black hair bespoke Boscastle heritage. So did the wicked grin she gave Eloise.

"I don't believe we've met." She eyed the damp splotches on Eloise's dress with devilish amusement. "I'm Chloe, sister to the two reprobates at the fishpond, and wife to the third. I assume the fellow they're drowning did something to offend you."

It was impossible to resist her mischievous warmth. Eloise, however, was too self-conscious about her drenched appearance to muster much charm on her own behalf. Her torn drawers spoke for themselves.

She shivered as a breeze cut across the garden. Her skirt clung in cold folds around her legs. So did the tattered hem of lace that hung limply from her ankle. "Here," Chloe said in concern, and pulled her lightly spun woolen shawl off her shoulders. "Put this on. It doesn't match your dress, but then—"

"Nothing matches this dress," Eloise muttered. "But thank you. I am Eloise Goodwin, by the way, and I—" Well, she couldn't think of a way to explain exactly who she was in relationship to Chloe's brother. She wasn't certain she understood it herself, and heaven knew what his family would think of her becoming Drake's mistress.

"You're what?" Chloe prompted, her eyes straying from the sight of her husband shaking the man in the pond like a dead rat.

Eloise hesitated, quite distracted herself by the act of masculine aggression that was unfolding before the two women. Drake had pulled off his expensive evening coat, and his white muslin shirt was molded to the planes of his muscular shoulders and chest. His cravat dripped water onto his broadcloth pantaloons, and he stood with his legs braced apart in a dominant stance.

She felt a queer fluttering deep in her belly. Her protector. He was every inch a dangerous, virile male. A man who followed only his own dark moral code. She could only imagine the demands he would make as a lover, and if this was any example of the lengths he would go to defend her, then she didn't stand a chance. Her heart was his.

"I—I'm—"

Some preternatural sense of being watched penetrated her concentration. She glanced around without even thinking. Only now did she realize that the small audience gathered on the terrace had descended the steps to observe the proceedings at the pond in shocked silence.

She didn't know any of the guests watching, did she?

Three elegantly gowned ladies, and an older, quite distinguished-looking gentleman. The youngest woman, of a delicate build and red-gold hair, stepped forward slowly to regard Eloise.

No, no, no. Blood rushed to her face as she met the woman's startled look. Not her. She stood rooted to the spot, praying that she would not be recognized in this deplorable state.

Viscountess Lyons. Drake's dignified sister, the very last person in the world she would wish to witness her embarrassment. She could only imagine how it must look, the conclusions a lady would draw. Eloise dripping like a drowned rat. Drake, Devon, and Dominic drowning a rat in the pond.

"Emma!" Chloe cried enthusiastically, stepping in front of Eloise to greet her sister. "How lovely to see you." And in a lower voice she added, "I don't know if your companions are people of importance, but I strongly suggest you take a detour around the fishpond."

Eloise risked another look at Lady Lyons, her heart sinking. Well, there was no point in hoping that the viscountess had not recognized her. Or in trying to pretend that she had nothing personally to do with the incident at the fishpond.

She drew a breath. "Good evening, Lady Lyons. This is an unexpected pleasure."

"Unexpected?" Emma's blue eyes settled on her with disconcerting steadiness. "Yes. But I'm not certain that what has happened here is a pleasure."

Chloe sent Eloise a championing smile. "Well, not for the fellow in the pond, perhaps."

The viscountess, Emma, should have known that there were too many Boscastles at the party to avoid a scandal. Whenever more than two of them were gathered in one place, the devil came into active play. In this case, Drake and Devon had the added influence of their brother-in-law, Dominic, who was certainly not a man to be crossed.

The situation might not have been quite so alarming had Emma been alone. But the Earl of Heydon and his pompous old countess had insisted on a walk in the garden. If Emma had not been desperate to receive their offer of financial help for the academy, she would not have been nearly this distressed. She could only pray that her potential benefactors had poor eyesight and would not realize that her two wilding brothers and her brother-in-law were drowning a man in the fishpond.

Or that her sister, Chloe, was watching the exhibition with an unladylike satisfaction. Or that the bedraggled-looking person standing beside her was the young woman Emma had planned to employ as assistant headmistress of her budding academy.

An academy whose bud would likely be nipped in its infancy if Lady Heydon, who rarely visited London, realized just how scandalous the Boscastle family was.

"My goodness," said the gray-haired countess, peering over Emma's shoulder, "it would appear that there are four young men in the fishpond. What could they be doing?"

"Best not to ask, I expect," the earl replied, his eyes twinkling with the mirth of a misspent youth.

Emma moistened her lips. "And as I was explaining, I personally select each instructor after an extensive series of interviews and verified references. Our dancing master, for example, taught at the French court—"

"Good God!" the earl exclaimed in delight. "It looks as if they're bobbing for apples. What fun. I'd like to play, too."

The countess drew a breath through her compressed lips. "That's a man's head, Henry. Not an apple."

"A man's head," he said with a chortle. "Well, that looks to be even more fun."

Emma closed her eyes with a shudder at the sight of Percy's pale, gasping face, and her two brothers on either side of him like a pair of gargoyles. How had Eloise Goodwin become involved in this?

"A y-year?" Percy sputtered.

"Well, a year or certain death," Dominic said with a heartless grin.

"Death in a fishpond?" Devon said, shaking his head. "Think of the indignity."

Emma opened her eyes, muttering, "Yes, *please*. Someone should have thought of the indignity."

Then she looked directly at Eloise, who wore an expression of guilt on her face if ever Emma had seen one. "Miss Goodwin," she said in a disparaging undertone. "I did not expect to find you involved in something like this."

Eloise raised her chin in resignation. "I suppose that

you're finished with me now. I understand. You'd probably like to tell me never to darken your door again, but you're too polite. Well, I do not blame you."

Emma frowned. "That's a little dramatic, Miss Goodwin, and not entirely distant from my true feelings, except that I am more inclined to tell Drake to stop darkening doors. Or drowning men in fishponds." She narrowed her eyes in distaste. "That's Percy Chapman, isn't it?"

"Yes," Chloe answered, putting a protective hand on Eloise's forearm. "And I don't know the whole story, but I would guess he deserves to be drowned."

"Not at a ball in front of countless guests!" Emma said in despair. "Why, Miss Goodwin, why? How could you have allowed yourself to become drawn into this? And where on earth did you get that dress?"

Eloise exhaled, looking for all the world like a victim facing her executioner. "I was only doing my duty, Lady Lyons. And I can't explain the origins of this dress except to say that apparently it is ill-fated."

Chapter Nineteen

🌿 🌿

Eloise trudged up the steep stairs to her room. The house seemed unnaturally quiet; she was grateful not to encounter any of the servants, who would ask her how the evening had gone. She hadn't the heart to discuss it. In fact, she was glad to see that Thalia had not yet returned home. She would be with her fiancé and his family. Properly chaperoned. Protected.

Percy Chapman would remain in exile long enough for the wedding to take place. The bride and groom would leave London and live happily ever after on Sir Thomas's country estate. One hoped.

That part was up to Thalia and her husband, God bless his unsuspecting soul. Eloise had done her duty.

And sealed her fate into the bargain.

Clearly after the evening's misfortune at the fishpond, Lady Lyons would not offer her a position. Who in her right mind would? She would have felt more sorry for herself if Drake hadn't gone to such dramatic lengths to avenge her. Lord help her, she loved that wicked man. If she'd ever doubted it, she knew tonight what she felt for him when she saw how unhesitantly he came to her assistance. Of course she understood what he wanted in return.

She walked into her room and closed the door behind her. How could she possibly pretend this was only a sexual arrangement? How soon would it be before he broke her heart?

She pulled off the shawl that his vivacious sister had given her in the garden. Devon, Emma, Chloe, and even Gabriel—every Boscastle she had met was beautiful and compelling. It seemed to be bred into their bloodline. She wondered with a wistful sigh whether she would ever carry Drake's child. The thought filled her with ambivalence. She believed in marriage with all her practical heart, and to bring a child into the world without a proper home did not seem right. She'd always assumed that if she bore a child, she—

She had not left the wardrobe door open, had she? Open wardrobe doors only invited moths, and Eloise owned few enough sensible woolens as it was.

She unhooked her damp, horrible dress and walked across the room to the wardrobe with the bodice and sleeves hanging around her waist.

She pulled out a pretty sage-green night rail, one of her few indulgences, then closed the wardrobe door.

And there before her stood the stuff of nightmares, Ralph Hawkins, the man who had ruined her life, with a carving knife gleaming in his hand.

Drake was striding toward his carriage when his sister Emma caught up with him. He turned, staring down at her angry, delicate face. He reminded himself that he loved her dearly. In fact, he would defend her to the death, in a heartbeat, but the two of them together were as compatible as fire and ice. She disapproved of everything he did, and let him know it. He thought she was an infernal nuisance and tolerated her only because . . . well, because she was his sister.

He frowned, motioning his footman away. "I'm late for an appointment, Emma. The lecture will have to wait."

"An appointment? At this hour?"

"It's past your bedtime, isn't it? I'm surprised to see you out after dark. Aren't you afraid that breathing all this night air will corrupt you?"

"Get inside the carriage," she said in a clipped voice. "We've had enough of a public spectacle for one evening."

He sighed and followed her into the dark interior of his carriage. She sat opposite him, her blue eyes cool with condemnation. He stretched his long legs out across the seat and moodily resigned himself to the inevitable.

"You know, Emma, widowhood doesn't suit you at all. We need to get you married."

"Take your own advice," she retorted, rearranging her shawl over her arms. "And sit up properly when you talk to me."

He refused to obey, regarding her with a stubborn indolence. "What's got you in such a snit?"

"You."

His hard mouth quirked into a half smile. "I'd have thought the self-righteous Lady Lyons would approve of banishing a blackguard like Percy Chapman from Society."

"You were not dousing that idiot in the fishpond out of the goodness of your heart."

He pretended to look hurt. "Of course I wasn't. Lest I forget, I don't have a heart, as you and everyone else in the family are so fond of reminding me."

"Don't make yourself out to be a martyr. You play the role of disillusioned rake too well to take a different part."

"God forbid," he murmured. "Me, a martyr."

"Why her?" she demanded. "Of all the eligible young women in London who would be only too glad to play your games, why Eloise Goodwin?"

His smile slipped a notch. "Why her? Why not her?"

"She's a decent woman, Drake, and she's worked hard to establish her good reputation in a society that does not reward personal sacrifice. Her family turned her out of their home six years ago, and she's been alone ever since."

He faltered. This was a little more than Eloise had revealed to him. Turned out of her home? What could she possibly have done? She wasn't exactly what he'd call a rebellious personality. Or was she? "What happened between her and her family?" he asked guardedly.

"I didn't ask. Her references are authentic, she has an excellent record, and don't you dare change the subject. Why? Of all the women to choose from, why do you select her for seduction?"

He feigned a look of utter boredom and swung his legs off the seat. "Who said anything about seducing her?"

"Oh, you are a devil. I can imagine all too well what happened this evening. Percy made her an indecent proposal. And you, having already claimed her as your next mark, flew into one of your violent furies and decided to cool his ardor in the fishpond."

"Jesus," he said, his gaze heavily lidded, his expression unfathomable. "From martyr to villain in the blink of an eye."

"At this particular party of all places," she continued, lifting up her white-gloved hands in despair. "A fortnight ago Percy Chapman would not have looked twice at a woman like Eloise Goodwin. But once she began to associate with you, she was not seen as quite so virtuous."

He was quiet for several moments. "Well, you know what they say. By the time a woman is seen in my company, her reputation is already in ruins."

"Her reputation was spotless. I intended to offer her employment at the academy, which, by the way, will probably never exist now that my sponsors have observed the Boscastle family in action at the fish pond."

He sat up abruptly, biting off each word that he spoke. "Once again, you have absolutely no idea what you're talking about."

"Then enlighten me."

"I—" He sat back heavily on the seat. He really didn't know why he bothered. "First things first. Eloise was *not* defending herself against Percy. She was defending her client."

"Thalia Thornton." Emma made a face. "What an unbearable twit. She's lucky to have landed Sir Thomas. He seems a decent sort."

"Yes. However, Percy had been threatening to reveal some damaging secrets of a personal nature about Thalia at the party. Eloise was attempting to dissuade him when I intervened. She did not want Percy and Sir Thomas to meet."

A glimmer of grudging approval brightened her gaze. "That explains tonight's unfortunate incident. But it doesn't explain your involvement with Eloise."

"I'm not sure I care to explain it." He shook his head, murmuring with a wry smile, "Or that I understand it myself. I've asked her to be my mistress."

"And she accepted?" she asked quietly.

He turned away. He had no idea why he'd told her as much as he had unless it was to protect Eloise. "Aren't you going to be missed by now, Emma? I'm sure that at this very moment some guest is committing a social gaffe that you should remedy."

She muttered something under her breath that might have been an obscenity. Then again, Lady Perfect being her overbearing self, it could have been Bible scripture. All Drake knew was that the words *God, hell,* and *devil* were used along with his name in her mumbled epithet.

She hit him on the knee. "Has she agreed to be your mistress?"

He *tsked* at her. "Hitting is not acceptable behavior for a viscountess."

She hit him again, hard enough for him to take notice. "What about murder?"

"Stop." He caught her wrist in a gentle but unbreakable hold. "The virtue of every woman in London is not your concern."

"I'm talking about the virtue of Eloise Goodwin."

"Well, I'm not. Keep your nose out of my life for a change. My affairs are not your concern. Neither are hers."

They glared at each other, as opposite as two human beings could possibly be except in their loyalty to their line. He saw her disdain for him in her eyes, and he could not believe how it hurt him. Dammit, he shouldn't care what his meddlesome sister thought. She was the standoffish aberration in the family, not him. Everyone else rather enjoyed their sins.

"You're just like him, you know," she said softly. "You're more like our father than anyone in the family."

He smiled, refusing to show her how deeply her remark had penetrated. "I'm not sure whether that was supposed to be an insult or a compliment."

"I'm not, either." She pulled her wrist from his hand. "And now I shall return to the party to repair whatever damage has been done." She rose from the seat, glancing down at him in chagrin. "I only wish that you had chosen a different woman, Drake."

Eloise was too shocked to scream. She'd convinced herself that Ralph wouldn't return. How long had he been hiding in her room? She managed to stagger back, the blood in her veins frozen and immobilizing her reflexes. She barely had the presence of mind to pull her bodice over her chemise.

"Surprise, Ellie." He threw his knife down onto the bed, his eyes full of mockery. "Nice to see you again."

Her heart began to beat in sick fear. She swallowed over the tightness in her throat. "I can't say I return the sentiment."

"Been out having fun, have you?" he asked softly.

"I was doing my job," she said, backing woodenly into the bed. She'd dealt with aggressive young men in the course of her career. She knew most of them were all bluff and bravado. But this was Ralph; he'd come all the way to London to find her, and he'd been waiting in her room. No one had ever threatened her with a knife.

There was a danger in the air that warned her this was very different from anything she had faced before.

"You look tuckered, love. Not taking care of yourself, are you?"

He moved toward her. She reached behind her for the knife, lost her balance, and fell back onto the counterpane. Ralph bent over her, his eyes dark with cruel humor. "That's it, Ellie. Let's have a lie-down together."

"What do you want?" she whispered dryly, suddenly more disgusted with him than afraid. He smelled of gin and stale sweat, although his neck cloth was clean and meticulously folded. He'd always been a vain little bastard, she thought.

"I'm out of funds, and you owe me."

She leaned away from him in relief. Money. Oh, God, that was all he wanted. "I don't have money right now. I haven't been paid in a month. You'll have to come back later."

"You could give me something else." He stroked the side of her neck with his fingernail. Eloise cringed, remembering how different it had felt when Drake touched her, remembering how he had defended her tonight. She should have told him about Ralph, but shame had stopped her. Shame and the hope that she had left the past behind.

"What's this then?" Ralph asked, his finger lifting the pearl necklace that encircled her throat.

"What does it look like?" she whispered.

"I'm almost sorry I didn't marry you, Ellie," he mused, "except that you've gotten a bit too forward for my taste. I like my girls docile and dumb. I like—"

He went to stroke her cheek, then stopped, his hand

arrested in midair as he found himself staring down the barrel of one of Lord Thornton's flintlock pistols that Eloise kept underneath her bed. She had braced her elbows on her knee so that he couldn't see how awkwardly she was holding the weapon.

"I wish now I'd let Mildred and her cousins murder you when they wanted to."

His face darkened. "When I get my hands on that witch, she'll wish she had killed me. You were a sweet girl once, Ellie. You—"

"I'm not a sweet girl anymore," she interrupted him. "I was a companion once to an elderly baroness who loved hunting more than life itself. I'm perfectly capable of blowing off your ballocks. One at a time, if you prefer. Is that sweet enough for you?"

He smiled uneasily.

She leveled the pistol at his face. "I don't think you'll ever find Mildred, but if you do, I hope she finishes what she started."

He straightened, but Eloise wasn't about to trust him. He had hidden in her room and threatened her with a knife. She kept the pistol trained on him even as he reached the door. "You will leave through the garden, Ralph."

He snorted, bumping against the doorknob. "Why should I?"

"Because I'd rather kill you than let anyone know that I was associated with you."

"I don't know the way out," he muttered.

She allowed herself to breathe. He was still a sniveling coward. "I'll show you. And there are two other men asleep downstairs who will come if I scream."

She must have sounded convincing because he followed her from the room and tread cautiously down the stairs without another word.

At the garden gate he hesitated, reaching out awkwardly to embrace her. "Give us a kiss good-bye."

She pushed the pistol into his ribs. "Get away from me," she whispered in contempt. "And don't ever come back, or I'll send Lord Drake after you."

He drew back into the street, his eyes narrowing. "Lord who?"

"Nobody you're ever likely to meet in the low places you frequent." She shoved the gate shut. There was an unfamiliar carriage pulling around the corner. "I think that's him over there now," she whispered from behind the gate, her entire body shaking in relief. It wasn't Drake's carriage, but he didn't have to know that. "Get out of here before he sees you."

Grayson Boscastle, the Marquess of Sedgecroft, and his male entourage descended from the carriage onto the street as if they owned it. Flanking him were his two younger brothers, Lord Heath and Lord Devon. Close behind the impressive trio followed their brother-in-law, Dominic Breckland, Viscount Stratfield.

Grayson was the largest in physical size of the group, golden-haired and charismatic, comfortable in his position of command, his massive framed draped in a black woolen overcoat. His brother Heath was no less lethal for all his reserved strength and introspective nature. Devon was the youngest, playful, sensual, an untested element whose military prowess had proved that he could turn dangerous at the drop of a hat.

Dominic stood rear guard, his rough face watchful

and quietly approving. He fit quite well into this family and pitied anyone who challenged them tonight. Only a fool would attempt to disturb this unholy group of vital men banded together for the good of one of their own. Still, for all their audacity, not one of them had wanted to let Drake know that they were secretly investigating the cause of his recent suspicious behavior.

It was Devon who had called this emergency cabal to discuss Drake's preoccupation with a woman who had already involved him in a duel. Drake had never invested this degree of interest in any female before and kept his attachment a secret. Ergo, she was a source of family curiosity, and concern.

It was also Devon who spotted Eloise at the garden gate with a man who did not appear to be a servant in the house. He shook his head, passing his spyglass to Heath. "That doesn't look right, does it?"

Heath was quiet. He was the least likely of all the Boscastle brothers to leap to conclusions. "There is a definite air of the clandestine about it."

"She seemed so straightforward and sweet," Devon said with a frown. "I would never have suspected this of her."

"There's nothing sweet about sneaking a man in and out of your house late at night," Dominic observed dryly.

Heath turned to stare at him. "Spoken as one who did quite a bit of sneaking himself in and out of my sister's bedroom?"

Dominic's teeth shone in a grin. "At least I married her afterward."

Grayson grunted.

Heath shook his head in amusement and raised the spyglass back to the house, murmuring, "Now *that* doesn't look very encouraging at all."

"What is it?" Grayson demanded.

"The man is trying to embrace her," he answered after a pause.

Dominic frowned. "Perhaps it's her brother or a close cousin."

"And perhaps Miss Eloise Goodwin isn't what she seems," Grayson retorted. "I, for one, find it hard to believe that Drake has given up a practiced courtesan for a—a practical companion."

"It does raise suspicions," Dominic said. "However, she is quite an attractive woman. At least from what I could tell of her at the fishpond."

Grayson folded his arms across his chest in displeasure. "I vote that we find out more about her."

"So do I," Devon said.

Dominic raised his hand. "Do I have a vote?"

"Of course," Grayson said magnanimously.

"Then I cast an aye."

Heath followed the unidentified man's movements down the street through the spyglass. "Then we're agreed. We will investigate the young woman's background."

"Let me do it," Devon said quickly. "You all have wives to answer to, and I started this business."

Heath lowered the spyglass with a sigh. "I'm happy to help."

"So am I," Dominic said.

Grayson nodded. "As am I."

"No." Devon gave his eldest brother a confident smile. "Let Dominic and me do this. We'll learn more by subtlety than by committee. Besides, if we're found out by any press reporters, this affair will end up in the papers, and Drake will suspect we've been spying on him."

Heath laughed. "Which we have."

"Still, there's no need for him to know that," Grayson said with an arrogant grin. "At least not yet."

Chapter Twenty

꙳ ꙳

Eloise could not fall asleep after Ralph left. In fact, she was still awake three hours later when Lady Heaton and her son brought Thalia home. She heard the three of them laughing in the hall below and then Thalia coming quickly up the stairs. Finally she drifted off, her last thought not of Ralph, but a pleasant one, of Drake demanding that she be ready for him in the morning, although perhaps after everything that had happened tonight at the party, he would forget.

But if he remembered he would ask for her decision, and she was growing weaker by the hour. He had proven himself as her protector at the party. He had come to her defense without any hesitation, and now it was her turn to either accept or refuse his offer. He would protect her against Ralph, but it would take courage to explain that part of her life to him. She was feeling very cowardly at the moment.

A woman alone and unprotected was vulnerable without question. But once she gave herself to Drake, she would become vulnerable in other ways. No matter what he demanded of her in return for his protection, she would not be able to remain emotionally detached.

She fell asleep deciding that she would make demands

of him, too. For one thing, he'd be forbidden to visit any bordellos. And he couldn't simply seduce her on sofas when he felt like it.

She came awake with a jolt of shocked awareness less than an hour later. She hadn't heard the door open, but the warm masculine figure lying against her on the bed was no dream. Neither was her—her nakedness? Her eyes flew open.

Drake's heavy-lidded gaze met hers, flaming with unmasked sensuality. His right hand drifted down her back to her bare bottom. She stared up into his darkly shadowed face, her body both relaxed and alive at the same time. How long had the devil been lying here in her bed? And where in the name of heaven was her night rail?

She struggled for her voice, her heart beating heavily in her breast. "I thought you said you would come tomorrow."

"I couldn't wait." He dipped his head to kiss her softly on the lips. "Will you forgive me?"

How could she not forgive him? He was here, in her bed, and she should not have felt this wicked happiness. But now she was safe. "Someone might have heard you."

"Everyone's asleep," he said, stroking her bare hip with a languid caress. "I waited to make sure."

Her mouth trembled as he lowered his head to kiss her again; his tongue delved between her lips at the same instant he slid his hand between her legs and pushed two fingers inside her engorged folds. She gave a startled cry of surprise as her body adjusted to the warm penetration.

"It seemed like forever until morning," he whispered. She ached with anticipation. She wanted to forget everything that had happened earlier in the evening. The pleasure he offered was a perfect excuse. He was strong and—he thrust deeply again until she whimpered and gave herself up to pulsations of heat that broke over her in waves.

He closed his eyes in bliss and let her convulse against his hand, her fragrance intoxicating his hungry senses as he whispered, "I'm forgiven?"

He angled his head to kiss her. He had never felt this tenderness for a woman before. He refused to consider what it meant, how this affair might end. He knew her hesitation to trust him came from a reasonable fear that he would hurt her, abandon her, use her. Rakehells broke hearts every day.

Yet there was no guarantee that she would not do the same to him, as much as he hoped she would never change. He wanted her to stay honest and unsophisticated. And his alone.

"Drake." She whispered his name, her face pressed to his shoulder.

He smiled. She was so deliciously soft and open. "What?"

"I'm *very* glad you're here."

Something in her voice penetrated his haze of heated anticipation. He drew his head back to gaze down at her. "Are you?"

She kept her face hidden against his shoulder. "Tonight was horrible."

"Oh, that." She meant the incident at the party. She was probably wondering if she had taken a wild man as her lover. "It's over. I've talked to Emma. She thinks quite highly of you. In fact—"

"Just hold me."

He frowned. "Darling, I *am* holding you."

"Well, hold me tighter," she said in a muffled voice.

"You don't have to please anyone but yourself anymore, Eloise," he said indulgently. "Except perhaps for me. I'm going to take care of everything."

"Promise?"

He kissed the top of her head. "Of course."

"I need to explain a few things to you first," she whispered after a long pause.

He grinned inwardly, his body aroused and aching. Was there a woman alive who did not want to talk at the most inconvenient times? "Can it wait an hour or so? I'm a little preoccupied."

He turned her onto her back and studied her naked body like a victor who reveled in the spoils he had won. He couldn't seem to think clearly when he was with her. And yet when they were apart, he could think of nothing else but her.

I need this woman.

When he'd seen her standing at the fishpond tonight, the torn lace at her feet, he had been consumed by a rush of bloodlust and protectiveness more powerful than any emotion he had ever known.

"I wanted to murder Percy with my bare hands tonight," he mused quietly. "If Devon and Dominic had not been there—if you hadn't been watching—well, I don't think Percy would have left the party alive."

"If I hadn't known you before," she said softly, her eyes slowly opening to look at him, "I might have been afraid of you. You were very impressive."

His dark eyes glinted. "You aren't afraid of me though, are you?"

"No."

"You never have been. Not from the first night I met you."

"Why would anyone fear you?" she whispered.

"I'm not about to destroy your illusions," he said with a cynical smile.

"I don't have any illusions," she said softly.

He realized again that it had not been her innocence or inexperience that had captured him as much as her understanding of who he was. He'd never pretended to be a saint to anyone, but he knew he wasn't the world's worst sinner. Yes, he had the devil's temper and a tendency to days of dark moody despair. He wanted her to accept this from the start.

"You're awake now," he said. "I can no longer claim the advantage of sleep."

"I'm awake," she agreed.

He drew a breath. Anticipation and another more keenly edged emotion deepened his voice. Despite his promise to be patient, he had to have her answer now.

"And your decision is made?"

"You knew there was never any doubt."

The decision had been made. She would be his mistress. Perhaps she felt vulnerable and should have taken more time to consider his offer. Perhaps she would regret her answer. For years she had been afraid to trust her instincts. She had been cautious and guarded in all her affairs. She had observed life. She thought she had learned quite a lot about people. And she trusted him.

She loved him. She had lived long enough to understand the difference between physical attraction and love.

She lifted her hand to his white satin waistcoat, meeting the steel muscle shield of his chest. She wanted to touch him. Surely he expected her to. But she could not ask how to go about it.

For a moment she could not gauge his reaction. Then suddenly he pulled off his evening coat and cravat, unbuttoned his waistcoat and shirt with a knowing smile. Her gaze traveled down his chest to his flat belly as he slowly unfastened his pantaloons. His thick organ jutted out from a shadowed triangle of dense black curls, and powerful muscles striated his thighs.

She concentrated on calming her heartbeat, the wild pulsing of blood that pooled in her lower body. His gaze lifted back to hers.

"Be my woman," he said.

He finished undressing, breathing hard, the shadows of his broad shoulders falling over her like a warm caress. Her heart tightened as he lowered himself to the bed. The touch of his hard male body against hers was pure bliss. She felt her entire being soften in welcome, in invitation.

"I can't wait," he whispered roughly. "Do you mind?"

"Do what you want," she said, moving restlessly beneath him. "Do everything. Anything."

He pushed her legs wide open and braced himself above her. She lifted her hands to his shoulders, shivering as he rubbed his swollen cock against her belly, then teased the entrance of her sex with the knob of his shaft. She felt her body respond at the sensual torture. She heard him inhale sharply as she traced her fingers over the ridges of his back in tentative exploration. He pushed her thighs even further apart and grasped her bottom, pressing between her sex lips to her core.

She gasped, arched, her hands gripping his tightly

muscled hips. His eyes were half-closed, and she raised her shoulders off the bed in surprise as her body accepted him.

"That's it," he whispered. "Take me. Trust me."

He flexed his back and tightened his hold on her hips so that she was completely exposed, unable to move. His cock pressed deeper into her cleft. He rotated his hips and withdrew, than pressed deeper, muttering, "Try to relax a little. I know it hurts at first, but it won't last forever."

Forever.

The word echoed in his mind and in the beat of his heart until the moment when all thought receded. Then, his head thrown back in sexual resolve, he thrust and let his instincts take over. Her hips bucked; he forced her down, his hands gentle but firm. A haze of sexuality enshrouded his brain. He was lost in her, giving as much of himself to her as she had to him. But it felt like the most natural act in the world. How could it be? He'd known her for such a short time, but this was new to him.

Eloise stared up into his hard, sculpted face as her body adjusted to his size. Inscrutable emotions smoldered in his dark blue eyes. He was an intense, sexual man who made no apologies for what he was, and she had understood that from the start. It hadn't altered her course. She had given herself to him anyway, seeing more in him than perhaps even he realized.

But she was his now. She hadn't been able to fight what she felt for him. Nor could her body resist his eroticism. She reveled in the way he had mastered her. Their joining was more beautiful and wild than she could have imagined. The intimacy of passion was beyond anything she had expected. She had never guessed the physical act was both earthly and exhilarating.

It amazed her that she could take his thick organ inside her. His penetration had stretched her until she wondered if she would be torn, but now only a stinging heat lingered, and she did not wish to dwell on it. Daringly she traced her fingertips down his spine. He reacted to her touch by rolling his lean hips and thrusting upward.

Her breath caught at the uninhibited movement. He would shatter her. She moaned, although it was from pure arousal, not from fear. He sought her mouth and kissed her until she stilled. But his body did not stop its relentless drive, and she gripped his pumping hips to anchor herself. He surged deeper. His lovemaking was fierce, intense, and graceful. His beautiful face was a mask of unbridled male desire.

She wanted all of him. More. She raised her hips invitingly. He groaned against her mouth. She knew a moment of satisfaction that her untutored skill could elicit a powerful response.

She moved again, guided by instinct, the desire to please him. He shuddered, driving deeper until she was whimpering with the need that burned in her blood. She felt the muscles of his back tighten, and she guessed by the dark tension on his face that he was exercising great control.

His deep voice broke through her sensual reverie. "I could die inside you. I could die coming just like this."

His words inflamed her. He was open in his sensuality, and she accepted that. She bit her lip, thrashing her head as he surged into her, uninhibited and aggressively male.

He was like a battering ram that had penetrated into her deepest reaches, his virility more than she could resist.

There was nothing else. Nothing but the unrestrained union of their bodies, a mystical joining, and then release. She came apart beneath him, convulsed as he stared down at her in undisguised satisfaction. She gave in to the pleasure that streaked through her body. Surrendered as he gripped her bottom and pumped until the moment when she thought she would lose consciousness; then he took his own fierce pleasure.

His seed flooded her womb. She felt the breath sough out from his body in a long exhalation. The swelter of raw sensations in her own body slowly ebbed away into a receding tide of throbs and pulsations and the warm trickle of semen between her legs.

Her body did not belong to her anymore, and yet she felt only a strange exaltation. Her protector. Her lover. It wasn't the life she'd planned for herself. Who would have thought that Eloise Goodwin had it in her sensible heart to fall so irrevocably in love?

Had he known? Expected it? Was it something he would demand of a mistress? A mistress. A sense of sadness overshadowed the pleasant warmth that had begun to steal over her. Loving him felt right, but the role she had accepted did not. Yet it had been her choice.

He disentangled himself from her warm body and smiled down at her, feeling the beat of his heart slow to a steady echo. "Well, Miss Goodwin," he said as he kissed her lightly, "I'm very glad now that I didn't have to wait until morning." He rolled onto his side and gazed around the tiny room. "Although I don't fancy either of us spending another night here. Where would you like to live?"

She sat up on her elbows. "I haven't thought about it," she said quietly.

He glanced back at her appraisingly. "Think about it now. I want a place where we will meet in private, and—"

"I know what a mistress does," she whispered, her gaze traveling over his body.

He caught her around the waist and grinned. God, he felt good. "You certainly do, and I'm glad you're entering this affair with a practical perspective. I only hope you won't be sorry."

"So do I," she said earnestly.

He laughed at that, leaning down on his elbow to look at her. "What made you decide to say yes? Was it my heroic intervention at the party tonight? If drowning idiots in fishponds wins your favor, I could probably arrange to do it on a regular basis. London is full of them."

She laid her head against his shoulder, smiling reluctantly. "Fishponds? I hadn't noticed."

"No. Idiots."

"Oh, yes. I have noticed that. Every party has its share."

He threaded his long fingers into her thick brown hair. "You won't be going to any more parties alone, and I meant what I just said. I hope you won't be sorry."

"Are you trying to warn me not to fall in love with you?" she asked after a long, uncomfortable pause.

His hand drifted down her nape to her shoulder. "Hell, no. I'm too selfish to wish for that. Let yourself fall in love with me."

"It might be too late to stop," she said in a wry voice.

He smiled tenderly, and his grip tightened on her shoulders. She thought she loved him. He should be jaded enough by now not to let it matter. But oddly it did. He wanted sex, affection, and anything else she had to give. "Why did you decide to accept my offer?"

She gave a little sigh. "Starvation and the threat of living on the street might have played a small part."

"So I'm better than a bowl of broth and Cheapside?" he asked, frowning down at her in mock disappointment. "That's not exactly the highest compliment to pay a man who's been trying his damnedest to seduce you."

"And succeeded." He felt her wriggle upward onto the pillows as if she had just noticed something on the floor. He turned his head and realized she was staring at the hideous dress she'd worn at the party. It sat in a wrinkled heap with either a pair of scissors or a knife buried in its stiff folds.

He chuckled. "What happened to the dress?"

He felt a slight quiver go through her and reminded himself that a gentleman should never make fun of a lady's appearance, not even in jest. Lord, who would have thought she'd have that sort of reaction to a few ill-made remarks? "Can I tell you in the morning?" she whispered, tilting her head back to look at him.

He hesitated, and his amusement melted away. Were those tears in her beautiful eyes? "Oh, God, Eloise," he said hoarsely. "Don't cry. I'll buy you a thousand other dresses. I didn't mean anything by it. You know what a tease I am. But, yes, by all means, tell me about the dress in the morning if you wish. Or never mention it again."

He wasn't sure exactly what it was he'd said, but it must have been the right thing, because she smiled at him and fell back willingly across the bed as he moved over her. Perhaps she was merely emotional because it was their first night together, and she had just given her virginity to a man who probably didn't deserve such a gift. It didn't occur to him there was more to her reaction than he could guess. In fact, he never would have suspected that she was keeping a secret from him had his godblessed brothers not decided to interfere.

Chapter Twenty-one

❧ ❧

Lord Devon Boscastle and his brother-in-law Dominic had followed their prey into a low-class tavern nearby in Covent Gardens. A drizzling mist had brought out the ripe smell of stale beer, boiled fish, and offal rotting in the gutter.

Devon glanced around the badly lit establishment in disgust. He was rather afraid he would catch a deadly ailment merely by breathing the air. Dominic was scraping his boot heel across the filthy floor as if he'd stepped on something nasty. Or someone. A wasted soldier lay sprawled out under a table, snoring in oblivion.

Devon's sharp gaze penetrated the smoky gloom. A short, wiry figure in a shabby brown woolen overcoat sat alone in the corner, calling out to a barmaid, who pointedly ignored him.

"Ah," Devon murmured, "there's our mystery man now."

It took two rounds of beer to loosen the man's tongue. By the fourth, Ralph would have sold his mother's soul and danced naked on her grave.

"It's not the money, mind you," he said, wiping his nose on his coat sleeve, "it's the principle of the thing."

Devon's chiseled mouth slanted into a cynical smile. "Who needs principles?" he murmured, refilling Ralph's tankard to the brim.

Dominic grinned. "Especially when women are involved. So, you were engaged to this young Desdemona."

Ralph took a loud slurp from the tankard. "Desdee who? Her name was Ellie. Eloise Jenkins. And then she met up with Mildred. The pair of them humiliated my manhood. Made a mock of me, them two witches, and Mildred was the worst."

Devon arched a dark brow. "Mildred?"

"I don't think I understand," Dominic said, leaning back on his chair with an indolent smile. "You were engaged to Eloise *and* to this Mildred, at the same time, and *you* perceive yourself as the injured party?"

"Exactly," Ralph said, his face mottling in anger. "And if you don't think it was an injury to my male pride, then you've never been displayed bare-arsed on a dog-cart in front of an entire village."

"I can't say that I have had that experience," Devon murmured, avoiding Dominic's mordant gaze. "But what is it that you want from Eloise after all these years?"

Ralph spat on the floor. Dominic's upper lip curled in revulsion.

"I reckon I'm owed something for my loss."

If Ralph had not been so drunk, he might have perceived the dangerous glint in Devon's eye. "What is it exactly that you think you're owed?"

"I dunno," Ralph said, his gaze skittering to a table across the room where an argument had just erupted. "I'm almost sorry now I didn't marry Eloise except she's gotten a bit too bossy for my tastes. Now, Millie, on the other hand, always did have a she-devil's temper."

"The woman who masterminded the dog-cart abduction?" Dominic asked, his upper lip curling into another smile.

Ralph shuddered. "Don't laugh, my boy. I still have nightmares that I'll wake up one night and find Mildred Hammersmith standing over me with the scythe she stole from her father's barn."

Devon ground his teeth. The conversation had exhausted the little tolerance he had for fools. "But as for this other woman—"

"Eloise—"

The three men ducked under the table as a chair came flying across the room. By the time Devon and Dominic judged it safe to reemerge, most of the cheap tallow candles in the tavern had gone out. Waxy billows of smoke wafted through the clamor of grunts, curses, and meaty fists assaulting flesh.

Devon and Dominic shot to their feet. "I think it's time to leave, don't you?" Devon asked, shoving an unbalanced body out of his way.

Dominic pivoted and threw a punch at a man lurching toward him with a broken bottle. "Good idea. What about the rat?"

Devon glanced around. Not surprisingly, Ralph had disappeared out the door into the unlit street at the first threat of danger to himself. "I don't think he's worth following. He's told us all we need to know for now."

Drake had disappeared by the time Eloise awakened the next morning. She didn't move for several minutes except to stretch her arms luxuriously and subside back against the bed. She stared around the room. How much warmer and more intriguing his presence had made her drab chamber.

He'd left without a trace. Not a boot or a button to mark his visit. But her body bore the proof of his passionate lovemaking. She ached deep inside with a warm awareness that made her want to hide under the covers all day and savor the aftermath of his seduction. She didn't want to leave her bed. She wanted to linger in the memory of last night for as long as possible.

She had felt so blissfully safe with his arms enfolding her, protecting her. She sat up slowly, her gaze lowering to the dress on the floor. And then she remembered. She hadn't forgotten, actually, but she had managed to put Ralph's visit from her mind.

She suffered a faint stab of remorse that she hadn't told Drake about Ralph. She had not wanted to ruin the night, but she was certainly going to tell him. It would be better all around if he knew. Dishonesty was not in her nature.

Several minutes later she tumbled out of bed and walked gingerly to the mirror. There was a bruised tenderness between her thighs to remind her of what she and Drake had done. Still, she felt almost beautiful . . . until she remembered that she still had her position as companion to consider.

She dressed hurriedly and peeked into Thalia's room to check that all was well. Thalia lay snoring across the bed in her ball gown, one slipper dangling from the tip of her big toe.

Eloise smiled to herself and quietly closed the door.

Her client appeared safe and content with her situation in life. It seemed that the evening had turned out well for both of them even if it had started out badly. Of course there was another day to face.

The entire household was waiting at the bottom of the stairs for her descent. Heston, the butler, was pretending to examine the hallstand. Mrs. Barnes was standing in the middle of the hall pretending to remind the scullery maid to buy an onion for soup. Freddie was polishing the life out of the brass doorknob with his sleeve.

"Well, good morning," she said, pausing briefly before she went into the parlor to sort through the post. "It is good to see all of you so industrious this early in the day."

Bluebell, the scullery maid, gave her a gap-toothed grin. "Some of us were industrious half the night."

"And some of us should mind our own affairs," Mrs. Barnes said under her breath.

Eloise smiled, more embarrassed than offended, and headed for the parlor door. As she opened it, her enrapt audience broke into light applause. She half turned, her mouth open, then shook her head and made her escape. It was distressing to realize that she had so little privacy. But how had they known?

Did she have "passionate affair" written all over her face? "Fallen woman"? Did the dear idiots actually believe that Drake's seduction had been an act of self-sacrifice on her part? She wished she could have convinced herself that her actions had been entirely altruistic.

She sat down at the table. Mrs. Barnes came in a minute later with a steaming cup of tea. "Some bacon, love?" she asked solicitously. "A tasty bowl of porridge to warm your innards?"

Eloise gave her a guarded look. "My innards are quite warm, thank you."

"I'll bet they are after what you've been up to."

"Mrs. Barnes, really."

"How about a nice piece of toast? I imagine you've worked up quite an appetite."

Eloise sighed and reached for the newspaper on the table. "Is this all that came today, Mrs. Barnes? No word from Lord Thornton?"

"The post hasn't arrived yet. Major Dugdale brought that over last night while you were at the party. He said there was something in it you should see."

Eloise frowned as she unfolded the paper. "Heavens, not another scandal sheet. Does that man have nothing better to do with his time?" she muttered as, against her will, she began to read the paragraph that the major had so thoughtfully circled in ink.

Which member of a notorious London family has taken a courtesan as his mistress? This infamous Cyprian is not hidden in his Castle, but in a well-known pleasure house on Bruton Street. The Christian name of our wicked gentleman rhymes with rake . . .

Rake. Drake. Castle. Boscastle. Eloise swallowed over the bitter taste in her throat.

"Look at this, Mrs. Barnes," she said in a hollow voice. "It's really quite unpleasant."

"Too many leaves in the tea again?"

"The *paper*. I mean the paper."

Mrs. Barnes fished her spectacles from her pocket. "I do love a bit of gossip."

Eloise eased her chair back from the table and rose to her feet. "Well, I don't. At least not this sort."

"Oh, my," Mrs. Barnes murmured as she slowly read the article. "Perhaps it isn't as bad as it sounds." She glanced up at Eloise with a hopeful smile. "Perhaps it's not true at all. You've said yourself the broadsheets are full of lies."

"But it is true," Eloise said quietly.

"How do you know, miss?"

"Because I went to fetch him from the pleasure house on Bruton Street the night we first met," she said morosely.

"You?" Mrs. Barnes said in shock. "You went to a bordello? Goodness, I've got to have a sit-down in the fresh air to ponder this."

Eloise picked up the paper. She had a few things to ponder herself. True, she'd known what kind of life Drake had led before she had entered their affair. But to find out that he had been openly pursuing this—her nose wrinkled in distaste—this courtesan—and her, at the same time. It was a cut to the heart. Had she been a second choice?

Even worse, according to the paper, he had been in competition with several other men for the courtesan's favor. Was he still chasing her? "Maribella St. Ives, indeed," she muttered. "If that's even her real name. I won't put up with this for a moment."

Mrs. Barnes eyed her approvingly. "That's better, love. I didn't think you were the sort to take a personal insult lying down."

Eloise pursed her lips. "Poor choice of words, Mrs. Barnes."

"Just make him understand you won't tolerate his misbehavior from the start. We'll mince words later."

Drake had returned home early to shave and change his clothes. He'd hoped to sneak out of Eloise's room undetected and spare her unnecessary embarrassment, but Thornton's servants had been spying on him from strategically designed hiding places all over the house.

Well, no point in denying the obvious. He'd flipped Freddie several gold coins when the young man had tried to duck behind the door to avoid his notice.

"Let the lady rest a little longer, Freddie," he said, winking at the astonished footman.

"Thanks, my lord," Freddie replied, and darted forward to open the front door. The day had dawned overcast and damp, a typical London morning. "And may I just say how relieved I am that—"

Drake glanced back, arching his brow. "That what?"

Freddie cleared his throat. "That Miss Goodwin has a trusted friend in you."

A trusted friend. Drake felt an unexpected warmth at the description of his relationship with Eloise. Friends and lovers. He liked the sound of that. He liked the comfort it implied, the way that being with her seemed to fill the emptiness he'd tried so long to ignore. Sex and friendship. Could anything be better?

"I'm glad she has a protector," Freddie added, following Drake out the door. "She needs one, my lord."

Drake thought nothing of the remark until a few hours later. He planned to visit his older brother Heath to suggest they meet Sir Jeremy Hutchinson at the club instead of boxing at Jackson's.

And then the rest of the day would be dedicated to Eloise. He wasn't sure exactly what they would do. Perhaps nothing at all, or a ride in Hyde Park. He only knew that they would be together, and he did not feel he needed to impress her. She'd all but admitted that she'd fallen in love with him.

Heath arrived just as Drake finished dressing. Unlike Devon, his older brother rarely dropped in unannounced. Drake motioned his valet, Quincy, out of the bedchamber.

"I was about to visit you," he said, straightening his neck cloth. "How is Julia?"

"She's well, thank you."

Heath met Drake's gaze in the looking-glass, and he knew something was wrong. He pivoted slowly. "What is it?"

"I was nominated to be the one to tell you."

"God." Drake made a face and turned to the window. "Well, get on with it. Emma gave her lecture last night. It's your turn now. At least I can count on you to be concise."

Heath circled the desk that dominated one side of the room. "Have I ever lectured you?"

"No. Not that I can remember." Drake half turned, his voice dry. "But allow me to save you the trouble. Yes, it's true. I'm having an affair with a woman who works as a companion. No. She is not my ordinary type, as Emma so bluntly pointed out. I have ruined her and take full responsibility. Do you need to know more than that?"

Heath sat in the ladderback chair. "I don't *need* to know anything about your private affairs."

"Good." Drake shrugged in annoyance. "Then what is the point in this visit?"

"How much do you know about her?"

Drake was momentarily taken off guard. Of all his siblings, Heath was the closest to him in character, intensely private, brooding, inclined to probe beneath the surface. Both men were suspicious by nature. Yet while Heath tended to be reflective and scholarly, Drake was more a creature of mood and instinct.

"What do you mean?" he asked bluntly.

Heath hesitated. "How long have you known her?"

"Long enough."

"For a casual affair, perhaps. But this seems more serious. Or am I wrong?"

Drake felt a stirring of unease. He trusted Heath's instincts more than his own. "Damn you, don't play with me. What do you know about her?"

"Only that a man left her house late last night," Heath said directly.

"Jesus." Drake laughed in relief. "Marriage has dulled your mind. The man was me. I spent almost the entire night with her."

There was a fleeting silence. Heath averted his gaze. "Before you arrived, I mean."

Drake did not react, but his mind methodically reviewed every detail of the evening. Eloise had been in bed when he entered her room, asleep. There had been no visible signs of another man's presence. She'd been wearing a white linen night trail, which he had removed and . . .

Her ugly ball gown had sat on the floor. Nothing unusual there, considering how he'd made fun of her.

No wineglasses on the nightstand. No love letters lying about. Nothing suspicious at all except that she had seemed a little fragile and emotional, not unusual considering the irrevocable step they had taken.

He shook his head in denial. "Not that it's anyone's business, but I swear that she had never slept with a man until I took her."

"I'm not trying to pry—"

He shrugged. "Perhaps it was her neighbor. The old bugger is always bothering her."

"No, Drake."

"Then who?"

Heath looked down at the desk. "Devon and Dominic followed her visitor to a tavern in Covent Garden. He claimed that he had been engaged to Eloise before she came to London. He appears to be after money."

Drake felt a deep flush work up his neck into his face. "Where is he?"

"He disappeared when a brawl broke out. It seems he was not a pleasant sort."

"I see."

"Do you want my help?"

Drake shook his head, the words barely penetrating. "I can handle this myself."

"Do you care about her very much?"

"Did I say that I cared about her?"

"No," Heath said thoughtfully, "but you didn't say that you didn't care, either."

He swore under his breath. "Now you're starting to sound like Devon."

"Well, I wish Devon had been the one to tell you." Heath came to his feet. "I disliked this duty very much, by the way."

He shrugged. His face felt as if it were cast in stone. "Why? I barely know her."

"Well, I'm glad at least that you aren't upset by the information."

"Did you think I would be?" Drake asked with a cynical smile.

Chapter Twenty-two

❧ ❧

Drake sat in his carriage as his driver set off through the London streets. Upset by the information? Upset that his *trusted* friend and lover had been entertaining another man last night? A man she had been engaged to marry?

No, he wasn't upset. He was devastated, enraged, so consumed with black suspicions, that he had to struggle to think straight. He could not believe that Eloise would deceive him. He trusted his instincts. Hell's bells, he'd trusted her. He *knew* there had to be a logical explanation why a man had visited her last night. And claimed he had been engaged to Eloise.

For the life of him he could not imagine what it could be.

Certainly she should have mentioned the visit to her lover. Being a trustworthy female, she should have confided in her protector. Unless she intended to keep the visit a secret.

Perhaps she had been too embarrassed, or hadn't thought it important enough to mention her mysterious visitor to him. Hadn't Emma claimed that Eloise was estranged from her family? Perhaps Devon had gotten the man's story all wrong . . . except that meant that

Dominic had gotten it wrong, too, and what were the chances of them both misunderstanding?

Or perhaps, he thought darkly, leaning his head against the cushion, there was more to Eloise Goodwin than met the eye. Well, he should have known that. He wouldn't have been this attracted to a shallow female. But he never would have pegged her for a duplicitous female, and after last night—

Last night. A raw shudder went down his shoulders into his spine.

He'd never enjoyed lovemaking as much as he had last night. He rubbed his eyes, the memory making his heart accelerate. In fact, lovemaking had been a misnomer for his past sexual encounters. Love had not entered into any of his previous relationships. Pleasure, respect, companionship, yes. Well, he didn't love Eloise, either. He wouldn't let himself.

The carriage turned the corner and stopped. He did not move. Sir Thomas was escorting his mother and Thalia to a small serviceable carriage in front of the house. The little group was laughing gaily; he caught a glimpse of Eloise standing at the door to see them off before she disappeared back inside.

He thought she'd seen him. In fact, he was sure of it. She had glanced directly at his carriage before vanishing into the house. He sat forward, his suspicions rearoused. She hadn't smiled at him. Had not even given him a covert little wave or a lingering look that said, I see you. Wait until they're gone before you come in.

He threw open the carriage door, not waiting for his footman to do the honors. Thalia, glancing over her shoulder with a concerned look, had just noticed him. He ignored her and strode across the street to the house.

What did he know about Eloise, anyway? Aside from the fact that he desired her with an irrational passion that had muddled his brain. He knew more about Thalia Thornton than he did about Eloise. Emma had learned more about Eloise in an interview than he had.

All he really knew was that he was insanely jealous at the mere possibility that there might be another man in Eloise's life. She was a warm-hearted, appealing woman. Why had he assumed she had never loved anyone before him? Had she been keeping her past a secret from him? Or had he merely not bothered to ask?

Irrationally he decided that he wouldn't be facing this dilemma if his brothers had kept out of his life. He knocked loudly at the door as Lady Heaton's carriage trundled off down the crowded street. Good. He would have Eloise to himself, and he wasn't leaving this house again until all his questions were answered.

The door opened. Mrs. Barnes, the housekeeper, had answered his knock.

"She's in the parlor," she announced without fanfare, then lowered her voice to a stage whisper. "I hope you've brought a present. Bit of mood this morning, we are. I expect it was all the excitement last night. And, of course, a certain *other* woman."

He scowled. As far as bad moods went, Eloise hadn't seen anything yet. And what the hell was the housekeeper prattling about? Was his entire life subject to the scrutiny of everyone from his sister to the servants?

She was standing at the window when he entered the room, her back to him. He allowed himself a few seconds to study her before he approached her. True male that he was, he felt arousal flood his body as he remembered the pleasure of bedding her.

His. No one had touched her before last night. He didn't care what anyone said. He had been her first lover. He knew it. He had taken her maidenhead. His brothers were wrong.

Eloise turned from the window, her mouth compressed. She was holding a paper in her hand. Actually she was crushing the sheet in her fist. He studied her face in surprise. She didn't look guilty. She looked . . . furious. At him. What did that mean? He was the one with the right to be angry.

He took her by the arms and kissed her before she had a chance to say anything. His hand slid down her back to her arse. She was resisting and responding to him at the same time, but suddenly he didn't care. He needed to hold her.

For a moment he forgot his jealousy, his suspicions. He ran his hand possessively down her arm, back up to her breasts as he kissed her. He didn't know why he thought that kissing her would clear his mind, but it had the opposite effect. He broke the kiss without warning and set her away from him. She looked breathless and more than a little disconcerted. Well, so was he.

His gaze pierced her. He had come here to have the truth from her, no matter what it cost. "We made an agreement last night, Eloise," he said curtly, watching her for the least sign of evasion. "We—"

She stuck the crumpled paper at his chest. "And just how many 'agreements' do you have going at the same time?"

He glanced down distractedly. He hoped she wasn't going to show him another sketch of Heath's infamous cannon-sized cock. Lord help him. How was a man supposed to conduct a serious conversation with his brother's rod staring him in the eye? "Don't show me that rubbish again," he said angrily. "And don't change the subject."

She shook the paper harder. "The subject was our agreement, and according to *this*, you've already drawn up a contract—"

He wasn't listening to a word she said. He wanted to know one thing, and one thing only. The question gnawed at his brain like acid. Did she have another love interest?

He raised his voice to drown her out. "You have a few questions to answer yourself, Eloise. And kindly stop waving that damned paper in my face."

She took a step back from him, apparently disarmed by his aggressive tone of voice. He couldn't help himself. His jealous doubts were tearing him apart, and if the infuriating woman would just answer him—

"The truth," he said coldly, closing in on her.

"The truth." Her eyes glittered. Suddenly she didn't look at all intimidated. "The truth. Ah, well, wouldn't that be nice? I'm waiting. Of course it would have been considerate of you to tell me *before* last night. However, in the interest of fairness, and because hitherto I have been known as a reasonable woman, and because even a dog deserves his day in court—"

He leaned into her, his eyes as dark as midnight. "Are you calling me a dog?"

"If what this paper says is true, yes."

"I don't give a damn about the paper!" he shouted. "I want to know exactly about you and this other man."

Eloise waved the wrinkled paper again. "And I don't give a damn if you don't give a damn! I want to know about this courtesan, this Maribella person—" She broke off, her startled gaze connecting with his. "What other man?"

He had to admit her astonishment looked genuine. He lowered his voice, although the black beast was beating its wings with evil fury in his face. "Do you have a relationship with another man, Eloise?"

"Do I have a what?" Her eyes widened, as if she had just discovered the secret to an ancient mystery. "Oh, I see now what this is all about. You're trying to throw me off the scent by accusing me of what exactly you're doing."

He walked her into the windowsill. "Never mind what *I'm* doing. What were you doing last night?"

"Have you been drinking, Drake Boscastle? You were here last night."

He glanced up. The shadowy bulk of Mrs. Barnes darted across the doorway. He took two steps back and kicked the door shut. Mrs. Barnes emitted a surprised but muffled squeak.

Eloise had moved into the center of the room, eyeing him as if he were an uncaged lunatic. For an absurd moment he envisioned her picking up a chair and cracking a whip over his head. Perhaps that was what he needed. He felt as if his emotions were erupting all over the place.

"What is wrong with you?" she whispered cautiously, circling the table.

He closed in on her. "Was there or was there not a man here last night before I came? A man you sneaked out through the garden gate in the dark?"

She stared at him, her soft red lips parting in surprise. Deny it, he thought wildly. Don't tell me it's true. Lie to me. *Give me any excuse on earth. I'll believe anything.*

"How did you find out?" she asked after the longest moment of his life.

He blinked. That was the last reaction he'd anticipated. Not even a pitiful attempt at deception, nor anything resembling a reasonable explanation. The entire morning he'd rehearsed this moment and swore he would not overreact. He had persuaded himself that his brothers had jumped to the wrong conclusion. He had pictured Eloise laughing off their well-meaning but unfounded suspicions with one of her sensible explanations.

The initial pain of her response flared into an unholy anger. "Who?" he demanded, all semblance of gentility discarded. "Who is he? Are you planning to be his mistress, too?"

She turned white. "It isn't anything like that at all." She edged past him to press her ear to the door. A moment later she gave a sharp rap at the panel and said firmly, "I know you're eavesdropping, Mrs. Barnes. You, too, Freddie. Go away right now."

Drake had wrenched off his gloves and gray silk-lined morning coat. He'd flung himself across the sofa, his arms folded behind his head. But he couldn't sit still for a moment. So he stood. Then he couldn't stand without starting to pace. So he sat down again. It was a miracle that he managed to lower his voice to a low roar when he spoke to her again.

"Who?"

"A man I was engaged to over six years ago," she said with a frown.

He frowned back at her. What right did she have to frown at him, anyway? She was the one who had a man visiting her in secret. "You never mentioned him before."

Freddie's voice interrupted them from behind the door. "I hear shouting in there. Are you all right, miss?"

"I am fine," Eloise said in irritation.

He cleared his throat. "Mrs. Barnes wants to know if Lord Drake is all right."

"I'm bloody fine," Drake said through his clenched teeth. "Now go the hell away."

"Here there." Mrs. Barnes banged on the door. "I demand to know what's happening in that room."

"Mind your own business!" Drake and Eloise answered at the same time.

There was a gasp of outrage from behind the door.

Then Freddie, in a consoling voice, said, "There, there, Mrs. Don't cry."

Drake threw up his hands. "Is it possible to have a private conversation in this house?"

"This is hardly a conversation," she retorted. "Not with you bellowing and kicking doors. And the servants are understandably concerned about your behavior. They are probably afraid you'll turn violent."

"That is a distinct possibility if you don't answer my questions."

Her mouth dropped open.

His gaze bored into her. "Explain all. I'm listening. Were you going to take this man as a lover?"

She paced to the sideboard. "Absolutely not."

"Are you involved with him?"

She spun on her heel. "You're an intelligent man. You ought to be able to answer that insulting question yourself."

He was silent. He didn't feel intelligent. He felt like an

absolute, raving idiot who couldn't think straight for his jealousy. And she still hadn't answered him. "Who is he, dammit?"

She started. "My former fiancé. His name is Ralph Hawkins. And he is not now nor has he ever been my lover."

"Well, he was here last night," he said flatly.

"Not at my invitation. I've had nothing to do with him or my family since I left home." She took a breath. He waited again. "Do you want the truth? Fine. I was sent away from home in disgrace."

His mouth thinned. "Well, this is getting better. How many fiancés do you have hidden away, if you don't mind me asking?"

She narrowed her eyes. "Do you have to interrupt me every few seconds with a snide remark?"

"Sorry," he said unapologetically. "You've forgotten your past. I appear to have forgotten my manners."

Her cheeks turned pink. "And what if I did have a past I wanted to forget? Would you be able to forgive me?"

"How the hell do I know unless you tell me?" He closed his eyes. "Oh, God. Just tell me the truth. Do you love him?"

"I thought I did once." She shivered at the memory. She had been a rather plump, ungainly girl of seventeen who'd felt too unsure of herself to refuse Ralph's offer of marriage. With three other sons to raise, her parents had been openly relieved when she and Ralph became engaged. True, he liked his drink, he had a brash mouth and a roving eye, but he'd built himself a sturdy cottage and had ambition as an estate manager. As a young man he'd seemed to have good potential as a provider.

Her father had been openly doubtful that Eloise could do better for herself. She'd had little poise, even less self-confidence in those days. Everything she had learned had come from practical experience in the ensuing years.

Drake lifted his shoulders questioningly and speared her with a ruthless stare.

"Do you love him now?" he asked bluntly.

She recoiled as if the suggestion was an insult. "Of course not. The rotten little rat has been blackmailing me. I hate him."

His face darkened. His voice dropped an octave, the depth of it sending a chill down her back. "He's been *what*?"

She swallowed. He did not look anything like her wildly beautiful lover of last night. His blue eyes burned with a hunger that made her want to hide under the table. "He's been threatening to reveal our past relationship to ruin my name."

Drake rose from the sofa and slowly advanced on her. Eloise did not move. "What past?" he asked with a cold, unmerciful smile.

"I just told you," she whispered.

"A woman's name is not entirely ruined over a broken engagement," he said softly.

She swallowed again. "Well, there might be a little more to it than that."

He raised his brow in feigned surprise. "Yes, I gathered that. Would you care to enlighten me?"

"I did try last night," she said, frowning up at him. "You were too intent on other things to listen."

She sighed at the memory. What a complex, moody man she had become the mistress of. And what a possessive one. Still, even if it was the way of the world for a gentleman to have more than one lover at a time, Eloise was not about to accept such behavior. It hurt too much to think of him pursuing another woman as she was falling in love with him.

"Eloise." His voice commanded her attention. "Explain why this bastard is trying to blackmail you. And why your family excommunicated you in the first place."

She wished she did not have to tell him. It was too mortifying to put into words. "It was a lifetime ago, you understand."

"It's been a lifetime since I've been waiting for your explanation," he retorted.

She shook her head in resignation. "Ralph became involved with another woman soon after he asked me to marry him. I didn't know it, but he'd asked her to marry him, too. She found out about his duplicity and came to me. She thought we ought to pay him back for his betrayal. At the time it seemed like a good idea. I didn't really think about the consequences. I was too angry."

"All right." He shrugged. "I've had enough practical experience to understand that passion can override common sense. As jaded as I am, however, I am not certain I understand what all this means. Was your revenge sweet?"

Eloise glanced away. "We humiliated him in public."

"Ah. How precisely?"

She fidgeted with one of the silk bows on her sleeve.

"Eloise?"

"Yes?"

"Your revenge," he said. "How exactly was it enacted?"

"It's really not easy to talk about."

"It isn't exactly easy to wait to hear you talk about it,

cither." He nodded. "Go on. It can't be that horrible. The man is still alive. What could two young girls possibly have planned that is so painful to speak of?"

"We bound him to a dog-cart on a Sunday morning and left him on a bridge where everyone in the village must cross for church."

Drake shook his head. "And that's all?"

She pulled a loose thread from her sleeve. "Well, I seem to remember that we hung a placard around his neck that listed his sins."

He continued to stare at her until she looked up slowly at his face. "He wore a placard," he prompted her. "And?"

Her voice was barely audible. "And . . . I seem to remember that . . . he wasn't wearing anything else."

Silence.

She thought by the expression on his face that he wasn't sure he believed her. He gave no reaction that Eloise could discern expect perhaps for the faintest glint in his eyes. Unless he was thinking that his new mistress was a madwoman. Well, in a way she supposed it was better to have the past out in the open. As humiliating as her past had been.

"There's more," she said, seeing no reason not to tell it all.

"Ah." He allowed the shadow of a smirk to settle on his lips—the sinful lips that had seduced her only last night and promised to protect her from the ugly world.

Eloise sighed. How she wished that she'd let Mildred murder Ralph when she'd been of a mind to.

"What else, Eloise?" he asked her in a perfectly even voice.

"We set fire to his bed."

He blinked, clearly startled. "Was he in it?"

"Of course not," she said in horror. "I just told you that he was tied up on the bridge."

He studied her for the longest time. "Was there any particular reason why you burned his bed?"

She frowned. "Mildred wanted to burn down his cottage, but I was afraid we'd be arrested, and the fire could have spread to the village. We decided that by burning his bed, we would express our disapproval of his deceit. And not hurt anyone."

"How could you be unaware that he was engaged to both of you at the same time?"

"Mildred lived in a neighboring village. Our paths would never have crossed except that one of her cousins decided to follow Ralph home on a whim. When Mildred found he was already betrothed, she came to me immediately."

Drake had to hand it to her. This was a hell of a defense. "I always knew you couldn't be as proper as you pretended, Eloise, but I never dreamed you were capable of this sort of . . . I'm not even sure how to describe it."

"Well, now you know. Does it make a difference?"

"It certainly does make a difference." He shook his head and pulled her firmly into his arms. "I'm going to be a faithful lover, or else."

She wriggled out of his grasp. She hadn't forgotten that he had been pursuing another woman. "Which brings us back to the subject of the newspaper." She pushed it at him. "Who is Maribella St. Ives?"

He glanced disinterestedly at the article. "She means nothing to me. She never did."

"Oh, really?" She wanted to believe him, he sounded convincing, but then wasn't that a rogue's strength? "According to this report, you went to considerable expense to impress her."

"That's true," he said evenly. "And she might even have become my mistress except that on the night of my assignation with her, I met you."

I met you.

They stared at each other in heavy silence until he smiled ruefully. "Don't you remember? You danced with me, and I lured you out into the garden."

She turned her face away, her heart aching. "Of course I remember. I also remember where you went later in the evening."

"Where am I now, Eloise?" he asked gamely.

She glanced around with a sigh. "I can't compete with a woman like this Maribella St. Ives. I'm a companion, Drake, not at all sophisticated."

"Perhaps I'm too sophisticated," he said in a low voice.

She wavered. Having been forced to defend herself, she wasn't certain she should let him off the hook so easily. "The newspaper said she's very beautiful."

He shrugged. "She is. But she isn't you."

She wandered over to the window and lifted the curtains to look outside. "Had you really been trying for months to meet her?"

"Yes."

She sighed again. At least he wasn't a liar. "I see."

He came up behind her. "But I've waited my entire life to meet someone like you."

She turned slowly to look at him. It might have been a poignant moment had the front door not suddenly slammed and reverberated through the house. She glanced back outside the window, her eyes widening.

"Oh, no. Mrs. Barnes is leaving with her bag."

"Why?" He didn't look as if he particularly cared.

"Probably because we both told her to mind her own business," she said in distress. "I've never spoken sharply to her before. I shall have to stop her."

He stepped in front of her. "Why don't you let her go? She's only a servant, Eloise."

"Some people might say the same of me," she said indignantly.

And then, in one of those frequent but regrettable instances when a man says the first thing that enters his mind, he replied, "Yes, but I'm not sleeping with Mrs. Barnes, am I? I'm not about to go chasing a housekeeper, not even my own housekeeper, down the street just because I asked her to mind her own business."

Twenty minutes later Drake brought Mrs. Barnes back to the house. She seemed less impressed by his profuse apologies for offending her than she did by the victory drive back home in his elegant carriage. It was the highlight of her career as a housekeeper to have a nobleman seek her pardon.

"Right to the door," she boasted to all the neighboring servants who gathered curiously outside the house to witness her return. "As if I were a duchess, mind you. Lord Drake is nothing but a gentleman."

Freddie carried her bag from the carriage. "I thought you said you'd never forgive 'im for telling you to mind your own business."

She floated toward the front door. "And right he was to tell me, young Frederick. A housekeeper has no call interfering with her betters."

"Aren't they coming in?" Freddie asked when the carriage set off smartly down the street, spiriting Eloise and her protector away.

Mrs. Barnes turned to wave broadly at Lord Drake's coachman and two footmen. They gave her grave respectful nods in acknowledgment. "I reckon his lordship can come and go as he pleases, my boy. And I reckon if our Eloise gets herself set up in a nice house, we'll be only too happy to follow, won't we?"

Chapter Twenty-three

※ ※

"That was kind of you, Drake." Eloise watched from the carriage window as Mrs. Barnes walked proudly to the door. "She'll probably worship you for life for making her feel important."

"Think nothing of it," he said airily, although it certainly wasn't the plump Mrs. Barnes's worship he wanted. It was yet another first for him, running down the street after a housekeeper and begging her in front of a crowd of astonished onlookers to forgive him.

Which, fortunately for his future plans, she had.

The carriage began to ease into the stream of traffic. Eloise saw the knife-grinder, who came to the house frequently, look up and stare at her in surprised recognition. "Where are we going?" she asked Drake.

"To my house," he answered. "If we're going to continue our conversation, I think we should do so without people listening at doors."

She looked at him. It was broad daylight, she had just become his lover, and the boundaries between her former life and new identity had already begun to blur. She had realized last night that she could not turn back. But that didn't mean that her old values could be easily discarded. In time, perhaps.

She did not know.

"Eloise," he said gently as if he could read her thoughts. "It won't matter to me what anyone else thinks. Are you brave enough to be seen with me in public?"

"I don't know that *brave* is the word," she said under her breath.

"Come to my house," he coaxed with a beguiling smile. "We will talk without interruptions."

"Only talk?" she asked, arching her brow.

He grinned but did not bother to deny what she suspected. "I believe we had our first argument today. Making love after a quarrel is usually a mutually pleasant way to make amends."

She hesitated. "Does Maribella St. Ives know you have taken me as your mistress?"

"I don't know." His seductive smile sent a warm tingle down to her toes. "She'll find out soon enough, won't she?"

And, God willing, he thought, it would be later rather than sooner. He had written Maribella a letter explaining as gently as he could that it would be best not to pursue their association. He would have told her in person but she had refused to see him again. Perhaps she did know that another woman was involved in his decision. Well, if she didn't know, she probably suspected as much.

The carriage pulled into the private porte cochere of his three-story Georgian town house, the iron gates clanging shut behind them. He spent as little time at home as possible, and he knew that bringing Eloise here today meant more than he could admit even to himself. In fact, Devon had joked that Drake must be afraid that he would grow roots if he stayed in any one place for long.

He wondered suddenly if it were possible for him to change, or if all the dire prophecies his family had made about him were inevitable.

Eloise stepped down from the carriage and stood for a moment in hesitation before following him. It was going to take time for her to ignore the rules of society she had obeyed for most of her life. Still, her curiosity about Drake was stronger than her misgivings. She had always judged her former employers by their homes. What would she learn about her lover?

The entrance hall was unadorned but for the rococo ceiling and bronze wall sconces of ancient gods and goddesses who gazed at her as she walked beneath them. As he led her through the lower floor, she realized this was truly a man's abode, with a billiards room and dark oak appointed library that bore the pleasant fragrance of cigars and expensive brandy. But there were few personal effects to soothe the soul or reflect the owner's character.

His face unreadable, Drake led her up to his bedchamber wing on the second floor. Eloise slowed her pace, and felt his strong fingers close around hers. There was a loneliness to his house that made her want to fill it with warmth. Did she know him at all? she wondered.

"It's all right," he said, his eyes glinting as if her hesitation amused him.

She could hear the unsteady throb of her heart in her ears. Loving a man like Drake—well, agreeing to become his mistress gave her only a temporary sense of security at best. There was no clear-cut precedent for her to follow. Could she learn to be a competent mistress as easily as she had learned the rules of etiquette?

Was she wrong to follow her heart when he had made her no promises beyond their arrangement? An arrangement. How hollow it sounded.

"What are you thinking, Eloise?" he asked, his shoulder braced against the door.

"I usually . . . well, whenever I have accepted a new position in the past, I've asked my employer to state exactly what is expected of me."

He smiled. "A reasonable enough question. And my answer, of course"—he opened the door and drew her into his bedchamber—"is everything. I expect everything of you."

Her gaze went to the large mahogany bed draped in dark green silk. "Everything? You couldn't be a little more specific, could you?"

He lifted away her cloak with another dark smile that sent a delicious shiver through her. "What I demand of you is your loyalty, your honesty, your company. And, it goes without saying, this—"

She stood, barely breathing, as his large hands skillfully undid her dress and unlaced the back of her corset. Next, her short-sleeved chemise, dimity lace drawers, and stockings dropped to the carpet. Thank heavens the curtains were drawn; she was standing flagrantly nude in the middle of the floor while he calmly went about the business of removing his own coat, waistcoat, and pantaloons.

"What can I expect of you?" she asked, staring at his broad back and hard, lean buttocks. His entire body might have been forged of steel. "I mean, I have a right to know, too, don't I?"

"What can you expect?" he mused. "I've promised you protection, security, and pleasure. We can draw up a formal contract if you like."

"For how long? You must have plans to marry at some point in the future," she said in a subdued voice.

"I never plan anything," he said with an idle smile. "I enjoy a sense of surprise. Don't you?"

"It depends."

He walked unself-consciously to his bed and stretched out before her. Her gaze traveled over his hard torso in unwilling arousal. Who would have ever thought that a man's body could be beautiful? But a beautiful being he was, a sleek study of tight, well-toned muscle and lithe strength. Young, agile, he was at the peak of his prowess, a man who reveled in his sexual power. And obviously wanted to revel in hers.

"Turn around for me, Eloise."

She did, facing a long looking-glass that sat in the corner. His dark, mocking reflection stared back at her in unadulterated preoccupation.

"Now walk over to the window," he instructed her.

"For any particular reason?" she asked, swallowing at his wolfish stare.

"Yes. Pour me a drink from the decanter on the desk. And for yourself if you like. You'll have to bend over to open the cabinet door. Take your time."

She allowed herself to exhale. It was easy enough to obey such a simple request. She'd done so a thousand times, although not perhaps when she was stark naked and conscious of the steamy heat between her thighs. But oddly the familiar act gave her courage to overcome her nervousness.

"There's port or sauterne." She reached for a cut-crystal decanter. "Which do you prefer?"

"I don't give a damn," he murmured. "I only wanted to see your arse when you walk."

She put down the decanter, pivoting in indignation. The devil had the gall to laugh. "Are you always this misbehaved?" she asked.

"I apologize for teasing you," he said. "Now come here and let me redeem myself."

She walked slowly toward the bed. *"Redeem?"*

"Hard to believe, isn't it?"

"I suppose," she said, "that depends on one's idea of redemption."

"Will you redeem me, Eloise?" he asked guilelessly.

She stopped at the side of the bed and stole another glance at him. He looked entirely comfortable in his naked magnificence, a man at ease with his sexuality. She, on the other hand, felt nothing but awkward. But her discomfort didn't stop her from responding to his beautiful male body. His wide shoulders tapered into a hard-planned chest sprinkled with dark hair and a flat abdomen. Between his heavily muscled thighs his thick manhood rose; Eloise remembered with a pang of desire how she had felt when he had possessed her, stretched and impaled her to the hilt.

She forced her gaze back to his face. He laughed again, deep and low. "Look all you like. I'm looking my fill at you."

He was, too. His lips curled into a sultry smile as he stared. His dark gaze studied her full breasts until her nipples puckered into hard, aching points. She gave a soft helpless moan and prayed he hadn't heard it. But his eyes lifted swiftly to her face, hot with sexual promise.

He crossed his arms behind his head, his muscular torso a study in elegant power. "Lift one leg onto the bed, Eloise," he said, the husky tenor of his voice weakening her knees.

"Lift—" It was shameless of him to ask; she would be exposed and open to his view, but the burning lust in his blue eyes rendered her breathless and unwilling to refuse.

She raised her leg, arching her foot, and stared in suspense across the room to avoid his disarming gaze. She could feel the heat of his scrutiny lower to the nest of curls between her thighs. Sweet flames flooded her belly. Instead of embarrassing her, his shameless eroticism only made her want him more.

He sat forward with a deep growl of anticipation; she glanced back at him involuntarily. His supple body moved in a perfect synchrony of bone, muscle, and sinew. The headboard behind him was designed of dark mahogany, the emerald green curtains looked like a primeval forest setting for a wild animal. She wondered suddenly how many other women he might have seduced here. And what she would have to do to be the last.

"What are you thinking?" he asked, his brow quirking in amusement.

"That I don't like the thought of other women in your bed," she said bluntly.

"You don't see anyone else hiding under the covers, do you?" he teased.

"You know what I meant."

"I've always been faithful to my mistresses."

She snorted delicately.

He slid to the edge of the bed, his powerful thighs

splayed wide, the muscles tightly corded. "I'm a generous man, Eloise. You will not regret your decision to take me as your protector."

"Pearls don't mean anything," she said in vexation. "Neither do beautiful dresses."

"You need a new wardrobe," he murmured devilishly. "That carpet you were wearing last night—"

She drew her leg onto the floor. "I didn't sleep with you last night for a ball gown!"

"God, I hope not." He was clearly trying not to laugh again. "Come here," he ordered gently.

She moved back self-consciously to the side of the bed where he sat in his glorious nudity. "Are you sorry you slept with me?" he asked, his gaze lifting to her face.

She sighed, weakening at his gentle tone. "No. I'm sorry that you have slept with other women."

He grinned. His sultry gaze moved unashamedly over bare shoulders and breasts again. "Go down on your knees before me, Eloise," he ordered her in a seductive voice.

She drew a shaking breath. Oh, the wickedness of him. "I assume we are not going to say our prayers together."

"One of us will pray for release," he said, his eyes glittering. "Who shall it be?"

She knelt, a shiver of anticipation rippling over her. "If this is to be a battle of sorts, I do not think we are equal opponents."

He stared at her downcast head and the sweet rise of her rump. "You possess greater weapons than you realize."

Her head lifted. She knew that she'd liked the intimacies that he'd performed on her to give her pleasure. It seemed natural to reciprocate, and while she had never been familiar with a man before, she'd lived in a great many houses where sexual matters, especially among servants, were discussed in frank, if whispered, detail.

"I've always been good at my job," she murmured, smiling up at him. "I take pride in my position."

He did not smile back. "Is that all I am to you?" he asked quietly.

"No." Her heart beat fiercely. "Not in the least."

"Good. Then continue."

She frowned at his imperious tone, even if it had the disconcerting effect of arousing her. But perhaps he was right. She was not without some skill or defenses. Hesitantly she slid her hands up the insides of his hard, powerful thighs. Her fingers curled around the knobby head of his organ. It rose thick and flushed in response against her hands. He exhaled and flexed his hips.

His body told her he liked her touch. Would he like her to perform the act that he'd done to her? She rose higher onto her knees and slowly took the silken length of him into her mouth. She had heard maidservants discussing how this pleasure was given to a man, how it could tame the wildest of their masters.

"Sweet Jesus," he whispered, his voice raw with disbelief. There was something about her desire to please and the softness of her mouth that undid him. He called on all his control to keep himself from thrusting down her throat. The tip of her tongue circled the crest of his cock. He released a tortured groan, his head thrown back.

She drew away without warning. Her voice was low with uncertainly. "Did that hurt you? I know how men are sensitive about their—"

He smothered a groan as her mouth brushed his manhood again. Her unskilled seduction had him shaking all the way down to his ballocks. A few more seconds of her sweet mouth caressing him, and he'd spill his seed. Gritting his teeth against the temptation to let her continue, he lifted her gently into his arms and rolled her beneath him on the bed.

"How," he demanded raggedly, one large hand moving down the contours of her belly to part her thighs, "did you learn to do that?"

She gasped in pleasure as his fingers slipped deep inside her warm sheath. "Did I do something right?"

His blue eyes gazed down at her in approval, and she waited, her heart pounding. Tenderly he rubbed his thumb against the nubbin of flesh that crowned her swollen pink folds. She shivered against him, her nipples hardening with the pleasure of his touch.

"You made me feel like an overexcited schoolboy," he admitted with a grudging smile. "I all but spilled into your sweet mouth. Have you ever done that to a man before?"

"Never," she said, flushing at the mere suggestion. Nor could she ever imagine performing it on anyone but him. "But I've walked in on enough trysts in my career as a governess to gather a few things." Of course, putting what she'd heard about into practice was another matter.

He was silent for several moments, holding her gaze. "I'd say you were very good at gathering for a governess."

She turned her head. She could hardly concentrate on what he was saying when his wicked fingers teased her sex and sent blood rushing through her lower body. The moisture between her legs betrayed his effect on her. She felt restless to take him inside her, but he seemed to enjoy prolonging this part of their lovemaking, arousing her to the point where she writhed in frustration, a prisoner of his skill.

"You'll never need to seek pleasure outside my bed," he promised her in a ragged voice.

And silently she told him the same.

He drove his fingers deeper inside her, bending his head to capture one pointy nipple between his teeth. Pleasure pulsed in the pit of her belly and spread through her in ripples. She raised her hips and rode his hand. The ache inside her intensified, as he'd surely intended it would, and she thought of what he'd just promised her. As if she were the sort of woman who could love another man, or give both heart and body to anyone but him.

He thrust her thighs apart with his knee and withdrew his fingers from her cleft. She twisted her lower body, restless, in search of relief, rewarded by the feel of his engorged member brushing the drenched curls of her sex. She was dying to take every inch of him inside her.

"Look at me," he commanded.

She did, shivering at his darkly beautiful face.

"You're going to be very sore tomorrow," he warned her.

Her breath caught in her throat. "I don't care. Just don't stop."

She ran her hands down his muscular back and clenched his lean buttocks, bracing herself for his penetration. He had already brought her to the brink of release with his hand, but now he deliberately tormented her, rubbing his engorged organ between her pink folds until she could not control herself.

"Please," she whispered, her voice breaking on a sob.

"Yes," he murmured. "Cry for me."

He studied her with a shuttered gaze for several moments before he closed his eyes, his mind, and gave himself up to pure sexual pleasure. He teased the pouting lips of her cleft with his swollen cock until she shook uncontrollably and thrashed beneath him. She sobbed in need. He bent lower to kiss her, his mouth absorbing the soft cries he wrung from her.

"Oh, my God," she whispered. Her hands tightened on his hips. "I don't . . . I can't take much more."

"No?" he asked in gentle mockery, slowly entering her. He rotated his hips and smiled at her moan of frustration. "Is that better?"

He felt her pleasure rising and flexed his back in anticipation. Had he ever met a warmer, more sexual woman? Hot blood pulsed through his groin. He would come if he did not exercise every drop of his will. She'd already begun to move her body with a sensuality that challenged his skills. Sweat broke out on his shoulders as he drove deeper inside her. Her lush bottom bounced with his thrusts, and just when she'd learned to anticipate his rhythm, he positioned her legs over his shoulders and surged.

She broke apart beneath him. Her body convulsed, clenching his cock in dewy heat that drove him insane. She moaned and arched to hold him inside her, and the unconscious sensuality of her untutored instinct tore through the last remnants of his restraint. His orgasm was explosive, a sweet violence that reached his soul, satisfying and unsettling at once.

Not just a sexual act. Something more. What? He didn't need to know, did he? It was enough to simply breathe and slow the erratic racing of his heart. To hold her in his arms and lay in drugged contentment with this desirable woman, his woman. He drew the scent of her, of sex, deep into his lungs. Why was this so different from his past affairs? God, it frightened him to feel like this.

He glanced down. Her eyes were closed, her delicate foot captured under his, her mass of heavy hair barely covering one plump, delectable breast. She was so unlike any of his previous mistresses. She wasn't like any of the shallow debutantes, either, that he was expected to marry. Did she fall somewhere in between?

"Are you sore?" he whispered, stroking her hip bone with his thumb.

"Hmmm."

"I'm curious about something," he said as his hand strayed to the cleft of her bottom. "What attracts a woman like you to me?"

She gave a little shiver at his touch. "Silly," she murmured, stretching her spine. "Why would you ask?"

"Indulge me with an answer. Why were you attracted to me?"

She sighed, curling her hand around his shoulder. "You mean besides the fact that you're rich, titled, and devilishly handsome?"

He kissed her lightly on the lips. "Swept you off your feet, did I?"

He swallowed as she leaned her cheek against his arm. Her skin smelled faintly of soap, and her body was flushed a becoming pink from their lovemaking. There was a softness to Eloise that brought out his most protective instincts, but wasn't he more liable to hurt her in the end than anyone else? Except for this vile bastard in her past. Drake's eyes darkened with pleasure at the thought of confronting him.

"I don't know," she murmured. "I thought you were a rake the first time I met you, but I also saw a man who has goodness inside him that he refuses to admit."

He shook his head. "I've deceived you indeed if you believe that I am good."

"Not all that good," she said, laughing. "You're also arrogant, cynical, and accustomed to having your way."

"Is there any other way?" he teased her, tightening his arm around her waist.

Her hazel eyes warmed in rueful amusement. "You're everything a proper young woman should avoid."

"Do you view me as your ruination?"

"I knew what you were the night we met, and I still danced with you."

"You weren't afraid of me then," he mused. "Or perhaps you were distracted by duty. You know me better now. Do you resent what I have made you become? Are you afraid of me at all?"

It was a test of sorts, she thought in surprise, a challenge to the loyalty he demanded. He wanted to know if she could accept him as he was. Didn't he understand that she had already done so?

"I'm only afraid that you will grow bored of me," she replied, relieved to realize that her integrity was still intact at core despite her fallen status.

Her eyes searched his face. She hoped he could see that she had nothing left to hide. She had given all of herself to him this afternoon. But did that matter to a man who could easily have any woman he desired?

"What *I* am afraid of," he said, the honesty in his

deep voice too stark to discount, "is myself. Of what I could become. But maybe you'll be my redemption, although certain members of my family have already called me a lost cause."

"At least you have a family to care one way or the other," she said wistfully.

"Well, perhaps one day—"

He stopped himself before he could say what came unexpectedly to mind. Perhaps one day . . . she would have another family? A child? His child? How had the unthinkable become a possibility? He hadn't intended to make this a permanent relationship, had he? His philosophy had always been to let the future unfold as it would.

He tumbled her back against the pillows, bracketing her between his arms. "Are you hungry? Would you like cake and champagne in bed?

"Decadent man," she whispered. "I'd be too worried about what the servants thought to enjoy it."

"You'll have to get used to it."

He smiled down at her, then deftly turned her over onto her front. She twisted around, protesting, but his hand was already between her thighs, stroking her with shameless intent. He was aroused again, admiring how her supple back flared into her sweet arse. It was all too easy to imagine her body carrying his child. She was warm, intelligent, and strong-willed. And any son or daughter Drake sired would surely need an iron hand.

"I can't believe we're doing this in the middle of the day," she whispered, then lifted her head.

He went still. They had both heard a door slam downstairs.

She sat up instinctively, clutching a sheet to her breasts. "Are you expecting anyone?" she whispered.

"No." He leaned back, staring over his bare shoulder at the door.

A woman's voice resonated from the entrance hall, strident with indignant fury. A man replied in calmer tones. One of the footmen, Drake thought, already half-way into his clothes.

Eloise looked at him in panic. "Who is that?"

He tossed her chemise, corset, and gown onto the bed, pulling on his jacket with his other hand. "God, I don't know. One of my sisters? Perhaps it's Emma, although she never calls without an invitation." And she never shrieked like a virago, either. Her lectures were always delivered with scathing dignity, which didn't make them any less painful.

Eloise paled and stuffed her corset under the pillow. "I thought you said you rarely had visitors."

She meant women, he thought, running his hand through his short black hair. His voice was deep with puzzlement as he helped her into her gown. "I rarely do."

The voices belowstairs climbed to a terse crescendo. The woman spewed colorful curses that would have put a sailor to shame. "That," Eloise said, squirming away from him, "does not sound anything like either of your sisters."

He threw a grim look at the door. He recognized the voice now, and could have kicked himself in the head for not realizing this could happen. He'd been stupid to think he could appease a woman like Maribella St. Ives with a generous settlement and written apology explaining that he did not want to consummate their arrangement. And hoped she would understand.

The screaming harridan at the bottom of the stairs didn't sound like an appeased woman. She was bellowing more like a vengeful goddess threatening to destroy the world.

He glanced back at Eloise in concern. Maribella would certainly fly into a rage when she realized why he had reneged on their agreement. "Believe me, I didn't foresee this happening."

She pinned back her disheveled hair. "What didn't you foresee?" she demanded, suddenly sounding like a woman who could more than hold her own.

"That she would not accept the end of our affair."

"I thought you never had an affair."

"We didn't." He straightened his neck cloth. "Except on paper. Please stay here. I'll take care of her."

She eyed him narrowly. "You'd be surprised at the persons I've taken care of in my career."

He drew a breath. "Let me handle her first."

She hesitated, folding her arms across her midsection. "Fine."

"You're not the sort of woman to confront a courtesan anyway," he added at the door.

"I'm a courtesan myself, Drake," she said, practical as always. "Perhaps she could give me—"

"You're *not* a courtesan," he interrupted, ducking out the door. "You're . . . mine."

Chapter Twenty-four

❧ ❧

Eloise cracked open the door to listen. It didn't take long for him to calm the woman down, she thought a little resentfully. What had he said to silence her? And what did she look like? Blame it on ancient female rivalry, but Eloise simply had to see for herself what kind of woman captured the attention of wealthy, powerful men from all around the world.

Was Maribella St. Ives as unbelievably beautiful as everyone said? Or did her attraction lie beneath the surface, a practiced sexuality that turned strong males into puddles of steaming lust at her feet?

Eloise burned to know. She had a right to know. An obligation, as Drake's mistress. Besides, it was too quiet down there. She couldn't bear the suspense, she thought as she slipped through the door.

All she wanted was one look. One peek from the top of the stairs, and she'd be satisfied.

Drake had managed to appease Maribella, if only temporarily, with his heartfelt promise that somehow he would make monetary amends for his behavior. She would have none of his promises. She demanded to meet her rival as a point of professional pride.

"It is only fair," she insisted, looking like a breath of winter in an ice blue silk gown with a trim of white Siberian wolf fur at her throat and delicate wrists.

He put his hands on her shoulders and gently guided her away from the stairs and back down to the sofa in the drawing room. How she knew that he'd brought Eloise here, or even that she existed, was a mystery to him. But then he'd never tried to hide his interest in Eloise from the start, another anomaly in the history of his affairs. He had made no secret of the fact that a lady's companion had caught his attention. Still, he wondered how Maribella had found out.

His question was answered a few moments later.

As he motioned his footman and butler to close the front door, he noticed a tall lanky figure pacing back and forth outside.

One of Maribella's bodyguards. The same limber ape whom he'd chased for spying on him and Eloise in Thornton's garden. Drake realized now why the ape seemed familiar. He was one of the bodyguards who'd been standing in the shadowy hallway of Audrey Watson's house the night of Drake's assignation with Maribella.

She'd sent her bodyguard to spy on him. He would have laughed at her nerve if he didn't have Eloise hidden away in his room. Without the most skillful maneuvering, the situation was liable to erupt into a full-scale disaster.

He had to keep the two women from meeting each other. No matter what it took, he had to stop Maribella from confronting Eloise. The pair of them could not have been more dissimilar if they'd come from opposite ends of the earth.

God's teeth, they'd loathe each other on sight. How

could he prevent them from meeting when they were both in the same house? He'd never had to resort to subterfuge in his past affairs. He could only blame his current dilemma on his obsession with Eloise. He had wanted her too badly to consider the consequences. Of course he couldn't have known that Maribella would confront him in such dramatic fashion.

Actually he should have known. The papers had described her infamous temper, her intolerance for deception. She was notorious for insisting that her lovers treat her like a queen. Well, he'd betrayed the damned queen, and she wanted his head on a platter.

He could handle himself with a temperamental woman. His concern was for Eloise. For all her practical experience in dealing with difficult employers, he doubted she had ever encountered a fury like Maribella St. Ives before.

"How could you do this to me?" Maribella shouted.

Her voice startled him from his reverie. She had uncoiled her slim form from the sofa to spring to her feet.

How could he get rid of her? he wondered. "Maribella, believe me, I didn't plan to hurt you."

"Hurt me?" She shook her fist in his face. "You haven't hurt me, you arrogant idiot. You have humiliated me. I have never been rejected by a lover before."

"But we never made love," he pointed out, praying that her voice didn't carry beyond this room. Eloise wouldn't be a normal female if she weren't listening to every word.

Her flawless white skin flushed in anger. "That makes it even worse. Did you consider my reputation?"

"Your reputation?" he said in surprise. Hell, the

woman was a courtesan. How the devil could his retracting his offer damage her name?

She strode up to him, her eyes blazing. "What is at stake is not my heart," she said. "Do not for one moment allow yourself to believe that I cared for you. The—"

"Well, then that makes it easier."

"—issue," she continued as if he hadn't spoken, "is my value on the market. You have lessened my worth by taking another woman, a little nobody no less, while dangling me on a thread."

He cleared his throat. "A very costly thread, too."

She circled his desk in agitation. He suspected she was looking for a letter-opener to use as a weapon. "You could at least have the decency to show me who has taken my place. Or is she too afraid to meet me? I'm perfectly aware you've got her hiding in your bedroom, for God's sake."

"I'm not afraid of meeting you," Eloise said in a composed voice from the doorway. "In fact, I'm probably as anxious to make your acquaintance as you . . . as you—are—"

She broke off midsentence. Drake pivoted, fully prepared to stand bodily between her and Maribella's notorious temper. For all the self-possession in Eloise's voice, she looked anything but composed when she stubbornly sidestepped him to enter the room.

"As you are," she repeated in a faint voice, staring at Maribella as if she were a spirit. "No, it isn't possible. It can't be. You're—"

"Oh, my God," Maribella said, throwing down the letter-opener she'd found in the desk drawer. "Ellie."

"Mildred," Eloise said, laughing and shaking her head in disbelief. "Tell me it isn't true."

Drake blinked, several times. *Mildred? Ellie?* The pair of them knew each other? Apparently quite well to judge by the way they nearly bowled him over to share an affectionate hug. He was frozen in shock where he stood. It had to be one of the worst situations a man could imagine, the two women in his life bonded by some past alliance, possibly joining forces in the future—against him?

"I never thought I'd see you again," Eloise said in an incredulous voice. "It's been years."

So Maribella was a fraud. She was a Mildred. He almost snorted. To think the male world, to think *he*, had been taken by a very clever woman, indeed. Mildred the milkmaid, for all he knew. She ought to have worked for British Intelligence with her talent for masquerade. Her other talents would have proven helpful, too, although he hadn't experienced them personally. He stared at her and Eloise, clearly forgotten in their emotional reunion, which might actually be a blessing.

How the devil did they know each other, anyway? Until this rather startling moment he'd assumed that the only thing the courtesan and lady's companion had in common was him. That had been an uncomfortable enough position in itself. But now he stood between them, through no duplicity on his part.

And then he put two and two together. He recalled what Eloise had told him about her past. He might be the man they had in common now, but another man had connected them before. The man Eloise had said was blackmailing her. The one Drake could hardly wait to pummel into a bag of pudding. He braced his shoulder against the wall, listening to their conversation. Being a man he naturally wondered what this would mean in terms of his enjoyable relationship with Eloise.

"Your hair is different," Eloise exclaimed, drawing back to examine her friend. "It's gone red. I hardly recognized you. And you've lost ever so much weight."

"I've been dying my hair for years," Maribella—or was it Mildred?—said. "Well, you know, since the incident. I wanted to put everything behind me."

"Yes," Eloise murmured, casting a guarded look at Drake. "The 'incident.' "

Mildred glanced at him, too, arching her finely plucked brow. "Does he know?" she whispered.

Eloise nodded vaguely. "Hmm. Yes, I just told him. I couldn't not."

"You've slimmed down, too, Ellie," Mildred said in an obvious attempt to change the subject. "But not too much. Some men like a bit of flesh on their women."

A moment of dead silence ensued. Drake pretended to study the ivory chess set on the sideboard.

Eloise shook her head in wonder. "You, Mildred, *you're* the celebrated courtesan he's been involved with?"

Drake glanced up. Mildred's red lips pursed in hesitation. "That's a gross misconception," she said. "Involved? Uninvolved is what he was with me, and now I understand why. But you, Ellie, you're the little tart who is stealing my business?" she asked fondly.

"Who called me a tart?" Eloise sent Drake an indignant look. "Did you refer to me as your tart?"

"No," Drake and Mildred said in unison.

Maribella—Mildred—strode right up to him and met his gaze. For a moment he thought she might smack him. Her delicate fingers tightened into an indelicate fist.

She must have been a raging hellion in her youth, this woman he'd almost made his mistress. Hadn't she set her betrayer's bed on fire? Well, she'd been setting beds on fire ever since.

Her sultry voice vibrated with menace. "If you harm one hair on Ellie's head, I will personally filet you into Boeuf au Boscastle."

He bent his head to hers, his dark eyebrows lowering. "No, you won't, and I wouldn't hurt Eloise if you threatened to cook my ballocks into oyster stew, *Mildred*."

She gazed up at him with a challenging smile. "I intend to make an official announcement to the newspapers that I have broken off our negotiations."

"Suit yourself." His family and few close friends had formed their opinions of him long ago. He didn't give a damn what anyone else made of it except Eloise. How was the fact that he had been involved, or uninvolved, with her long-lost friend going to affect *their* association?

It was a wicked bit of irony for the history books. He doubted it would elevate his status in her eyes.

"Does this mean that you're both going to forgive me?" he asked.

Neither of them answered him. They were chattering on about how long it took to dye one's hair red and how attractive Eloise would look with henna tresses to bring out the green in her eyes. And he wanted to take her into his arms and tell her not to change because she was so beautiful to him that he almost couldn't bear it. He didn't want anything to ruin her, not even him. He wished she'd never had a past to begin with.

"Should I leave?" he asked loudly.

Eloise stopped to look at him. He hadn't any notion what she was thinking, but he was damn glad he'd bedded her before she found out that Maribella was really Mildred. "If you don't mind," she said politely.

Mildred spared him a glance. "Ring for tea while you're at it, Boscastle. I need some refreshment."

"Ring for tea," Drake muttered on his way to the bellpull. He'd been dismissed from his own drawing room like a footman. Heaven only knew what would be said and decided about him while he ordered tea. Considering their past conspiracy, he wasn't sure the two women should be left alone.

He rang dutifully and gave the maid who answered him a forbidding look that sent her scurrying back to the kitchen posthaste. He had never ordered tea in his whole life. Maiden's water, that's what it was. He shook his head, then went outside.

Standing on the steps to their door was Mildred's young athletic bodyguard, the spry bugger who'd sent Drake on a merry chase through the streets of London. "You," he said in disgust. "I ought to have you arrested on the spot."

The fellow had the grace to hang his head in shame. "Sorry about that day, my lord. My cousin made me do it. You almost caught me, if it's any consolation. By damn, you're fast, and I ran races at the fair for—"

"It isn't any consolation," Drake said uncharitably, then, "Cousin? She's your cousin?"

"I'm afraid so," he said.

"In that case, I accept your apology. We can't always choose our relatives."

"My name is Albert, my lord." The young man

looked at him hopefully. "Do you think my cousin is safe alone in there with your—well, the woman you're keeping? I did hear voices raised."

Drake snorted. "The voices were raised at me. Your cousin and Eloise are getting along famously."

Albert gave him a faintly pitying look. "You're in for trouble now, aren't you?"

The reminder didn't serve to lighten Drake's mood. Nor did the sight of Devon barreling down the street toward the house in his phaeton. All he needed to top his unprecedented indignity was to have his younger brother gossiping to his friends and family about Eloise and Mildred. It seemed that every time he turned around, Devon appeared to bedevil him.

"Isn't this another bright spot in my day?" he muttered, blowing out a sigh.

Albert hunkered down on the step beside him, shrewdly eyeing the approaching phaeton. "Someone you don't wish to see?"

Drake laughed darkly. "Not at the moment."

"Would you like me to take care of him for you?" Albert asked, squeezing his hands into huge menacing fists. "I owe you a favor."

Drake gave him a hard glare. "That's my brother, unfortunately, or I might be tempted to accept your offer."

"Hell," Albert said, lurching to his feet. "Family. A pain in the arse. Would you like for me to leave the two of you alone?"

"Yes."

A few moments later Devon vaulted down onto the street from his phaeton. A pair of vendors selling lavender had converged on the corner to watch the two handsome young lords, well known for their manly charms and generosity. Drake ignored them. Devon flashed a broad grin that sent both girls into a spell of giggles and blushes.

His grin vanished as he turned to meet Drake's unwelcoming gaze. "Grayson sent me to make sure you were all right."

"Of course I'm bloody all right," he said impatiently. Which as far as Devon knew was the truth, and he wasn't in a mood to change his mind. "Why wouldn't I be?"

"Well," Devon said, "you're sitting on the steps of your house for one thing, and I don't think I've ever seen you do that before. At least not when you were sober. What's the matter?"

"Did I say anything was wrong? Everything is fine." Discounting the fact that he'd just been cast by past association into the role of the man who had broken Eloise's and Mildred's hearts. God only knew what mischief Mildred might talk Eloise into now. He shouldn't be surprised to find himself tied to a dog-cart and paraded nude through the streets of London with a placard around his neck.

Devon sat down on the step below him. "I'll come straight to the point. Heath and I have been spying on you and your paramour."

Drake's upper lip curled. Why had he known the moment he saw him that Devon was only going to make his day worse? Obviously Devon wasn't aware that Heath had already come to Drake, and his conscience was bothering him. Well, it was Devon who'd initiated this "spying" and Drake wasn't inclined to forgive him easily. "Pardon me. I think I must be hearing things. You did not just say that you've been spying on me and Eloise?"

"It was only for your benefit." Devon leaned back several inches, swallowing at the look of anger that darkened Drake's face. "Grayson did not want you to be deceived."

"Hell's bloody bells!" Drake thought he sounded convincingly shocked. "*Spying* on me? I knew it."

Devon slid down another step. "You ought to be thankful. I found out quite a bit about Eloise."

"Did you now?"

"I thought you ought to know. I wouldn't have spied on you without good cause."

Drake glowered down at him, reminding himself that one probably shouldn't commit fratricide in front of witnesses. Spying? During the war, Heath had been involved in intelligence affairs, as had Drake, to a lesser degree. Neither of them knew exactly what, if anything of that nature, Devon had done during his years in the cavalry. Devon had belonged to an entirely different regiment. It was hard to imagine the playful rogue dabbling in espionage. Especially when the subject in question was his own brother.

"Don't you want to know what I discovered?" Devon asked with an artless lift of his shoulders.

Drake turned his head, his expression morose. "If you're going to tell me that Eloise was considering becoming a courtesan before she became a companion, I'll kill—"

"Eloise?" Devon asked in alarm. "You'd kill a woman?"

"No," Drake said between his teeth. "I'd kill *you*."

Devon leaned back against the wrought-iron railing, visibly unsettled. "Why me?"

"Because you're the nearest human being within killing range. And if I find out that Eloise was considering—"

"—becoming a courtesan," Devon supplied.

Drake wouldn't have believed this conversation an hour ago. "Was she?"

"I don't know," Devon said, looking befuddled. "Ask her."

"I'm asking you, idiot. You're the one who said you had information on her."

Devon frowned. "Yes, but not that she was a courtesan. That's a shock to me. She seemed so decent. When did you learn that?"

"Dear God, help me."

"Praying won't change what she was," Devon said, shaking his head. "All you can do is forgive her. Besides, it's not like either of us have an aversion to courtesans."

Drake smiled unpleasantly. "Do you know what I have an aversion to?"

Devon held up his hands in self-defense. "If you hurt me, I won't be able to tell you what I found out. You do want to know, don't you?"

Drake exhaled. He thought he knew enough about Eloise. Discovering that she had loved another man six years ago did not sit well with him, as irrational as that might be. It wasn't his masculine pride, either. He didn't give a holy fig about the disgrace of what she'd done, or that she'd hoped to keep her past a secret. He realized how the world regarded a woman's mistakes.

He wasn't about to pass judgment. He wanted to protect her. He only wished she'd felt safe enough with him to be honest about her past. And if he ever found out that there was more to her story than she'd revealed, well, he wasn't sure what he'd do. He was in this deeper than he realized.

"Tell me what you know," he said to Devon. "And then I'll decide if I'm going to kill you."

Chapter Twenty-five

❦ ❦

Now that the initial shock of meeting each other was over, Mildred scrutinized Eloise in mild dismay. "A governess and companion," she said with a shudder. "What a frightful fate. I thought you'd have married a country sire by now and raised a passel of pretty brats."

"Well, I certainly never thought you'd become what you've become, Mildred." Or that again a man would bring them together.

Mildred leaned into her, her voice dropping. "There is no Mildred Hammersmith outside of this room. She ceased to exist the very day you and I parted company. I'll never go back home, no matter what I have to do, and to be honest, my life is not exactly unbearable."

Eloise nodded in understanding. "I'm not the same person I once was, either."

Mildred snorted in amusement. "Well, you haven't changed as much as I have. You're still a bit . . . well, reserved."

"I assure you," Eloise murmured, lowering her gaze a little wickedly, "I'm no longer as reserved as I was." If only until recently, and listen to her, practically boasting about her decline into indecency.

"Ah," Mildred said without any resentment at all.

"So you and Boscastle have become lovers. Well, if any-one was to be my rival, I'm glad it was you. I might have killed him otherwise."

Eloise breathed out a reflective sigh. Apparently she was still reserved enough to cringe at discussing her personal affairs with such candor. She had no defense, of course, except for love. Foolishly perhaps she had fallen in love with a man who had promised her nothing but his passion and his protection. Affairs such as this were commonplace to a woman like Maribella St. Ives. But no matter how long Eloise lived, she would never be able to separate her heart from the giving of herself.

"The wisest thing Ralph ever did in his wretched life was to ask you to marry him," Mildred mused, her lips pursed.

Eloise shook her head. She'd had years to consider the past. "Actually, I thought you would have been the better choice for him. You would have kept him honest. I'm not much on corporal punishment, which is what he seemed to need."

"Punishment? I'd have killed Ralph within two months after if I'd married him, and then where would I be?"

"He would have deserved it," Eloise said, thinking of the moment she'd discovered him behind her wardrobe, and the stark evil in his eyes.

"We can't go back and kill him now," Mildred said, her voice deepening conspiratorially. "Or can we?"

There was a pleasantly disgraceful moment when both women entertained the fantasy of murdering their mutual nemesis, thereby ridding the female world of a malignant troublemaker. But neither of them had homi-cide in her heart. They had worked too hard in their disparate professions to risk imprisonment, or hanging, for a worthless man like Ralph Hawkins.

They stared at each other, bound by more than their past, two women who could not have been more different. And yet their shared strength, that spark of unconventional rebellion, expressed so long ago, still linked them today. True sisters of the soul who had managed to survive in a society that could have crushed them.

Eloise looked up suddenly. "He's been here."

"Who—Ralph?" Mildred asked in shock, her aplomb slipping.

"Yes. He's in London." She hesitated. She hated to even acknowledge how he had frightened her. "He was trying to blackmail me. I don't know how he found me, but he asked about you. It seems he has never forgiven us for shaming him. He doesn't know who you are."

Mildred leaned back in her chair. "He'll ruin my reputation if he exposes me."

"You're a courtesan, Mildred. How much more can you be ruined?"

"I'll have you know I've worked damned hard for my notorious reputation."

Eloise started to laugh. "He has a family back in the country."

"Good riddance to him. It's fortunate for you that you've got Boscastle as a protector. You have told him about Ralph?"

"Yes. Of course. But what if Ralph should come back and recognize you?"

Mildred's red mouth formed a menacing smile. "I was planning on leaving London soon, anyway. Don't worry about me. I've always taken care of myself."

"And so have I."

Mildred was quiet for several moments, and Eloise could not help marveling at how she had changed since that day they had parted. She was breathtakingly beautiful and sophisticated, so self-assured that it was hard to believe Drake had not fallen under her spell. He had chosen her, instead.

"He must love you," Mildred said, as if she had read her thoughts. "Don't let him go, Eloise. I am almost envious of you."

"Only almost?" Eloise asked lightly.

Mildred broke into laughter. "Well, I do have an earl waiting in the wings, and I think I've been too spoiled by living as I please to answer to any one man."

By the time Devon finished revealing the few snippets that he'd gleaned of Eloise's past, which turned out to be nothing but a rough account of what she'd already told him, Drake decided it was high time he went back inside his own house to assert himself. Devon agreed, although he probably would have agreed to anything to make amends. He was clearly relieved that his brother had forgotten his recent threat to kill him.

He followed Drake inside, more because he wanted to get a close look at Maribella St. Ives than anything else. Drake was rather anxious to find out what she and Eloise had been discussing himself. Call him overly protective, or perhaps possessive, but he'd rather not have a professional courtesan exerting her influence on Eloise. He was world-weary enough for the both of them.

When he entered the house, Eloise was rushing past him in the hallway, dressed to depart in her cloak. He caught her by the arm and pulled her backward, afraid that he had lost her. "Whatever she said about me isn't true. Please don't go yet."

She caught her breath as he drew closer. "She didn't say anything, but I have to leave."

"Why?" he asked. He hadn't answered to anyone or anything since the war, and she only had to answer to him.

"Thalia and the servants will wonder where I've gone," she said, relaxing against him.

He breathed in the scent of her skin. He'd never known a sweeter fragrance, soap and a lingering trace of sex. "You don't have to work another day in your life."

She lifted her face to his as he leaned down to kiss her, then froze. "Your brother is right behind you."

Drake swore softly.

She wriggled free. He closed his eyes for a moment, allowing his emotions to cool. "Don't go," he said under his breath.

"I promised I would help with the wedding," she whispered.

"What wedding?" Drake asked blankly. "Oh, Thalia and Sir Thomas." He shook his head and smiled in resignation. "I'll take you back."

"No. We can't be seen together again in daylight. Everyone will know—" She glanced again at Devon, who turned his head away a little too quickly to reassure Drake he wasn't listening to every word. The devil danced in those Boscastle blue eyes of his, too.

"What will they know?" Drake asked. "That you're my new companion?"

"There's no need to be quite so obvious about it," she said in an embarrassed whisper.

He shrugged. In a few weeks everyone who knew him

would realize that he had taken her as his mistress. Not that he was a highly social creature who shared every detail of his private life. But he didn't intend to keep her a secret. "I shall drop you off at the door," he said firmly. He glanced up. "Are you staying, Devon?"

Devon cleared his throat. "Well, I thought perhaps I would stay for a while. If only to make certain that your other guest is not feeling ignored."

Drake laughed at the notion of anyone ignoring the tempestuous woman in his drawing room. "Please yourself, but do be careful. I wouldn't want her to have you for supper."

"Aren't you going to formally introduce us?" Devon asked, unable to suppress a grin.

Drake was about to refuse until Eloise smiled at him. "I don't mind," she said. "But you'd better ask Miss St. Ives for permission first."

Drake walked into the drawing room to discover Maribella—he still couldn't think of her as Mildred—standing at the sideboard surveying his chessboard.

He cleared his throat. "My younger brother would like to meet you. Do you mind?"

She half turned, her smile more amused than reproachful. "I'm not in the market for another Boscastle."

He smiled. "I hope you're not holding a grudge against me for what happened."

"Eloise?" She lowered the ivory queen she had been holding, her eyes warm. "I could kiss you for bringing her back into my life."

He hesitated. "I don't mean to sound rude, but I think

it might be better if you and Eloise don't actually meet in social circles."

"Good God," she said, choking on a laugh. "The devil has gone moral on me. Don't worry. I'm not going to corrupt her. In fact, I might be leaving London soon to go to France."

"Forgive me?"

She considered him coolly. "Only because the other woman was Eloise."

He shook his head. "I don't care what people say about me, but as far as the rest of the world knows, let's agree to tell anyone who asks that you've taken a new lover."

"I have taken a new lover," she said.

"So soon?" he asked, grinning in surprise. "I wouldn't have thought anyone could have met your requirements in so short a time."

"He hasn't," she replied. "But he's an earl, and the silly fool fancies himself in love with me."

He smiled at her. "You say that as if it surprises you."

"You didn't fall in love with me." She didn't sound accusing or even disappointed. She was practical, too, he thought.

"People will say I must have lost my mind to let you go."

"Perhaps you lost your heart," she said.

He didn't deny it.

"Eloise is nothing like either of us," she said. "She has principles, for all the good they'll do her."

"Which she has abandoned because of me," Drake said soberly. "Is that what you mean to say next?"

She met his scrutiny. He had a feeling that he was seeing a side of her she rarely showed. She was self-protective in the extreme, as beautiful as the world believed her to be. But she wasn't for him. Perhaps they were too much alike, he and Maribella St. Ives, cynical, guarded, pretending to feel nothing beneath a composed indifference.

She shook her head. "I only meant that she could never follow in my path. Eloise will make at most an imperfect mistress. She'll fuss and worry over you like a mother hen, and no matter how many jewels or seductive evenings you give her, she will come to feel the lack of what is missing in her life."

He said nothing. He understood women too well to even bother pretending he didn't understand what she meant. Or that he disagreed.

"I ruined her chance of a normal life by revealing Ralph's deceit," she said ruefully. "If I hadn't confronted her and drawn her into my revenge, she would have made the best of her life with him."

His face darkened. "You deserve accolades for that, not criticism."

She stared at him, and for a moment he glimpsed a vulnerability in her that he would never have guessed had survived her experiences. Her brittle detachment was merely a shield. "She deserves the wedding that was stolen from her, Drake. She should have married and had children." She gave a light dismissive laugh. "And that is the end of *my* sermon, and the end of you and me."

He smiled. He'd always ended his love affairs with a mutually satisfactory agreement, but this affair had never even begun. "Be kind to Devon, won't you?"

"From what I saw of him through the window, he looked as if he were capable of taking care of himself."

"Then I shall leave you to him." He turned toward

the door. He was eager to return to Eloise, to spend the afternoon hunting for a suitable house for her. "By the way, I want you to keep the gifts I gave you."

She laughed. "I fully intend to."

Drake wondered how long he could distract Eloise before she realized his driver had been instructed to take a leisurely detour on the way back to Thornton's house. Not long enough, apparently. He'd just hooked his finger into her bodice when she broke their heated kiss to whisper, "Isn't this the wrong way home?" She peered out the carriage window over his shoulder. "We just passed that same pie-seller a few minutes ago."

"It's amazing how quickly those vendors can move from corner to corner," he murmured, pressing her back against the squabs.

"Then the house behind him moved, too," she exclaimed. "In fact, this is the third time we've gone past that china shop. Are you going to tell me that it moved, too?"

He fought a grin. "Didn't the dish run away with the spoon?"

"Did you ask your driver to go in circles?" she demanded.

He shifted his shoulder slightly to block her view of the street. "Perhaps he's trying to avoid traffic."

"Perhaps you're trying to avoid an answer. How long were you going to allow this?"

He leaned back on his elbow, his blue eyes warm and devilish. "For as long as I possibly could. If you have to know the truth, I didn't want to take you back at all."

She shook her head and began to straighten her disheveled clothing. He resisted the impulse to stop her.

She looked so desirable that he was tempted to break his word and drag her back to his bed.

"You're not even sorry, are you?" she asked.

"I'm sorry that you realized we were driving around in circles."

"Did you actually instruct your driver to take a detour?"

"Well, not in so many words."

"That makes it even worse!" she exclaimed. "You're so practiced in wickedness that he anticipates your whims."

He paused, staring at her in pleasure. "Does that mean I have to take you back now?"

"Yes, it does."

"Are you sure?"

"Yes—"

"We could buy a pie on the corner and share." His voice low, he stroked his thumb beneath her jaw as if to coax her into his mood.

"You," she said, turning her head to hide a smile, "are one completely wicked man."

He drew his hand back to his side, sighing in regret, and rapped lightly on the roof of the carriage. She glanced back at him. "That wasn't difficult, was it?"

"Yes," he said in a disgruntled voice. "It was. It is."

The carriage stopped. Eloise realized that not only had they reached their destination, but that she was not at all the same person as she had been when she'd left Lord Thornton's house. Could she even pretend that she had not changed?

"I will walk you inside, Eloise."

"The servants will make such a fuss—"

"They will learn to obey me if I am to employ them."

The servants, she thought, would be no more able to resist obeying him than she was. All of them had already fallen victim to his Boscastle charisma. They would worship him like a dark demigod for rescuing them from the quagmire of poverty. She would worship him, too, but in different ways.

She cast a reflective glance outside the carriage as she made to rise. The house appeared quiet enough. She'd half feared that the entire staff would be waiting at the door with laurel wreaths to greet the man they hoped would become their new master.

"For some odd reason," she murmured, as if just realizing it herself, "the creditors have simply stopped calling. I have a horrible suspicion that I shall wake up the morning before the wedding to discover the house stripped down to the floorboards."

Drake opened the door for her. "It won't happen," he said with a droll smile. "I took care of the creditors three days ago."

"You? *You* paid Thornton's debts?" She gazed at him in astonishment. "Why?"

His devilish grin made her heart quicken. "So that my dutiful companion could walk away from her former position and not look back. I resent even your dedication to that duty. I am willing to pay for your full devotion, Eloise."

Chapter Twenty-six

❧ ❧

Old habits died hard. Eloise had lived a quiet existence for so long that she couldn't help feeling self-conscious as Drake walked her to the front door, his hand firmly clasping hers. How bold-hearted of her, entering her place of employment in broad daylight with the man who now claimed himself to be her protector. She faltered for a moment as Freddie answered her knock, blushing at his wide-eyed look.

She blushed again when Drake drew her back into his arms to kiss her one last time at the door. "Send for me immediately if there is any trouble," he said in an undertone. "And plan on spending the evening with me."

"I've been with you all day," she said softly. "What if I am needed?"

"You are needed," he said, his grin challenging her to disagree. "By me. Please don't forget it."

Flustered, she turned away to peel off her cloak and enter the hall, vaguely aware of voices coming from the parlor. She glanced curiously at her reflection in the ornate rococo mirror that hung on the wall. Did she look different? Did—

That mirror had not been hanging there when she'd left the house that morning. In fact, she'd never seen it before. She backed away, her shoes sinking into the unfamiliar plush Oriental carpet that ran the length of the hall.

The carpet had not been there earlier, either. In fact, neither had the long case clock that ticked away precisely in the corner. Had Boscastle done this? Had he refurbished the house during her absence to impress her with his generosity? It was a sweet gesture, but it seemed extravagant to furnish a house that would soon be empty. Thalia and her husband-to-be intended to live far from London on his modest country estate.

She walked pensively toward the parlor and hesitated in the open doorway. Freddie followed at her heels, his voice anxious.

"He made me promise not to tell you," he said over her shoulder. "It's supposed to be a surprise. He's come home, but you didn't hear it from me."

He? Eloise stared blankly the well-dressed gentleman who stood at the parlor window, his hand at his chin in a contemplative pose. She whitened as if she were staring at a ghost.

"Lord Thornton." She glanced distractedly at Thalia sitting on the sofa. "Is that really you?"

He pivoted. It was Horace Thornton, but not in the familiar form of the dissolute rascal she remembered. This incarnation was dressed in an expensive superfine coat and tight black pantaloons. His brown hair was artfully styled in short curls, his neck cloth folded in flawless lines.

"Eloise," he said, extending his hand in supplication. "Dear Miss Goodwin."

How dare he "dear" her, she thought in indignation. How dare he return after abandoning his sister and dependents as if they were no more than dirt beneath his highly polished Hessians. Oh, that the irresponsible rascal had outfitted himself like the Prince Regent while they warded off his creditors.

She voiced none of these thoughts, of course. Eloise was too well trained in hiding her feelings to even raise her voice.

"Well," she said unenthusiastically, "the prodigal has returned at last."

"I deserve your condemnation." He hung his head. "I have been no better than a dog."

She wasn't about to contradict him. "If you wish to apologize, I suggest you start with Sir Gabriel and your sister."

Thalia snorted at the suggestion. "He swears he's reformed. I don't believe him for an instant."

"I have reformed," Horace said, scowling at his sister. "And I will offer a public apology to Sir Gabriel as well as to the members of my club the first thing in the morning."

"That is the proper thing to do," Eloise said with a sigh.

"You don't even wonder where I've been?" he asked.

"It crossed my mind," she said, glancing at Thalia. What charade was this? the two women seemed to ask each other. They had grown not only closer during his absence, but stronger, too.

"I went to the country," he said. "I rusticated to have a long think."

"You might have thought of us," she said bluntly.

"I have thought of you," he said in a quiet voice. "In fact, I have thought of little else."

She felt an unwelcome prickle of heat at his admis-

sion. She sincerely hoped that she'd misunderstood him.
"We were afraid you had taken your own life," she said
in a subdued voice.

"I believe I might have found it," he replied.

She wanted to sit down. No, she wanted to walk out
the door and run after Drake. Why had she insisted on
leaving him?

"What about your debts?" she asked pointedly.

"I have repaid every one of them."

Her brow arched. "How?"

"Do you remember the investments I made two years
ago?"

She shook her head a little impatiently. Horace had
forever rambled on about his wagers and investments.
None of them had ever paid off. Was it possible—?

"I have a proposition for you, Eloise," he said, his
hands knotted behind his back. "A personal offer that
will allow you to retire from service altogether."

"A proposition?"

Thalia threw down the magazine she had been perus-
ing, her eyes widening in warning. Then to Eloise's disbelief, she rose, strode straight up to her brother, and
slapped him soundly on the face. "How dare you."

"*Ow.* Bloody hell. What was that for?" he asked, his
hand lifting to his reddened cheek.

"For making Eloise an indecent offer," she retorted.
"I'm sure she was too offended to slap you herself, so I
did it for her. It was high time someone did. You abandoned us, Horace."

He blinked. "Eloise would never have slapped me."

Thalia shook her head. "Is that right? Well, perhaps
she's changed since you deserted us. Perhaps she's even
been forced to sacrifice her decency to save us."

He cradled his jaw. "Then the rumors of her and Boscastle are true." He turned to regard Eloise, who was rather horrified at their display. "Is it true, Eloise?" he asked quietly. "No, don't answer me. If you have indeed been forced into an unspeakable situation, it is my fault."

She wasn't about to argue. She could hardly admit that her affair with Drake was the most wonderful experience of her life, or that her decision to become his lover had less to do with Horace's irresponsible behavior than the leading of her own heart.

"What is done is done," she said, avoiding his gaze, and hoped that would be the end of the discussion.

He bowed his head. "I deserve your condemnation. Will you at least hear what I have to say?"

There was no point in denying his request, even if she doubted that anything he could say would make a difference. "Go ahead," she said with a sigh.

"Thank you. May we sit together on the sofa?"

"If you insist."

"I have an offer to make you, Eloise," he said.

She sat awkwardly, Thalia plunking herself down between them.

She had to force herself to listen politely. She couldn't imagine anything Lord Thornton could offer that would tempt her. A position at a friend's house so he could salve his conscience? A pittance to pay her off? Or perhaps he'd promise to give her glowing references for her next job. He couldn't very well give her references for the position she'd taken as Drake's mistress, however.

He rose unexpectedly to his feet and began to pace before the sofa. She thought absently that he was not an unattractive man, especially now that he appeared to be sober and serious about reforming. Perhaps if he found someone to love him, he might even become—

"I want you to be my wife," he said without warning.

She could not have been more stunned if the cast-iron chandelier had dropped on her head. "Your what?"

"Oh, Eloise." Thalia stared at her in delight, then smothered her in an ecstatic hug. "I won't lose you, after all! My *sister-in-law*. An auntie for my children, and you can take care of them while Thomas and I travel around the world! Horace, you aren't the heartless dog that everyone thinks you are. You're the most wonderful brother in the world."

"What is your answer, Eloise?" he asked, clearing his throat but looking somewhat pleased at his sister's exuberant reaction.

"I'm speechless," she said. "However, I—"

He glanced meaningfully at Thalia. "Do you mind leaving us alone? This is a private moment."

She jumped to her feet, her hands clasped in glee. "Yes, of course. You want to court Eloise. Oh, it's too perfect. I wish I'd thought of it myself. Now you don't have to become a courtesan, Eloise. You can be close to me forever."

She danced from the room on a cloud of fantasy, grinning at the group of servants who were eavesdropping unabashedly in the hall. Eloise frowned at them in reproach. So did Horace as he crossed the room to close the door on their blatant curiosity.

"I'm sorry, my lord," she said, shaking her head as if trying to make sense of his behavior. "You have taken me by surprise."

"I understand about you and Boscastle," he said with a deep sigh. "You need not apologize or explain how it happened. He is a rake who has taken advantage of you. I am entirely at fault."

Eloise lifted her hand to the pearls at her neck. Yes, Drake was a rake, and if he'd taken advantage of her, well, she wasn't about to blame anyone but herself for allowing him to do so. She would never have been attracted to Lord Thornton under any circumstances.

"I can't think of a worse pairing," Horace added. "Boscastle is cunning and worldly. You're—"

Eloise rose to her feet as he foundered for words. "What am I?" she asked, one hand on her hip.

"Well, you're not worldly," he said. "Which is actually a compliment. You're rather gauche and unsophisticated, in an endearing way, mind you. I suppose it comes from being raised in the country. That's one of the reasons I think you and I will suit."

She didn't know whether to laugh or cry at his approach. For a man proposing marriage, he had the finesse of a cart horse. "You think that we are compatible because you're a country bumpkin at heart like me?"

He looked taken aback at her bluntness. She had never spoken so openly to him before. "I'm afraid Boscastle's company has brought out a cynical side of you, Eloise."

"I have always been a little cynical, if you must know."

"You certainly never called me a country bumpkin before," he said, sounding hurt.

"Not to your face, perhaps." Now that she'd begun to be honest with him, she found it difficult to control herself. "Actually, I called you far worse when you disappeared."

"Mull over my offer for a few days," he said obstinately.

"There is no point."

"Boscastle will never marry you."

The cruel barb stuck right to the core of her heart. She steadied herself inwardly. "This is foolish, my lord. You and I do not love each other."

"Perhaps we could learn," he said, his voice rising in such desperation that she retreated a few steps. "Don't you understand, Eloise? We are both ruined in Society's eyes. We have no choice but to escape London and live our lives in obscurity."

"Leave London?" she repeated in disbelief. Not to mention Drake, who would certainly have a word or two to say in the matter. Something about this whole proposal did not make sense. "As flattered as I am by your offer, I cannot accept."

"But I need you, Eloise." His cheeks were flushed with emotion. "Actually, I need a wife," he confessed miserably. "My uncle lent me the money to repay my debts only on the condition that I marry a decent woman within a month."

Eloise truly wanted to throttle him. "And here I was ready to forgive you, to pity you, you jackanapes. Besides, I'm not a decent woman, as of last night. You'll have to find someone else."

He sank down onto the sofa, his head in his hands. "No decent lady wants to marry a cheater, Eloise. You have to help me. I'm bloody desperate."

A few weeks ago she would have softened at the sight of his hopelessness, but now she felt, well, she felt sorry for him, but not enough to marry the silly fool. "Pull yourself together, my lord," she said in a gruff voice, marching to the door. "We have a wedding to plan."

"Ours?" he said hopefully, lifting his head.

She studied him in vexation. "Your sister is getting married, not us. Furthermore, it seems to me you need a mother more than a wife."

"Will you help me?" he asked, rising to follow her.

"To find a mother?"

"No." He frowned. "A wife."

"How am I supposed to do that?"

"Nobody wants anything to do with me anymore," he said in a fretful voice. "Not even you, Eloise, whom I considered to be my rock, my anchor."

"Your rock was apparently set on a shifting shoal."

"You aren't going to tell your new protector about my offer, are you?" he asked fearfully. "I mean, I wouldn't want him to turn violent on me."

Eloise twisted the doorknob. "I won't say a thing on the condition that you behave properly until Thalia is married. Agreed?"

"Do I have a choice?"

She opened the door onto the hallway. Thalia and the servants who had congregated to listen scattered like insects exposed to sunlight. Behind her she heard Lord Thornton mutter, "Damn Drake Boscastle. How can a mortal man compete with the devil himself?"

He couldn't, Eloise thought with a sigh of resignation. Nor could a mortal woman resist him.

Chapter Twenty-seven

⚜ ⚜

Later that same evening Freddie stood in Drake's private study, recounting every word, with a touch of East End embellishment here and there, of the scene he had overheard between Eloise and Lord Thornton.

Drake rested his head back against the caned chair, his angular face hard and forbidding in the candlelight. In fact, Freddie thought, his lordship looked downright demonical in a certain shadow, and a sane man would not want to cross him when his features took on that sinister aspect. But then Freddie was no moron, no matter what his father had called him on the day that he'd left home.

He'd gotten on Lord Drake's good side from the start. He rubbed a speck of dust off the desk with his sleeve, hiding a grin of self-satisfaction. Freddie had a grand vision of himself as the head footman in a house like this. Let his father call him a moron when his firstborn son was parading about in silver-braided knee breeches. He might even get himself a powdered wig to wear over the mop of flame red hair that he'd inherited from his gin-sop sire.

Drake tapped his pen on the desk. He was furious, Freddie could tell, even though he kept the lid on his temper. "Describe to me again Miss Goodwin's reaction to this proposal," he said in a deceivingly unaffected tone.

Freddie snorted. "God love her, she was beside herself, she was. Almost heaved him out the window like a chamberpot full of old piss, she did."

Drake's finely molded mouth curved upward at the corners. "A chamberpot full of old piss. My, my, Freddie, who would have ever thought you were a poet?"

Freddie broke into a full grin. "She slapped him, too, right across the chops."

Drake dropped his pen. "You witnessed this through the door?"

"Hell, no, but I heard it. Sounded like a jawbreaker, too. I've never seen her raise a hand in anger before so I reckon she'd saved it up to give him a good one."

"You did not see her today, either," Drake pointed out, clearly in a black mood over what Freddie had told him. And what normal male wouldn't react in the same way?

"Look, the woman turned him down, whether I saw it or not," Freddie said. "She told him plain enough that he needed a mother, not a wife."

Drake chuckled reluctantly. He could easily picture Eloise giving Thornton the set-down he deserved. The man was a coward and ne'er-do-well, but what had prompted his sudden proposal to Eloise? How dare he return to the household he'd abandoned and assume she would marry him? He hadn't shown her the least consideration before. Had he been secretly lusting after her all those months she had worked for him?

"Is she alone with him now?" he asked suddenly, surging to his feet.

"She's helping Miss Thornton get ready for a party."

"What party?" Drake asked, his hand already on the bellpull.

"Lord Mitford's, I think."

Drake smiled slowly. Lady Mitford was a close friend of Emma's who was always pestering him and Devon to attend her dreary affairs in the hope of marrying off one of her insipid debutante nieces. Devon frequently accepted her invitations because he was an outgoing, playful type who had a talent for bringing out the best in even the most tiresome females. Drake had attended once and had practically dropped dead from boredom.

"Are you planning to go, too?" Freddie asked eagerly.

Drake laughed. "Damn right I am. Perhaps I'll even invite my cousin Gabriel to add a little pepper to the pot. Sir Gabriel has a legitimate grudge against Lord Thornton. He caught him cheating at cards and challenged him to a duel."

"No wonder they call you a devil, my lord," Freddie said in heartfelt admiration. "You'll have the two of 'em at each other's throat while taking care of private matters."

Drake didn't bother to deny it. He'd intended to take Eloise to a play tonight, and perhaps even convince her to spend the night with him afterward. And he hated to do it, but sooner or later he would have to introduce her to his family. He thought he'd start with Heath, the brother least likely to make her feel uncomfortable. Grayson was likely to overpower her. Unfortunately the formality would have to wait. Fortunately Drake was of a malleable enough character that the change in plans did not disturb him in the least. He wouldn't be a

Boscastle if he let a little competition get in his way. He looked forward to a satisfying evening.

Eloise was privately amazed that Lord Thornton had the gall to show his face in public after his social disgrace. But, she reminded herself, she was in no position to judge. Lord and Lady Mitford's small party tonight marked her last official appearance in London as an invisible companion; even at Thalia's wedding Eloise would be expected to remain behind the scenes.

As was her custom, the moment that she reached Lord Mitford's town house, she separated from Thalia and Sir Thomas and went directly to sit with the other wall-flowers in attendance—lady's companions, spinsters, and unsuccessful debutantes who pretended not to mind their neglected status. She wondered idly how long it would take before Society discovered that she'd become the mistress of a notorious rakehell.

Regrettably she did not have to wonder for very long. No sooner had she taken her seat than the seven other women already present subjected her to petrifying stares worthy of Medusa.

"Good evening, ladies," she said, fixing her own gaze on the dance floor. Thalia was dancing happily enough with her betrothed. Lord Thornton had presumably gone off in search of a willing bride to solve his woes. "How was your stay in Sussex, Mrs. Burton?" she asked one of the senior matrons as a matter of courtesy.

The pasty-faced woman granted her a sly grin. "Not as exciting as your stay in London has been lately. Or so we've heard."

All but one of the other ladies twittered like a flock of sparrows eyeing a tasty ladybird. Eloise decided to ignore the rude remark and take the high road. "Well, one cannot believe everything one hears."

Another woman who served as a companion and was a few years younger than Eloise murmured, "If we believed only half of what we've heard about you, it would be scandal enough."

Eloise compressed her lips. High road, she reminded herself. Just because she'd become a fallen woman did not mean that she had to grovel in the dirt with her critics. "The weather is unseasonably warm this time of year, isn't it?" she asked in a pleasant tone.

Mrs. Burton snickered. "I'd say it was positively scorching in certain parts of the city for certain people."

Eloise managed a strained smile. "Perhaps you should return to the cooler climes of the north country, dear."

The other ladies exchanged glances. They may not be members of the ton, or wives of distinguished gentlemen, but they maintained their own social standing within their select group. Eloise's leap into mistressdom, with a highly desirable lord and all its attendant wealth and luxuries, had put their collective noses out of joint. Only if she'd married above herself would they have resented her more. It was not likely that her protector would make her an honest woman, but such things did happen. Boscastle certainly had the means to support Eloise for life even if, as expected, he discarded her after his initial infatuation wore off.

Her more gentle-hearted friend, Mary Weston, touched her wrist. Mary was in her thirties, steadily employed as a companion, but she had not allowed her status to sour her disposition. "They're only jealous, Eloise," she said softly. "Never mind what anyone says."

Mrs. Burton *hrrmph*ed. "Jealous? Disgusted and dismayed is what we are. What will she do when her protector tires of her? No decent family will have her in their home. Nor will a certain academy."

Eloise's simmering temper neared the boiling point. How dare the old harridan mention the academy. Oh, that was unfair. "I have turned down that position, Mrs. Burton."

The woman smirked. "Your loss perchance will be my gain. I have applied and passed a heartening initial interview with Lady Lyons."

Eloise might have done something truly dreadful at that moment had Drake not suddenly materialized from the sea of dancers. Her heart leapt into her throat, and invisible fire raced through her body as his dark masculinity cast a spellbound shadow over the room.

He was the antithesis of what a gently bred woman should desire. A wicked vision who had stepped out of her most private fantasies. She heard the women around her gasp in scandalized shock. Or was it a delight they could not dare express? Was Eloise the only one of them who perceived that behind his veil of alluring darkness flickered the faintest spark of light? She could not be sure if she had only deceived herself. That elusive glimmer of goodness might be as misleading as the will-o'-the-wisps that ill-fated fairy-tale heroines followed in the woods only to be lost themselves forever.

She was already lost. She loved the devil no matter what he turned out to be.

He sauntered up to the small awestruck group with the indolent grace of a wolf surveying a herd of deer. There wasn't a woman among them, young or old, who did not secretly respond to the unabashed sensuality that radiated from him.

But his gaze singled out one woman alone. He looked only at the voluptuous brown-haired beauty he had chosen as his mate.

He held out his hand to her. "Dance with me."

It wasn't as much a request as a playful command, a seductive reminder of the first night they had met. She rose, strangely not feeling embarrassed, but elated. His sensual mouth quirked up in a smile of pleasure.

The tips of her fingers tingled as his hand closed over hers. She was aware only of him. She didn't care what anyone said about her. One look at his hard, chiseled face, and she gladly surrendered herself. It thrilled her that he did not bother to hide the dark longing in his eyes. He had chosen her.

"What a pleasure to see you again, Miss Goodwin," he said in a warm, deep voice. As if they had not been naked in each other's arms only a few hours ago, lost in fierce lovemaking. "I had no idea you were attending the party tonight."

The rest of the world faded away. Eloise could not miss the note of disapproval in his voice that she had not notified him of her plans.

"I'm surprised to see you here, my lord," she said as he drew her around the dance floor. "And I had no idea myself that I would be coming."

He subjected her to an intense look. They were out of earshot now, and the performance he had put on did not need to be prolonged. His hand tightened possessively around hers. "I heard Thornton proposed to you today," he said, his square jaw taut with emotion. "Did you think I wouldn't be here?"

She realized suddenly that he was leading her from the ballroom, and without the least discretion. All she could do was walk at his side, his hand gripping hers, pretending that it was the most normal thing in the world for a lady's companion to be lured away by a scoundrel. "I thought we were going to dance. And how did you hear about Thornton?"

He didn't answer, guiding her through a door to a long darkened hallway. "Oh," she said, her eyes narrowing, "it was Freddie, wasn't it? Well, I hope he told you that I—"

Seconds later she was pulled into an oak-paneled study and into his strong arms. He kicked the door shut and locked it as he kissed her, his body molded to hers. She knew they'd been discussing something, but suddenly it didn't seem important.

"What are you doing here?" she whispered, her hands locked around his neck to draw him even closer. "This isn't the kind of party I'd think you would enjoy."

He gave her a slow, wicked smile. "I was looking for a woman," he replied as he ran his hands expertly down the sides of her opulent breasts to the firm cheeks of her bottom.

"What do you want this woman for?" she demanded, struggling to draw her breath. Her heart had been racing since the instant she'd seen him tonight.

"I'll show her in a moment." He cupped her arse in his hands with a deep groan, drawing her belly against his arousal. "You don't happen to know where that idiot Thornton went, do you? I have a feeling he's avoiding me."

He caught her by the wrist and led her with him across the room. The musty aroma of books and brandy hung in the darkness, a potent background perfume to their desire. With a shiver of forbidden expectation

Eloise realized that he was going to seduce her in a stranger's study, and she was going to let him. In fact, she felt faint with anticipation.

"I have no idea where Lord Thornton is," she managed to whisper, "but I happen to know he's looking for a woman, too. Do you think it could be the same one?"

His blue eyes darkened to smoldering black obsidian. "If it is, he can't have her, although I understand he asked. Do you know if she accepted?"

She trembled as his eyes pierced hers, the naked passion he allowed to show weakening her knees. "Would she be standing here with you now if she had?" Or barely standing.

"Thornton would not be still alive if she had," he replied in a rough voice, using his lower body to walk her backward.

"Did you really come here just to see me?" she asked softly, stumbling over a footstool.

He caught her swiftly. "You know I did. It's been torture."

"Torture?" she teased. "It's only been a few hours."

He grinned. "I meant that being at the party was torture. Do you know how many elderly ladies have asked me to dance? For some reason I appear to have been marked by a group of extremely aggressive widows."

"Did you turn them down politely?" she asked, laughing at him.

"I didn't turn them down at all," he replied. "I barely managed to escape with my shirt. I don't know why the ancient ones aren't afraid of me. They seem to regard me as an adventure."

"You'll have to keep your promise to dance with them."

"Couldn't I just make a quiet escape?"

"Perhaps they'll forget," she whispered, lifting her hand to his face.

He grasped her around the waist. "I had to see you again. I couldn't stay away."

"I'm very glad."

"I've never—"

Never what? she wondered. But before she could ask, his mouth covered hers, sensuous and demanding, setting her blood on fire. His tongue thrust between her lips in burning possession. His hands roamed over all the secret hollows of her body, her breasts, her bottom, pushing between her thighs to where she ached for him to touch her.

He exhaled against her throat. "Ah, this is what I need, to feel you there again. I've been imagining being inside you again all day. Did you think about me, too?"

"You know I did," she whispered, beyond shame, her body quivering in response. She could feel her heart shaking, her breasts swelling inside her gown. Even his warm breath against her skin became a caress. He was so open in his passion, so masterful she could deny him nothing. It was almost a relief when she felt him pulling her to the sofa, lowering her over his muscular forearm to the cushions.

"We're going to be missed," she whispered, not really caring as she wound her arms around his waist. His body felt warm and hard. She wanted to slide her hands under his shirt to touch his chest and draw him closer.

"I could stop if you insist," he murmured.

She moaned unwillingly as he leaned over her, the most sexual man she had ever met. "Most definitely not. One is obliged to finish what one starts."

"You're so sensible, Miss Goodwin," he murmured. "Now spread your legs like a good mistress."

He unhooked the back of her gown, then her corset, shoving the satin sleeves and boned undergarment to her waist. The act temporarily imprisoned her arms. As her heavy breasts tumbled free, he bent his head and sucked hard at each of her nipples in turn. The fierce pleasure stole her breath. She felt wicked and wanton, hot sensation flooding the private places of her body with humid desire. It was all she could do not to beg him for relief.

"Oh, my God," she whispered. She raised her hands to stroke his powerful shoulders. "Do you know what people are going to say about me?"

He licked wet circles around her tender, elongated nipples. "They should see you now, shouldn't they?"

She laughed, completely under his spell, every nerve ending in her body wound tight. "No, you devil."

He raised his head to smile at her. Before she even realized it, he had rucked her skirt up to her waist and kneed her thighs apart. She closed her eyes as he lowered his head to kiss her belly. She strained upward, not caring how crude she must look. She didn't think she could take another second of waiting.

"Do you want something?" he asked wickedly.

She opened her eyes, helplessly exposed to him, her sex lips pulsing and slick. "Yes. You."

"Are you wet enough?" he whispered.

"What do you think?" she asked fretfully.

"There's only one way to find out."

He tangled his fingers in her thicket of curls, then slipped his hand lower over her tender mound. A shudder of anticipation rocked her. His strong fingers plunged into her sex, stretching her, spreading her open for his penetration. She bit her lip to smother a cry. She needed him inside her. She arched her hips to relieve the aching pressure only to feel him slowly withdraw his hand from her cleft.

"Devil man," she whispered, her senses throbbing in panic. "Don't stop . . ."

He rolled back onto his feet, smiling down at her delicious, disheveled appearance. This was how he wanted her, he thought. He could practically bring her to orgasm with a look.

He was almost over the edge himself. Who would not be undone by her eagerness to please? He unfastened his pantaloons and leaned over her. She whimpered as he flexed his hips and teased her plump inner folds with his engorged shaft. His thumb circled the sensitive nub of her sex until she writhed, her eyes dilated with desire. Still, he withheld what she wanted.

"Not yet," he whispered, staring down at her in satisfaction.

She sobbed, her eyes glazed. "When?"

He clenched his jaw, his own control slipping as he brought her closer and closer. He waited, his fingers toying with her nipples until he felt her quiver in climax, her body straining into his. Only then did he follow the wild desire of his body. His eyes black, he gripped her hips and drove his thick cock deep inside her. Her cries of helpless pleasure enhanced his own enjoyment. Too late he reminded himself that his passion for her could produce a child.

"My God," he whispered in a rough-edged voice. "I've never known anything like this before."

She wet her lips, her eyes locked with his. Her inner

muscles gloved him, tightening around his shaft as he thrust deep into her warmth.

She shivered, half-trapped in her clothes, lifting her bottom to meet the rhythm of his languid thrusting. He was in control and let her know it. He ground his hips in slow deliberation, prolonging their pleasure. She aroused him with her eagerness, her hunger, more than any other woman he had known. Left to his own hedonistic devices, he would have loved her all night long, would have devoted himself to her discovering her secret desires.

But a muted noise impinged on his concentration from somewhere in the house. He laced his fingers with hers and lifted her hands above her head. Her breasts pressed against the damp wall of his chest. She closed her eyes, quivering beneath him.

He withdrew, intoxicated, and for a moment neither of them breathed, immersed in pure sexual pleasure. Then she arched her spine and raised her hips to draw him back inside her. He heard footsteps outside the door and without a moment's hesitation, impaled her to the hilt. She gasped, her legs locked around his waist to withstand the force of his thrust. He closed his eyes, and his mind went blank. Moments later he felt the blissful release of his seed pouring into the depths of her body, their hands still joined.

"I want you with me all the time," he whispered fiercely.

She trembled, sinking back onto the sofa.

Under other circumstances he would have gentled her in the afterglow. But even as his racing heart resumed a normal rhythm, he pulled her off the sofa and onto her feet. He did not need to explain the reason for his haste.

She was completely presentable before he'd rebuttoned his pantaloons and smoothed back his hair.

He drew her briefly into his arms at the door. It occurred to him again that he'd taken no care to prevent making a child. He'd always used precautions in the past—what was happening to him? Why did the possibility of a pregnant mistress hold this sudden appeal? Did he want to follow in Grayson's footsteps?

Previously when he had envisioned his future, it was as if he were staring into a lonely veil of darkness. For the first time he saw a tantalizing glimmer of light in the shadows. Was he holding the source of that light in his arms?

He should have run for his life the moment he met her. It was too late now, he thought as he buried his face in her neck.

"I thought I heard someone in the hall," she whispered, pushing him away. "We can't stay in here all night."

Sensible. She brought him back to earth, or was it back from hell? He breathed in her clean scent, then reluctantly released her.

"You go first. I'll give you time to return to your group of stone-faced spinsters." He unlocked the door and gazed outside to make sure she had free passage. "Go."

She edged around him. He thought that any man who looked closely enough at her would guess that she had just been tumbled. "You aren't going to break your promise to dance with your admiring widows?" she asked over her shoulder.

"No, I'm going to break Thornton's"—he stopped at

the look she gave him—"bad habits. I'm going to find Horace and have a serious talk with him."

She backed away from him. "Well, please don't conduct your conversation in the fishpond this time."

"Don't worry about Horace, sweetheart," he said, leaning against the door jamb with a languid grace that belied how badly he wanted to chase her. "I promise to be a perfect gentleman."

Chapter Twenty-eight

❧ ❧

Horace gazed at the dark, lean-muscled figure that strode toward him like a predator and decided that his death was at hand. "Boscastle," he said, swallowing over the painful lump in his throat. "My God, it's good to see you again. I expect you thought I'd never come back. I was going to stop by tonight and see you, but now that you're here . . ."

For a dangerous moment he allowed himself to be deceived by Drake's easy smile. Was it possible? Could he fool a Boscastle and escape the wrath he knew he deserved?

"What I thought," Drake said, almost conversationally as he shoved Horace with one hand into a darkened alcove, "is that you had enough sense to remain in hiding. And"—he twisted Horace's neck cloth around his wrist—"that if you were stupid enough to return, you would realize there are certain people you could never, *ever* cross with impunity."

"C-Cross you? I'd never dream of crossing—"

Drake pulled the neck cloth tighter. "Not only did you try to cheat my cousin, but you left me to defend your damned honor."

"I meant to thank you for that, by the way—"

"And you abandoned your entire household to creditors, leaving two young women defenseless and alone."

"Well, now I'd hardly call Eloise defense—" He fell into terrified silence at the cold fury on Boscastle's face. "By God, you're right. I am an utter cad. Kill me now. But, please, make it as painless as possible."

Drake shook his head in disgust. "I really ought to."

Horace thought he was going to faint. He'd never understood why Boscastle had befriended him in the first place. It had to be because of his deceased brother. He knew he was a complete idiot, and that he hung precariously on the lowest rung of the social ladder.

He swallowed convulsively. "You've been good to me, Boscastle. You were a friend when I did not deserve one. But I want you to realize that I'm reformed, a man reborn—"

Drake's eyes glittered dangerously. His hand twisted the neck cloth like a noose. "I don't care if you've been resurrected as the Lord himself, you are to leave Eloise alone."

Horace trembled. He would later tell himself that he imagined the scent of sulfur and brimstone in the air. "Do you think that I would dishonor her?" he choked out, wisely deciding not to point out that Drake's conduct could be interpreted to have done just that.

"You have certainly dishonored yourself," Drake retorted.

"I—I didn't realize," he said haltingly. "I didn't think a man of your stature would care about my sister's companion. I didn't know, Boscastle. I swear it. I'll never talk to her again. I'll lick your bloody boots clean, but please don't kill me. I didn't know you cared about her that much. She's a lovely woman, a bit of a bully at times, but I won't go near her if it upsets you. I just didn't realize that you cared."

Drake released his grip, his face dispassionate. The relief in Horace's eyes would have been laughable but for one stunning fact—until the words were flung in his face, Drake had not realized how much he cared about Eloise, either. He hadn't dreamed that he was capable of feeling such emotions for any woman. Well, it seemed as if the dark beast had finally come to rest on his shoulders. And he had a feeling it was there to stay.

Eloise had just dropped off to sleep with a contented smile on her face. Her last image of Drake as she left the ballroom was of him being waltzed about in circles by a spry, silver-haired widow who had apparently been waiting for him to make good his promise. Oh, lovely man, Eloise thought as she drifted off. What she wouldn't give right now to feel—

—a pair of bare feet burrowing between hers? She came fully awake, not daring to move or even open her eyes. She might have convinced herself that her nocturnal visitor was indeed her indecent protector, who showed every sign of being as insatiable a lover as the gossip sheets claimed.

But surely Drake had not grown such sharp toenails in a few hours' time. Nor would he sneak into her room to snuffle piteously into the pillows as this unwelcome bed partner had begun to do.

She sat bolt upright in annoyance. "Miss Thornton, *really*. What is the meaning of this inconsiderate visit?"

"Oh, El-oh-eeeze," Thalia wailed, throwing her arms around her neck and knocking her back against the headboard. "I had the most wretched dream. Hold me until the horror passes."

Eloise untangled the girl's slender arms from around her neck. "I shall do nothing of the sort. You are not a child, and I should dearly love the chance to dream myself. It is very late, and we are to awaken early for the alterations to your wedding dress."

"My wedding dress," Thalia wailed, pressing her head to Eloise's bosom like a child. "That's what gave me the wretched dream. What am I going to do?"

Eloise felt goose bumps rise to her flesh. She repressed the urge to slap the girl senseless. Her voice dropped to a stark whisper. "Don't you dare tell me that you're having second thoughts about marrying Sir Thomas again after all the trouble you've put me through."

Thalia rubbed her nose. "He seems so terribly old sometimes, Eloise."

Only because Thalia appeared to be an infant in comparison, Eloise thought rather unkindly. "He is but two years older than you. That hardly makes him an ancient. This is simply a case of bridal nerves."

Thalia made a face. "How would you know? You've never been a bride. Or are likely to become one unless you marry my brother, who by the way, was threatened by Boscastle tonight at the party. Your lover appears to have a rotten temper."

Eloise sighed. It was such a wonderful way to be awakened, really, being reminded that marriage and respectability were no longer possible to one of her disgraced status.

"You must ignore your doubts and concentrate on your upcoming nuptials," she said in a firm voice. "We have barely any time to plan the ceremony and reception."

"Not much more than a week," Thalia murmured, biting her thumbnail.

"What?" Eloise whispered, certain she had misunderstood.

Thalia gave an enormous yawn. "Didn't I tell you? Thomas has gotten a special license so we can be married here in London at his mother's house. It's vastly extravagant of him, but I think he's afraid I'll change my—"

Eloise slid out of bed. "It isn't possible. There's so much to do."

"You'll manage, Eloise. You always have. That's one of the reasons I thought you'd make a good wife for Horace." She settled back against the pillows. "I suppose you're right. Second thoughts aren't unusual when a young girl is giving herself away for life. But then you've already given yourself—"

Eloise had stopped listening. There was so much to do that her head was spinning. She'd hoped to steal a few afternoons to spend with Drake in the upcoming days. He wanted to find her a suitable house, to have her portrait painted on Bond Street, to take her to the theater and to the park. He wouldn't be pleased if she kept putting him off, but with Thalia showing signs of balking, he would have to understand.

Thalia curled up under the covers. "Don't be upset, dear Eloise. If I refuse to marry Thomas I can always follow in your footsteps. You could serve as my companion in my dotage. Then again, I don't really mind his kisses. Perhaps marrying him won't be as bad as I fear."

Eloise stared down at her in coldhearted resolve.

"Not marrying him will be worse than anything you've ever feared, I guarantee you."

Thalia pulled the covers up to her chin, not looking at all intimidated.

"Horace is right, Eloise. You can be quite a bully at times. May I sleep in your bed tonight?"

"Only if you promise not to change your mind again."

"I do love you, Eloise. And I wish that my brother deserved you."

Eloise sat down on the bed and sank back against her pillow. "Then go to sleep, and tomorrow we'll have to see about trimming your toenails."

Drake had gone straight home right after the party. It was the first time in a year or so that he hadn't felt compelled to stay up until dawn chasing some worthless distraction. If he'd had his way, though, he and Eloise would be drinking champagne naked in bed and watching the sun rise over her beloved city.

He'd have his way soon enough, he supposed. He'd already made several inquiries about setting up a proper house for her. He had several friends who leased lodgings for their mistresses in Half Moon Street. It was quiet, close enough to the park and shopping to please a woman. But it wasn't close enough to please him, and somehow the idea of putting her in a place that would be used only for sexual convenience felt wrong.

Wrong. Sweet God above. Was Mildred's accusation of belated morality true? Although one could hardly accuse him of morality after what he and Eloise had done behind closed doors tonight. But it hadn't been enough. He'd wanted to stay with her afterward, to find her beside him in the morning when he rose. He'd wanted to talk and just, well, just be with her.

He stopped at the door of his study and saw two men conversing in the candlelight. The tall younger man arranged casually across the sofa was his brother Devon. The heavyset older man standing before the fireplace was Evan Walton, the Bow Street detective whom Drake had asked to investigate the whereabouts of the man who'd threatened Eloise.

"Good evening," he said, tossing his greatcoat and gloves onto the chair. "I assume you have something to tell me."

The detective came right to the point. He appreciated the extra money he was paid to supplement his poor salary. He also held the Boscastle family in high esteem. "We found him, my lord. He was staying in a nice enough hotel on Dover Street, which he could ill afford. Were it not for the fact that he refused to pay his rent, thereby infuriating the landlady, we might never have learned his location at all."

Drake felt his anger rising. He'd hoped to enjoy a few private moments with Ralph Hawkins before the police took over. "Is he at the station?"

"Unfortunately, no. He left London on the stage to Bath. I thought you'd be glad to see the last of him."

"You're certain he's gone?" he asked, frowning.

"Well, he got into a ruckus with a post boy and was almost asked to get off the coach. It appears he quieted down. That's the last we heard of him."

"I see." He couldn't fault the detective's work, but he would have felt better if he could have confronted Ralph

Hawkins in person and dealt with him to his own satisfaction.

"We'll keep a watch out for him, in case he returns," the detective said. "Sorry to disturb your evening, but I thought you'd want to know."

"I did, Walton," he said. "You've done a good job. Thank you."

Several moments of silence elapsed. Drake glanced questioningly at his brother as the other man left the house. Devon was reading a newspaper, his neck cloth loosened, his chiseled face scrunched in a cynical frown. "Word from Vienna?" he asked, leaning up against the desk.

"No." Devon looked up distractedly. "Quite a few words about you, though. Did you know that Maribella St. Ives is in negotiations with the Earl of Chesleigh?"

"Devon, you did not come to my house to read me the scandal sheets before I went to bed. What are you doing on my sofa at this hour of the night?"

"Nothing, really. I played cards with Gabriel at the club. I thought I'd stay here tonight if you don't mind."

"Why aren't you at your own house? God, don't tell me there's a cuckolded husband on the hunt for you?"

Devon threw down the paper and rose, stretching his arms over his head. "It's because of Emma, if you want to know the truth. I don't know how much longer I can stand living with that woman and her academy. She's got my entire home full of young girls about to be launched. She's holding a mock house party to teach them social niceties."

"Your house full of young women?" Drake sent him a mocking smile. "Exactly how does this present a problem?"

"It's a problem when one is forbidden to look, touch, or tease," Devon said grumpily, sinking back down onto the sofa. "It's bloody utter torture, actually. It brings out all my bad instincts."

Drake shrugged, pushing away from the desk. "Then stay here. I'm going to bed."

Devon's voice stopped him at the door. "There's another rumor going around town about you," he said in a more sober voice.

Drake turned. "Oh?"

"It's only the men at the club," Devon replied, looking decidedly uncomfortable. "Some of them are taking bets on how long your new mistress will last."

"That's nothing new."

"Yes, but a few others, not me, mind you, are wagering that this is the woman who's going to lead you to the altar."

"Let them wager," he said, and walked out the door, his face faintly amused.

Devon stared after him in a mild state of shock. That wasn't the vehement denial he'd expected. In fact, it sent a chill right down his back. If he'd made a similar comment only a few months ago, Drake would have laughed him into the ground. But now—there went another chill. God knew what had gotten into Devon's sibs lately, nearly all of them married and happy about it, too. Whatever their ailment, he hoped to heaven it was not contagious, and that Drake wasn't showing symptoms of their horrifying malady.

Eloise spent the next few days in a state of flurried activity. Not unreasonably, Sir Thomas had insisted on moving up the date of his wedding, which meant that his bride-to-be had less opportunity to change her mind. Nor was there time to send out proper invitations, or even to arrange a decent reception. Of course, St. George's in Hanover Square as the church of choice was out of the question.

True to form, Lord Thornton proved himself to be of absolutely no help. He avoided Eloise like a case of cholera, apparently convinced that if he so much as accidentally bumped into her, Boscastle would draw and quarter him. Drake interrogated her about him the few times she was able to meet him during that frantic week.

"Did he talk to you at length?" he demanded as they strolled through a bookshop on Bond Street.

"He hasn't uttered two words to me since the dance," Eloise replied. "Whatever you said that night must have scared him to death."

"He hasn't touched you in any manner?"

"Most certainly not," she laughed, ducking under a ladder.

"Did he want to?"

Eloise paused. "How would I know? He goes mute when I enter a room."

He met her on the other side of the ladder. "But did his eyes suggest that he wanted to touch you?"

She backed into the circular counter, laughing again. "I believe he was staring at his feet the last time I looked."

"And what were you staring at?" he asked.

"At him." She shook her head as if realizing what he'd tricked her into saying. "I mean I was staring at him staring at his feet."

He glanced past her suddenly and realized that a group of his friends had gathered around the corner to spy on him and Eloise. He frowned, and the young men quickly picked up their books and began to peruse the pages in avid concentration.

"We've been discovered," he said in annoyance.

"I'm sorry," she said, obviously not certain what he meant.

"It was bound to happen." He grasped her elbow and guided her back against a bookshelf. "Actually *you've* been discovered."

Her eyes widened under the brim of her bonnet. "Doing what?"

He swung around without warning. Five opened books lifted simultaneously to conceal the curious stares of the young men holding them. Eloise looked at this audience in amusement until Drake's cold glare sent the quintet scurrying off into all directions.

"What was that about?" she whispered. "Do you know them?"

"Unfortunately. They must have followed us here. I don't think that between them all they can read three words." He took her elbow again and walked her from the shop onto the pavement.

"Do people always stare at you like that?" she asked, trying to peer around him to see if he'd been followed.

"They're not looking at me," he said in irritation. "They're hoping to get a good look at the woman who has usurped Maribella St. Ives."

"The woman who—"

"You," he said, his scowl deepening. "You've already been described in the papers."

"Have I?" she asked, not sounding anywhere as displeased as she ought to. "What am I described as?"

"I thought you didn't approve of such filth."

"I don't," she said, lowering her gaze as one of Drake's friends exited the bookshop and glanced at her.

Drake led her toward his carriage. "You were described as a mysterious young goddess who challenged the supremacy of Hera and won."

She laughed in delight. "Really?"

His eyes glittered warmly. "Yes."

"What did I win?"

He lowered his head to hers, then narrowed his eyes as a tall familiar figure crossed the street toward them. "Don't turn around," he said under his breath. "Just climb into my carriage and turn your head the other way."

She tensed, whispering, "Your brother again?"

"Worse." His arm gripped her with instinctive possession. He might have been willing to play his cousin Gabriel's harmless games of rivalry in the past, but Eloise was different. She wasn't some squire's daughter they were trying to impress, or a sack race to be won. He granted Gabriel a passing glance of acknowledgment, but there was enough male warning in it that his cousin slowed his pace.

"Coming or going, cousin?" Gabriel asked pleasantly.

Drake kept his hand firmly on Eloise's shoulder, exerting pressure when he sensed she wanted to look around. "We were just leaving, Gabriel. Sorry we don't have time to chat."

Gabriel smiled. "Well, in that case, don't let me delay you. It's a pleasure to see you again, Miss Goodwin." He glanced down at the paper folded in his hand. "Or is it 'goddess'?"

"It's neither to you, Gabriel," Drake said bluntly. He

turned his back pointedly as his carriage rolled up to collect them.

"I didn't mean any offense," Gabriel said with a wicked grin. He watched Drake guide Eloise into his carriage. "I merely wanted to offer you both my congratulations."

Chapter Twenty-nine

※ ※

Eloise woke up before dawn on the morning of Thalia's wedding. Her first act, after completing her own toilette, was to reassure herself that the bride-to-be had not disappeared during the night. Thalia had seemed so complacent during the past few days that Eloise was a little afraid to trust her. But there she was, snoring fitfully in her bed when Eloise peeped in. There were no other bags packed except for the modest wedding trousseau sitting by the armoire.

She's getting married, Eloise thought in elation. She didn't think she could be more relieved if she were taking the holy vows herself.

The small private wedding was to be held at Lady Heaton's residence at noon on Cork Street. It would not be an elaborate affair. Eloise would have been satisfied if the baronet and Thalia had been married on the pavement. Just as long as the ceremony took place.

Thalia refused to eat breakfast. She wept into her teacup and wished aloud that her mother were alive to see this day. "Well, dear," Eloise said distractedly, "at least your brother will be there to give you away. You'll be represented by one member of your family."

Thalia rose from the table, still in her dressing robe. "I

think I'd almost prefer to have Freddie the footman stand in his place. He's been more like a brother to me than Horace."

Eloise rose swiftly to nip this rebellion in the bud. "That is no way to talk. Anyway, Freddie and the other servants are no longer in Lord Thornton's employ."

Thalia narrowed her eyes. "Are they working for Boscastle now?"

Eloise hesitated. "I believe they might be."

"Are you at least going to attend my wedding, Eloise?"

"It really is not done, dear, but I will if you insist." In fact, Eloise would stand at the altar and recite the damned ceremony standing on her head if need be. "Now, come on. We've only two hours before the carriage arrives to collect you. Your brother has already left ahead of us to allow you privacy to dress."

Devon poured himself a cup of steaming black coffee from the silver pot and glanced with curiosity across the table at Drake. "You're not going to the wedding, I take it?"

Drake smiled archly. "No. Thrashing the bride's brother would probably not be appreciated."

"I didn't think you'd go. You hate weddings as much as I do."

Drake nodded vaguely, sifting through the mound of letters and invitations on the table.

"Aren't you the one who said they made you suicidal?" Devon asked conversationally.

Drake folded his arms behind his head and stared up at the ceiling. "Did I?"

"Weddings invariably make women cry. I've always

wondered why. It's the groom who should be shedding tears. The mere thought of marriage makes me weepy." He glanced curiously at his brother as if to prompt an inappropriate response. "Drake?"

He glanced at Devon, his brow furrowed. "What?"

Devon paused. "Did you hear a word of what I just said?"

"Yes." Drake tossed a letter onto the table. "Weddings turn you into a waterworks."

Devon smiled uneasily. "Right. At which point you are to vigorously agree and proclaim your desire to remain a bachelor for the rest of your life."

"What time is it, anyway?" Drake asked, suddenly restless and unsure why. He wanted to see Eloise and knew she would be fulfilling her final obligations until late in the day. He wouldn't be surprised if that damned brat Thalia insisted Eloise accompany her and her husband on their honeymoon.

He would put down his foot at that point. In fact, he'd never been this patient or understanding about a woman before. It couldn't be a good sign.

"By the way," Devon said, waving a spoon in Drake's face, "I saw Maribella at Audrey's last night with her earl."

"Oh?"

Devon grinned. "She sent her best regards and mentioned she might be leaving England next week."

"All's well that ends well." Drake still could not think of the flame-haired courtesan as Mildred Hammersmith, or that she and Eloise had been rivals cum conspirators before he'd known either of them. She wanted to be known as Maribella St. Ives, and that was how he would remember her.

Devon tapped his spoon on the table. "She also told me to remind you to protect Eloise or else."

Drake did not reply. Devon dropped his spoon with a clatter. "Grayson and Jane have invited the family to dinner tonight. Would you like to come with me and leave early before the lectures start?"

"I might not be able to make it at all." Drake reached behind him for his jacket. "There's something I have to do."

Devon shoved his chair back, his face a little troubled. "I could go with you. I don't have plans for the afternoon."

"No." Drake was already to the door. "I have to do this alone."

"Do what alone?" Devon asked in bewilderment, staring into the silence that answered him.

"Heavens above!" Eloise exclaimed, backing away from the parlor window. "The carriage is already here for you, and, oh, it looks as if it's going to pour. Hurry up. You cannot be late for your own wedding."

She whirled around, realizing that she was talking to herself. Thalia had been standing behind her only a few minutes ago.

"Oh, where are you?" she called impatiently into the hallway.

"I'm right here," Thalia said in a nervous whisper, as she rearranged her lace half veil before the hallstand mirror. "Where are Thomas's footmen to attend me? It isn't proper to walk to my wedding coach unescorted."

"I've no idea," Eloise muttered, her silk-lined cloak thrown over her arm. "Please stop preening. You may do that at Lady Heaton's house."

She opened the door. The cloudy gray sky looked unpromising for a wedding, and a chill wind blew a paper across the pavement. A pie-man hurried by ringing his handbell.

Thalia took two steps forward and scowled at the serviceable if unwieldly carriage parked in the street. The coachman stared straight ahead, his shoulders slumped as he gazed into the dreary day. "Is that the best Thomas could do? It's not much better than a beer-cart."

Eloise sighed. "You'll have to take that up with him after the wedding. That is, if we make it there on time. Perhaps he's saving his nice carriage for your country drive."

Thalia stood tapping her white-satin-shod toe on the step. "Why did my brother leave so early, anyway? I never saw him come home last night."

Eloise glanced away. "I'm not entirely sure what time he came home. Are we going to the carriage or not?"

Thalia balked. "What if Horace has started gambling again?"

"Listen to me," Eloise said in an undertone. "It does not matter. You are to begin a new life as a wife and country gentlewoman. Lord Thornton shall either rise above his vices, or he shall sink."

"Who'll give me away if he doesn't show up?" Thalia asked.

"The baronet's uncle will be there. I think Lady Heaton understands that your brother's behavior is not your fault." Eloise nudged her toward the door. Major Dugdale had just emerged from his house and was fast approaching, a newspaper in hand. "Quickly. That old gossip is on his way here."

Thalia put her hand to her bare neck with a gasp.

"My mother's locket. I planned to wear it in her memory."

"We'll get it after the ceremony," Eloise said. "I'm sure Sir Thomas won't mind stopping by."

"No," Thalia said with tears in her eyes. "I want it now. I want to know that she's with me today."

Eloise glanced at Major Dugdale, then grasped Thalia's arm and dragged her back inside the house. The major pounded at the door. Thalia pounded up the stairs. Eloise began to pace the hallway.

"Hurry up," she muttered. "I know it's going to rain, and it will take forever to get there. Please hurry. Did you find it?"

There was no answer. The major appeared to have given up and returned to his house. She could hear Thalia upstairs pulling out drawers, talking to herself. A door closed from the direction of Lord Thornton's room. Then silence.

"Thalia?" Eloise called, pivoting toward the stairs. "The locket was on your dressing table this morning. You must have found it by now. Did you look on the floor?"

Silence again. And then—what was that sound? A cry? Oh, merciful heavens. What had happened now?

Eloise hesitated, then ran up the stairs to Thalia's room. The door was locked, but she could hear Thalia moving about. She pounded until the door slowly opened.

"What in the name of—"

She knew before she could finish that something was wrong. The room was in shambles, not in its usual untidy tableau of fans and feminine attire. Thalia was standing by the bed, a look of silent horror on her face.

Her light lace veil lay on the floor, and tears slipped down her ashen cheeks.

Eloise started to approach her, then a movement caught her gaze from the cheval glass in the corner. It reflected the image of a man hidden behind the door. A taunting grin lit his face as his eyes met hers. A carving knife glinted in his hand.

Eloise threw Thalia a reassuring glance, even though her own heart was thudding in fear. There were two of them against one man, she thought. They would have to keep calm. She would not let Ralph Hawkins hurt this girl.

"One scream from either of you," Ralph said, as he came forward to slam the door shut, "and I'll make you and your little lamb here sorry, Ellie."

Thalia was shivering in her thin white muslin dress. She lifted her eyes to Eloise in hurt disbelief. "You *know* this monster? Did you let him in? Have you been hiding him here?"

"Of course not," Eloise said, not moving.

"Know me?" Ralph smiled at Eloise with unmasked malice. "Does she know me? Ellie and I were going to be married once upon a time. We were a fairy-tale couple. She promised to be my bride, didn't you, love?"

"Eloise?" Thalia whispered, her voice shaking. "Is it true?"

"But you didn't marry me, did you, Ellie?" Ralph went on, not looking at Thalia. "You lost your mind."

He backed Eloise into the wall before she could answer. His voice was rising. From the corner of her eye she saw Thalia cover her ears to block out the sound. "You ruined my life," Ralph said, his mouth twisting, "made a mock of my manhood."

Fat globules of rain began to pelt the windowpanes. The temperature seemed to drop by several degrees. "You weren't a man that I could mock you," she said with a calmness that belied her racing heart. "If your life is ruined, you have only yourself to blame. And it has nothing to do with a young woman you've never met."

"I'm not worth spit to anyone at home," he said. "That's your fault."

He shoved her against the wall, his hands grasping her shoulders. "You didn't have to let it ruin your life," she whispered as his fingers tightened around her neck. The pulse in her throat beat wildly. She knew what a man was. For all their wild ways neither Drake nor any of his brothers would ever hurt or threaten a woman.

"People laughed at me," Ralph said, his face flushed with rage at the memory. "I couldn't work for years afterward. I had to move my business. Who's going to hire a man who was shamed by two women? Even the barmaids laughed when I went into the tavern for a pint. 'Where's your placard, Ralph?' they'd say. 'Any hot coals burning in your bed today?' "

The rain pounded harder against the windows. Eloise wondered how long the coachman would wait for them outside. Wouldn't he grow suspicious, knock at the door? He wouldn't sit outside in the rain indefinitely. Why had she been anxious to ignore Major Dugdale? Surely Sir Thomas would grow anxious when Thalia did not appear at the house. But the bad weather would snare traffic in the streets. He would understand, and wait. He would be patient and willing to wait for hours.

Ralph's voice snapped her from her trance. His callused fingers dug into her skin as he shook her hard. "I've spent years imagining this moment, imagining making you sorry for what you did to me. Do you like cleaning chamber pots? Is this a better life than I could have given you?"

She met Thalia's gaze in the mirror, sending the girl a silent message to be strong. "I don't clean chamber pots." She brought her hands up slowly between his outstretched arms, then slammed them down upon his wrists and pushed him in the chest. "Run, Thalia! Get out of the house now."

Her shove unbalanced Ralph, but unfortunately not long enough to do any good. Thalia hesitated, then bolted for the door. Ralph flung out his arm and caught her in the abdomen to send her sprawling across the bed. He raised the knife in his other hand, and pressed it against Eloise's throat. She swallowed reflexively. Why today? This was to be the beginning of a new life for Thalia. She tore her gaze from the sight of the girl crying quietly on the bed.

"How could you?" she demanded in a deep, indignant voice that sounded so much stronger than she felt. "It's her wedding day. She's supposed to be getting married at this very moment."

He raised his chin, sneering at her. "*We* were supposed to get married. You didn't seem to worry about missing our wedding day."

"We'll give you money," Thalia whispered, rising up on her elbow. "My brother will give you whatever you want."

"I want my pride back." He sliced a thin line from the shoulder of Eloise's padded pale blue satin gown to the flounces at the elbow of the sleeve.

She closed her eyes. There were no weapons in the room. She had returned the pistol she'd taken from Lord

Thornton's room when he'd returned home; Horace had presumably gone to Lady Heaton's house. And she had told Drake that she could not possibly see him until after the wedding breakfast. She had promised him that once she and Thalia had said good-bye, she would leave her former life behind and give him all the attention he demanded.

Surely somebody would come.

But not in time.

Her buttons scattered on the floor. "Take down your hair, Ellie," he said, the tip of the knife dipping between the warmth of her breasts. The cold metal shocked her.

Unwillingly she opened her eyes. Her gaze darted back to the bed. Thalia had hidden her face in her hands, clearly too terrified to attempt an escape. Ralph prodded her, pressing the blade to her breast. Her hair, he'd said. She raised her arms, her movements as stiff and wooden as a marionette. She was wearing Thalia's great-aunt's old-fashioned pins that pricked her scalp but kept her unruly curls in place.

She pulled them out slowly, one by one. Their dull points pricked her palms, but would not work as a weapon. Her hair fell free.

"Now, the dress," Ralph said, breathing hard.

"The dress," she repeated. The two words echoed in the room. She felt as if she were dreaming. No. This was a nightmare. She should be attending a wedding ceremony right now, then overseeing the traditional breakfast that would follow. Prawns, champagne, and paper-thin slices of mouth-watering pink ham, laughter, and congratulations. She and Thalia had not eaten a thing all morning, too nervous and rushed. Her stomach cramped now, but not from hunger. She placed her fingers around the glittering butterfly brooch that Thalia's great-aunt had left Eloise on her death. The pin slid free.

Help me, Udella, she whispered silently. You must have left me this brooch for a reason. Show me what to do with it.

Chapter Thirty

❧ ❧

Drake stood in the doorway of his house and stared out into the wet, windswept street. He wondered what Eloise was doing right now. Standing guard over Thalia to make sure she reached her betrothed's side? Or was she guarding herself from Horace Thornton? All Thornton needed was a few drinks and a sentimental setting to weaken again. Perhaps Drake should make a surprise appearance.

But it was a hell of a day for a wedding, and even worse for a walk or ride in the park. It was, however, perfect weather for making love in a comfortable bed with the woman he desired.

Damn it. He couldn't stop thinking about her. She had no idea how much he resented giving her up for even this last request. Sacrifice had never been part of his nature. He needed her, and blast her obligations. But it was another symptom of how he was changing, that he would grant her the time to fulfill what he perceived as a pointless duty. Her duty should be to him.

Why did she have to be so stubbornly loyal and dependable? Even as he pondered the question he knew that Eloise's character was the very thing that had made him fall in love with her. Well, one of the things. And it dawned on him that the Boscastles chose their mates from some deep instinct that was not as happenstance as it appeared.

He was in love. How else in God's name could he explain standing in the pouring rain like an idiot who didn't care what he looked like to the passersby who were sensibly running for cover?

Raindrops pummeled him, soaking his glistening black hair, his face, his broad shoulders. Did rain wash away sins? he wondered, breaking into a reckless grin. What had he thought a few moments ago?

It was a hell of a day for a wedding.

He spun around, practically knocking over Freddie who apparently had been standing at the ready to offer Drake his greatcoat. "Why aren't you at Miss Thornton's wedding, Freddie?" he asked, shoving his arms into the proffered sleeves.

"The staff decided we was best needed here, my lord. Besides, waitin' on all them bawling ladies couldn't possibly be as exciting as serving you. Are we are going out? To a certain Bruton Street address, perhaps?"

Drake allowed a smile to curve his mouth. "I fear I shall disappoint you if you hoped to see the darker side of life at my side. Those days are behind me."

Freddie responded to this enigmatic remark with a rather confused smile. It was clear the lad did not grasp the import of what Drake had just told him.

"Lead me into darkness or light, my lord," he said diplomatically. "I shall serve you well."

"Then begin by having my carriage brought round. And ask Quincy to lay out formal attire for when I return."

Freddie's eyes widened in anticipation. "Is my lord attending a special affair this afternoon?"

Drake grinned devilishly. "A wedding."

Freddie looked deflated. "Miss Thornton's, I gather."

"No, *my* wedding, you rascal. Now hurry up before we are both drenched like a pair of waterfront rats. It's raining in case you hadn't noticed."

Devon arrived back at Drake's town house at the height of the storm. He'd been involved in other pleasurable activities with a certain young lady from Paris. In fact, he and the oh-so-willing mademoiselle had been in the midst of a promising carriage ride in the rain when Weed, the officious senior footman to his older brother the Marquess of Sedgecroft, had interrupted them.

"Not now, Weed." He gave Weed a meaningful look through the carriage door as his young French temptress cuddled against him to get warm. Her small, apple-firm breasts rubbed his arm. "We are in the middle of a conversation."

His lanky frame huddled in his cloak, Weed remained unmoved and handed Devon a folded note from Grayson. He gazed out into the rain as Devon scanned the note in silence.

> *The Elders have met and decided that Drake should be watched due to behavior most peculiar. As you are in frequent contact with him, we have nominated you for this duty.*

" 'Behavior most peculiar,' " he said in exasperation. The note smacked of an emergency, and certainly dashed his hopes of a rainstorm seduction. He couldn't argue, but what were Grayson and his two older sibs, Heath and Emma, alias the Elders, afraid Drake might do? Did they think he might blow his brains out like poor Bertie Potter did last month? The possibilities put a damper on his desire.

Half an hour later he was dashing across the street to Drake's home in such a rush to avoid a soaking that he almost knocked over the man standing at the door. It was Evan Walton, the Bow Street detective and close friend of the family. He took one look at Walton's gruff, troubled face and prepared himself for something unspeakable.

"Did they send you here, too?" he asked, swallowing over the huge lump in his throat. He shouldn't have let Drake escape earlier. He'd known something was on his brother's mind. "Are we too late?"

"Too late for what?" Walton sounded peevish, which was understandable enough as it seemed by his sodden appearance that he'd been knocking at the door for quite some time. He was soaked all the way down to his scarlet vest.

Devon didn't bother with protocol. He opened the door without waiting for anyone to answer and ushered the detective inside. Nor did he bother to excuse himself before searching the study, then the upstairs drawing room for a sign of Drake. Four minutes later he discovered every servant in the house gathered in Drake's bedchamber.

"Dear God," he muttered grimly, hanging back in the doorway. "I think I'm too late. They're all drawn around his bed to pay their last respects."

Except that the servants bustling about the large

drafty room looked anything but respectful. Drake's valet, Quincy, was whistling a lighthearted tune as he laid out a set of formal clothes on the freshly made bed. A maidservant bustled hither and thither with a dust rag and beeswax. Another arranged a bouquet of hot-house flowers in a Wedgwood vase as if she were an artist whose life depended on the outcome.

"What the devil is going on in here?" he asked, recovering his wits.

"Oh, Lord Devon," the busty maidservant cried over her floral masterpiece as she noticed him. "Isn't it the most exciting news in the entire world?"

He stared at the bed, which clearly did not have his brother's dead body lying upon it. Furthermore, no one in the room seemed the least bit mournful—in fact, the lot of them looked downright merry.

Their unnatural cheer should have warned him. Instead, it hammered a nail of fear into the center of his carefree heart. "What news?" he demanded of the grinning maidservant, finally working up the courage to enter the room.

She whitened, darting the valet an anxious glance. "It wasn't a secret, was it?"

Quincy's mouth turned down at the corners. "Apparently not, as it was a mere *footman* who broke the news to me and not the master."

"What news?" Devon repeated, leaning his hip against the bedpost. He hadn't passed out even when he had held a friend down to have the man's toe amputated during the war. He might drop into a virgin's swoon now if what he suspected was true.

"Lord Drake is getting married," the maidservant said, busily dusting.

"Married?" he repeated in a bleak voice. "To whom?"

"Why, to his mistress, of course," she replied. "Practically one of *our* own. It's ever so lovely. Aren't you going to the wedding?" She was chatting away so much that Quincy sent her a quelling look.

"I wouldn't have gone even if I'd been invited," Devon said numbly.

He backed out of the room as if it were contaminated with the plague. And well it might have been. His siblings were dropping their sinful souls at the marriage altar like flies. God forbid it should be catching. He felt as if he should be holding a scented pomander to his nose in one hand and a Bible to his heart in the other.

He stumbled down the stairs. His first duty would be to inform the Elders. And he didn't know what the hell he'd do then. Probably stick his head in a bucket of gin for a week or hide out in Audrey's.

Walton was pacing at the bottom of the staircase. "Is Lord Drake available, my lord?" he asked gruffly.

"Not to us," Devon retorted.

The man scowled. "In that case I shall impart my information to you. I trust you will notify your brother straightaway what I am about to reveal."

Devon heard a distant rumble of thunder and thought it an appropriate background accompaniment to Drake's wedding. There should be bats in the air and coffins creaking open in all the graveyards of London. His brother and best friend might as well be dead to him forever. "What information, Walton?"

"It seems that Ralph Hawkins did not leave London at all. Another man got on the stagecoach in his place. Unbeknownst to us, Hawkins came into a little cash and paid his landlady what he owed in arrears. I thought Lord Drake ought to be made aware."

"Yes. I shall tell him immediately." That is, right after he sent a message to Grayson alerting him of a family crisis, and *if* he could find Drake. Devon did not intend to walk in on his brother's wedding. He'd probably burst into tears like a bridesmaid himself if he had to watch his favorite partner in sin getting leg-shackled.

It was the unfamiliar touch of Ralph's heavy fingers on her breast that penetrated Eloise's haze of paralyzed horror. She jabbed his wrist, three times, tore a jagged trail up the side of his neck with the bent pin of her butterfly brooch. She had stabbed him in the ear when he finally reacted, pummeling his fists at her face.

She ducked, and raised her arms to protect herself from his blows. "Go, Thalia, now. For God's sake, get out of the house while you can!"

She should have known the girl would not heed her advice. For once, Eloise was glad. Thalia launched herself off the bed and gripped a heavy ceramic chamber pot in both hands. She swung at Ralph's head with her eyes closed, then proceeded to hit him on the shoulder with the heavy vessel.

"Eloise has never cleaned chamber pots!" she cried, finally opening one eye.

He reared around, broken pieces of ceramic in his hair. Blood trickled down his ear onto his neck. Eloise swallowed and stabbed him in the shoulder for good measure. He swore at her and drew back the knife.

"Don't you dare," Thalia said through her teeth, a Valkyrie in a wedding gown. "Don't you dare touch Miss Goodwin's bodice like that again!"

He lunged at her with a feral growl. "I'll show you what I'll dare, you little bitch. I'll show you both—"

The door. Someone was at the door. Eloise was afraid to even look around, praying that the pounding from below was not the rain, nor even the coachman, who would surely not be so bold as to enter the house alone. Praying that when the knocking stopped abruptly it did not mean that whoever had been there was gone.

Chapter Thirty-one

❧ ❧

Drake hadn't guessed that anything was wrong inside the house. The waterlogged coachman had complained about the weather, women, and weddings in general. Drake did not know himself exactly what time the ceremony was supposed to begin. He hadn't paid attention when Eloise had spoken of it. He'd only cared that afterward he could have her to himself. It didn't seem at all unusual to him that the ceremony would not start on time.

Thalia wouldn't be the first bride to be late to her wedding. Ordinarily he wouldn't have given the fact that she was dallying a second thought. But he had his own wedding to attend. The special license he'd obtained on his way there was safe inside his vest pocket.

The front door to Thornton's house was unlocked, and no one answered his questioning hello. He called back for Freddie to wait outside in the carriage. If Eloise still insisted on attending Thalia's wedding, he might as well escort her himself. That way he could spirit her away the moment the vows were exchanged.

"Eloise?" he called again into the quiet house.

The storm had eased up, although the light patter of rain on the roof amplified the silence that greeted him.

He brushed off his wet coat and strode toward the parlor. "Where is everyone?" he muttered.

A noise from upstairs, the dull clatter of an object shattering, arrested him in his tracks. It could have been Thalia in the throes of a temper, but his instincts said it was not.

He ran first up the stairs to Eloise's room. One glance inside revealed that it was neat and unoccupied. Another muffled thud drew him farther down the hall to a closed bedchamber door. He was so intent on reaching it that he did not react to the familiar voice calling him from below, footsteps in the entry hall.

"Eloise?" he shouted. "Thalia? Bloody answer me! Are you in there?" He thought he heard a stifled cry. He wrenched the doorknob several times in panic.

The door was locked. He threw his shoulder up against it, heard the hinges groan, and a woman's cry for help from inside. Another shoulder joined forces with him. He glanced in gratitude into his younger brother's concerned face.

Devon stared at him. "I almost bloody killed myself to get here."

"I'm glad you did," Drake said, his jaw tense. "Ready?"

Devon nodded.

"One, two—"

Three. The door splintered open at their combined strength, the panels rent in irregular pieces. Drake had no idea what he expected to find; instinct drove him. Wedging his way between the jagged opening, he stepped over the doorsill into the room. His heart was beating hard enough to feel its pulsations through his entire body.

And if anything had happened to Eloise, his heart might as well stop beating because there was no bloody point in his life without her. Hadn't he wanted her to stay with him today? If he'd lost her—if he was too late— He blocked the possibility from his mind.

His gaze searched the room. Where was she? *Where was she?* There, beside the bed with Thalia. He reassured himself that both of them appeared safe, if clearly distraught.

His face hardened as he shifted his attention to the shabbily dressed figure backing away from him at the window. For a moment he savored the fear that flickered in the other man's eyes. Ralph Hawkins. Betrayer of women. Blackmailer. The worst kind of coward.

The man had good reason to be afraid. Drake made no effort to mask the murderous impulses that he felt. From the corner of his eye he saw Eloise pinning a butterfly brooch back on her dress. Her face looked chalk white except for a vivid red mark on her cheekbone. Ralph had struck her. The bastard had left a bruise on her face.

Drake went wild. He shoved Ralph down onto his knees before Devon could rush the two women from the room. He'd always been a fair fighter, he at least gave his opponents a decent chance, but this involved Eloise, and the groveling animal on the floor had hurt her. He pounded Ralph's head against the floorboards in a frenzy of revenge, almost afraid of the violence he felt.

Ralph was groaning incoherently, no longer attempting or even capable of attempting to fight back. Drake heard Eloise calling to him through his dazed fury. But he intended to finish this until either the man underneath him was dead, or he couldn't move. His blood was on fire with the need to avenge his woman. He would have cheerfully dispatched Hawkins to hell had a heavy but respectful hand not fallen on his shoulder.

"Lord Drake," Evan Walton said quietly.

He didn't want to stop. He didn't want to be calmed or to listen to reason. He wanted to purge all the wildness inside him in this one act of vengeance. He wanted—

"Lord Drake," Evan Walton said again, his hand firm but not restraining. "I'll take over from here. You have a wedding to attend, do you not?"

Drake half expected to find Eloise and Thalia in understandable hysterics when he stepped into the hall. But Devon, bless his charm, appeared to have settled the pair of them down. He stared hard at Eloise, afraid to ask her if he'd been too late, if Ralph had taken his revenge too far. She was brushing Thalia's hair back into a cluster of curls and rearranging the girl's veil around her pale face. His sensible, practical mistress. He thought he might be more upset than she was.

She stopped and came into his arms when she saw him; he knew by the way she trembled that she was merely hiding what she felt. He gripped her to him and closed his eyes, his voice rough with emotion. "Did he hurt you?"

"No," she whispered, burying her face in his damp shirtfront.

He exhaled into her hair. His thoughts would not settle. Thank God he'd come in time. Thank God she and Thalia had been together. He hoped to God he did not have Hawkins's blood on his jacket, that it would not stain her dress. She wouldn't have time to change, and he didn't want to wait any longer than necessary to marry her. "Are you sure he didn't hurt you?" he asked urgently.

She nodded, and he could have gladly gone back into that room to rip out Ralph's heart when he heard the catch in her voice that she could not control. He sensed she was doing her best to remain composed, but she was more subdued than he'd ever seen her. He could barely keep his own anger from flaring up again. It burned all the way to his bones. "He frightened us, that's all," she said. "But we're late—"

He drew back to grin down at her. "I know. For a wedding."

She regarded him in surprise. He studied her face in concern. A small bruise already showed on her cheek, purple-blue against her creamy skin. He wanted to keep holding her against him, not so much to reassure her as himself. "You've decided to come to the wedding?" she asked guardedly.

"Yes. Ours." The moment he said the words, he knew it was the best decision he'd ever made and he would never regret it.

"Ours?" She stared up at him as if he were entirely mad. Which he might be. But it was a light, welcome madness in contrast to his familiar mood.

Thalia and Devon were staring at him, too. He grinned again, feeling like a fool. Distractedly he ran his hand through his tousled hair. He was not accustomed to this sense of self-consciousness. "Do I look bloody awful? I feel it."

Eloise bit her bottom lip. Her eyes gleamed with tears. "You look bloody beautiful, if I do say so myself," she said brokenly, and Drake would have kissed her tears away then and there had it not been for their awestruck audience.

Devon coughed behind his fist. "I couldn't agree more, Drake. You've never looked lovelier in your life."

Drake gave a chagrined laugh. He would never stoop to admitting to his brother how much he appreciated his support. He suspected the young rascal knew. "What are you doing here, anyway? You're always showing up where you're not invited."

"The Elders sent me to spy on you," Devon said reluctantly. "You've no idea how I rushed."

"The Elders set you on me again?" Drake's gaze wandered back to Eloise as she broke away from him to lead Thalia downstairs. Family matters would have to wait. He hoped that Grayson would understand. "What did they expect you to find?" he asked in an undertone, more curious than angry.

"They were afraid you were about to do something dangerous," Devon admitted hesitantly. "Were you?"

Drake met his brother's worried look. "Eloise and I are going to be married."

Devon staggered back against the wall in mock horror. "Oh, my God, they were right."

"No brotherly hug to congratulate me?" Drake asked dryly.

"You must be joking." Devon held up his hands in the sign of the cross as if to ward off the ultimate evil. "Stay away from me. I won't be contaminated."

Drake shook his head in amusement and turned toward the staircase. "You'll probably be next, you idiot. If it can happen to me, it can happen to anybody."

Devon followed him to the banister. "Don't count on

it. The only way I'll ever get married is under threat of imminent death."

"A possibility," Drake retorted, grinning rudely.

"I'd rather be buried alive."

"That's what I said not all that long ago."

Devon braced his elbows over the balustrade. "It's not too late. We could make an escape for the coast."

"I heard that." Eloise's disparaging comment drifted up from the hall below.

"My God," Devon exclaimed. "Can you imagine her and Emma together in the same house? Life will be absolutely unbearable."

Drake paused at the bottom of the stairs. "Do me a favor. Don't tell the Elders yet."

"Why not? You can hardly keep getting married a secret."

"I could for at least a few hours, assuming you could stay quiet for that long." Drake watched Eloise escort Thalia to the door.

"What about a best man?" Devon wondered aloud.

Drake motioned Eloise to wait for him. Poor Devon looked so perplexed that he felt sorry for him. Of course Devon would be over his misery by evening. Life went on. "Freddie the footman can stand as your proxy."

"By damn, Drake. The family is going to murder me if I don't tell. You've put me in a hell of a position."

To the amazement of Eloise, and probably the anxious but patient groom, Thalia's marriage went off smoothly after its initial delay. None of the few guests commented upon the fact that the bride's wedding veil hung askew or that she had blown in from the storm almost two hours late for the ceremony.

Nor would one have ever guessed that the glowing young girl who took her vows had just bashed a vile man on the noggin with a chamber pot to save her beloved companion.

The companion would certainly never tell. Sir Thomas remarked over and over that Thalia looked radiant. So did her brother, Lord Thornton, who made his own belated appearance a few minutes after Thalia. He arrived accompanied by a handsome if somewhat on-the-shelf lady he introduced as his fiancée. He confided in Eloise that he'd met her at Vauxhall Gardens the previous evening and had proposed to her on the spot.

Eloise barely had a second to congratulate them on their sudden engagement and drink two glasses of champagne before Drake whisked her from the house. She caught one last look at Thalia standing with her new husband. Thalia glanced around Thomas and smiled at her. She smiled back.

"Duty discharged," Eloise whispered. "God bless them both."

The rain had stopped. Feeble rays of sunlight cast a gleam upon the cobbles on the street. Eloise dabbed at her eyes. Drake glanced at her in concern. The bruise on her cheek had darkened. "He'll never come anywhere near you again, Eloise," he said. "I won't ever let anything happen to you."

She gave a delicate sniff. "It's not that. Or maybe it is. I'm happy for Thalia. Sir Thomas loves her enough to overlook all her faults. I believe they will make a good life together."

"Do you believe the same for us?"

She studied his hard, masculine face. Had she ever seen such an earnest look in his eyes before? She was suddenly overcome with what she felt for him, by the realization that he wanted to marry her. It was what she had hoped for, of course, and now she had to let herself believe it. "I wasn't sure you were serious. I thought perhaps you had gotten carried away when you came to the rescue."

"I was carried away the moment I met you." He looked out into the street, his voice deep with emotion. "I wouldn't have made you a marriage proposal unless I meant it. And it had nothing to do with the fact that I found you in danger. I was already on my way to propose to you."

"Actually, you did not ever propose to me, as I recall. You more or less said we were getting married, and that was that."

He stepped out into the street to watch a hay cart trundle past them. She wasn't sure if he was uncomfortable discussing his feelings or if something had distracted him. But clearly he wasn't paying attention to her all of a sudden. What had changed his mood in the few moments they'd been talking?

"Where did my carriage go?" he muttered.

Eloise leaned around his shoulder. "There's a carriage turning around the corner now."

"That isn't a carriage," Drake said. He pulled her back onto the pavement. An elegant vehicle bearing a coat of arms and drawn by six white horses bore down on them, taking command of the street. "It's a traveling circus."

"A what?" Her voice was muted by the precise clatter of approaching hoofbeats. She was rather impressed by the bewigged coachman and imperious-looking footmen, despite the disapproval she sensed from Drake at this display. She admired those who took pride in their positions and secretly loved the splendor of the aristocracy. "Is this someone you know?"

He gave an evasive shrug, edging back toward Lady Heaton's house. "Come to think of it, we should have at least had a bite of that wedding cake. We ran off like a pair of beggars."

She glanced back curiously at the carriage. "What are you talking about? You could hardly wait for the clergyman to end the ceremony."

"Well, yes." He slapped his flat abdomen. "But I'm feeling a bit peckish now."

"For wedding cake?" she asked skeptically.

He grabbed her arm. "I'm famished for it," he said at the same instant the elder footman stepped down from the impressive carriage and strode toward them, fastidiously avoiding a rain puddle. Heaven forbid, Eloise thought, that a drop of muck should spatter those black knee breeches.

She stood in expectant silence. It was not that the footman, as imposing in his gold-braided livery as he was, intimidated her. She could hold her own with the working class, thank you, no matter how resplendently garbed. It was the fact that Drake seemed, well, a little afraid of this servant who intrigued her. Who was this man? What did he want? A crowd of pedestrians had gathered on the pavement to stare.

The stone-faced footman bowed before her and snapped his fingers over his shoulder. Another footman opened the carriage door and unfolded the steps, his movements practiced and precise.

"His lordship's carriage awaits my lady's pleasure," the senior footman announced to the street in general.

Eloise sighed in appreciation. She did love a surprise. Was this why Drake had seemed so distracted? "How thoughtful of his lordship." She glanced with a pleased smile at Drake, whose mutinous scowl looked anything but romantic. "Drake, you shouldn't have," she whispered.

He glared at the footman. "I didn't."

"Then—" She broke off as the footman practically lifted her over the steps and handed her into the spacious interior of the carriage. The leather curtains had already been drawn to ensure privacy. Drake, she noted, was following her in hard-lipped silence.

This couldn't be an elopement, she thought. It was more like being taken captive in a polite sort of way.

"Am I being abducted?" she asked Drake over her shoulder.

"We're both being abducted," he said as he settled onto the opposite seat. And by the look on his face, he did not appear to be pleased about it at all, which meant that it was as much a surprise to him as it was to her.

The carriage took off at a smart pace. Eloise lifted the curtain. Pedestrians and lesser vehicles drew to the side of the street to allow them passage. The crossing-sweepers stared and hoped for a coin to be tossed down at them.

"I assume this is the marquess's carriage," she said in an undertone.

He nodded, obviously disgruntled. "Yes. The Marquess of Arrogance has summoned us."

She glanced at his dark, displeased face. "What does that mean?"

"It means that Devon cannot keep a secret, and I'm going to strangle him."

Eloise adjusted the seams of her gloves. "A Boscastle summons." It was to be a full day of trials. "I hope that I'm not the cause of this family dissension."

He swung over to sit beside her, his smile reassuring if rueful. "My siblings and I have been at one another's throats from the day we were born. Grayson is an actor at heart. He can do nothing in half measures."

"I would hate to come between you and your family," she said haltingly.

"Let me take care of the Boscastles." He frowned, gently grazing the bruise on her cheek with his forefinger. "Does it hurt?"

"Only a little."

"I don't want you to feel anything but pleasure on our wedding day."

"We haven't—"

He silenced her with a deep, tender kiss. She should have stopped him, but it was more tempting to burrow up against his strong chest and simply forget everything unpleasant that had preceeded this moment. Of course she couldn't forget herself completely. Not in the marquess's carriage with that cold fish of a footman liable to report back every detail to his master.

She drew a breath and tilted her head back. "Are you really serious about marrying me?"

"Yes."

She shivered as he traced his knuckles down her throat, then lazily descended to the tops of her breasts. He offered safety as well as sinful pleasures. "Don't you think we should have a proper engagement?" she asked softly.

His dark gaze traveled over her. "Why?"

"It would give you time to think," she said, holding his gaze. "I was barely your mistress for a week."

His hand slid over her breasts to her belly. "Long enough to be carrying my child."

Another tremor of pleasure coursed through her. What he said was true. They had been incautious and unprepared for their passion. "You're the son of a marquess, Drake. I'm a country magistrate's daughter, a disgraced one at that."

His broad shoulders lifted in a shrug beneath his coat. "Have I ever told you that I have an absolute passion for justice? As well as for disgraced women."

"I do have a sense of fairness," she conceded, and tried not to smile. "But you know what people will think. Besides, wedding a disgraced woman is different from making her your mistress. Marriage makes everything far more complicated."

"Perhaps. But men marry their mistresses all the time. Dukes marry actresses, and I'm no stranger to disgrace. I'm also old enough to know my own mind."

She wanted to believe every word he said, and somehow if he believed it, then she could, too. "What will your friends say?"

The devilish warmth in his gaze was melting her defenses. "They'll meet you and ask me if you have any sisters. They'll talk to you and be stricken with envy. I shall have to beat them off with a police baton."

Eloise bit her lip to keep from laughing. "That's highly unlikely—I will be shunned in most circles."

"Then we will never leave the house."

She closed her eyes. He slipped his arm around her waist, his voice wickedly coaxing. "I won't give up. I'll stand outside your window morning, noon, and night begging you to marry me."

"They'll put you away if you do," she whispered, already weakening.

"Would you be so cruel as to have me confined for loving you?"

"No," she said after a long moment.

"Then the answer is yes?"

As if the rogue had ever doubted it, she thought. "Yes. It's yes. But what will your family have to say when you introduce me as your fiancée?"

His brows drew together in a frown. "Actually, I'd been hoping to avoid that part of our engagement."

Her heart seemed to drop. She felt a flush of unpleasant heat flood her face. His family would *not* approve of her, of course. He was marrying beneath him, and nothing could change that. Even his liberal-minded siblings would discourage this match. "You'd rather they didn't meet me? Am I supposed to be a secret wife?"

He took her chin in his hand. "Correction. I'd rather *you* did not meet them." He started to laugh. "I think you misunderstood me, Eloise. I'm not afraid that the Boscastles will disapprove of you. What I'm afraid of is that they'll change your mind about me."

She smiled, her brow arched. "I doubt it, but how? What could they possibly say?"

He cleared his throat. His family could recount quite a few damaging stories actually. "Just don't listen to anything they say about my wicked years."

"Your *wicked* years?" She asked in feigned shock. "And what are the current ones known as then?"

"Contented." He stared down at her, struggling to explain what he felt until he realized that she understood. The loving passion that sparkled in her eyes spoke for itself. He was humbled by what had happened between them. She had brought out a capacity for love inside him that he'd never wanted to admit. Had it been there all the time? His throat ached. "These will be called my contented years, Eloise. Because of you."

She lifted her face to his. "And mine, too," she whispered.

Chapter Thirty-two

🌿 🌿

Drake kept telling himself there was nothing he could say to adequately prepare Eloise for meeting his family. Roman gladiators must have suffered the same bewildering survival instincts when thrown to the lions. Of course, he would be there to defend his mate. Let the Boscastles rip him to shreds first. She had endured enough for one day. Every time he saw the bruise on her face he felt a red fury rise inside him and an instinctual desire to defend her again. Well, this was a different sort of battle, and they would face it together.

The carriage stopped at the elegant Park Lane mansion. Once upon a time its owner, Grayson Boscastle, the Most Honorable the fifth Marquess of Sedgecroft, had been a fun-loving scoundrel who had scoffed at convention and set London on fire with his countless indiscretions. He had been an ally in misadventures and a friend in general to his siblings.

Now, he was a faithful husband and overprotective father who took his role as family patriarch far too seriously for Drake's liking.

He glanced apologetically at Eloise as they entered the spacious, high-columned hallway. Weed's heels clicked on the marble tiles. How could he possibly prepare her for the inescapable fate of his unforgiving ancestry? "Please remember that I am not responsible for my bloodlines. And don't believe everything they tell you about me."

She was so engrossed in admiring the Italianate wall architecture that he suspected she didn't take in a single word of his warning. "I've already met your brother, Lady Stratfield, and Lady Lyons," she murmured. "I think you're exaggerating a little."

"Exaggerating." He exhaled as the double doors at the end of the endless corridor swung open. "A little."

A voice announced, "Lord Sedgecroft will receive you now."

He pulled her back. "This is your last chance. We can still make a run for it."

She glanced up at him in mild reproach. "I cannot believe this of you. Your brother is only a man, marquess or not. How intimidating can he possibly be?"

Drake laughed in defeat. "I don't know that he's intimidating, at least not to me, as much as he's—well, he's a presence. Anyway, you have to face the Boscastles *en force* sooner or later. It may as well be now."

Intimidating.

That might have been the first word that came to mind when Eloise was introduced to Grayson Boscastle, the Most Honorable the fifth Marquess of Sedgecroft. A presence? Oh, definitely. But in a very entertaining way.

She saw his resemblance to Drake instantly in his compelling blue eyes and masculine vitality, the chiseled bone structure and riveting personal magnetism. But there the similarity ended. Her Drake was dark, intense, his allure subtle and more underplayed. The marquess was a golden-haired lion of a man, his presence charismatic and surprisingly warm.

"So you're to be my sister-in-law," he said, leaning against the windowsill with a winning smile that might have left another woman breathless.

"The pleasure is mine, Lord Sedgecroft," she said in a perfectly composed voice as she met his curious gaze. He was summing her up, she thought. Judging her character on the basis of this meeting. She was surprised that she didn't feel more nervous. Her ease, she decided, was a measure of his charm, and Eloise found that her years of passing interviews had taught her how to withstand such scrutiny.

He straightened. Eloise turned her head and noticed several other figures filing into the elegant drawing room. She recognized Lady Lyons, of course, and Chloe Boscastle, with her husband, Viscount Stratfield. They were, she thought, a killingly beautiful bunch. Devon strolled in a few moments later and flung his long-boned frame across the sofa.

"Don't fault me for this, Drake. I was threatened with thumbscrews and other instruments of Boscastle torture. I had to tell him."

Drake poured himself a glass of sherry at the sideboard. "Of course you did, you coward."

"We couldn't let you elope," Grayson said, his grin magnanimous and a little manipulative.

Another woman entered the room, introducing herself quietly to Eloise as Jane, Grayson's wife. Eloise took immediately to the lovely marchioness. She possessed a straightforward appeal and gentle self-assurance that counteracted her husband's overwhelming presence.

Jane embraced her warmly. "You are a brave woman

indeed to marry our black sheep. Welcome to the family."

The beautiful raven-haired Chloe grinned with rueful humor. "If my family does not convince you that you are making a dreadful mistake before the ceremony is over. Whatever privacy you have previously enjoyed is gone."

Drake set down his drink. His smile was strained. "Ceremony? Did you say ceremony, Chloe?"

There was silence. Grayson met Drake's gaze. "Of course you'll want to be married in the family chapel. We're only waiting for Heath and Julia to arrive. The minister is already here. I do hope you don't mind that I took care of the details for you."

Eloise drew a breath at the dangerous tension in the air. Had she caused it? Not for anything would she wish to create a divide between Drake and his family. It was understandable that the marquess would at least question this marriage.

Drake's mouth curled into a sardonic smile. He lifted his glass but did not drink. "The family chapel?"

For an instant Grayson's aplomb seemed to slip. He cast an almost helpless look at his wife, Jane, who said, with a persuasive smile, "Of course. You must not drag Eloise out in public. If you elope there shall be reporters hounding you all the way home."

Drake stared down at his sherry. "I have procured a special license," he said guardedly. "I meant for it to be a private ceremony."

His statement could have been taken in many ways. Eloise held her breath and hoped it would not be a gauntlet thrown down. The last thing she desired was to start her marriage at odds with the Boscastle family. Her marriage. She was almost afraid to let herself believe it.

She would become his wife and belong to this awe-inspiring family.

"I understand your desire for privacy," Grayson said in an even-tempered voice. "That is why I believe it is best to have only the family in attendance. I would be honored if you'd agree."

It was an olive branch offered in peace, a gesture of acceptance, and perhaps, Eloise suspected, one that did not come easily to a man like the marquess. But would Drake regard it as such?

Another silence swathed the room. Drake swirled his sherry, then laughed in surrender. "How can I refuse? Eloise?"

Eloise exhaled with her entire body. "You can't."

Jane regarded her husband with warm approval, and Chloe clapped her hands in delight.

Emma rose from her chair, having remained silent until now. Etiquette was naturally on her mind. "Well, now that the place has been decided, I think that we shall have to find a suitable dress for the bride." She glanced askance at Drake. "I assume that this crucial detail has been neglected?"

"Well," Drake said, shaking his head, "I—"

"I didn't think so," Emma said with a sigh of dismay.

"The typical Boscastle male is more concerned with undressing a woman than with what she'll wear to a wedding," Devon commented from the sofa.

Emma rolled her eyes. "I'll thank you to keep your off-color remarks to yourself."

Jane swept across the room to the door. "Heavens, surely I must have something suitable in my wardrobe."

"Darling," her husband Grayson murmured, "if one were to judge by your bills, you own enough cloth-

ing to outfit all of Wellington's troops with a wedding
trousseau."

It felt peculiar to Eloise to be on the receiving end
of all this attention when she had spent years serving
others. The marchioness brought out practically every
gown from her personal wardrobe. Her lady's maids ran
back and forth through the elegant suite to drag in even
more dresses that Jane had not yet worn.

A modiste and two assistants were summoned and
sworn to secrecy. Someone—it was Chloe—brought in a
bottle of brandy and gave Eloise a glass to fortify her
nerves.

Emma spent an hour hunting for a pair of elbow-
length white kid gloves and brocade slippers to match
the cream silk gown with a gold tissue underskirt that
had finally been chosen for Eloise. The marchioness
had a willowy figure that childbirth had only enhanced.
Eloise was surprised at how well the dress draped her
own ample form.

"I had it made for me in the early months of my con-
finement," Jane confided. "I've never worn it, but it does
look perfect on you."

Eloise gazed at her reflection in the gilded pier glass.
The shimmery light material sculpted her curves in becoming folds. The belled-lace sleeves that draped over
her wrist made her think of a Renaissance princess.

"Do we have a veil?" the modiste inquired as she sur-
veyed the bride-to-be with weary satisfaction.

The question sent everyone from the room on a veil
quest except for Eloise and Emma. Their eyes met in the
mirror. Just because Emma had been quiet did not mean
she would not eventually voice her thoughts.

"Lady Lyons, I don't know what to say," Eloise said, deciding to take the initiative. "I know you are disappointed in me."

Emma surprised her by laughing. "It is a vast disappointment to me that the academy shall not be able to count you as one of our staff."

"I'm desperately sorry about the incident at the pond."

"No doubt Percy deserved it," Emma said, tucking one of Eloise's wayward curls behind her ear. "I was too hasty to judge you. You were protecting your client at the risk of your own reputation. Loyalty like that is more precious than gold. Or good standing."

Eloise sighed. How long she had waited to be acknowledged for her job by someone who understood what *really* mattered. "I am flattered that—"

"It is, however," Emma continued a little ruthlessly, "a profound relief to me and the parents of the young ladies I attempt to civilize, that rogues such as my brother shall be taken out of social circulation, as it were."

Eloise laughed, narrowing her eyes. "I'm not entirely sure how to take that remark."

"I'm not entirely sure how it should be taken." Emma stepped back from the mirror, a petite figure whose deceptive fragility bore the impact of a lightning bolt. "But if anyone is to marry the blackguard, I am grateful it is a woman of your character."

Eloise softened. "Oh. Thank you."

Emma smiled. "You are very welcome. I understand that you went through a hellish experience only a few hours ago, and yet here you are, perfectly composed. Good job, my dear."

"Well, I did have a wedding to attend."

"A wedding takes precedence over nearly everything—rakes, ruination, riots, possibly even war. Everything except the birth of a child," Emma said in a rare moment of unguarded emotion. "A wedding signifies the magical start of a new life. I hope that you will forget what happened to you earlier today."

Eloise nodded, not trusting herself to speak.

"And," Emma added, "I hope that you and Drake will know only happiness together."

It was the second wedding that Eloise had attended that same day. The first had been an act of duty that she had worked to bring about. This was a dream, an act of grace. The sinfully beautiful man standing at the altar belonged to some gossamer-spun fantasy. So did the footmen in powdered wigs and formal knee breeches who guarded the doors of the private Park Lane chapel. And Freddie. Her dear mop-headed friend looked so in awe of his surroundings that she had to smile.

Grayson walked her down the nave to give her away. His sturdy arm gave her courage. For a moment she thought wistfully of her own father, of how he had cut her so completely out of his life. Perhaps one day they would reconcile. His last words to her had been, "You are a stubborn girl who will find herself in trouble one day if you don't change your ways."

Well, she'd proven her papa right.

There at the altar waited the trouble she had found. Her dark and decadent Boscastle. The one man on earth she could not resist. How fortunate she had not changed her ways. How fortunate that deep in her practical heart she had always believed in fairy tales.

Her heart beat wildly now beneath her cream silk bodice as she reached her beloved troublemaker's side. His tall frame towered over her. He wore the same dark broadcloth frock coat with light woolen pantaloons that he had been wearing when he had rescued her. His gaze held hers until nothing else seemed to exist but the two of them.

He did not smile but gently took her hand in his. The gesture warmed not only Eloise but the few guests who witnessed the intimate ceremony. Drake had never been known as a demonstrative man. Only those who loved him realized the significance of this marriage. He had always walked an uncertain path, but at least now he would not be alone. Surviving was really all he'd done, and he had worn a convincing façade. His family had been frightened for him.

Suddenly from somewhere in the chapel he heard the happy gurgle of his nephew. Rowan, survivor of gas and Grayson's overprotectiveness. Another Boscastle to carry on the wicked line. He broke into a grin. Well, perhaps he'd produce a few of the wicked demons himself. After all, Eloise had experience dealing with unruly persons. She had certainly brought him to heel.

Oh, God, she took his breath away. Her oval face glowed with happiness, even if the bruise on her face reminded him of how close he'd come to losing her. He swallowed as he remembered finding her in that room. Even now he felt ill at the image of her terrified reflection in the mirror as he'd opened the door.

He'd promised to protect her. He would take his wedding vows to heart. Was it possible that not long ago he had not cared whether he lived or died?

"Dearly beloved," the minister began, and from the corner of his eye Drake saw his cousin Gabriel slip into a pew with another Boscastle cousin, the fair-haired Charlotte, one of Emma's students at the academy. He returned his attention to the ceremony.

Who had invited them? He didn't know. Family was family, and—was that Freddie in knee breeches at the vestry door? All the ceremony lacked was Maribella St. Ives to make it a traditional Boscastle wedding.

His heart missed a beat as he heard Eloise take her vows. His own voice was steady but thick with emotion. Then, as he bent his head to kiss his wife, he caught a glimpse of Devon sinking down in the pew, his hand covering his eyes as if he could not believe what he saw; to Devon's left sat Gabriel with an inscrutable smile on his face.

At any other time Drake might have leapt across the pews and knocked their heads together. Fortunately he had other plans.

"Eloise," he said as he brushed his lips against hers, "let's escape before they corner us."

"Highly unlikely," she whispered, and it was indeed several hours later before they excused themselves from the endless rounds of champagne toasts and well-meant words of advice to be alone at his town house.

Evening had fallen over London, a soft misty night in a city of endless possibilities. Eloise draped herself across the bed with a luxurious sigh and finished the glass of champagne her husband had poured her. "Am I drunk?" she asked happily, unhooking her wedding dress with abandon.

He locked the door and leaned against it as she wriggled out of all her clothes. What a view. His wife subsiding naked onto her side. Candlelight sculpted the hollows of her body. A rose-tipped breast, the enticing curve of her hip, her thighs slightly parted. His gaze drifted over her inviting pose with a conqueror's satisfaction. She might have been a goddess as the gossip papers alleged, except that she was very human, attainable, and his.

"I think it's time for us to celebrate," he said, shrugging out of his coat.

His naked wife rose diligently to remove his neck cloth. "I'm right here," she murmured.

"Forever?" he asked, settling his arm around her voluptuous backside to kiss her deeply.

"Even longer." She breathed a soft sigh of approval into his mouth. "Love me, Boscastle," she whispered. "Forever is starting at this moment."

Drake was only too delighted to fulfill his wife's request that he make love to her. Hadn't one of his brothers once told him that practical women were the most passionate? Spilling her over his shoulder, he bore her back to their bed and tumbled her down onto the green silk coverlet. She laughed and fell in a graceful sprawl, her beautiful body flushed and beckoning. He stared at her, and his lungs struggled for breath.

His wife.

Her inviting smile weakened him.

Could she make the darkness that so often rose inside him go away? Probably not. But she would make going through it easier to endure. She would be the light to keep his vision clear, his step steady until the day he drew his final breath.

He'd never thought he would fall in love like this, believed himself incapable of it. But then he had danced with Eloise on a whim. He'd only meant to pass a few moments with a pretty woman who looked a little in need of distraction. As the fairy tale went, he was supposed to have swept her off her feet. The opposite had happened.

Love is horrible. Don't let it happen to you.

But it had happened. He couldn't have stopped it if he'd tried. The panic and love on Grayson's face had frightened him that night in the nursery, but it had also forced him to see the truth. A Boscastle in love was a terrible thing to behold, a beast who resisted his transformation until the last moment.

Love is wonderful.

Horrible. Wonderful. And whatever love was, it was part of life, and it made him want to live.

His wife reached up as if reading his mind and unbuttoned his pantaloons. He sucked in his breath at the possessive tug of her hands at his hips, eagerly freeing his aching erection. Every blood vessel in his body expanded, pulsed with the delicious power of arousal. He'd never had her to himself like this. It was time to show his bride how diligent he would be in his duty to her, too.

He kicked off his drawers and black pantaloons. She slid her hand under his shirt and waistcoat, loosening the buttons, her eyes inviting him to make love to her. As a gentleman he had to accept.

He leaned over her and parted her thighs, his smile a wicked promise. She was warm and open, glistening wet even before he stroked her into breathless readiness.

"My heart," he said, "I love you more than anything."

"I love you," she whispered back, sitting up to cup his face in her palms.

He kissed her until he felt her hand slide down his chest to his throbbing cock, and suddenly he could not wait. Her touch was his undoing, the key to his heart and all he desired. He gripped her generous heart-shaped arse in his hands and lifted her to him.

"On your knees, wife," he whispered, his arm sliding beneath her breasts to support her. She hesitated slightly before she assumed the submissive pose. But when she glanced back at him over her bare shoulder, her eyes were kindling with a passion that matched his own.

"Like this?" she asked in a curious voice.

His heart clenched in his chest as he looked down possessively at her graceful back and dimpled bottom, the petals of her pink cleft drawing his gaze lower still.

His body shook with desire as he ran his fingers down her bottom to pry her thighs even further apart. "That's very nice," he said in a thick voice, delighted at her compliance. He sank into her sheath, feeling her spine arch in pleasure. "I love the way you feel inside," he added hoarsely. "As if you were made for me." And he meant it in every way.

He thrust then, his head thrown back. She accepted every inch of him to the hilt, challenging the stamina and skill that had served him so well in the cavalry. But this was the sweetest ride he'd ever taken, and he was in no particular hurry to make it end.

Nor was she, moving in rhythm with his bucking hips, arching her back to absorb every hard thrust until he brought his left hand between her legs to pinch her secret bud. Her pleasure crested. He triumphed in her soft cries of surrender and the shudders that tore through her belly, the contractions of her inner muscles that would soon milk him dry.

"Eloise," he said fiercely. He bent his body over hers to bite the back of her neck. The next moment his mind went blank and he convulsed, his spine aching as he flooded her passage with his seed. His heart seemed to stop beating. The breath in his throat caught as he gave himself up to pleasure.

She folded at the knees; his damp body lowered to the bed and crushed her warm curves. Somewhere in the misty distance a church bell pealed, and a carriage rumbled through the streets. He drew several harsh breaths and smiled into the darkness, shifting onto his side to touch her face.

"I never knew I could be this happy," he said, drawing her against his shoulder.

"Your family," she murmured, sighing in contentment, "are the most wonderful people I've ever met. I knew you were exaggerating about them."

His deep laughter filled the room. "Then we've all got you fooled. Everyone was on his best behavior today, but you wait until Christmas, or the next time all of us are in the same house." His hand moved tenderly over her soft belly. "We might even have our own little Boscastle by the end of the year. Would you mind?"

"Nothing would make me happier."

"Then don't say you weren't warned when our baby turns out to be a devil. Being born a Boscastle is a life sentence."

"You weren't really the worst of the lot, were you?"

"Who knows?" His hand skimmed her hip bone. She was heat and softness, his love and light. "Even if I was, someone else is bound to take up the torch. I'll wager at this very minute one of them is scratching at trouble's door."

"And you?" she asked, tracing her fingertip across his lips.

He shuddered and felt the warmth of her touch penetrate the shadows of his soul. "I'm more than satisfied right where I am."

Read on for a scintillatingly sexy sneak peek at

The Sinful Nights of a Nobleman,

the next sweeping romance
in the Boscastle Family series
by Jillian Hunter.

Coming in fall 2006 from Ivy Books

Devon had just dismissed his valet for the evening, when he spied a note that had been slipped under his bedroom door. He debated going out into the hall to catch the messenger, but decided against it. Secret notes passed between admirers were not an unusual occurrence at a sophisticated society affair. Pranks and impromptu little parties within the main house party were the primary reason most of the haut monde guests attended in the first place, although no one ever admitted it.

Devon had politely declined a handful of offers so far; his interest had narrowed to the one lady who had been encouraging and eluding him for the past five weeks. Their last conversation earlier in the evening had led him to believe her capitulation was at hand.

He'd thought, however, that she might withhold her surrender for at least another day. In Devon's experience, a slow prelude to sex usually made an amorous conquest all the more intense.

Still, he wasn't about to offend his admirer by playing coy, when the evening and following days promised so much pleasure.

Crossing the room, he bent to pick up the folded paper and break open the still-soft seal. The carefully worded message confirmed his belief that the lady was more impatient for a night of lovemaking than her evasive tactics at the party had let on.

My dear Devil,

We are both old enough to admit and yet young enough to act upon our desires. Despite my reputation, I am a private woman at heart. If your pursuit of my attention is more than a fleeting temptation, meet me tonight at a quarter past midnight in the east tower where we shall enjoy privacy to reveal our true intentions.

I trust that I have not misread your interest.

Will you wear your infamous domino for me?

L

The paper bore the rather overpowering scent of lilies, her namesake fragrance, but oddly not a perfume that she had ever worn in his company. It seemed a little unsubtle to drench an invitation in cologne when she'd been leading him on a chase for over a month.

He dropped the letter on the desk on his way to the oak armoire. Casually he removed his long-tailed evening jacket in favor of the highwayman's hooded cloak and half-mask that had rendered him one of London's favorite scandals.

He should have expected that Lily Cranleigh would find his short-lived career as a highwayman an aphrodisiac. She had made several references to his past in their conversations. Still, who would have thought that a single regrettable interlude could ignite so many fantasies in the hearts of women scattered throughout England, most of whom he'd never met.

He shook his head in amused resignation. Ironically, he'd been hoping to impress Lily with his subtle wit. It hardly seemed fair that he should reap continued profits for committing a crime he would prefer to forget.

But the fact remained. His masked counterpart had brought many an aloof lady to her knees, which only went to prove that there really was no rest unto the wicked. Or unto the Boscastles, if one chose to recognize the difference.

*   *   *

It seemed to take Jocelyn forever to wend her way through the lonely castle hallways, then up a steep staircase to reach the east tower. The sounds of revelry in the west wing grew faint, only the piping notes of a flageolet still clearly audible. When she had first received Adam's note, she'd thought the notion of a midnight summons romantic and adventurous.

Who would have guessed her proper suitor capable of such a passionate gesture?

It went without saying that if a proposition to tryst in the tower had come from any of the other young men at the party, she would have been offended. No one had ever tendered her such a wicked offer before.

But Lord Adam Chiswick was both a brave officer and an honorable man who'd made no secret that he intended to ask for her hand at the house party. Secretly, Jocelyn was a little pleased that he was showing this reckless streak. Never once had she guessed that such a lively spark smoldered beneath his endearing predictability.

Which made his invitation to meet in secret all the more irresistible. To judge by his spidery handwriting, he was as nervous about an illicit encounter as she was. Had she not been convinced that a marriage proposal was in the offing, she would have flung the invitation in his face.

And he'd asked her to wear a mask to protect her from being identified on the way here, bless his gentlemanly upbringing.

Suddenly she stood before the black arched doorway. A shiver of anxiety diminished her sense of anticipation. What if they were caught? They would be forced to rush into their marriage and—

Before she could change her mind about proceeding with the rendezvous, the door opened and she gazed into the room. She could only perceive a dark-clad figure standing against a backdrop of even darker shadows.

"Be careful," warned a baritone voice that sounded familiar and yet strangely more masculine than Adam's—except on the fortunately infrequent occasions when he gave his impression of Wellington as a party favor.

She lifted her hand self-consciously to her mask. "It's as dark as—"

An iron-grip closed around her wrist and drew her effortlessly into the tower. The door shut behind her with a heavy thud that reverberated through the soles of her feet. She half-stumbled, feeling herself steadied by that firm grasp again.

"This was a hell of a place to meet," he remarked dryly, his mouth against her cheek. "There isn't even a bed to—"

"A bed?"

His voice. It sounded—well, heavens above, no wonder his voice was so unexpectedly deep and muffled, considering he wore not only a mask but a handsome black hooded cloak that swathed him from head to mid-calf. He must be wearing a new pair of boots, too, that boosted his height. She had to admit she was privately delighted by his daring get-up. He didn't seem at all himself. Had the costume brought out his masculinity?

His big intrusive body walked her backward against the wall. She drew a deep breath as he demanded, "Am I going to have to take you prisoner? Or do you surrender yourself to me without a struggle?"

She giggled in disbelief. "*What?*"

"Do you want to pretend you're my hostage?" he asked in an amused whisper. "I didn't have enough notice to make preparations for your captivity." He turned his head as if assessing the dark. "I suppose there might be a tapestry tassel I could use to subdue you."

That voice. Oh, God. A shiver ran through her. Oh, dear God.

"'Subdue'—your *hostage*?"

"Shall I tie you by the wrists or by the ankles?"

That voice. Her throat closed.

"Or both?" he offered rather politely.

"You did *not* just say you intend to bind me with a tassel?" she asked hoarsely.

"A tisket. A tassel. What does it matter? Just as long as we don't leave telltale marks on that lovely flesh."

"Who are you?" she whispered.

"You're not allowed to know my identity," he answered in a stage whisper.

She shook her head, shivering again. She could not decide whether her befuddlement stemmed from shock or from the fact that his gloved fingers had set off in a wandering foray down her cheek to her shoulders, only to dip in the valley of her breasts and wickedly circle her nipple. A wave of faintness swept over her.

The hooks and eyes of her gown, which had taken the maid a dedicated quarter-hour to fasten, sprang open as if by a wizard's touch. Cool air mingled with the touch of warm leather to caress her skin.

Half-naked, she thought. A stranger in masquerade had just loosened her gown. Her voice unsteady, she said, "This game has gone too far."

"Then I'll play whatever game that pleases you," he replied, his firm mouth trailing down her mouth to the tops of her breasts. "Do you want me to hold you up or hold you down?" With his free hand he wrenched off his hood. "I could have chosen a far more comfortable place for us to meet, by the way."

That voice. It did not belong to Adam, muffled or not. Nor did the knowing caress that teased her breasts before sliding down her belly to the hollow below.

"You aren't Adam," she said, her bones dissolving the instant she spoke the words, even though somewhere deep inside she'd known it from the moment he'd taken her into his arms.

He hesitated, irony vibrating in his low velvet voice. "And you're not Lily."

"Lily?" she echoed faintly.

"I'm flattered, actually, that you went to all this trouble to arrange a tryst. But if you desired me, there wasn't any need for deception. I would have most likely come out of curiosity."

"Deception?"

"Unless intrigue is the element that excites you," he added.

His eyes glinted as if to mock her through the slits of his mask. A gasp rose in her throat. The next thing she knew he was bending her backward, over his sinewy forearm in a position of subjugation. The steel-hard muscles of his thighs tightened and locked her to him. He angled his body closer until she felt his shaft thicken against her belly.

His hard mouth descended on hers in a deep, devastating kiss that would have silenced her had she been capable of speech. Indeed, she was submerged in too many sensations to wage a defense. She wanted to blame her breathless disequilibrium on the darkness that engulfed them. But even the darkness did not allow her to continue pretending that the strong body molded to hers belonged to the man she had come here to meet.

"Let's do away with our masks, shall we?" he murmured. "As a matter of fact, let's do away with the dress you're wearing."

"It's *you*," she said in a strangled voice.

Who in attendance at the house party was devious enough to lure her to the tower using a respectable gentleman's name? Who but a master of immorality and subtle persuasion would not only have dared, but succeeded?

"Devon Boscastle." She stared up into his beguiling face as he removed his mask. His beautiful mouth quirked into a grin.

"Jocelyn." He added insult to injury by breaking into laughter. "It is *you*. Well, slap me sideways."

"Of course it's me," she said, straightening indignantly. "As if you hadn't lured me here."